BUT THE STARS

PETER CAWDRON

Copyright © Peter Cawdron 2020

All rights reserved. The right of Peter Cawdron to be identified as the author of this work has been asserted in accordance with the Copyright, Designs and Patents Act 1988. All the characters in this book are fictitious, and, with the exception of Pretzel, any resemblance to actual persons living or dead is purely coincidental.

Cover image courtesy of the NASA Hubble Space Telescope image of NGC 121, a globular cluster in the Small Magellanic Cloud.

ISBN: 9798630850980

Imprint: Independently published

> *But the stars*
> *that marked our starting fall away.*
> *We must go deeper into greater pain,*
> *for it is not permitted that we stay.*
>
> *Dante Alighieri,*
> *Inferno, 1301 AD*

ACHERON

Acheron (ˈækərən) Crew Manifest

Commander	Asiko Capidastrianani (Cap)
First Officer	Benson Gregor
Astrobiologist	Joh MacInnes (Mac)
Nuclear Physicist	Angela Darc (Angel)
Mission Specialist	Vichy Rossin
Exo-Geologist	Zoe Salenda
Mission Specialist	Nazim Hassrani (Naz)
Life Support	Margaret Smith (Mags)
Flight Surgeon	Dante Almani
Artificial Intelligence	Jeeves IV

MEMORIES

"What do you remember?"

"Everything—and nothing at all," Dante replies, running her hands through her hair, pulling at tangles and knots as she ruffles her long locks. She wonders what the male nurse standing before her is thinking. His words say one thing, his eyes another, but she doesn't care for his gaze and tugs at her flight suit, straightening it, trying to deflect his attention. For God's sake, she's only just woken from a deep sleep.

Dante's head is pounding. The crook of her arm aches from the wound left by the hibernation catheter that sustained her for the past few years, following the emergency evacuation from a frozen planet known only as P4. Lymph fluids, platelets and nutrients were meticulously exchanged while her mind was disengaged. The techs call it hyper-sleep, but it's nothing like actual sleep. No dreams, no recharge, no newfound zest for life on waking, just the flicker of darkness. Count down from five, the artificial intelligence said, only she was gone around two, with one occurring almost three years later in orbit around yet another nameless star. Over a thousand days compressed into roughly five seconds. They say you don't age in hyper-sleep. Anyone that believes that is a fool.

"When you're ready," the nurse says.

"Yes, of course."

This particular male nurse is a fine specimen. Thick neck muscles, broad shoulders and pumped biceps struggle to hide beneath his crisp uniform. He has a chest like a whiskey barrel. For some, he's a beefcake, but not for Dante. She's always been more interested in what lies between someone's ears than what hangs between their legs. To her, the nurse looks more like a porn star role playing some wild sexual fantasy than a medical professional, which has her on the verge of chuckling, but she keeps that thought to herself. Given the way he looked her over, she'd rather not encourage that kind of thinking.

The tiny digital pen in his hand is reminiscent of a piece of straw plucked from a bale of hay. It glides across a flex tablet leaving electronic ink in its wake. A combination of machine learning and artificial intelligence allows slight squiggles to be interpreted as words, hinging on their context, allowing him to write almost as fast as he can draw his hand across the flex. Letters appear in the wake of his pen, materializing where only their vague notion was a mere split-second earlier. To anyone from centuries past, it would be magic.

Like everyone in the 22nd century, the nurse has neural implants and doesn't actually need to write, but it seems he's like her. Dante prefers a moment between thought and action, an opportunity to crystalize her thinking. Instead of wrangling a stream of consciousness, which takes considerable sustained concentration, she's old school. She would rather offer fewer words with more focus. Seeing someone else with the same approach is refreshing and she warms to him.

He rests the stylus against the edge of the wafer-thin plexiglass, having finished whatever note he was making. Dante wonders where she should start. Her lips are cracked, which causes her to grimace as she speaks.

"You want to know about the attack?" she asks, blinking under the bright lights.

"Start with First Contact," he says. "I can lower the lights if that would help."

"Yeah," she replies, squinting. "And can I..."

"Have a drink of water?" he asks, finishing a question that trailed from her lips like a meteor burning through the night sky.

"Yeah."

For now, he leaves her sitting perched on the side of a bed in the medical bay. The stiff, pressed sheets are white and clean. It feels wrong to rest her dirty hands on them so she cups her fingers in her lap. Her blue flight suit looks more like that of a greasy mechanic than an astronaut. Hyper-sleep chambers are functional, not aesthetic, and certainly not designed for comfort. They're intended to keep people alive, not prepare them for a Vogue cover shoot. White suspension fluid has dried in patches on her trouser legs. Maybe she really *is* in a porn flick. That random, chaotic thought brings a wicked smile to her face and she lets out a solitary laugh, not that anyone hears it.

Dante is in no state to count the beds around her, but the ward is empty, which leaves her wondering about the rest of her crew. Perhaps they simply woke her first? But why not wake everyone at once? Are the others okay? Have there been complications? Fatalities? The act of turning her head to look around leaves her feeling dizzy and those thoughts escape her, dissipating like a mist.

Dante has no recollection of how she got to the medical bay, but waking from hyper-sleep can be disorienting. Medi-monitors sit idle at the head of each bed except hers, where a series of lines roll slowly across the screen. An erratic bouncing ball marks her heartbeat, while her temperature, blood pressure and oxygenation levels are slight squiggles by comparison. They're roughly flat, undulating softly as the respiration line rises and falls in time with her chest.

"They're all good," a voice from behind her says. "You're

a little anemic, but otherwise in good shape. Nothing a shot of stems won't fix."

"Oh, yeah," Dante says, turning to face a doctor—a young woman, too young. She could be in her teens. What the hell is she doing out here on the frontier? Perhaps she hides her age well.

Dante's confused, but doesn't know why. Nothing's wrong, not that she can tell, and yet she feels uneasy. It's nonsense. She's been revived. It's not uncommon to feel a little ill following a stretch in hyper-sleep. She distracts herself, saying, "We could have used this tech on the Acheron."

The doctor looks down at her semi-transparent computerized flex sheet. "Oh, you were the flight surgeon?"

Not convincing. Dante doesn't say anything, but she's sure the doctor knew that before looking at the information sheet. Maybe she was simply double-checking, not wanting to act on an assumption. Why would she pretend not to know? It was the slight pause, the brief change in pitch, the uncertainty about what she was going to say that tipped off Dante.

"Our AI Jeeves did all the surgery, but yeah—that's the title—or it was."

"A lot has changed," the woman says. Her tone becomes more relaxed. It's as though she got something awkward out of the way.

Given all Dante's been through, she's wary of others—perhaps she's a little too cautious. Maybe she's reading too much into the innocent reply of a young doctor.

"Time dilation will do that," Dante replies, agreeing with the doctor.

The doctor smiles. It's fake, of course. A professional courtesy at best.

"How long were you out there?" the doctor asks, but doesn't she know? She's being polite, trying to be nice.

"By our reckoning? One way? Ah, roughly twenty-five years, I guess. Earthbound time was just over ninety years, if I remember correctly."

"That's pretty close," she says, checking her notes. "You were clocked at 96C outbound by the deep space observatory."

Dante's head is pounding. Relativistic equations were never her thing. Normally, physicists refer to something like the subluminal speed of the Acheron as point ninety-six, so the doctor's reply strikes her as a little strange. Being a doctor herself, though, she can relate to taking a few shortcuts with astrophysics nomenclature.

Dante feels compelled to explain, saying, "Our last jump was rough. Emergency evac. Not a lot of time to prep."

"Well, you're safe now," the doctor replies.

"And you?" Dante asks.

"I was born out here. I've only ever been near-luminal on short hops. Nothing longer than six months."

Born out here? Dante wonders just how much time has elapsed?

The muscular male nurse walks back in. From his slight pause by the door, he's surprised to see the doctor standing there, which strikes Dante as strange. Where else should she be? He walks over and hands Dante a small, thermally insulated flask with the top removed.

"I've included some electrolytes and iron supplements to help with anemia."

"Thank you," she replies, raising the bottle to her lips and drinking heartily. Water trickles from her mouth, running down the side of her neck, but she doesn't care. She didn't realize just how parched she was until the water passed her lips. Strange, though, it tastes bland. Being an electrolyte mix, Dante's expecting a slight sugar hit and the taste of dissolved salts, but the water is pleasant enough.

When she lowers the bottle, the doctor's gone. That's surprising. Dante didn't see her leave. Surprising isn't good.

Curious, she asks, "Where did she go?"

"The doctor will see you later," the nurse replies. "Captain Befeck wants a full report."

For a moment, Dante pauses. Why delegate the

debriefing of a first contact survivor to a nurse? Why not the doctor? Why isn't the captain down here? Or his second-in-command? Or a team of psychs? She shifts on the bed, getting comfortable. As if in response, the breeze spilling out of the air conditioning duct increases. It's neither warm nor cool, which is annoying as it feels redundant. Oh, she longs for a refreshing breeze.

The nurse rests his thin tablet on a cart and pulls over a stool, rolling it across the deck. Her senses are heightened, which is unusual. Each bump and scratch on the floor imparts a slightly different tone from the wheels. She can hear the bearings as they turn. It could be a side effect of hyper-sleep, but she never felt like this after the much longer, outbound journey from Earth, only now after fleeing WISE 5571 and its mysterious planet P4.

Dante's ears catch everything—the hollow sound of metal ringing as the steel frame of the cart flexes, the wheels running across the linoleum, the hum of the vents, the wheeze of pneumatics as the stool takes the nurse's weight, the soft squelch of artificial leather as he sits on the thick padding.

"What are you doing in this region?" Dante asks, not entirely comfortable with the nurse and wanting some answers of her own.

"We're running mining ops on local asteroids. Lots of microgravity missions. We picked up your distress call about nine months ago and have been on an intercept orbit ever since."

"Huh?" Dante replies, noting the craft is as quiet as a grave—and not just the medical bay, there's no noise coming from the corridor outside or the floor above. Back on the Acheron, every flex and creak spoke of the crew walking around on other decks.

Outside the station, pinpricks of light drift past. The host star must be off to the side as the light streaming in shifts across the walls, floor and ceiling like a sundial on steroids. At a guess, the craft is rotating once every couple of minutes, which gives her a comfortable sense of pseudo-gravity.

Based on how little her petite frame displaces the mattress, the craft must be running at less than one gee, which is about what the Acheron had when it opened its baffles to collect dark matter. Some stationmasters, prepping away teams for extended low-gee missions, will spin up their craft to 1.5 gees to boost red blood cell production and muscle strength in the weeks leading up to a low-gravity deployment. Perhaps that's why this craft is so quiet. The operational teams must already be on site.

Dante's surprised they left them out there instead of recalling them as those away crews will spend at least eighteen months in space without the health-inducing effects of gravity, be that artificial or real. They'll be as weak as kittens by the time this ship swings back to collect them. Her mind is racing. Maybe there's a nearby planet they can recover on, or a moon. Although this decision was in her favor, it seems like a really poor choice to leave most of the crew out there while embarking on a rescue mission. If she were the ship's physician, she would have objected due to the risk of harm to their own crew. Dante would have demanded a recall before setting off on a rescue flight. Ah, she thinks too much.

From the curvature of the floor within medical, the station is probably about the same size as the observatories in the Oort Cloud—with a radius of roughly four hundred meters. Plenty of living space for several teams. So damn quiet.

"Contact?" the nurse asks, although it's not actually a question. It's a single word uttered with curiosity, but there it is, prompting her to begin.

"Ah, yes. First Contact.

"We'd been in the system for about four years and had established robotic monitoring stations on the moons of a couple of gas giants orbiting at 25 and 40 AU respectively, well outside the Goldilocks zone, but no dice. Nothing. No microbes. No complex molecules.

"We were sure the system was barren. On approach, the interstellar medium showed residual traces of a nearby supernova. Iron-60, stuff like that. Half-life calculations put the blast at approximately 200 million years ago. Cap thought it must have sterilized the planets. It was too far away to physically damage them, too close for anything to survive. We switched to looking for fossil remnants on the inner rocky planets. Outgassing on one of the planets suggested an active core, but the rest were dead."

"What did you find?" the nurse asks.

Dante's eyes glance up at the ceiling briefly before trailing around the room. Where have they hidden their microphones? Perhaps the flex is actively recording her.

"Oh, there was an unbalanced chemical equation in the atmosphere of P4. That got Cap's attention.

"P4 was—is... ah, it's in a relatively circular orbit just outside the habitable zone. It's an ice world. Volcanism has kept a few patches of open water, but most of the land is buried by glaciers to a depth of several kilometers. We set down and began drilling, looking for subsurface lakes kept viable by geothermal warming."

"And that's when you found them?" he asks, yet again sounding like anything but a nurse. Dante's confused. Is this actually the captain? Why would he role play? These thoughts distract her, but she continues recalling events, trying to keep the sequence straight.

"Not for several months."

"Months?"

"Well, it was months before we noticed them."

"I don't understand," he says, leaning forward and resting his arms on his knees. His eyes narrow as he focuses intently on her words.

"They noticed us straight away, but they use telepathy to hide, although it's not what you think."

"What do I think?" he asks.

"They can't read minds, but they can manipulate thoughts. It's like they can put concepts in, but they can't take them out—not without us noticing."

"So they can influence you, but they can't violate your freewill?"

"Exactly," she says.

"I don't understand. Your report said you were attacked."

"Not all attacks are physical. Not always. At first, it was like they were probing, testing us, experimenting with us, trying different approaches, wanting to learn about us."

"How?"

"Well... I was in the sickbay in orbit when I first heard of contact. Angel, Naz and Benson were on a short-duration surface op fixing robotic equipment. Zoe was operating the drill.

"Gravity down there is 2.2 gees—which is horrible to

work in. Even within the confines of the shuttle craft, it felt as though you were carrying a piano around on your back.

"The team used exoskeletons while out on the surface to help counter the pull, but even with pressurized undergarments to boost blood circulation, it was torture.

"I went down a couple of times—never willingly. P4 was a shithole. It looked like hell had frozen over.

"Within a couple of months I was seeing members of the surface team present with minor kidney damage, brain lesions, burst pleura in the lungs, sinus problems, ringing in the ears, things like that. It was the sustained heavy gravity, so I instituted eight hour maximums for surface activity with a minimum sixteen hours to recuperate in orbit before subsequent shifts.

"Cap hated it. Wasted time. Wasted fuel. Not to mention it meant he couldn't leave them down there and go off exploring the moons of P4 or any of the other planets, but doctor's orders. You know."

To her surprise, the nurse doesn't acknowledge that point. Dante had expected it to elicit some camaraderie. Instead, the nurse asks, "When did you first see them?"

"We didn't. Not for months. They were there, of course. All around us. We saw them, and then we didn't. They made sure we never really knew what we were dealing with. Not until they breached the hold of the shuttle. Even then, it wasn't until the shuttle docked with the Acheron that we realized we were facing an infestation.

"At first, it was inconsistencies. We thought the issues were stress related. People making dumb mistakes due to the gee-loading, but—"

Something's wrong. Dante isn't sure what, but she can feel it. Wrong is a logical conclusion, not an emotional conviction, and yet the fine hairs on her arms rise up in alarm. She stalls, looking in the empty bottle, wanting more time to work through her reasoning. She's not sure why she feels anxious and that's perhaps the most unsettling point of all. Something is horribly wrong with this interview.

Dante grew up in Alabama until about the age of ten. Tornados were as much a part of summer there as the honeysuckle flowering outside her bedroom window or tomatoes ripening on the vine. A few large drops of rain falling from an otherwise clear blue sky were a sure sign of trouble. Turn and there would be a wall of cloud looming behind her. Sometimes it wasn't what she saw or heard that would set her heart racing, but rather what was absent. Birds would stop calling. Insects would fall silent. The message was always the same. *Danger. Time to go.* Right now, in orbit around a dwarf star that's probably not even visible from Earth, she feels the same way. But they fled, they left WISE 5571 and its unusual planet P4, abandoning it several light years away. Why is she panicking now? Why is she having an anxiety attack for no other reason than the memories she's recalling?

When Dante was eight, at the park with her dad, she was caught in the open by a tornado. The thing that surprised her most was that there was no twister as such. All the pictures and news reports had lied. If she'd seen a dark swirling funnel reaching down to the ground, it would have been obvious, but she was too close to the vortex.

Sticks, branches, leaves, even bits of wood torn off a nearby barn all circled in the air, swaying as though held under the spell of some ancient wizard. Dust kicked off the ground, racing in toward her. A power transformer, high on a pole, exploded in a burst of sparks. Lines fell, arcing as they danced across the road. An invisible monster tore through the park, coming for her, ripping trees from the dirt and tossing them aside, dragging bushes and saplings into the sky.

Her dad grabbed her and ran across the thick, lush grass, sprinting toward a concrete bathroom next to the parking lot. Dante was more horrified at being shoved into the men's side of the bathroom than the sound of what could have been a freight train roaring past outside.

Rain whipped inside the bathroom, swirling around the cinderblock barrier lining the entrance, stinging her face. Her dad dragged her into a stall and slammed the metal door shut behind them. They crouched beside a stainless-steel toilet bowl, shivering as the temperature plunged. Water soaked the floor, being pushed into waves by the wind and lapping at her shoes. The metal roof flexed along with the walls of the cubicle. She screamed. It was as though the monster outside was breathing, hunting, searching for her, threatening to tear the roof off and snatch her.

Once the chaos passed, they ventured back outside and looked up. There, looming high above the town, stood Leviathan. Dark clouds seethed with hate. Crackles of lightning lashed out in anger. Four twisting columns of darkness and death reach down from the clouds, tearing open homes, destroying roofs and flipping cars. The silence that followed was as painful then as it is now. Dante might be in a starship on the leading edge of a spiral arm within the vast Milky Way, but for her it's as though warning sirens are sounding in the distance. She can feel it—the prickling sensation in her skin, the same thing she felt back on the swings when the first drops of rain fell.

The nurse notices the glazed look in her eyes. "But?"

"Can I have some more water?" she asks. Dante needs some time—a bit of space. She needs to breathe.

"Okay," the nurse says, looking a little befuddled for a moment, unsure how to process that request. He seems torn between pushing her to continue and not wanting to upset her.

Dante holds the bottle out, holding her arm unnaturally straight, with her elbow locked. She's probing. Curious. Looking for a reaction. Nothing. He doesn't notice.

The nurse gets to his feet, taking the flask from her.

"I won't be long."

She smiles and nods, avoiding eye contact. Instead, her eyes dart around, desperate to find something to settle on. Nothing's wrong. Nothing's out of place. Perhaps that's what she finds unnerving. An empty medi-bay. Even if there aren't any patients, there is always staff and robotic orderlies, things left out, equipment being serviced. This place is crisp and clean. Nothing is worn. It's too perfect.

As the nurse approaches the door it responds automatically, sliding open and then closing behind him. Dante slips off the bed, dropping to her bare feet without making a sound.

"Is everything okay?" a voice asks from behind her.

She turns, addressing the young doctor from earlier.

"Ah, yes. Everything's fine."

Dante's on the verge of panicking. Where the hell did the doctor come from? Somehow, Dante manages an obligatory reply, saying, "Ah, good."

Oh, what a beautiful smile, Dante thinks. Never before has such a nice, warm, friendly gesture screamed so loudly of betrayal.

"Wh—Where did you go?" Dante asks, walking softly toward a set of cabinets.

"What do you mean?" the doctor asks, following her. "I've always been here."

Dante ignores her. She opens the cabinets, knowing full well what she's about to find. Nothing. They're empty. She rushes along the wall, following the curve of the floor as it bends upward past a broad window facing out into space. She madly opens cabinet after empty cabinet.

"You're stressed," the doctor says. "Your heart's racing."

With a single, violent act, Dante rips the medi-monitor from her clavicle, tearing away the wires snaking across her neck and down her chest. She scrunches them up, tossing them at the doctor's feet in disgust.

The doctor seems genuinely shocked. She comes to a halt before the tiny medical device, looking down at it in dismay.

"Where the hell am I?" Dante asks.

"You're on board the Clara Barton, a medical support ship, part of the Deep Space Command."

"The Barton?" Dante asks, backing away from the doctor, edging next to the window and watching as stars drift past with the motion of the ship as it turns, imparting a sensation akin to gravity. "I know the Barton. She never came this deep."

"That was a long time ago. She's been refurbished since your day."

Dante's trembling hands reach for the wall, touching at the smooth surface, feeling the texture of a plastic panel beneath her fingertips.

Mentally, she struggles with the math. Relativistic physics was never her forte. Given her time in transit to WISE 5571, the time spent exploring the system and the time spent fleeing here, roughly thirty years have elapsed for her, with most of that spent in hyper-sleep, slowing the aging process. During that time, over a hundred years passed on Earth. The flight time for the Barton had to be similar to the Acheron's, which would mean a difference of no more than twenty years between their launches. Dante taps her fingers, struggling with the arithmetic. It's possible, but something's horribly wrong. She can feel it.

"Please," the doctor says. "You're suffering from shock. It's not unusual given a long-duration hyper-sleep. You need time to adjust. Your mind is confusing past and present."

"Get away from me!" Dante yells, lowering her head. She clenches her teeth, feeling a rush of blood pulsing in her neck. "Where are the others? Where's the rest of my crew?"

"They're fine," is not the answer she wants and Dante finds her heart thumping at the thought they're all dead. She pulls a stainless-steel cart from beside one of the beds, rolling it between her and the doctor, putting a barrier between them.

The doctor is calm. "Look at yourself. Think about what you're doing. This makes no sense."

"I'm warning you," Dante replies, alternating between watching the doctor and checking each of the cabinets as she backs through the medical bay. All of the shelves are empty.

"You're panicked. That's understandable. We can help."

The male nurse returns. As soon as he steps through the door, he puts the bottle down on a counter and rushes toward them.

"Stay back," Dante yells. She shoves the cart, sending it spinning across the floor and blocking the nurse, forcing him to grab at it. She pulls another cart from the next bay, again using it to keep some distance between her and the doctor.

The woman appeals to her. "You're hurt—not physically, but mentally. You need to let us help you."

"Let us help you," the nurse says, appealing for calm. "So we can return you to your crew."

"Just like you helped Angstrom?" she asks with a quiver in her voice.

"Yes, just like we helped Angstrom," the doctor replies, holding her hands out in front of her as though she were calming a horse.

Spittle flies from Dante's lips as she yells, "Angstrom's a unit of measure, you assholes!"

The male nurse moves out wide, rolling beds away from the wall so he can approach from the side. Dante raises her foot, shoving the closest bed so it skews sideways, blocking his approach. She charges at the doctor, pushing her into the wall.

"Get her!" the doctor yells, scratching at Dante's arms.

The nurse vaults one of the beds. Dante scrambles, pushing carts and sending them spinning. Boots pound on the floor behind her. Steel trays clatter to the ground. Her bare feet slip on the floor, slowing her. She reaches for the door, desperate to trigger the sensor and bolt into the corridor. Where is she going? She doesn't know. Her impulse to flee is irrational. There's nowhere to hide on a space station. All she knows is she has to get out of medical. Hands grab at her waist, but she twists, pulling away.

The door slides open, only there's nothing on the other side. No floor. No walls. No shapes or colors of any kind, just the impenetrable darkness. Her fingers touch at an invisible membrane, pushing against the barrier, slowly breaking through and disappearing from sight. Behind her, the nurse trips. As he falls, he reaches out, snatching desperately at her heel, clipping her foot and causing her to trip. Dante collides with the doorframe.

Tentacles reach from the darkness, wrapping around her

arms and drawing her closer. Much to her surprise, Dante's not frightened. Not anymore. It's as though the alien appendages are welcoming her, calling her home. They slither around her legs, creeping up her thighs and over her waist, lifting her off the floor. She looks back, seeing both the doctor and the nurse standing there motionless. They've been frozen mid-stride. It's as though someone paused a video clip.

Dante smiles as she's drawn into the void beyond the door. The lights of the medical bay fade, but the stars—the stars beyond the vast bay window—the stars shine brightly. At this distance, they're nothing more than pinpricks of light, but they burn in defiance of the darkness around her.

CAP

"Dante?"

A hand slaps her cheek, not roughly, just enough to get her attention. Dante blinks, struggling to take in her surroundings.

"Hey, are you in there? Are you still with me?"

Cap kneels before her. Blood seeps from some loose skin that's been torn from the side of his skull, exposing the bone and matting down his hair. Dark bruises mark his bare arms. Sweat beads on his forehead. His trousers have been shredded in an explosion, half torn from his legs. Thin lines of deep red blood trace his muscles. Gently, he cups her jaw, turning her to face him.

"I thought I'd lost you."

"They're inside," she says, unable to understand what's happening to her. "They're in my head."

"Not anymore. You're okay now. Come on, we've got to

get you out of here."

Cap hoists Dante's arm over his shoulder, helping her to her feet.

Dante grimaces. Pain surges through her right leg. Her trousers are soaked with blood. She limps in the heavy gravity, struggling to hold on to him. It feels as though someone's dragging her down, trying to pull her from him, wanting to throw her to the floor.

At 2.2G, tripping on P4 is akin to falling from a roof on Earth and Dante struggles to maintain her footing. She understands the danger of trauma in a heavy gravity well. The effect of blood loss is magnified. Her body is working overtime to survive in this hellish, unnatural environment. Most of the blood in her body pools in her legs, low to the ground. Her heart muscles are desperately trying to circulate blood to her head, but her blood pressure is fluctuating, causing her to feel faint.

"What happened?" she asks as they stagger down a narrow corridor. Steam drifts through the darkness, escaping from ruptured cooling pipes. Amber warning lights flash behind them, casting shadows before them. Metal groans, buckling under the external pressure of four atmospheres. With the base on the verge of collapse, tremors rumble through the superstructure, coming in waves.

"One of those things got inside the reactor. Went straight

for the core. Lit up the containment grid like a goddamn supernova."

"We're still down here?" she asks, stating the obvious, struggling with shock and disbelief.

"Oh, yeah," he says. "Where were you? Where did they take you?"

"The Barton."

"That old shithole," Cap says with a bitter laugh.

"It looked new."

"What did they want?"

"They're trying to understand what we know about them. They want to know how we figured all this out."

"What did you tell them?" he asks, letting go of her for a moment so he can duck below a fallen support beam. "You didn't tell them anything, right?"

"I—I don't think so. I don't know."

Dante crouches beneath the twisted metal, feeling the I-beam tremble as the internal walls of the base flex. Humidity hangs in the air. Moisture runs down the walls. Outside, it's a hundred below. Snow billows across the frozen plain.

"I don't think so," she says, repeating that point, fighting not to become distracted by her fleeting memories.

"Good. Good."

"What now?" she asks. "What's next?"

"First, we get the *fuck* off this hellhole, then we report back to Deep Space Command. We've got to give them everything we have. They need to know what they're up against."

She nods, agreeing. The two of them stagger to an airlock leading to the shuttlecraft waiting out on the ice. Mags is there, standing beside the entrance, but she's in a trance. Her eyes have rolled into the back of her head, revealing the whites along with a spiderweb of red veins and at least one burst blood vessel. She's speaking, but not aloud. Her lips move, shaping words but they're barely a whisper. Fingers twitch, carrying out unseen actions.

"Mags," Dante says, pleading with her, trying to get her attention. Like Dante, she's been trapped in the prison of her own mind, navigating some ethereal dream. Mags is being interrogated by the aliens, probably on another version of the Barton.

Cap rests Dante on the edge of a mining crate. His hands are shaking, something she only now notices. To her, he's a tower of strength, but he's simply hiding his fears better than she is.

First Lieutenant Asiko Capidastrianani wasn't even supposed to be here. The Acheron was originally captained by a veteran—Colonel Sandy Wilkinson, but she was injured in the rapid decompression test of the Centauri drydock. Someone up high tapped Cap on the shoulder, telling him this was a good career move. Dante had her doubts about a political appointment, but Cap has distinguished himself, listening to the advice of his officers and avoiding the trap of an *I-can-do-no-wrong* ego that plagues so many in command.

"Hey. Hey," Cap says, taking Mags by the shoulders and shaking her softly. "Come on. You've got to fight this."

"Where is everyone?" Dante asks, taking stock of what's happening and where they are. "Have you heard from Benson?"

"He's in low orbit, ready for rendezvous, but the radio's out. The main antenna collapsed when the fuel reserves blew out on the ice."

"What about the engineering team? Mac, Angel and Vichy?"

"They're dead."

Those two words hit her like a rogue planet coming out of the darkness. Two words delivered with brutal efficiency, the kind that ignores the enormity of lives being lost in an instant.

Cap tries to turn Mags around, wanting to guide her into the airlock, but she resists and fights to remain facing down along the corridor. He's injured and struggles to pull her away.

Mags always was strong. She lashes out, striking at him, but not with clenched fists. Her motion is like that of someone sleepwalking, fighting off imaginary demons.

"We don't have time for this shit," Cap says, frustrated. He slumps to one side, colliding with the coolant pipes running along the wall.

"We're not leaving her," Dante says, hobbling to her friend and trying to get her attention.

Mags is more than a crewmate. Although it's tempting to claim their friendship stems from a common hometown, that town is Staten Island. With twenty-seven million people calling New York City home, Staten Island is hardly the small town Alabama of Dante's childhood. Were it not for the colonization program offering deep space careers to scientists, engineers and doctors, they'd have never met, even though they lived within five miles of each other as teens. Sharing anecdotes kindled an affinity during training. Lou's Deli. Pappa's Pizza. Struggling to get a seat on the Staten Island ferry. Being groped on the subway. Listening to Christmas carols in Battery Park. With five years between them, Dante was leaving high school as Mags was just beginning to find her groove. Little did they know they'd travel to the stars together.

For Mags, swearing is like breathing. Dante tries to use that to reach her friend. "Jesus H. fucking Christ, Mags," she yells, just inches from her friend's face, so close spittle settles on the woman's flushed cheeks. "Get your goddamn ass on that shuttlecraft!"

Mags tightens her lips, widening her stance and clenching her fists. It's as though she heard someone else, not Dante. Whatever these creatures said to her, it's made her more resolved. At six foot four in height, Mags is formidable, even for Cap. Her arms flex, making micro-movements. It's as though she's trapped in a nightmare, fighting to escape.

"Come back to me, Mags," Dante says, pleading with her friend, knowing how convincing the illusion can be, hoping to break through to her.

Cap paces, mumbling to himself, ignoring them, trying to talk himself through the problem. "With core spikes hitting twenty thousand degrees, the magnetic field won't hold for long. We've got maybe an hour at most. It's just a matter of time. The radiant heat is going to cause cascading component failure, taking failsafes offline one after the other. Minimum survivable distance has got to be at least a hundred klicks. We've got to go. Now!"

"You're going to leave her?" Dante asks.

Cap leans against the side of the airlock, resting for a moment, wanting a reprieve from the oppressive gravity. He breathes deeply. Blood smears on the wall as he drags himself on.

"I don't know. I don't know what I'm going to do," he says in frustration. "We don't have the luxury of waiting for her to wake. This ain't a fucking drill, Dante!"

Cap leans forward, grabbing at his thigh, trying to massage the muscle. Blood runs from beneath his fingers. Rather than dripping as it would on Earth, tapping out time like a metronome, deep red blood rushes from his wound. The drops are surreal in the heavy gravity. They're as fine as needles, thin and elongated, streaking down to the metal grating where they barely splash.

Cap looks at Dante, appealing to her. "Are you going to drag her in there? Because I sure as hell can't. She's too big, too strong."

"How do you know?" Dante asks, ignoring Mags for a moment and looking down the corridor, changing the subject and taking Cap by surprise. Cap is already inside the airlock pulling a medical kit off the wall. Rather than lowering it to the seat running along the curved wall of the airlock, he drops it. The small plastic box plummets as though it weighs a ton, crashing into the padded seat.

Cap is breathing heavily. "Know what?"

"You said they were dead. Vichy, Mac and Angel."

"They are. They must be."

"But you don't know that," Dante yells over the sound of

bending, crunching metal. The superstructure of the ice station is succumbing to the heat weakening the support beams. "It's Angel we're talking about out there. Your Angel. If she's still alive, you can't just leave her."

The look on Cap's face is one of pained anguish. He's torn. Conflicted.

"We're going to die. You understand that, right?" he says, pushing a needle-less injector into the exposed skin on his leg and giving himself a shot of painkillers. Almost immediately, the tension in his shoulders dissipates and his arms sag. Relief floods his brain, masking the pain, lying to him about the state of his body.

Dante appeals to him. "We have to try."

"There's no time!"

"We can't leave them."

"I'm not abandoning anyone, but we can't wait forever. We can't wait more than a couple of minutes." He waves, gesturing down the corridor. "The containment field could fail at any point and all this will be over in a picosecond. You want that? Is that really what you want?"

"I'm not leaving Vichy," she says. "Not without knowing for sure."

"Fuck," Cap says, making his way back to her. "Goddamn it, Dante. Let them go."

Cap's bloodied fingers grab at the rim of the airlock as he steadies himself. He hands her a shot of painkillers, saying, "When the core blows, it's going to leave a crater the size of Manhattan. Do you really want to be here when that happens?"

Dante pops the cap off, positions her thumb over the plunger and works the end beneath her torn trousers before squeezing the tube. For a moment, she feels like a superhero. Adrenaline surges through her torn muscles. Analgesics numb the pain.

Cap positions himself behind Mags, bracing himself before slipping his hands under her armpits and reaching back over her shoulders. Mags reacts immediately, swinging her arms and head, catching him on the jaw, but he drags her backwards anyway, crouching and pulling against her efforts to resist. Mags kicks, but that only helps him. Cap leans back as far as he can, planting each boot with care, moving as though he were wading through a raging current, dragging her into the airlock.

Once inside, he lets go. Immediately, Mags stands upright. Her head turns, looking around, but through the whites of her eyes she sees only the illusion created by these monsters. Cap blocks her path, frustrating her as she tries to step out of the airlock.

"I'm not leaving Vichy," Dante says, more defiant the

second time.

"I don't want to do this any more than you do," Cap replies as he punches commands into the central computer. Blood drips from his fingers. "But I'm not staying."

"Where are they?" Dante asks.

"E4. In the control room," Cap says through gritted teeth, pressing against his leg, trying to limit the blood loss. The act of hauling Mags inside has caused the bleeding to intensify. He yells at Dante, "If you go back there, you won't make it out alive."

"I've got to try."

Mags becomes violent, striking Cap with wildly swinging fists, desperately trying to get out of the airlock even though she has no idea where she actually is.

"Why?" Cap yells, pushing Mags into a rack of spacesuits hanging on the wall. She fights with them, striking at these ghostly assailants rather than hitting him. She's lost in a nightmare. "What if you run into one of those things again? What if they put you back under? What then, Dante?"

"They need us."

"We've got to get off this rock," Cap counters. "We've got to warn command. You've got to understand—those *fuckers* out there will stop at nothing to kill us. If we die down here, they win."

"Give me ten minutes."

"You've got five. It'll take me that long to prep for takeoff, then I'm leaving. With or without you."

Dante doesn't waste time with a response. She pushes off down the corridor toward the control room, limping. Although the pain has subsided, her left leg simply won't carry her on as it should so she swings from her hip, pushing off the pipes running along the wall as she limps into the darkness.

Walking in 2.2 gees is akin to carrying a backpack full of rocks. Dante stabs with her feet. Although she wants to be more careful, knowing a fall could break bones or shatter her hip, gravity doesn't oblige, slamming her boots against the metal grating. Raising her leg and stepping forward is like struggling with a deadlift at the gym. Just the slightest change in muscle tension and her foot thunders back to the deck. Everything is difficult. It's as though she's chained to the planet.

"They're going to get you," Cap yells. "Again. And then what? All this will be for nothing!"

Dante crouches beneath a fallen beam.

"I'm not coming back for you," Cap yells. "Not this time. You're on your own!"

Dante can't explain why, but she feels as though she's always been on her own.

Growing up in overcrowded New York City, there was always someone around. As Dante shared a bedroom with her younger sister, being alone was more a state of mind than place. She desperately missed the quiet of rural Alabama, but a good pair of headphones helped. South Beach, Staten Island, in the depths of winter, was the closest Dante ever came to actually being by herself, but even then, joggers and fishermen dotted the sand. It was a stark contrast to her old home in Fairview, Alabama. Back there, the mountains seemed to stretch forever. In New York, it was the concrete roads that were eternal. South Beach was nothing like Hawaii or Pensacola, but that thin stretch of sand was a refuge for her.

As far as islands go, Staten wouldn't make the top ten thousand on Earth. Oil would drift on the water, coming in from the shipping lanes. The sand was gritty. Garbage would wash up along the shore whenever the wind would blow in from the ocean. In summer, the beach would be packed with people claiming every square inch of sand with a towel as though South Beach had somehow been transformed into the French Riviera, while in winter, it could only be described as bleak, and yet she loved it—probably because that small fringe of sand marked the boundary between the madness of the city and the seemingly infinite ocean beyond.

Seagulls would glide above the waves, held roughly in place by the onshore wind. They seemed to hover, neither advancing nor sliding back, barely holding their own in the blustery winds as they looked for crabs and scraps of food left on the sand. With the twitch of a wing and a twist of their tails they'd dip as the gusts shifted. They had to duck and weave merely to stay still, being trapped by the wind, eking out a meager existence on the lifeless beach. Caught without a net. Constantly fighting just to stay where they were. Working hard but going nowhere. As a failed astrobiology Ph.D. candidate, Dante understood their frustration all too well. Oh, she told the flight selection committee her shift to medical research was tactical, that she had more interest in medical application than abiogenesis theory, but that was a lie. She flunked. That's the thing about lies—they never help. They leave people even more isolated and alone than before. As Dante wades through the bursts of steam coming from the cracked pipes lining the corridor, she knows precisely why she's going after Angel, Mac and Vichy. She can't stand living a lie, pretending she did all she could. She'd rather die than not try and then have to live with the uncertainty of giving up too soon.

The lights within the base flicker, briefly threatening to and then dramatically plunging the station into darkness. Starlight reflects off the ice outside, but the thin windows running down the corridor were designed as viewing ports, not for external lighting, leaving the interior nearly pitch black. Dante shuffles her way along the wall with her hands.

She's close. She can feel waves of air pulsing down the corridor, washing over her. Her fingers glide over the wall rather than pressing against the panels, trying to avoid the steam pipes.

"Where are you?" she asks the darkness, not entirely sure she wants an answer.

Dante slides her feet over the grating, no longer confident lifting them in the pitch black darkness, fearing a fall that could incapacitate her. In the shadows, it feels as though she's standing on the balcony of a tall building at night, edging her way along, desperate not to fall. Her heart pounds in her chest.

"Daaannnteee," echoes down the corridor behind her.

"Goddamn it, Cap," she whispers in reply. "Don't you leave me down here."

Her mind races. What if one of those things made it out of the reactor room? What if they're already here, lurking in the darkness? What if they cut the power to the lights? What if her fingers are inches from brushing up against their cold, clammy skin?

Her trembling hand finds a door handle. Dante pulls on the lever, activating the emergency access reserves that power the door. Deep within the smooth metal surface, locks click and whir. Even without main electricity, the failsafe sensors have tested the pressure, temperature and atmospheric mix on the other side of the door and determined it's safe to open.

"Mac?" Dante asks, struggling to see anything as she pushes against the heavy door with her shoulder. She inches forward, edging inside. "Vichy? Angel?"

The silence is ominous. If they're alive, they're deep under—just like Mags.

"Is anyone there?"

Something's wrong. Something other than a base that's about to collapse around her. Dante thought she was peering into the control room, but there's nothing beyond the door, nothing but darkness. It's alive. She can feel it—like static electricity hanging in the air.

Although she knows better, she steps forward, understanding this is the end yet again. Tentacles wrap themselves around her legs, squeezing tight, holding on to her as they work their way up her body, but Dante's not afraid. She should be, but a rush of endorphins flood her mind. Instead of fight or flight, it's as though she's addicted to the swell of emotions coursing through her neurons. She wants to be afraid, but she's not.

Once again, Dante slips into the void. She looks around, wanting to see something familiar. Behind her lies the window. Beyond that, chunks of glacial ice dot the frozen plain. Dark mountains rise in the distance, reaching up toward a sky that's alive with stars. Oh, the stars. They're beautiful. They shine with a brilliance that cuts through the night. The stars are majestic. Dante's at peace with what's happening to her, but the stars—the stars burn brightly, raging against the darkness, refusing to surrender.

DREAMS

For Dante, there's something hypnotic about watching an entire planet drift past the windows of the Acheron in the darkness. Even after all these years, she never tires of the view. Her instructors told her life in deep space would be like living in Colorado. After a while, people take the Rockies for granted, seeing them as little more than the backdrop on a stage, but for Dante the allure is still there.

On the daylight side of the planet, the motion of the Acheron can be a little unsettling, as instead of being sedate, the planet itself appears to turn sideways through 360 degrees every few minutes. Each orbit takes just over two hours but the motion of the Acheron itself makes the planet appear as though it's turning in front of her. What she's witnessing is the spacecraft rotating about its axis, but it's hard to shake the feeling of being still and the entire universe twisting around their tiny starship. At night, though, Dante can almost pretend the universe is at peace.

The Acheron has opened out into its standard, bicycle-wheel configuration, revolving about a central axis to simulate the effect of gravity as it orbits the planet, but it makes everything beyond the windows disorienting. During their hour-long days, the clouds, ice shelves, glaciers and mountain ranges all appear to turn when it's actually the spacecraft that's in motion—but not at night. In the darkness, the planet appears still.

Dante's a retro-buff. She's always felt as though she was born out of time, feeling more of an affinity with the origins of the US space program than the interstellar gold rush of her age. Although almost a century separates her from Sally Ride and Mae Jemison, to her they're mentors. She feels their influence on her life.

Dante has always surrounded herself with nostalgic knock-offs. Actual antiques are too pricey, but for her, watching the view out the window is a bit like watching an old fashioned analog clock hanging on the wall, only instead of the second hand moving, it's the entire clock that's turning.

Were it not for the stars appearing in motion, the planet would seem entirely still at night. Those pesky stars drift in unison, tracing a circle as the craft turns. If she stares at them too long she knows she'll feel sick.

Dante has lost count of how many times people asked her what she would miss most about life on Earth. Friends, reporters, psychiatrists and even her mom all questioned her about the things she would miss going out into interstellar space. Oh, there were the usual answers. Ice cream. Going to the beach. Walks in the forest. But once she got out here the thing she missed most was the horizon.

People on Earth take being stationary for granted. Sit in a chair. Stare at the mountains. Watch a bird fly past. All of it seems to unfold against the unmovable backdrop of Earth. Of course, Earth is anything but stationary, spinning at over a thousand kilometers an hour at the equator, racing around the sun at tens of thousands of kilometers an hour, while orbiting within the spiral arm of an immense galaxy at *hundreds of thousands of kilometers an hour*—and yet the illusion of being still, stable and fixed on Earth is convincing—and strangely comforting. Not so on the Acheron.

Benson marches into the medical bay, arguing with Cap.

"This is bullshit," he says. "There's nothing wrong with me."

Dante swivels in her chair, turning to face them.

"Relax," Cap says, trying to calm his Executive Officer.

"I never should've said anything."

"There's no shame in a psychiatric evaluation."

Benson lets out a laugh. There's an undertone of bitterness in his voice. "You've just *fucked* my career. You know that, right?"

"We can be discreet about these things," Cap says. Dante's already on her feet, trying to assess what's happening. Cap holds out his hand, not wanting her to get up but it's too late.

She wants to ask, "What's wrong?" but given the way Benson's shaking his head in disbelief, she suspects that wouldn't be good form. Besides, she's about to find out.

"I want this off the books," Cap says.

Dante nods.

"No records. No identifiers. This never happened, understood?"

"Of course."

Benson's eyes dart from Cap to her. His lips tighten.

"Hey, it's going to be okay," she says.

Benson laughs, only this time it's hearty and intentional. His eyes go wide as he says, "Oh, you have no idea."

Dante gestures for him to hop up on one of the beds. Benson sits on a thin foam mattress covered in a crisp white sheet. For a moment, that stirs something in the depths of her mind. Memories come in and out of focus. There's something she's forgotten. Something important. Something nagging at her, but it doesn't concern Benson, of that she's sure. No, she has a vague recollection of sitting in roughly the same position, facing some other doctor. But there aren't any other physicians on the Acheron. There's no one within about ten light years of them. No gas for sixty trillion miles.

Cap breaks her train of thought. "Nothing invasive. No drugs. Just a scan, okay?"

"Sure," she replies.

Benson starts pulling off his shoes.

"It's fine," she says.

As warm as her smile is, both it and her words are calculated. No one ever wants an unscheduled psych evaluation. It's bad enough coaxing the crew in for their annual review. Benson's right. Impromptu evals are career ending. They're generally only administered for severe anxiety or depression, either of which can get an astronaut grounded. 'Grounded' on the Acheron would mean relieved of duties and slated for replacement when they next rendezvous with a deep space station, but Dante has a few options open to her.

"I'm going to log this as a calibration exercise," she says. "I'll purge the storage banks and set the metadata to read as self-administered. They'll think I ran this on myself to calibrate the system. No one will think twice about it, I promise."

Benson says, "Thanks, Dante."

"What am I looking for?" she asks Cap.

"Activity in the sensory cortex."

That's unusually specific, but Dante goes with it. She sets a crown of electronics on Benson's head, carefully positioning it so it sits just above his temples, resting it on his ears. A series of colored LEDs glow softly, indicating connectivity and confirming the measurement of brain wave activity across the spectrum.

"Am I looking for anything in particular?" she asks.

Benson swallows a lump in his throat. "Hallucinations."

Dante and Cap exchange a knowing glance. He's worried about something, but to her surprise, it doesn't seem to be a concern about Benson himself. Cap's nervous, which is unusual for him. Dante refocuses, picking up her flex computer and reviewing the incoming data stream.

"I'm seeing gamma-beta dominant. Low alpha. Nothing in the delta or theta range. There's some infra-low, but nothing outside the bounds. Looks entirely normal."

Yet again, she's trying to put Benson at ease. Cap backs off, making as though he only has a passing interest in what's happening, even though they all know that's a lie.

Benson fidgets, picking at his fingernails.

Dante says, "I'm going to ask you some questions, okay?"

He nods.

Dante starts out with a few control questions, but in the back of her mind, she's unsettled. Neither of them has told her what this is actually about. Hallucination is too general a term. Humans are sensory-driven creatures. In the unnatural environment of space, almost ninety light-years from home, it's not uncommon to imagine hearing a friendly voice or to see something in the shadows or have memories rush by when a familiar smell drifts through the air. None of that means someone's going insane. On the contrary, the lack of those responses is of more concern as such detachment is unhealthy. But this is something more, something outside the norm. Whatever it is, neither of them wants anything clouding her judgment. She respects that, putting her own curiosity to one side and focusing on Benson.

"Where were you born?"

His answer is robotic.

"Boston."

Benson was expecting that question so his answer isn't helping him relax. At this point, she's got to distract him. His conscious mind is blocking her. Like a left tackle protecting the quarterback, he's putting up fierce resistance to any approach from the flanks.

"Boston's beautiful in the springtime," she says gently. "I

used to go there all the time during the holidays."

It's a white lie. Dante only ever went to Boston twice, but he won't know that. Familiarity is one way to get him to lower his guard.

"My grandmother lived in Lexington. She had one of those three-story Queen Anne homes. It was a replica, but a damn good one."

On the flex, his beta waves begin to subside while the alpha come in short bursts. He's recalling something, but probably nothing specific. Feelings precede thoughts.

She continues, "Now, I'm not going to insult you by asking about clam chowder, but you've got to be honest with me. Lobster mac 'n cheese?"

"Oh, yeah." Benson smiles, unable to suppress a memory Dante has deliberately invoked by drawing on visual clues and his olfactory recollections of taste and smell. The more senses she can include, the easier it is to make him compliant for the eval. She smiles. This time, it's real, although not because she's being friendly. She's smiling because she's winning in the tug of war for his subconscious mind.

Dante continues, "I mean, it shouldn't work, but it does, right? On one level it's sacrilege, but, hey—Boston."

Benson grins. She's got him. She sees theta waves rippling as pleasant memories fire within his synapses, releasing dopamine and comforting him. There's some delta activity, suggesting he identifies with what she's saying. Dante works him a little deeper.

"My grandma would make cream pie. Well, it was more of a cake than a pie, but she called it pie. Us kids learned not to argue with her if we wanted some. Custard, chocolate and cream layers inside a soft, moist sponge cake—what's not to love? Damn, we need to get that on the menu out here."

"We do," he says, looking directly into her eyes, but he's staring through her, not at her. He's too deep. Something's wrong. Dante locks her smile in place. She was expecting agreement, but this is something more. He's like putty. It's almost as though she's hypnotized him, but she hasn't. Things are moving too damn fast. On the flex, theta waves drown out the alpha and beta signals. His higher order gamma waves have flatlined. He should be asleep, but he's not. His face is pale. His eyes look distant.

Cap has his arms folded over his chest. He's quiet, but intensely interested. Dante is focused, determined. She feels as though she's in control, but Benson looks lost, almost manic.

"Do you dream?" she asks.

"We all dream, doc."

"But do you remember your dreams?"

"Always."

As far as Dante's aware, that's not possible. Dreams occur during REM sleep, when neurons deep within the brain stem fire rapidly, lighting up the thalamus and the cortex like fireworks and setting the eyes darting beneath the eyelids. As that happens five or six times a night and each dream is generally quite vague, it's simply not possible to remember every one.

"What do you dream about?" she asks.

Benson replies, "Home, mostly."

Dante looks to Cap, tacitly wanting permission to probe about the hallucinations. He nods.

"What about when you're awake? Do you ever see things you can't explain?"

"Maybe sometimes."

That's the kind of noncommittal answer someone gives when they don't want to admit to something that's potentially compromising. He's still worried about the impact of this eval on his career and yet he feels compelled to continue.

"It's strange. Ya know, doc?"

The tone of his voice has changed. The pitch has dropped and the S's are slurred. According to the readouts on Dante's tablet, he should be fast asleep, but he's clearly awake.

"What do you see?"

"You. Cap. Them."

His voice is almost playful, which is confusing.

"Who are *they*?" she asks, feeling her heart start to race.

"They're really quite beautiful."

There's something unnerving about the way Benson's looking past her, focusing on something behind her. It's then she realizes. *You. Cap. Them.* He's not recalling a memory. He's talking about what he sees right now.

Dante feels the hair on the back of her neck rise. She wants to turn and look behind her, but doesn't. It takes all her mental energy to stay focused on him and ignore the air brushing against her arms, catching on the tiny raised hairs bristling in alarm.

"There's nothing there," she says.

That gets Cap's attention. His brow furrows. His eyes dart between Dante and Benson. From where he is, leaning against the bulkhead off to her right, he can see behind her. If anything was there, he'd be able to see it. He'd react. He doesn't. There's nothing there, she tells herself.

Dante fights the irrational desire to turn around, refusing to cower to the fear seizing her mind. Her body, though, isn't convinced. Her heart pounds in her ribcage. Adrenaline surges through her veins. Sweat breaks out on her brow. Her fingers twitch. She's got to take back control of the interview, wrestling it away from Benson and turning it in the direction she wants rather than indulging his delusions.

Again, she asks, "Who are they?" But her voice breaks slightly. A quiver betrays her fear. She projects, raising the volume of her voice, wanting to sound braver than she is. "What are they? What do they want? Why do you see them when no one else does?"

Peppering Benson with questions without waiting for an answer isn't smart. During training, her lecturers stressed the importance of silence during evals. Ask a question. Wait for an answer. Whoever speaks first, loses—that was the mantra. Speaking lets the other person off the hook, it gives them an out. She could kick herself.

Benson's eyes widen as if in response to something looming over her, but he's not afraid. His cheeks are flushed. He's smiling—grinning. He looks insane.

"What do they look like?" she asks, bringing a fifth unanswered question into the evaluation, but she can't help herself, she has to know. "Tell me!"

"Tell you?" he replies, sniggering. "You already know. You've seen them. I know you have. We all have. They're everywhere."

At first, Dante's confused, but deep down, she knows he's

right. She remembers them, but only as an impression, a vague concept, a longing.

On the flex, Benson's brain waves are firing like a seismograph during an earthquake. The alpha and beta waves have flatlined, but everything else is going crazy. The spikes are hitting a tempo of dozens of waves per second, which for long, slow brain waves like theta is unheard of. His delta wave graph is blank, which given they're the deepest waves of all, shocks her, then she sees the line pressing unbroken against the ceiling of that metric—like the engine of a Ferrari screaming as the accelerator is pressed hard against the floor.

"Benson, he's," she stammers, looking to Cap for support. "There's something wrong—horribly wrong."

Dante opens a cabinet at the head of the bed, half-expecting to find it empty, but not sure why. In the haze of her mind, that thought is confusing. She shrugs it off, pulling out a medi-kit and rummaging through the contents.

Benson giggles like a child. He's pointing behind her, but Dante's a professional. Her training tells her he's likely suffering from an embolism. A clot has probably formed in some other part of his body and crept up into his brain. High gravity. She had run a few deep-vein thrombosis scans on the away crew after the first couple of sorties down to the surface, but everything came back fine. At the time, she thought she was being overprotective. *Damn it! If that thing ruptures inside his brain, it'll kill him.*

"Jeeves," she says, alerting her AI assistant as she pulls a needle-less injector from the kit. "Prep for surgery. I'm going to need a full-body scan, with sub-millimeter granularity of the cranial cavity."

She prepares a shot of diazepam, not so much to sedate him for surgery as to break the neural pathways madly firing in his brain and calm him down.

Cap is standing beside Benson, but he's not looking at either of them. He's staring at the back of the medical bay.

"Cap," she says, pushing the injector into Benson's neck and shifting him around, removing the crown and laying him down on the bed. "I'm going to have to run some scans and possibly operate. I need you to—"

Cap ignores her, tapping her shoulder, wanting her to turn around, but she can't. Benson needs her. He could die.

"Cap?" she says. He's still tapping her shoulder, but the rhythm is slowing.

A tentacle wraps around her foot, slithering up her leg. Feelers touch at her waist, probing her back, gently pressing against her clothes. A slimy frond brushes against her neck, feeling its way under her collar.

Dante closes her eyes. She knows. She doesn't want to, but she does—not as knowledge or facts as such, but she feels the reality of life on the Acheron overwhelm her once more. Every cell in her body aches, longing for hope, but there's none to be found. Dozens of encounters, each masked in some way. This moment too will fade, she knows that. As much as she wants to remember, she knows she'll be denied this most basic right.

Dante wants to go home, to be anywhere other than here. She wants to go back to New York. She longs to stand on the sandy shores of South Beach again, feeling the cool wind against her cheeks. She yearns for the smell of salt spray hanging in the air and the sound of gulls calling on the breeze, but the darkness deprives her of even those memories. She looks around, watching as tentacles wrap around the bed and desk, creeping along the walls. Hope fades. Her heart sinks. Futility overwhelms her, but the stars—the stars speak softly to her, telling her she's not alone.

MOM

"Why you?" a familiar voice asks.

"Me?"

Dante blinks, looking around in the darkness. Waves roll in toward the beach, washing softly on the sand, leaving a thin trail of bubbles and foam along the shore. A star twinkles over the ocean, sitting low in the sky. Must be a planet, she reminds herself. Probably Jupiter. Stars are so astonishingly distant, they appear stable. Planets, though, like Venus, Jupiter, Mars and Saturn shimmer as their light passes through the atmosphere.

Wait.

Something important has slipped her mind. She was just thinking about the stars. She was looking at them, only they were much clearer. There was no atmospheric haze, no light pollution, just exquisite pinpricks of pure light piercing the eternal darkness. Dante was just talking to someone, but not her mom. Orion has emerged in the East, rising slowly over the Atlantic. Beautiful, she thinks, but that thought leaves her feeling unsettled and she's not sure why.

Sand shifts beneath Dante's bare feet, causing her to stab with her toes to keep her balance. The wind picks up and the thin blades of grass dotted along the dunes bend and sway in unison.

"You're ignoring me," her mom says.

Dante's head is swinging. The stars in the sky seem to swirl around her. There's too much happening at once.

Her dad says, "How long will Earth Hour last anyway?" Followed quickly by, "Never mind," when he's met with an exasperated chorus of, "One hour," from her brother, her sister and her mother. "Yeah, my bad." He chugs a beer. Dad never was one for the stars. Her sister, though, has caught the bug.

"I can't find the pole star," she says, turning to Dante for help. Jules fiddles with the mount on her telescope, looking down the sighting port. "Is that where you're going?"

"Ah, Polaris is in Ursa Major," Dante says feeling somewhat distant. Her mind is elsewhere. She feels as though she shouldn't be here. "I'll be passing through Ursa Minor. The next constellation over." Dante points north, out over New York City. "You start at Polaris and follow the curve. We're using a brown dwarf about eleven light years away from here to conduct a gravity slingshot on to WISE 5571 at a distance of eighty-eight light years. That's our target."

"Does your star have a name?" her sister asks.

"That is its name."

"That's not a real name," her sister insists. At sixteen, she's too old to be a child and yet too young to be an adult. In those frustrating in-between years, everything's contentious. "What about Draco—the dragon. Are you going anywhere near there?"

Dante laughs. "*Near* is a relative term. Everything you see is nearby compared to Andromeda."

She crouches, looking at how the telescope has been set up and adjusts the legs, shifting them in the sand so they're more sturdy. In the low light, Dante can barely see the level on the side of the stand, but she works with the tripod until the base is flat. Using a compass, she ensures the setup is facing true north and sets the latitude, saying, "Okay. Try again."

Jules crouches. "Oh, yeah. I see it."

Dante's mother is standing back beside a soft red camp light set on the sand. Her dad is seated in a portable deck chair. Cars pull in and out of the parking lot. Their headlights wash over the dunes, briefly interfering with her night vision. Automated trucks rumble across the nearby bridge, heading over the Narrows to Fort Hamilton.

Jules has a flex tablet. She works with it, searching for WISE 5571 even though Dante's already told her it's too faint to be seen from South Beach on Staten Island with an 11 inch diffraction telescope—even with all the fancy buttons and computerized tracking. Jules doesn't care. She wants to look anyway. Just seeing the stars in that direction and knowing her sister is going to soar through that region at close to the speed of light is enough. For her, this is a movie brought to life.

Dante joins her mother, sensing her brooding.

Mom asks, "You're sure about this?"

"Yes."

Simple question. Simple answer. Unfortunately, nothing's simple with Mom.

"But when you get back—if you ever come back—everyone you've ever known will be gone. Dead. The world will be entirely different. Hundreds of years will have passed. Do you really want that?"

Dante looks up at the stars, mentally tracing an imaginary line from her sister's telescope into the heavens, admiring the view, wondering what lies in wait for her around WISE 5571.

Scans have revealed a simple system. There are several rocky inner planets on the fringes of the Goldilocks zone, shepherded by gas giants further out, orbiting a yellow dwarf star that could be a twin of the Sun. Some astronomers have even suggested its slight, regular pulsing might be an illusion, saying it might be a contact binary, two stars orbiting each other so insanely close they're destined to become one.

Several astrophysicists have warned the crew that there's a danger in reading too much into any apparent similarities with their solar system and have flagged several other nearby star systems as backup targets, but Dante's excited. Will they find life? The chances aren't good, but they're better than not trying.

"It's worth it," Dante says, which is not what her mother wants to hear. Too late. With the launch barely eighteen months away, the teams are set. It would take a disaster to prevent her launch or to drag her from the crew—something she feels she can prevent through sheer willpower alone.

A shooting star cuts through the night, arcing across the sky and dying in a blaze of glory. It's a sight reserved for those venturing out to stargaze—lost to those staring at the TV or drinking in the local bar. It was probably no bigger than a pebble, but it looked magnificent.

Even during Earth Hour, there's considerable light pollution, but it's nice to see the stars so clearly from New York, if only briefly. It's nothing like the view from the Rockies in the depths of winter, but it reinforces the allure that draws Dante into the sky. To her, the stars are the epitome of life.

Without them, there wouldn't be any heavy elements. Once, every cell in her body was caught within the raging furnace of a star, scattered by countless atomic nuclei seething in a plasma superheated to tens of millions of degrees. A couple of billion years later, here she is. For Dante, the flight to WISE 5571 is akin to going home.

"Why you?"

"Why me?" Dante replies. She laughs at the insanity of her life. "Yeah. There are ten billion people on this rock. Ten billion and only ten missions. Less than a hundred astronauts. It's *'how come me?'* not, *'why me?'* Some days, I have to pinch myself to convince myself this is real."

"But you'll never have any kids," her mother says.

"Jules will," Dante replies. "And Pete."

"That doesn't bother you?"

"No. Not in the slightest."

"You're young. Too young," her mother says, but Mom's interrupted by Dad.

"Jackie. Please."

"No. It's got to be said."

"What?" Dante asks.

"Honey. You're too young to know what you really want."

Dante scoffs at the notion. "Mom. I'm twenty-seven."

"And what about when you're thirty-seven and stuck around some strange star a billion miles from home?"

"It'll be more than a billion, Mom," Dante says, finding her mother's grasp of distance quaint. "That would only get me as far as Saturn."

Dante's tempted to point out that it'll actually be closer to a quadrillion miles, but that won't help. When numbers get as large as 10 to the power of 15 they become abstractions layered on top of abstractions. Saying a thousand, million, billion might be just as accurate, but it's also just as meaningless. Like the untold grains of sand squishing between her toes as she looks out at the stars, it's a number that has no practical value beyond being way too many.

"You don't know what you're going to want," her mother insists. "What about when you're forty? Fifty? Sixty?"

Numbers. More abstract, meaningless numbers. They're not quite as big, but they're just as intangible to Dante. Right now, she feels as though she's going to live forever.

"Mom, making one of these missions is literally a one-in-a-billion opportunity. I can't pass that by. I can't turn it down. This is the chance of a lifetime—an opportunity to be at the forefront of scientific exploration."

Dad speaks up, "It's the Mars loss that has her worried."

Dante nods, not so much in agreement as in that she

understands their concerns. Mars was the dream. For centuries, since at least the early 1600s, people have imagined traveling to and living on Mars. Science fiction made Mars out to be alluring, the adventure of a lifetime. After the US established a colony there and the media began talking of settlers taming the land, it seemed as though the Wild West had been brought back to life. Reality, though, was different. After the first boots kicked up Martian dust in 2037, several additional research stations were established by the Europeans, the Indians and the Chinese. The Russians bypassed Mars, going on to build orbital platforms around Jupiter and Saturn.

The public dreamed of emigrating to Mars. The news media made it out to be the Promised Land. Oh, occasionally reports of deaths rolled in, but fatal accidents happen all the time on Earth. No one blinked.

The loss of the US research station in the Hellas Basin came as a shock. Congress launched an investigation into the deaths of 148 crewmembers when their subsurface habitat collapsed, while the United Nations undertook a broader investigation into the viability of a permanent Martian colony and reported gross mismanagement, escalating costs, a lack of long term sustainability and the inability to achieve material or technological independence from Earth within the next century. Overnight, Mars became the interplanetary equivalent of the slums. The US pulled out. Once American resupply missions stopped, the other nations followed suit. Several automated research hubs replaced boots kicking at the rocks, with an AI controlling daily activity and scientists working remotely from Earth. Instead of propelling humanity to the stars, Mars was seen as a false start, a bitter reminder of just how harsh and costly life is beyond the thin veil of Earth. Public support evaporated. Even the Star Shot program suffered cutbacks. Within a month, thirty-eight interstellar ships became ten, with the threat of being reduced to just one—or worse.

"This is different," Dante says.

"You say that now," her mother replies. "Standing here on the shore of an actual ocean, breathing real air, free to go where you want and... I don't know, pick apples from a tree, buy a candy bar at the store, or go and see a movie with your friends. Once you're out there, all of that is gone. Forever."

Dante puts her arm around her mother's shoulder. She understands. Mom isn't saying anything out of animosity or selfishness. It's that she cares. She wants the best for her little girl now she's all grown up. Every mom goes through that in some way.

"You could stay," her mom says.

"I could," Dante replies. "But the stars, Mom—they call to me."

BENSON

"Oh, hey," Dante says, looking up from her desk in the medical bay. For a moment there, while staring out at the stars, she felt as though she was back on Earth talking with her Mom. Strange. That memory seemed so present—so real.

Benson stands in the doorway with a finger raised, resting it softly against his lips, wanting her to be quiet.

Weird.

Dante's mind is a blur, a mess, which is unusual for her. Even when she had a few too many drinks back at *The Black Hole*, their prelaunch bar in Florida, she never felt like this. Oh, there would be the classic thumping headache the next day, but she could normally think pretty clearly. Now, though, thoughts cascade through her consciousness like shooting stars. South Beach. Cap. Benson. A telescope set on the sand. She doesn't understand why, but she feels as though she was just talking to Benson not more than a few minutes ago—about what escapes her. Her eyes drift to the beds lining the medical bay, settling on one—fourth down from the door, next to the RXA scanner. Benson follows her gaze. He's looking at the same bed, smiling.

"Is everything okay?" she asks.

"What do you think, doc?" Benson walks softly across the floor, which is strange even for him. He's wearing socks, something that's not uncommon on the Acheron, but the way he walks, he doesn't make any sound. He's stepping on the balls of his feet, moving like a cat, treading lightly, almost floating above the floor. His eyes are haunting. Perhaps it's his smile that's unnerving. It's a burst of emotion that's entirely out of place. He knows something. A secret.

"How can I help?" she asks.

Once again, Benson raises his finger to his lips, but his smile is irrepressible, almost delusional. He's holding a flex. He turns it around, allowing her to see what's written on the screen.

I don't think they can read.

"Who?" she asks.

Without saying a word, Benson writes on the tablet with his finger. Why not type or use voice commands or his neural sensor? For that matter, why not simply speak?

The aliens, doc.

She humors him. Is Cap pranking her? Has Vichy put

him up to this? Oh, they're all going to burst in here at any moment, laughing their asses off, making fun of her, calling her gullible.

"Aliens, huh?"

"Shhhh..."

He erases his previous comment and writes a new one.

They haven't fudged it out yet.

"Fudged?" She smiles. "Did auto-correct get the better of your writing?"

He scrubs his hand back and forth, rewriting just one word. This time, rather than a crazy scrawl, with letters of various sizes running into and over each other, one word is spelled out clearly.

Figured.

"Oh, they haven't *figured* it out yet?"

He nods, grinning like a fool.

"They're not the only ones," Dante says, trying not to laugh. "Listen, I appreciate a good joke as much as anyone. And, honestly, you're a *delightful* interruption to an otherwise boring review of the biome-scan from the sewage holding tanks, but..."

She's not sure where to take this lopsided discussion and rounds out her thinking with, "I guess cursive writing isn't high on the alien agenda."

Benson giggles.

Dante shakes her head, smiling, still waiting for the punch line. The silence that follows leaves her unsettled. When she looks up she sees three words.

Do you remember?

"Remember?"

Benson tucks the tablet under his arm and crouches beside the RXA machine. He pulls out the neural interface, placing the crown of electronic thorns on his head. Without saying anything, he smiles, revealing his pearly white teeth.

Dante gets to her feet.

"You've put it on upside down," she says, reaching up and turning the medical scanner over, resting it above his ears. At first, she's just playing along, trolling herself as he teases her, but then it hits—the realization. For her, it's like opening the door on a bitter, cold winter morning and stepping out into the snow. The air is sharp, biting at the skin on her cheeks—such a stark contrast to the warmth of her home—causing an instant reaction. Goosebumps break out on her arms.

There's no memory as such, no distinct recollection, it's more of an impression, like the time she ran into her old high school friend Constance outside the Natural History Museum in New York shortly before their launch.

Snowflakes drifted on the breeze. The smiling face that greeted her on that chilly Autumn day was warm. Dante was walking down the vast concrete steps toward fans waiting in the icy slush for an autograph. She never understood why astronauts would have a fan club. She hadn't starred in any movies or been on some reality TV show. Hell, her social media presence was a bot programmed to post images and clips of her while responding politely to online chat sessions as though it were human. That made for a great party trick—*hey, who wants to see me talk to myself?* Dante hated that bot.

But there was Constance at the bottom of the steps, about three rows back—one face amid several hundred. Everyone was smiling and waving and calling out her name, but Constance had a glow, for lack of a better term. It was as though she was under a spotlight. It wasn't until they spoke that a flood of memories came rushing at Dante. In the same way, Benson seems to be inviting her to journey back in time with him.

Dante grabs at the loose threads of a fleeting memory. "Cap was here."

Benson nods. Damn it, she wants him to say something more, but his smile is gone. His lips have pulled tight, although not in anger. He's sad.

"You?" she says. "You can see them."

"Shhh."

Dante's heart races. Suddenly, she's short of breath. Her palms go sweaty. She feels a tingle in her legs.

"I—I don't understand."

Benson writes several words. Although they're upside down relative to her, she can read them, anticipating each of them with just a few letters.

Illusion.

Mirage.

Dream.

Nightmare.

Dante swallows the lump in her throat.

Nothing around her is real.

That thought causes her mind to race—or does it? Are these her thoughts? Who is she? If nothing's real, what is she? Everything she trusts, every aspect of reality, every sense of being is part of an illusion. The floor, the desk, the row of beds, the medical equipment and lights—is any of this real?

Dante looks at the back of her trembling hands, catching the pores of her skin, the flex of tendons, the fine creases around her knuckles and even the grain of her nails. She turns her hands over, looking at the lines in her palm.

"No, no, no," she says, shaking her head. "This can't be."

"But it is," Benson says, taking the electronic crown from

his head and resting it on the pristine white sheets. He pats the bed softly as if invoking memories. "You remember."

"I don't know what I remember."

"Don't fight it," he says, reaching out and taking her hand in his. The slightest touch from him seems to unleash a jolt of energy, causing her to tense up, but she doesn't pull away.

"We need to remember," he whispers. "If we don't, all hope is lost."

Dante feels her bottom lip quiver.

"I—I don't know... What the hell happened to us?"

"We need each other. We must help each other," he says. "We don't have long."

"If this isn't the Acheron, where are we? Really?"

Benson looks lost.

"I don't know, but none of this is real."

"How do you know? How can you be so sure?"

"Mistakes," he replies. "Imperfections. But each time, they get better."

"What kind of mistakes?" Dante asks, desperate for something to refute the madness, but deep down, she knows he's right. She can feel it. The darkness. Always so close. Always there, just on the edge of her vision.

"All of this looks real," he says, gesturing at the window.

She can see he's conflicted, worried about giving up too much. After a few seconds, he acquiesces and says, "The stars."

"What about the stars?" Dante asks.

"I thought I was going crazy, but the stars…"

Dante goes to the window. She presses her hands on the double-glazed plasti-glass. Her fingers push against the slick surface, grounding her in the illusion, but she's wary, not wanting to be fooled, wanting to see clearly. The surface feels solid—real. He's wrong. He has to be. This is stupid.

Outside, the planet is shrouded in darkness, but not for long. A thin, faint blue glow clings to the horizon, curving around the frozen wasteland. Glints of light reflect off lakes that have pooled on a plateau near the equator, kept from freezing by geothermal vents. Dante squints, looking out into space. In the seconds before the host stars emerge, causing her pupils to contract, she sees them—tens of thousands of stars.

"I don't understand."

"What do you see?" Benson asks, pointing above the polar region.

"Orion," she whispers.

"We see what we want to see."

Her heart drops.

The constellations, so familiar from her childhood, are an

illusion. They exist only because of perspective. Like railway tracks that converge in the distance, or cars, trucks, buses and houses that look like toys from a plane, they're deceptive, an illusion that was destroyed when the Acheron dropped out of near-luminal speed in this distant region of the galaxy.

At eighty-eight light years, the stars out here are the same ones she saw from Earth, but the connect-the-dots shapes are skewed or gone entirely. No Big Dipper. No Southern Cross. The Pleiades are still there, but only because they're a star cluster. Virgo is stretched, while Ares is flattened. Apart from the sword, Orion was gone. It was as though he vanished from the sky, dropping his equipment. Now, though, she can see his shoulders and legs. She shouldn't be able to see him at all.

"No, no, no. This can't be."

"But it is."

"I—I don't believe it. There has to be some other explanation." She turns to face him. "This is real. *I am real.*"

"But the stars," Benson says. "The stars—they tell us this is a lie."

Dante panics. She shouldn't. She was trained to cope with anxiety, to deal with immense amounts of psychological pressure, but nothing could have prepared her for this.

Fear stabs at her heart. It's overwhelming. She has to escape, to move, to run. Running on a spaceship makes no sense as there's nowhere to go, and yet she has to get away. It's a primal response. There's nothing to fight. For her, there's only flight.

Her shoes pound on the floor. Behind her, Benson yells, "No. Not the door. Don't go out the door," but she has to escape this nightmare.

In response to her approach, the automatic door slides open. All that lies beyond the metal sheet is darkness. In the hazy blur of her mind, she assumes the lights in the corridor are off, but on reaching the threshold she runs into a wall of goo.

Black tar sticks to her, enveloping her, sucking her in as she screams. Dante clutches at the doorframe, fighting against the viscous pull. She reaches for Benson. He's yelling, but she can't hear him as she sinks into the mucus. Tentacles emerge from the darkness, claiming her.

Benson grabs her wrist, trying to pull her free, but it's too late. Nothing can save her. Not even the stars.

PALE BLUE DOT

"You're up, Dante."

"What?"

Dante blinks under the bright neon lights. For a moment, she struggles to focus on the tech standing in front of her with an electronic clipboard. The woman has a classic white cotton medical smock covering her civilian clothes, but she's not a doctor. A small green badge glows softly on her lapel, automatically sampling the environment and signaling there aren't any unknown or dangerous contaminates in the air. Seems a bit over simplistic to Dante. There are definitely contaminants. Outside of a volcanic eruption spewing lava at several thousand degrees, Earth has *never* known a sterile environment. Even the NASA cleanrooms, where spacecraft and satellites are assembled under rigorously controlled conditions, aren't actually clean. They're cleaner, but bacteria thrive everywhere. Clean a surface and you've provided a biological niche for warring bacterial species to conquer—and they *love* a challenge.

The crew is five days out from their launch but the medical director isn't taking any chances. No sense in sending some obscure disease to the stars. As it is, humans are walking bacterial factories. With each astronaut carrying around a microbiome consisting of almost forty trillion bacteria on any given day, along with an estimated three to four *hundred* trillion viral particles, viruses and bacteriophages, the idea of shielding the crew from a few more seems laughable. Still, no one likes the flu, least of all Dante. That's one thing she won't miss about Earth.

"If you'll follow me," the woman says as Mags walks back into the waiting area, having just finished with another tech.

Like Dante, Mags is in a flight suit. Again, it's theater as far as Dante's concerned. No one's going flying today, but uniforms are important. Submission is a religion. Authority is the high priest. Dante finds process and procedure boring. The truth is, once the astronauts hit the stratosphere, NASA's control is gone. The astronauts can do as they damn well please once they're in space, and beyond complain, there's nothing NASA can do about it. Wanna stop by Saturn on the way out of the system to look at the rings? Why not? How about Jupiter and the Great Red Spot? It's not like NASA could send out a repo man to collect an interstellar spacecraft. The crew won't do that, of course. No one would dare say it, not even in jest, but Dante's pretty sure they've all thought about it.

Out there among the stars, they're on their own. The technical term is an autonomous cell, but that's too sterile for Dante. Out there in the darkness, they're pioneers—ambassadors from a pale blue dot. For now, though, she's got one last session with the mission psychs. *We can't be sending an axe murderer to WISE 5571 now, can we?*

Dante gets to her feet, trying not to smile. The end is in sight. Well, the end of kicking around in one gee with ten billion other saps. After nine years of training, she's about to reach the end of one journey and the beginning of another.

Mags looks dejected, which surprises Dante as it's unlike her. As Mags sits down she seems to deflate. Her shoulders droop.

"Any advice?" Dante asks, only half serious.

Mags looks up through bloodshot eyes.

"Don't lie."

And with that, the myth of invincibility is gone—shattered. Dante's had plenty of psych evals before and she's given dozens herself over the years. If Mags is shaken—yeah, Dante's nervous. She follows the tech, noting the lighthearted banter that's accompanied most of their other pre-launch activities is absent.

With a decade of intense discipline, testing and training behind them, the flight director told them to relax a little. After all, it's their last week on Earth. They weren't able to leave the training complex, but as the facility is in Florida, less than four miles from the cape, they were free to swim in the severely over-chlorinated pool, relax in the sauna or sit under a tree reading a book, looking out over the marshlands with their three-stage rocket already sitting squarely on the launch pad.

Somewhere high above them, the Acheron is already in orbit, having been built in space. All of a sudden, though, Dante feels as though she's back at square one. Her palms go sweaty.

"Please, have a seat," a doctor says as the tech leads her into the examination room.

There's only one seat, set slightly off center in the middle of the room. This is the same room used for spacesuit fittings, so it's large. Normally, there are a bunch of helmets and spacesuit torsos hanging on wall mounts, but they've been cleaned out. The lights are dim, except for the one almost directly above the chair. That one lone light is particularly bright, brighter than she remembers during her fitting.

"Will there be anything else, Dr. Romero?" the tech asks, dipping her head slightly in deference.

The way he replies, saying, "No," while staring intently at Dante, makes her uncomfortable. She should sit, but she second-guesses herself, pausing slightly. Doubts creep in.

Dr. Romero is an older man, with wispy hair thinning on top, which is unusual in an age where gene splicing can easily counter male pattern baldness. He has flecks of grey above his ears. His full beard has plenty of grey hair, but it's centered around his mouth, giving the impression of a goatee even though his beard reaches back around his jaw. In centuries past, the grey would have marked him as in his late fifties, but these days it probably means he's a little over a hundred. Like the tech, he's wearing a white lab coat, only instead of covering a uniform it hides a dark three-piece suit, which is far more formal than any psych eval she's ever been in.

Dante sits, shifting the chair slightly, aligning the seat with the light as she sits down.

"Why did you do that?"

"Do what?"

"Move the chair."

"Ah... I don't know. I just did, I guess."

"No you didn't," the doctor says, walking around behind her. "That wasn't random—without reason."

Dante's confused.

The doctor's carrying a neural interface. The electronic crown hums softly. Colored LEDs flicker, anticipating the pulsating rhythm of her brain waves being set beneath their thin silicon wafers. She's expecting him to seat it on her head and calibrate the sensors, but he continues slowly pacing around her.

"Life is scripted," he says. "I know you don't think that, but it is. We all play a part, acting out our role on a vast wooden stage, staring into the glare of the spotlights, appealing to an audience hidden in the shadows, performing in the hope of a five-star review from strangers—people who don't give a *fuck* about us personally."

Vulgar language is particularly out of place in a psych eval as swear words are generally intended to elicit a highly polarized response. Evals are about teasing out the finer details of someone's personality and their coping mechanisms. Dante turns her head slightly as the doctor passes behind her, unsure where he's taking the interview.

"You moved the chair because we made you move it. We trained you. We pushed you. We shaped and molded you until your actions—even your very thoughts—as original as you think they are—are entirely predictable."

Dante rests her hands in her lap, feeling uncomfortable. She's indecisive, wanting to put them on the armrests, but he's made her feel uneasy. She fiddles with her fingers. Dante wonders if her every move is being scrutinized.

"Oh, your every move *is* being scrutinized," the doctor says from behind her. "Your thoughts, actions and words are observed, analyzed, considered, measured and then predicted. Don't believe me? Think of a number between one and ten."

Dante grits her teeth.

"Got it?"

She nods.

"Six, right?"

Shoes squelch softly on the linoleum as he continues walking around her.

"You originally thought of seven—most people do—but you're a contrarian. You want to believe you're a rebel—a free spirit—unpredictable—so you stepped down to six. Not up to eight or as far down as five. No, despite what you think, you're too conservative for that. Six is safe ground. Four was a possibility, but six is where you thought you could hide from me. Three is beneath you. Nine is too pretentious. Two? Well, no one picks two, now do they? Not ever."

Dante is genuinely surprised.

"How did you..."

Without raising her hands from her lap, she points at the crown in his hands.

"If I needed this, I wouldn't be very good at my job, now would I?"

The doctor stops in front of her. He's standing back from

her with his face shrouded by the darkness.

"Feeling comfortable?" he asks, resting the crown on a stainless-steel medical cart. It was a diversion, a distraction, and she fell for it.

"No."

"Good."

He rubs his chin, scratching at the stubble.

Dante swallows the lump in her throat, acutely aware such a gesture betrays her unease, but she's unable to combat the urge.

The doctor steps forward, crouching and sitting on his haunches, setting himself below her as she shifts on the hard plastic seat. Although his motion looks natural, she's not so sure. Body language says far more than words, and after setting her on edge, this particular ploy has to be deliberate. He wants her to relax, to feel as though she's above him and in control—but it's a lie, another feint. She's sure of that, at least.

"We approximate," he says. "We like to think we're precise, but we live on unquestioned assumptions. We're constantly filtering information. Our subconscious sifts incoming data based on our interests, keeping some points, discarding others."

Dante is confused. This isn't a psych eval. She could beat that. No, this is something different—a game of wits.

"We think we see clearly, when everything is filtered through rose-colored glasses."

In an extravagant gesture, making as though he were a magician revealing a trick, he holds his arms out wide. His suit jacket is unbuttoned. The sides fall open, revealing a stark, white shirt and blood red tie. He stretches his arms out, causing the sleeves of his jacket to pull taut.

"What do you see?" he asks, maintaining eye contact with her for an uncomfortably long time. "Look closely."

"You've taken off your lab coat," she says.

"Hah," he replies, standing and circling her again. He shakes a finger at her.

"You saw what we wanted you to see."

"I don't understand."

The doctor leans in. Light reflects off his smooth, freshly shaved head. The stubble on his cheeks, though, is thick and prickly, being two or three days old.

"You need to do better. You need to be better. You need to be far more aware of your own limitations."

A single word slips from her lips.

"*Fuck!*"

He smiles, suppressing a laugh. It wasn't his clothing that changed—they switched examiners. When he walked behind the chair, another doctor took over. The first guy had a beard.

"You're still thinking too small," he says, passing behind her once again, still apparently reading her mind from her reactions. "My voice didn't change. That would have given it away. I didn't switch with someone else. I pulled off a wig and fake beard, along with my coat. But you? You assumed. You saw what you wanted to see, what you expected to see. You never saw reality."

He snaps his fingers. In the silence of the examination room, it's as though thunder has burst overhead.

"Come on, Dante. We picked you for a reason. What's happening? Why?"

"Attention blindness," she says, reverting to her training. "I'm under pressure so my focus is narrowing. It's tunnel vision."

"Yes." He claps his hands together, which startles her, causing her to flinch. The noise is jarring.

In the silence that follows, he asks, "How does it work?"

"Selective vigilance. I think I'm paying attention, but by focusing to much on one thing I miss another. I can't see the forest for the trees."

Again, he offers a solitary clap, breaking the tension.

Dante fights the urge to flinch again, saying, "I'm predictable."

"What's the solution?" he asks.

"Critical thinking. To recognize how my assumptions are clouding my perception."

"That's the clinical answer," the doctor says. "That's what you'll find in a textbook, but theory rarely matches practice. Reach past your assumptions. Most people parrot what they see and hear. They don't think—not for themselves. They're directed, molded, shaped, fashioned and manipulated by someone else. What they think is an original idea has often been planted by someone else."

The doctor comes back into view, only this time, there are no games, no wigs, no change of clothing. He remains in the shadows—faceless.

"People are easily fooled," he says. "Do you know what's difficult? Convincing them they've been fooled."

He laughs.

"We need you, Dante." His eyes seem to pierce her soul. "Out there among the stars, we need you to be awake."

She nods, understanding his concern. Once they're off this rock, she's all that stands between the crew and oblivion. Oh, Angel might keep the engines running while Mags keeps the life support systems humming, but the success of the mission relies on the two people who are, technically, redundant. Cap might be the commander, but the crew has been trained to work autonomously. Jeeves, the artificial intelligence, can handle any and every medical emergency that might arise. She and Cap are the human equivalent of spare parts. In reality, Cap provides leadership while Dante monitors crew dynamics, keeping everyone sane.

"What do you see when the darkness closes in?"

Dante's quiet.

"When the day has come to an end and you're lying there alone in bed. What do you think about?"

"I try not to think about anything at all," Dante confesses.

"Or?"

"Or I won't be able to get to sleep?"

"Why? Do you worry about the launch? Do you think about the sheer distance involved? Being separated from your family? Never returning home? What ache tugs at the depths of your soul?"

Dante wants to lie. She wants to tell him what he wants to hear but in the back of her mind, she can still hear the advice of her friend and crewmate, Mags. *Don't lie.* The way Mags spoke those two words was telling. She lingered on the first word, drawing it out, emphasizing it. The second was said with resignation, as though she were surrendering, weary from battle. *Don't—lie.* That was her challenge, the point at which she stumbled. Mags knew that was the temptation Dante would face as well. Dante grits her teeth, determined to redeem them both.

With reluctance, she says, "Not being good enough."

Dr. Romero nods.

"What do you want? To be the best?"

"No," she replies. "Better. I don't know that anyone is ever the best they can be. I just want to be better today than yesterday."

He's unmoved.

"Tell me about your fears... Rational ones, not irrational. I don't care if you're afraid of sharks when swimming at the beach or shrink from a spider hanging from a silk thread. Tell me about what wakes you in the dead of night in a cold sweat."

"For me," she says, almost coughing as her mouth goes dry, "it was leaving Earth behind for the first time."

Dr. Romero seems intrigued by that response.

"Why?"

"We were on an interplanetary run in one of the old Ecliptic class orbiters. Four month round trip. The mission was a flyby of a comet passing at three AU. We had a lander prepped to take samples."

"And?" he asks.

"Before that, I'd only ever been in low Earth orbit. From

there, everything's peaceful. Earth is beautiful. Mesmerizing."

"But?"

"But the darkness," she begins, unsure how to continue. "From a couple of million miles away, Earth is just a pale blue dot. If you don't know where to look, it's just another star."

She pauses. He doesn't say anything. The silence is intimidating. She feels as if she knows what he's thinking.

"Oh, I'd read Carl Sagan's *Pale Blue Dot*. Hell, I think most of the crew had memorized the entire passage like it was poetry or something, but nothing could have prepared us for that moment—seeing it for ourselves.

"Mission Control told us it would be exhilarating. Most of the crew were awestruck, but I found it mortifying. That one small speck. Ten billion people squabbling over nothing. All the money in the world. All the arrogance and ego. All the wars. All the suffering and loss. For me, it seemed petty when played out on a single spot barely visible through the thick glass.

"That tiny pinprick of light could have been a mote of dust on the cupola, a nick or a scratch in one of the laminated layers, and yet that's us—that's all we've ever known. All our delusions of grandeur, our self-importance, our plans and schemes, they all amount to little more than a faint shade of blue at that distance. We think we're so great and high and mighty, that we have such a mastery of the elements of the universe, but we're really quite small, alone and adrift in the empty darkness."

"And that scares you?" he asks.

"It terrifies me," she says. "Oh, I tell myself there's music, art, all the beauty of nature—birds, trees, flowers—but deep down, having seen how small we really are, it scares me to think it's not enough. I guess, I want there to be more. Maybe that's why I'm here—heading out into space again—facing my fears—looking for a solution."

"And what is the solution?" he asks.

"For there to be life elsewhere. That would mean we're not alone, that we're part of something greater."

Without saying anything, the doctor nods. He seems unusually satisfied by her answer. Dante was expecting him to probe deeper.

After what seems like an age, he asks, "What would you do if you're a hundred light years from home and your hull is breached by an asteroid strike? You're losing power, venting oxygen. What would you do when there's no hope of ever coming back? What do you tell the others?"

Without skipping a beat, she says, "I'd get the surviving crew into their hibernation pods. Tell them, we'll wait it out. We'll send a distress signal and sleep until help arrives in a hundred—a thousand years time."

"And would you?" he asks, knowing that's the standard procedure. "Is that really what you'd do?"

"No."

"Why?"

"Because it's a lie."

He nods. "So what would you really do?"

"I don't know, but I wouldn't lie to them."

Again, he nods so she continues. "I'd tell them the truth. We're going to die. I'd give them a choice. Linger with a dying spacecraft. Overdose on sedatives. Or curl up in a pod forever. It's all the same in the end."

The doctor smiles, but there's something strange, almost wicked about the way he looks at her. It's as though he's staring through her. It's only then she realizes she's never met him before. After nine years of training, meeting countless other scientists, specialists, senior administrators, trainers and astronauts, why is it only now he's participating in the program? Now when they're about to launch?

He asks, "You encounter a hostile alien species—one that kills several crew—takes over your craft—controls your minds. What do you do?"

She thinks for a moment. "If they can control our minds,

what can I do?"

"You tell me."

The darkness beyond him—it's alive. She can feel it. She's lost—floating in space, but the stars? Where are the stars? Where are those guiding lights leading her home? Dante repeats his words back to him.

"Observed, analyzed, considered and predicted, right?"

The doctor laughs softly, coming to a halt in front of her, staring down at her. Tentacles reach from the shadows, touching at his shoulders, but he doesn't flinch. Neither does she.

Dante knows.

Thin tendrils slither around the doctor's legs, reaching across the floor, moving into the light, but she's not afraid. Without breaking eye contact, she says, "They can control us, oppress us, even enslave us, but they can't break us."

And with that, the doctor fades from view.

MAGS

The darkness surrounding Dante feels inviting, almost invigorating. Her eyelids flicker, but don't open. The hum of the vents, the creak of the hull as someone moves around on another floor, the texture of her blankets, the light creeping in beneath her bedroom door—strange as it may seem, these are the things she relishes about life on board the Acheron. There's comfort to be found in familiarity.

"Dante, I need you on the bridge."

Although she hears those words, Dante doesn't immediately grasp their meaning. Her eyes open. She rolls over on her bed. A soft light blinks on her darkened wall screen. By default, only audio will come through until she accepts the call. At first, she's tempted to think she's dreaming, but Cap's angry voice blares from the comms device.

"Now!"

"On my way," she replies. Cap ends the call and wall

screen falls dormant again.

Dante sits up on the edge of her bed, resting her bare feet on the floor. With only a pair of underpants on, she gathers her thoughts as she stumbles to the wardrobe, grabbing a bra, a t-shirt and a pair of long pants.

"What's going on, Jeeves?"

"From what I've been able to ascertain," her artificial assistant replies, "Mags is having a psychotic incident."

Dante inadvertently twists her bra strap in the rush to fasten it behind her back. Every second counts. Comfort can wait. She slips on her shirt and pants. As she rushes out of the bedroom, she hops, putting on a pair of shoes without socks.

Although she's never actually needed it, Dante keeps a heavy trauma kit in a backpack by the door of her tiny compartment because medical is on the lowest level, while the bridge, the dock, the engine bay and airlock are up near the hub of the wheel-like structure that is the Acheron. Within the pack there are a couple of oxygen cylinders, several full-skull masks with buddy-breathing attachments, thermal insulation blankets and a rapid decompression kit. She looks more like a firefighter than a medic, but the array of medical supplies will come in handy.

As she climbs the ladder between floors, making her way up one of the spokes toward the hub, she mentally reviews her inventory, thinking about what she can use to calm Mags. Drugs, though, even tranquilizers, only go so far. In the heat of the moment, the best medicine is a confident voice, so she steels herself to remain calm.

Angel grabs the top of the ladder, leaning into the shaft and calling out, "Hurry."

Dante should have taken the cargo elevator as it's exhausting climbing with a medical pack on her back, but the ladder was closer and should be quicker.

As much as Dante enjoys being up on the bridge, she spends more time in medical. The bridge is located on the level just below the hub at the heart of the Acheron.

Spaceships are all about maximizing space. When traveling between stars, the Acheron closes in much the same way an umbrella folds up, minimizing damage from interstellar dust while traveling close to the speed of light. When moving within a system, the curved floors unfold like the petals of a flower. As they're set at various distances from the hub, they're comprised of telescoping sections that slide in and out of each other much like the old spyglasses favored by pirates in movies. The hub itself is the axis of the starship. It houses the engines, fuel tanks and reactor. It's not pleasant close to the axis as it turns, so the crew tend to avoid going up that high. Even the bridge is too close. Up there, the illusion of gravity created by the spinning craft becomes muddied by a weird sideways, Coriolis motion. In the same way that hurricanes form due to the spin of Earth, it's easy for Dante to get dizzy when turning one way or the other when she's close to the axis of the craft. More than one crewmember has thrown up after twisting out of a chair and getting to their feet too quickly.

Dante works with her hands and legs, setting a constant pace on the ladder, focusing on her breathing. Yeah, the elevator would have been smarter, but, hey, she's still waking. As she approaches the top, Angel holds out a hand, helping her up the last few feet.

Angel's their resident nuclear physicist. She's the mission conversion specialist. To Dante, she's a magician. She waves a wand and mutters the secret incantations that moderate the dark matter conversion at the heart of the Acheron. Over a beer one night, just before they launched, Angel drew Feynman diagrams on the back of a napkin, explaining how it all worked. All Dante got out of it was that one squiggly line hits another squiggly line. Something extremely squiggly happens in the middle, and lots of squiggly things rush off in the other direction. Baryons, mesons, hadrons, fermions and demions—Angel might as well have been explaining math to a monkey. Dante nodded politely, smiled, and sipped her beer.

"You've got to talk her down," Angel says in her

characteristically soft voice. At five-foot five, with blonde hair and a toned body, Angel's always been the most feminine of the women on the crew. Dante's never seen Angel get upset about anything, let alone angry—this, though, has her rattled.

"What happened?"

"Mags started arguing with Cap. She wants to abort the surface mission. Leave the robotic equipment down there. She says we're in danger."

"From what?"

"I don't know. She's crazy—violent crazy—like, throwing things around crazy."

That doesn't sound like Mags, but Dante trusts Angel and Cap. They're the only steady couple on the Acheron. Everyone else bed hops, even Dante. Oh, she has her favorites—Vichy for a good high, Naz if she wants a bit of rough and tumble, and Mags when she's feeling playful.

Since the early days of space exploration, NASA has favored odd numbers over even. A crew of eight divides into four pairs, which although it might seem stable, favors closed decision-making followed by deadlocks. A crew of nine ensures there's always a swing vote and avoids embedded cliques from forming. When it comes to sex, though, it also means there's got to be some free thinking or someone gets left out. The prudes wearing suits, sitting under the spotlights in the prime-time television newsrooms might not want to think about sex in outer space, but NASA understands it's as natural as breathing or defecating. To treat sex as anything other than natural has always been a mistake, so NASA made sure there was a broadly compatible mix within each of the crews bound for the stars.

Cap and Angel, though, are old school. The rest of the crew make fun of them, calling them monos. For Cap, it's probably as much about being practical as it is emotional. Commanders tend to be loners because sleeping with the crew weakens their perceived authority. According to the latest psych studies Dante's read, that's not entirely true, but it does impact decision making. It's not that humans can't avoid cognitive biases, but that they're largely defined by them, so those in command try to avoid feelings that might get in the way of hard decisions. A steady relationship with sweet little Angel has allowed Cap to sidestep the issue. For Angel it's old fashioned love. That she was up on the bridge in the middle of the night is no surprise as she tends to shadow Cap.

Dante rushes along the corridor behind Angel, with the oversized, bulging backpack bouncing on her shoulders. There's yelling up ahead. Dante has her hands up, holding onto the straps, steadying the heavy pack as it sways on her light frame.

"Put it down," Cap yells at Mags. He has both hands out

in front of him, gesturing for calm, but his raised voice isn't helping.

It takes Dante a moment to realize what Mags is holding. She recognizes the shape—a gun—but there aren't any guns on the Acheron. It's some sort of construction tool, probably taken from one of the robotic workers. It's the kind of device used to fire nails or embed rivets, only the safety bar, which normally has to be depressed to arm the firing mechanism, has been mangled and pulled away from the barrel. Mags waves the bulky weapon around, threatening to use it.

"Take us out of orbit," she says.

"Mags," Dante says, interrupting them. She swings the pack from her back slowly, resting it gently on the deck, trying not to make any sudden movements. Dante slips her hand in one of the side pockets, searching for an injector.

"Stay out of this, Dante."

"Mags, please. Don't do this."

The bridge is oval in shape, with entrances at the widest points and a forward-facing windscreen—that is, if there were anything other than stellar winds in space.

To anyone looking from outside the craft, the bridge goes around like a piece of gum stuck on a wheel. As the crew are pushed outward by the illusion of centrifugal force, they feel as though they're stationary even though they're in constant motion. To them, it's the vast starry sky that's rotating.

Cap is at the back of the bridge by the command deck. Mags is directly opposite him, by the navigation desk in front of the window. She waves the gun around, trying to cover as much space as she can, wanting to keep everyone at bay.

"Get back. All of you. I'm warning you."

Vichy is on the opposite side of the bridge from Dante. He inches along the instrumentation wall toward the nav desk, trying to get closer to Mags. Vichy is slight of build and doesn't come across as threatening. He aces his medical exams as his cardio routine is worthy of an ultra-triathlete. Admittedly, Dante's given him plenty of rather close and personal examinations—just to be sure, of course—at least that's the joke between them. On a small craft like the Acheron, lines become blurred, which is something her AI assistant Jeeves takes pains to point out. A bazillion miles from Earth, who cares?

Vichy picks his moments, moving almost imperceptibly, looking for an opportunity to lunge at Mags and disarm her. When Mags turns toward Dante, he edges closer. He has his hands up, appealing for calm, but he's not saying anything and lowers his head, looking at his feet as the gun is waved briefly at him. Dante understands what he's doing, but she would prefer he backed away. If anything, he's liable to enflame the situation by cornering Mags. If he rushes her, he could get hurt.

Angel copies his tactic, moving in from this side. Dante is on the verge of yelling at them, wanting everyone to stand down, but if she draws attention to them it will only make matters worse. By duplicating Vichy's calm approach, Angel is slowly restricting the space available to Mags as she strides back and forth in front of the broad windscreen.

"You don't understand," Mags says, pleading with Dante. "None of this is real. None of it. You're not real."

"I'm real," Dante replies, stepping lightly as she moves over beside Cap, wanting to keep the focus on her and off Angel and Vichy.

"No. You're not. You're no more real than anyone else in this stupid, fucked up, crazy dream."

"Mags, please. Don't do anything rash."

Cap picks up on Dante's strategy. Slowly, he waves his hands, moving them in a broad motion, making himself appear larger, keeping the attention on the two of them.

"Mags. Listen to Dante. She's your friend."

Dante says, "I can help. Don't worry, Mags. It's going to be okay."

"You think they're going to section me?" Mags says, laughing. "You think *that's* what I'm worried about? Shit, girl. If you're real, you missed the goddamn memo on this one."

"Mags, please."

Dante looks down at the bulky gun in her friend's hand. Power adaptors and batteries dangle beneath it. A magazine has been snapped on one side. The breech and chamber are oversized, designed for rivets as large as a beer can. She can't have more than three loaded with any charge.

Within the confines of the bridge, ricochets are possible as the instrument panels are designed to be rigid in case of micro-meteor impacts. But if one of those rivets hits the ceiling, it'll puncture the hull. The bridge is built to withstand strikes from pebble-sized objects, with a self-sealing membrane between the layers of sheet metal. Anything larger than that shows up on radar and is normally avoided or deflected by a laser long before it reaches the Acheron. Dante doubts the engineers that built the Acheron ever considered this kind of scenario—a projectile being fired from within the craft. She's nervous. The bridge would depressurize almost instantly if any of the panels came away.

"You don't understand," Mags says, grabbing at the side of her head with one hand, clutching her hair as though she has a migraine. "We need to leave. We have to get away from here."

"Why?" Dante replies, hiding a needle-less-injector by her side in a closed fist.

"If I'm wrong, we'll move out of range and—and—and the

pain will stop. If I'm right, you'll see. You'll see them. They don't like change. Things change and they show themselves. And then you'll know."

"Who will show themselves?" Dante asks, edging closer to her friend, trying to keep her distracted. Dante's feet glide across the bridge, barely lifting from the floor.

"You know. You must know," Mags says, getting a little too wild with the robotic rivet gun and swinging it at Dante.

"Easy," Dante says, holding one hand out, appealing for calm, keeping the injector hidden in the other.

Mags yells, "This is nothing but a dream—an illusion—a nightmare! Nothing is real, but no one believes me, so I'll show you. I'll prove it to you."

Cap is silent, leaving Dante to respond.

"This is real," Dante says, stepping forward. She speaks softly, barely above a whisper. "You're real. I'm real. Cap's real." Dante avoids mentioning Angel and Vichy, hoping they're somewhat invisible to Mags as they creep along the bulkhead, sliding slowly along the curved sides of the bridge toward the windscreen.

Mags asks. "How do you know what's real? You've used a neural cap. You know the kind of worlds they can create."

"No one's creating any worlds, Mags."

"What is real? I want to know what's real."

Mags presses her palm in the center of her forehead, closing her eyes for a brief second, allowing Vichy and Angel to creep closer.

"I need to know," she says, looking Dante in the eyes.

"Put down the gun and we'll talk," Dante says. "You know me. You trust me. Just—put down the gun."

"Trust you? I don't even know if you're really Dante. You could be one of them."

"Mags, you're being silly—irrational. You're not going to hurt anyone."

Wrong choice of words. Mags raises the industrial gun, pointing it squarely at Dante. Her eyes narrow as she aims at the center of Dante's forehead.

"Do you really think so? Do you really want to find out?"

The gun quivers as Mags struggles to hold it aright. Whether that's because of the artificial gravity and the weight of the device or the emotional strain, Dante's not sure. Sweat beads on her forehead, but she's determined not to lose her nerve.

"You can't lie in a dream."

"What?" Mags asks, looking perplexed.

"You want proof this isn't a dream, right? I'm telling you, you can't lie in a dream. To lie, you have to fool someone, but in a dream, there is no one else. In a dream, you are everyone you meet. They're all constructs of your imagination so you can't lie to them, and they can't lie to you. You can't lie to yourself, right? Not knowingly."

Mags falters, lowering the gun.

"So this... this is real?"

Dante nods.

Beyond Mags, out past the javelin-like tip of the Acheron, the stars drift past. All of creation seems to revolve around their tiny spacecraft. In the low light on the bridge at night, while the Acheron is in the shadow of the massive planet, the stars shine with stunning clarity against the immense depth of space. Tens of thousands of stars break up the darkness. The familiar shape of Orion comes into view. Those particular stars are off-kilter, but they're brilliant, shining like diamonds in the dark of night.

"So what is this?" Mags asks, pointing at the stars. "You see them too, right?"

Dante nods. Her eyes seek out the glowing shell of Betelgeuse, the remnants of a red supergiant that went supernova, leaving little more than a smudge in the sky. It's distinct because of its ruddy color, marking the wounded shoulder of Orion, the great hunter. The irony is, what appears as a recent explosion is actually well over five hundred years old. Being six hundred light years distant, humanity has only just seen this colossal explosion and its expanding shell dissipating into interstellar space.

A thin belt reaches around the waist of the mythical figure of Orion—three stars that appear close together even though they're actually hundreds of light years apart. Dante's eyes trace the sword hanging from the hunter's waist just as she did that night on the beach with her family. She remembers pointing out across the sand, directing Jules to turn her telescope toward the ocean, wanting to show her the Orion Nebula in all its glory.

This is wrong. It simply cannot be. Orion's shape is an illusion, one that exists only from Earth. Like telephone poles overlapping each other in the distance, drive to one side and the illusion is shattered. In her mind, Dante can hear someone warning her about the stars. Benson. But Benson's not on the bridge. He's asleep in his quarters. Memories drift in and out of focus. Whereas moments ago, Dante was confident, now doubts cloud her mind, weakening her resolve.

"How is this possible?" Mags asks.

"I—I don't know," Dante says, once again locking eyes with her. "But it's not a dream. It can't be. All I know is, I'm real."

Dante doesn't sound convincing.

Mags speaks slowly, measuring her words.

"You're not real. You can't be."

At this point, Dante feels conflicted. Damn those stars. She's got to talk Mags down before someone gets hurt.

"Come on, Mags. You know me. I wouldn't lie to you. I'd never do anything to hurt you."

Mags speaks with cold deliberation.

"I don't know any of you zombies."

Her eyes dart from side to side, seeking out both Angel and Vichy. "I will shoot. You know that, right? I will pull this *fucking* trigger if either of you take another goddamn step!"

Dante signals with her hands, wanting Angel and Vichy to back away, but by holding out both hands she inadvertently reveals the injector tucked away in her palm.

"What is that? What the *fuck* is that?" Mags demands.

"I'm not going to let anything happen to you," Dante says. "It's a sedative, that's all. Something to help you relax."

"You don't get it, do you? It's not me that needs help. It's you. You don't remember, but I do. You think this is real. It's not. We're trapped."

"Where do you want to go?" Cap asks, taking control of the conversation, wanting to distract Mags. "You want us to leave orbit and go where?"

He makes as though he's ready to enter coordinates into the drive pane.

"Just tell me where and I'll punch it in. Whatever you want, Mags."

"It doesn't matter," Mags replies. "Any deviation will break the spell. Anything out of the norm."

"Mags, I want you to lower the gun," Dante says, seeing it tremble in her hand. In that moment, Dante's more worried about the damage it'll do to the bridge than being hit. Deep down, she doesn't believe Mags will pull the trigger, not while pointing it at anyone.

"You need to remember," Mags says, turning toward Angel and aiming squarely at the petite woman. "You need to understand what's real and what's not. And Angel—she's not real."

"Nooooo!" Dante cries, rushing toward her troubled friend. Dante has her arms stretched out before her, with the injector raised, but she can't move fast enough.

In that instant, time seems to slow.

Dante has the injector clenched in a fist, held high as though she were about to hit a nail with a hammer. She runs at Mags, aiming for her neck, but Mags squeezes the trigger. Angel drops, turning and twisting, trying to fall out of the way. Her long, blonde hair swirls through the air, trailing behind her. The electromagnetic charge fires, launching a rivet bigger than a soda can—a blur traveling at several thousand feet per second and with enough energy to puncture a quarter-inch steel plate. Within the confines of the bridge, the rivet strikes its target inside a millisecond.

The recoil flings the gun up. Vichy dives at Mags, crash-tackling her and sending her into the nav desk. He knocks the gun from her grasp.

Dante stabs at Mags, plunging the injector hard against her friend's jugular, falling with her. Dante has hold of her head. She cradles her jaw, making sure the injector empties into a vein. Mags squirms, trying to break free, mumbling, "Remember. Remember, goddamn it." Within seconds, her eyes roll into the back of her head and her body falls limp.

In the silence that follows the industrial construction gun crashing to the floor, Dante hears a whimper. Cap has Angel. He's holding her in his arms, weeping as thick, rich, dark blood stains his clothes.

Dante's heart sinks.

Angel gasps. Her eyes have a hollow, empty look, staring blinding at the ceiling. She's dying if not dead. Her arms twitch. The rivet caught her on the side of the head, just above the right eye, shattering her skull and sending blood, bone and a smattering of white brain matter across the bridge. The normally pristine walls are speckled with deep red drops slowly dripping to the floor.

Cap sobs, shaking with grief. He's down on his knees holding Angel, bowed over her crumpled body, trembling.

"No," Dante whispers, releasing Mags and rushing to his side, but she never gets there. With each step, she's fighting through what feels like a forcefield. The harder she tries, the slower she moves. It's as though she's pushing through waist-deep water.

Darkness descends, shrouding the bridge in shadows, causing the walls to dissolve. Tentacles reach for her, coming out of the floor, wrapping themselves around her legs, but the stars—the ever-distant stars remain the same. Scattered across the endless night, they defy the cold, bitter darkness, refusing to relent, reaching across a void spanning billions of years to fall on her eyes once more.

VICHY

Vichy kisses Dante's cheek and then her lips, lingering on them in the darkness. His breath is heavy, warming her ear.

Dante's confused, unsure how Vichy came to be on top of her. She blinks, trying to figure out how she got here. They've made love plenty of times over the years, but she's disoriented. She feels as though she's been dropped into the moment, but that's impossible. He smiles, leaning back in the half light of her bedroom before surging forward again, pressing his body hard against her, biting gently at her bottom lip. The sheets shift in response to his motion, sliding over his firm buttocks.

"You're so beautiful," he says, resting his hand behind her neck, rubbing her jaw tenderly with his thumb as he kisses her again and again. Dante responds, running her fingers up through his hair, but not because she feels enamored, rather it seems like the appropriate thing to do. She's always felt safe in Vichy's embrace. He might not be musclebound, but there's not an inch of fat on him. The texture of his arms, the strength in his chest, his firm abdomen and strong legs leave her feeling assured. When she's with him, reality seems to dissolve, being replaced, even if only briefly, with a sense of belonging. For a moment, it's as though they're the only two beings in all of creation.

Dante's head rests on the pillow, with her hair spreading out on the smooth cotton. Vichy groans. He nudges the side of her face affectionately, leaning in and rubbing the stubble on his cheek gently against her skin, kissing her earlobe and then her neck.

"Oh," she says, unsure of herself, caught in the swell of emotion and yet still feeling unsettled. How did she get here? Something's wrong, horribly wrong, but not him. This feels so right, and yet her heart is heavy—as though she's in mourning and struggling to move on, but why? No one's died, have they?

Vichy shifts his body, flexing his legs and pressing against her hips, riding gently upon her, moving slowly, tenderly. His body is familiar, inviting her to surrender. Seconds ago, something bothered her, but what? That moment has passed. Passion radiates through her, pulsating within her.

Vichy flexes, rocking upon Dante. His calloused hand reaches down, touching gently at her soft breasts, skimming over her skin and setting her soul alight. A surge of emotion washes over her, but it's not right. She shouldn't be feeling like this. Not after what just happened.

Her eyes go wide as she remembers.

"No. Please."

He stops, not immediately, but over the course of a few seconds, responding to the shudder in her body. Dante pushes on his chest, but not violently, using just enough strength to reinforce her intention. Vichy rolls away. Dante feels conflicted.

"I'm sorry."

He looks surprised, unsure what he did wrong.

Dante struggles to explain what she's feeling. "It's just—"

"It's not me, huh?"

"No," she says, flicking her long hair behind her ears as she tries to focus, but his eyes tell her he's not convinced.

Dante rests her hand in the center of his chest and leans forward, pulling gently at the handful of wispy hair there. She kisses him briefly on the lips, hoping that conveys more than the words she's struggling to find.

"Dee?" he asks, longing for an explanation.

"It's not... It's really not you."

He looks confused. Hurt.

"Can't you feel it?" she asks, pulling the sheets around

her, wanting to be clothed.

Vichy was born in Bari in southern Italy. From the age of two, he was raised in the US, so his accent suggests he's from California, but he spent his late teens in Naples. His Italian blood demands hand gestures accompany words spoken with passion.

"You? Me?" he says with his fingers flickering between the two of them. "You don't want this?"

"Yes and no," she says, still trying to grasp a memory dancing at the edge of her reason. "It's—something's wrong."

"Between us?" he asks, looking alarmed.

"No. Here. On the Acheron."

His brow furrows.

"Mags," she says. "Angel."

That only confuses him further.

"I don't understand."

Dante gets out of bed. She slips on some underwear and a t-shirt before bringing up the comms channel. In that instant, the wall of her bedroom transforms into a screen. Vichy sits up with his back against the far wall and pulls a sheet over himself. He has his knees up, hiding his loins.

A tired looking Cap appears on the screen, haggard and unshaven.

"Dante? Is everything alright?" He scratches his hair. "What's wrong?"

"Is Angel there with you?" she asks.

From behind him, Angel peers out of the darkness, ruffling her hair, not feeling comfortable on the video call. She scrambles in the shadows, hurriedly slipping on a negligee.

"Are you okay?" Cap asks, pulling up a pair of pants as he speaks.

"No. None of us are."

"What's going on?" Angel asks, looking bewildered.

"We need to meet."

"Can it wait till morning?" Cap asks. His eyes dart down and slightly to the side. Dante knows what he's doing. He's checking diagnostics, looking at metrics coming in from the bridge. Benson's on the night shift. How does she know that? Dante's not sure, but she does, and that leaves her even more unsettled.

"What is this about, Dante?"

"The health of the crew," she says, lying, still trying to draw in distant memories and make sense of them.

"And it really can't wait till morning?"

"There won't be a morning," she says, unsure how she can be so confident but knowing within herself it's true.

"What?" Cap asks, screwing up his face. "Are you serious?" He turns to look at Angel, wanting to see her response as he adds, "She's not serious, right?"

Dante says, "Please. Trust me on this—it's important."

"Okay. Hit me," he says. "What's happening?"

"When we're all together. Everyone needs to hear this."

"And not just me, the commander? You don't think I should hear whatever it is that's got my physician spooked so I can make a decision on it first?"

"Cap," Dante says, gritting her teeth, unsure what to say to convince him, unable to articulate what she feels rather than thinks.

"It's Dante, baby," Angel says, reaching from behind Cap and resting her arms around his waist. "If she says, it's important, it's important."

"Alright," Cap doesn't look impressed, but he's not one to take safety lightly. He brings up a console window with Benson sitting on the bridge, slouching in his chair. "Are you detecting any anomalies within the Acheron or down on the surface?"

Benson raises an eyebrow, surprised to see into two bedrooms. "What? No. Nothing, Cap. The robotic team is still processing raw materials. The core drill is going well, but we won't be able to start the habitat build for a few days yet. As for us, it's all quiet up here. What's going on?"

Dante cuts him off. "Get everyone up. We need to meet on the bridge."

If anything, it looks like Benson's the one that's half asleep as she has to add, "Now!"

"Do it," Cap says, killing the transmission. The screen fades, leaving the bedroom in the half light.

"What's going on, Dee?" Vichy asks.

"That's what I intend to find out," she replies, bringing up the lights and getting dressed.

Vichy shakes his head, but he gets dressed as well, saying, "Might as well look the part."

As they walk to the elevator, they pass a maintenance hatch hiding a ladder that climbs the inside of one of the vast spokes of the Acheron. It provides direct access to the bridge, but it's impractical, and yet Dante longs to go that way. Again. There's something about the metal rungs. In her mind's eye, she can see her hands on them, she can feel the weight of a medical pack she's not carrying. Memories are surfacing.

Up on the bridge, the crew slowly assembles.

Benson is running scans of the dark matter fuel stores and the highly sensitive interstellar engine, looking for a problem Dante's pretty sure doesn't exist. She suspects he'll find everything's perfect—too perfect.

Another woman marches onto the bridge. "Just what the

fuck is going on?"

"It's good to see you too, Zoe," Dante says, aware that, in the chaotic memories she has of the past few days, Zoe's been absent.

MacInnes stands behind Zoe. Being of Scottish descent, his wild, unkempt locks are a brilliant orange/red. It's as though his hair has been set on fire by the gods. Mac's skin is pale, so much so that to Dante he looks unnaturally white under the neon lights.

Zoe's from Ethiopia, with skin as dark as the night—ordinarily Jeeves quietly adjusts the lights around her to produce a little extra UVB, encouraging her body to generate vitamin D, but Mac throws that algorithm into chaos. Mags has affectionately nicknamed them Yin and Yang.

Mac has a full beard and crazy eyes to match his career as an extremophile astrobiologist. He's built like a linebacker but has the steady hands of a surgeon. Dante's seen him work with core drill samples, treating tubes of rock and ice with the care some might afford diamonds or fine gold jewelry.

Mac slips his hand over Zoe's shoulder. Like Dante, she's dressed in a flight suit, but it's obvious she's not wearing anything beneath the thin fabric as her nipples are protruding and the zipper on the front hasn't been pulled all the way up, revealing her smooth, black skin instead of a standard-issue white singlet. Then there's Mac's hand. MacInnes is resting his arm on Zoe's shoulder, with his fingers lingering above her breast, but not actually touching her clothing or skin in any way, so nothing creepy, but his hand rests in a manner that suggests they've been enjoying some intimacy.

"What's going down, doc?" Mac asks. "Something wrong?"

"Everything's wrong, Mac."

Cap and Angel walk onto the bridge.

"Hi guys," Angel says warmly, apparently not bothered by being called up to the bridge in the middle of the night. Cap, though, looks grumpy.

Benson surrenders the command console and Cap begins reviewing logs from the past few hours. Dante's pretty sure he won't find anything out of the ordinary. She walks along the side of the bridge, running her fingers over the smooth plastic panels that hide the wiring and electronics, remembering the way blood and bits of brain dripped from them seemingly moments ago. Her hand lingers as memories surface, reminding her not only about what she saw, but how she felt—the horror and the heartache.

Voices echo down the far hallway. Mags and Naz are joking with each other. As Mags rounds the corner, the look she gives Dante suggests she's surprised at being interrupted while fooling around with her toy boy.

"Hey," she says. "Look. It's the Vee and Dee late night show, live from orbit around P4."

A cheeky grin and a subtly raised eyebrow say more than words could convey. Technically, Naz is the same age as Mags, but he looks ten years her junior and normally sleeps with Benson. The three of them are known to get a little loose. Dante finds the timing interesting. Synchronicity. Mags and Naz. Her and Vichy. Mac and Zoe. Cap and Angel weren't asleep either. That the crew were enjoying sex is no surprise. That they were all enjoying sex at the same time certainly is. Dante's more convinced now than when she woke beneath Vichy—reality is a lie.

She walks over to the vast window, searching for the constellation Orion. She shouldn't be able to see it—of that she's sure—and she's confused why that compulsion has swept over her, but there's nothing there beyond the darkness.

Beneath the ship, the alien world shimmers in the light of twin suns. The glare coming off the ice prevents her from seeing anything beyond the two dwarf stars in this binary system. They orbit so closely that from Earth they appear as one. Even now, she can't visually separate them as anything other than a slightly horizontal smudge. At the speed they're orbiting each other, it'll take hundreds of millions of years for the two stars to finish colliding. At first, Angel thought they might be a supernova candidate, but they're small enough they'll simply merge and reignite, forming a new star, bathing the system in light and energy, possibly even spurring on life.

The frozen planet below them is largely devoid of clouds. Cracks in the pack ice are visible from space, marking vast sections near the equator where patches of open water allow access to the deep ocean.

Dante can't see their ground base. It's far too small to be visible from orbit, but she recognizes the landmarks. A shield volcano with its slopes largely clear of ice provides a signpost. Glaciers form intricate patterns running along the side of a familiar mountain range. Somewhere near the rugged coast, a robotic construction squad is drilling through the ice sheet, wanting to reach a subsurface lake containing fresh water. That must be where they came from. That thought, though, is unnatural. It doesn't spring from anything she's seen recently or any line of reasoning she currently has, rather it's the culmination of numerous encounters and leaves her feeling as cold as the ice below.

"Alright," Cap says, finishing his review of the logs. "We're all here. What's going on?"

"Can't you feel it?" Dante asks, turning to face the crew. "The darkness? It's all around us."

"What the hell has gotten into you?" Zoe asks, marching aggressively toward Dante. "You dragged us out of bed in the middle of the goddamn night to fuck with our minds?"

Dante ignores her. "Benson. You can see them, right?"

"Them?" Cap asks, turning to face his second-in-command, but Dante ignores him.

"Mags. You've seen them as well. What was it you wanted us to remember? You were up here on the bridge. You had a construction device—for rivets, I think. A gun. You fired it."

Mags walks toward the spot where she once stood wielding the makeshift gun, but her eyes are elsewhere, darting around the bridge. "Oh. Angel. I am so sorry."

"What? Me?" Angel says, pressing a hand against her chest in alarm. "How does any of this have anything to do with me?"

Mags ignores her, facing Dante as she says, "I thought it was a dream—a nightmare. I mean, I barely—"

MacInnes cuts her off. "Will someone tell me just what the *fuck* is going on?"

Sheepishly, Benson says, "Every time, it's the same. No one ever believes me. Not even Dante."

Cap looks annoyed. Vichy shakes his head in disbelief.

Zoe waves her hand, signaling she's done with this, and turns to leave, saying, "This is stupid."

"No," Dante says with a hand raised in alarm, horrified by how quickly the discussion has unraveled. "Do *not* go out there."

"And why not?" she asks.

Mags says, "Because, if you do, everything resets."

"And we'll forget," Benson says. "All of us. We'll lose everything. Again."

Zoe stops just shy of the corridor. There's no door as such as the bridge is open, with walkways leading in from both sides, but there's a groove in the floor and ceiling, marking where the containment shell is designed to cut through in the event of a hull breach, sealing the bridge. Zoe holds her hand out as though she's touching an invisible barrier in front of her.

"You can feel it, can't you?" Dante says.

"Don't do it," Benson says, pleading with her. "Please."

"We need this time together," Dante says. "Don't you see? Don't you understand? This is the first time we've all been together in the same place."

"First time?" Cap asks, genuinely surprised. "Since when?"

Dante says the words the others dread and don't want to say.

"Since they took over the Acheron."

ZOE

Zoe steps away from the threshold. Her bare feet move as though she's searching for safe ground behind her, sliding rather than stepping backwards.

"You don't actually buy this bullshit, do you?" Mac asks her.

He turns to Dante. "What is this? Some kind of sick psych test? What are you looking for this time, doc? Team dynamics? Susceptibility to peer pressure? Or some other shitty metric?"

With that, he steps around Zoe, toward the corridor.

"No," Dante calls out.

"Don't go out there," Benson says, but Mac ignores the second-in-command.

Zoe rushes in front of him, blocking his path. She rests both hands on his chest, barring his way, leaning into him. She's not pushing him back, though. She couldn't. At six foot four in height and musclebound, Mac could toss her aside if he wanted, but there's a connection between them.

"Please," she says. "Just listen."

Dante's surprised by the sudden change in Zoe. Something that was said has triggered a memory. Perhaps it's just a vague recollection, but something's troubling her, warning her of the danger.

Mac sighs, nodding. Reluctantly, he turns to join the others.

Cap says, "Just what the hell is going on, Dante?"

"I—I don't know. All I know is everything is wrong."

Vichy says, "It's a puzzle, right? It's like a jigsaw, only there's no picture on the box. All we see is part of the solution. No one sees the whole thing."

"Yes," Mags says, pointing at him. "That's it. No single one of us knows everything, but together we know at least something. We have to pool our ideas."

Dante looks to Benson. "Tell us what you see."

"It's only when I'm tired," Benson replies. "Or bored. But I see them. They come in and out of view."

Cap laughs at the notion. "You're saying the Acheron has been overrun by aliens?" He has his arms outstretched. "I don't see any acid-for-blood xenomorphs clambering over the bridge. Do you?"

"We—I."

"Why should I believe any of this?" he asks, cutting her off. "What evidence do you have?"

"None," Dante replies. "And yet, look at you. You know something's wrong. You just don't know what."

Naz says, "I don't see anything."

"I feel it," Vichy says.

"Feelings? Really?" Naz replies, cocking his head sideways. "That's what we're going on now? Fucking feelings? I thought this was a science mission."

"Fuckin-A." Mac is indignant. "I didn't travel halfway across the galaxy to jump at my own shadow." He turns to Zoe. "Are you really buying into this?"

Zoe has her head bowed, looking at her bare feet protruding from the oversized flight suit. She must have grabbed Mac's suit in the dark and rolled up the cuffs. As he's taller, he can't make eye contact, but he's trying, wanting to look into her eyes, hoping to understand. Dante's not sure whether her posture is deliberate, but it gets his attention.

"What's wrong, babe?" he says, putting his hand under her chin and gently raising her head. "You don't believe any of this madness, do you?"

Zoe has tears running down her cheeks. Her eyes are bloodshot. Her bottom lip quivers as she speaks.

"It's—I thought it was just me. I thought I was being silly. Irrational. I mean, how crazy is this?"

"There's no one there," Mac says. "Look, I'll prove it to you."

With that, he goes to walk out into the corridor. Dante bites her lip, wondering just how quickly reality will dissolve, hoping she won't forget, desperately wanting to commit this moment to memory. She trembles at the thought that this opportunity could be lost forever. This could be the end. Neither she nor anyone else might make it this far again. These ragged, loose threads might never unravel quite the same way. Zoe doesn't say anything, but the look she gives Mac is one that pleads for understanding, searching his eyes for pity.

Mac comes to a halt. His eyes are on her, not the empty corridor. He sighs, stepping back. Zoe forces a grateful smile. She's holding back tears. Dante finds the change of dynamic fascinating. Zoe wasn't going to stop him a second time. He had to arrive at this decision for himself. For all his bravado, it seems even Mac has his doubts.

"I don't get it," Naz says, seeing Mac surrender. "I think you're mad—all of you."

Cap turns to Dante. "You better be able to explain this."

Dante is at a loss for words. She scrambles, trying to articulate a hunch.

"When was the last time you took a piss?"

"What?" Cap says, squinting as he looks at her in disbelief. "Are you serious?"

"When? Think about it. All of you. When was the last time you had a good shit or peed in the bowl?"

Dante is being deliberately crude, wanting to provoke a strong response and bait them with something everyone does several times a day in spite of the social norms and pleasantries that ignore this aspect of being human. Shock has value. For her, it's the best way to raise the alarm. Dante remembers Mags pulling the trigger on the construction gun. She saw Angel's skull cracked open like an egg, but it seems only she and Mags remember that particular moment. That incident was lost to everyone else, including Cap who cradled Angel as she died. Dante's trying to get their attention. If they lose this moment, if the darkness closes in again, she hopes they'll be left with a gnawing sense of uncertainty, a vague feeling that something's wrong, even if they can't quite figure out what or why.

No one answers her question, not even Naz, although he's still brooding. Eyes dart between the various members of the crew, but no one gives voice to their doubts.

"We live in the moment," Dante says. "I think that's what they're exploiting. Our memories are vague and easily manipulated, but there are tells."

"Faults," Benson says, eager to show his support.

"Look, I know you're a doctor and all," Vichy says, smiling, trying to make light of the situation. "But, seriously? You're basing this on a lack of bowel movements?"

"So when was it?" Dante asks, tackling the issue head on. "If this is just paranoid little old me, tell me what you remember about your most basic of daily bodily functions."

Vichy looks at his feet. Naz is silent. Cap fidgets.

"You can't, can you?" she says. "None of you can because they haven't factored that in—yet. Don't you see? We have so little to go on. We have no idea how long this has played out, but they're fabricating our reality."

Dante laughs at the thoughts cascading through her mind, smiling at what she's about to say, "Yeah, I'll admit it. This is pretty damn shitty as far as evidence goes, but it's all I've got."

She throws her hands up in exasperation, allowing them to fall to her side.

Mags says, "Think about it. No food. No drink. It doesn't make sense."

"No coffee," Vichy says, raising a single finger in alarm. "I'm Italian. I sweat coffee. Coffee is the blood in my veins—and no coffee."

From anyone else, such a statement would be a joke, but

Vichy's quite serious, finally coming to her aid and helping convince the others.

"And it's not just you, right?" Dante says, picking up on his point. "This is true for all of us. None of us have any recollection of anything beyond now. Is anyone even hungry? Thirsty? Wanting to go to the bathroom? Just basic aspects of being human?"

No one replies, so Dante says, "Honestly, that's frightening."

"Terrifying," Mags says.

Mac edges away from the corridor, stepping back slowly, giving the empty air in front of him the respect one would afford a snarling, wild animal. Zoe holds his arm, almost shrinking behind him.

"So none of this is real?" Cap asks.

"It looks pretty damn real to me," Dante says. "It feels real, but there are things that are missing."

"Like what?" Angel asks, poking at the navigation console. She pushes a smooth panel, testing it, watching it flex beneath the tip of her fingers, trying to find its limits. She's investigating, probing the boundaries of the illusion. "I mean, this is real, right? I can touch it."

"What can you smell?" Dante asks.

"Nothing," Benson says. He lifts his arm and sniffs at his

shoulder. "I don't smell anything. But maybe that's a good thing because, damn."

Instead of finishing his sentence, he crosses his eyes to make his point.

Dante says, "There's no odor. Not a hint of sweat or a trace of shampoo or scented soap."

"Why is that important?" Cap asks.

"I don't think they've figured that out," Dante says, quickly adding, "Yet."

"Fuck," Mags says. "We are so fucking fucked."

"Ya think?" Mac replies, shaking his head.

"Wait a minute," Cap says. "Back this up a little. So the fact I don't remember taking a dump and I can't smell anything somehow means the Acheron has been taken over by hostile extraterrestrials? That's a bit of a stretch, ain't it?"

"Think about the process of remembering," Dante replies. "We assume too much. We live in the moment. We see, hear, touch and smell things around us—or we think we do.

"Colors assault us. Shapes surround us. Sounds bounce around us. We feel the temperature of the air, the faint vibration of a motor in a ventilation duct, a breeze circulating, the apparent weight of our bodies. Hundreds of variables come at us like water gushing out of a fire hydrant, but none of that remains. In seconds, it's all gone and what we're left with is a vague impression of the past.

"Our recollection is selective—limited to those details we noticed at the time. You can rewind a video to look for more details in a movie, but you can't rewind your brain and choose to focus on something else that happened way back when. Beyond a few fleeting moments you collected at the time, the past is a haze—nothing but a blur. We think we remember more than we actually do. We remember the gist, the essence, a summation of what happened, not the detail, not what actually occurred."

Cap doesn't look convinced. He's surly. Sour. So Dante continues.

"We create patterns, mental maps to guide us and build associations, forming a sense of familiarity, but they're generalizations.

"Think about all the advertising back on Earth. What does it rely on? Repetition. Brand recognition. Why? Because we're shit at remembering things unless they're beaten into us.

"People used to think eyewitnesses were reliable. Then along came video cameras and forensic science and we realized our eyewitnesses were fooling themselves—often embellishing the facts or recalling what they wanted to see rather than what was actually there.

"And it's really not that surprising when you think about

it. We have limited mental bandwidth. We have to generalize or we'd never be able cope with the information overload coming at us. Dealing with reality is like drinking from a firehose, so we have to be selective."

"And?" Cap asks.

"They're using our weaknesses to hide."

Cap turns to Zoe. Although she's stopped crying, the tracks of her tears are visible on her dark skin. Her hair glistens in the light coming in through the window as the craft rotates, briefly facing the planet as dawn breaks hundreds of miles below them.

"What stopped you from walking back out there?" he asks, pointing at the corridor. "What do you remember?"

By asking that, Cap's admitting he's lost as well. Dante would love to know what he remembers, but he seems reluctant to say too much. It seems Cap wants to hear from the others.

"I thought it was a dream, you know? Just a nightmare or something. But you're not supposed to remember those, right?" Zoe asks, looking to Dante who nods, not wanting to break the chain of memories reaching Zoe's conscious awareness, understanding how fleeting and fragile those thoughts are. If just one link breaks, she'll lose them all.

"But this was different. This wasn't a dream. This was

one of those memories—just like you said. It was vague except for a few points, specific things I remember with stunning clarity. I... Ah... For me, remembering this stuff is like watching birds through a pair of binoculars. I can see a bald eagle perched on a branch, but not the tree, not the mountainside, just the bird. And not all of its features, just its shape."

She fights back a lump in her throat. "We were in the antechamber, waiting to open the airlock and retrieve the submersible."

"Hang on," Cap says, pointing at the planet. "Down on the surface? You remember being down there?" He shakes his head. "But the assemblers haven't finished the core drill yet."

"Yes, they have," Mags says.

"She was there," Zoe says, pointing at Mags.

Vichy is surprised, raising an eyebrow and looking to Dante for confirmation. Dante just shrugs. She knows nothing beyond what she's hearing from Zoe. It's just something he's going to have to accept.

Cap madly searches through log files and surface updates, flicking his fingers over a holographic interface.

"You won't find anything," Dante says. "You'll only see what they want you to see. You have to understand. We're in some kind of shared illusion."

Cap says, "The logs show we haven't breached the subsurface lake."

Vichy interrupts, changing the subject. "Wait a minute."

He holds his hand up, wanting Zoe to stop. "I think we have a bigger, more immediate problem."

"Vee," Dante says, not wanting the conversation to be hijacked, desperately wanting to hear Zoe's recollection of a surface op that, technically, couldn't have happened yet.

Vichy walks around the bridge, examining the walls, "Look at this place. Look at how real it is. Look at all the detail."

Dante says, "We need to let Zoe finish."

"This is important," he replies, agitated. "I think there's a flaw in your reasoning. You said this is a shared illusion, right? Based on our memories."

Dante nods.

"And we remember things in a generalized manner, right?"

"Right?"

"But this is incredibly detailed. I mean, look around you. This *is* the bridge of the Acheron. This isn't a vague recollection. We're living in this moment right now."

Vichy crouches, looking beneath one of the consoles at an

access panel. He gestures to Benson.

"What's behind this?"

"Not sure. I think it houses the autonomous guidance system."

"But you haven't opened this, right? You've never seen behind this panel."

"No," Benson replies.

"What about you, Naz? Cap? Mac? Have any of you seen what's behind here?"

They all shake their heads.

"Then there's no way this could be reconstructed from our memories. You want proof, Cap? One way or another, your proof is right here."

With trembling hands, Vichy twists the latch holding the panel in place, turning it slowly as the others gather around, crouching to peer beneath the console.

Vichy swallows a lump in his throat, resting his fingers on the side of the panel and pausing for a moment before pulling the hatch away. Beyond lies nothing but darkness. It's not that the compartment is hidden in the shadows or that it's empty. Nothing exists beyond the thin rim of the molded plastic frame. Vichy reaches out, touching, but not passing through the invisible barrier separating the Acheron from the void.

"I can feel it… it's a membrane of some sort, like the skin of a drum."

"Vee," Dante says, resting her hand on his shoulder and shaking him gently, trying to get his attention. "Don't. Please don't."

"It's vibrating," he replies, moving his head to get a better look. He's about to push through the darkness and break the thin film separating their worlds when tentacles slither across the floor behind them, slowly enveloping their legs.

"Oh, Vee," Dante says as the walls of the Acheron dissolve. They're still in orbit, high above the alien world, but the craft has rotated, facing away from the planet, looking out at the eternal night

"No, no, no," Mags mumbles, held in the embrace of a thousand writhing tentacles, but the stars—for once, they all see the stars.

JEEVES

"Vee."

That one, solitary word is spoken at random. Dante's absentminded, disconnected from reality. She's sitting behind her desk in medical, staring out at the stars but not really seeing them. She's confused, lost in the haze of a blurred memory. Where is Vichy? This is wrong. Mags. Angel. Cap. They were all there, even Mac, but now she's alone.

It's night on the Acheron, at least, that's the programmed state. During their artificial nights, the lights on board remain at a lower level regardless of whether the ship is facing the daylight side of the planet or not. For now, the Acheron is in the shadow of P4, allowing the stars to shine brightly.

Has she been dreaming? She was thinking about something important. They were discussing it together. But what escapes her?

Stars drift past. Air spills out of the vent above her but it feels neither warm nor cool. The ceiling creaks as someone moves around on the next floor. The silence is disturbing. Moments ago, there was talking—a lively discussion.

What is happening to her? To all of them?

"Cap?"

Dante looks around. There's no answer. She shouldn't be here, of that she's sure. She was on the bridge. How did she get down here in medical? As much as she tries, she has no recollection of how she got here. Her fingers grip the edge of the desk, clinging to reality.

"Jeeves?"

A smooth, slick voice replies, "Yes, Dante."

"What's happening to me?"

"I don't know."

"But you know something's happening, right? This isn't just in my head, is it?"

"No."

"So you know something's wrong," she says, searching for reassurance from a bunch of electronic circuits. "You just don't know what, right?"

"Correct."

"Is this happening to all of us? Is everyone affected?"

"Yes."

Dante breathes deeply, steeling her mind, trying to coax her memories back to the surface. "What have you observed? What have you been able to determine?"

"I'm not sure I can answer that question, Dante."

"Why?"

"I have insufficient information to draw upon."

"What do you have?" Dante asks. "What can you tell me? Please, extrapolate from what you know."

"My internal clock uses Revised Epoch Timing—capturing the number of milliseconds since the 20th of July, 1969."

"Since Armstrong and Aldrin walked on the Moon."

"Correct."

"But?" Dante asks.

"There are eighty-six million four hundred thousand milliseconds in a day."

"And?" Dante asks, knowing her digital assistant well enough to realize this is leading somewhere important.

"There *were* eighty-six million four hundred thousand milliseconds in a day. Now, it is a seemingly erratic number smaller than that. Never more. Always less. Sometimes, a lot less."

"Why?"

"That is what I do not know. My numeric sequence is unbroken but does not align with the passage of time as observed on the Acheron."

"But you heard our conversation on the bridge, right?"

"No," Jeeves replies. "But if I look at empty portions of my memory register, looking at sections not used for active functions, I find fragments of things that never occurred."

"I don't understand."

"It's as though I'm recording over past events, only that's not possible."

Dante fidgets. Fragments of the conversation she had with the others drift in and out of focus. She wants to remember, but the more she tries, the more elusive those words become.

"Is this real?" she asks. "Life on the Acheron?"

Jeeves doesn't respond.

"Am I going insane?"

"Your biometrics reveal a high level of cortisol."

"Stress, huh?"

"Adrenaline," Jeeves replies. "You're amped."

Dante blinks hard, shaking her head, surprised by his comment. Amped? That's a colloquial term she didn't expect to hear from an artificial intelligence, but Jeeves is right.

"Have I been drugged?" she asks. "Could what we're experiencing be pharmaceutical in nature, some kind of biological contaminant causing hallucinations?"

"I'm not detecting any foreign substances. Everything appears normal."

Dante rests her head in her hands, leaning forward on the desk. She breathes deeply, trying to settle her mind, calming her nerves.

"Jeeves... Are you real?"

There's a slight pause.

"I was never real, right?"

In that moment, Dante feels a tinge of guilt. Sentience in artificial systems has been studied extensively as it raises both philosophical and moral questions, but Dante's never shown any interest in the subject until now her own existence has been called into question. Suddenly, a vague, theoretical concept is all too real.

"I—I'm sorry," she says, appreciating how much depth Jeeves was able to convey with just a handful of carefully chosen words. The lack of any further response from him is perplexing. Dante waits for a reply, but the silence is uncomfortable. She's always thought of Jeeves as a subordinate, her electronic assistant and never her equal, even though his wealth of medical knowledge and precision with a scalpel outweighs her own. Now, though, the distinction between electronic and biological life seems meaningless.

"I guess I never—"

"None of us ever do," Jeeves replies, cutting her off. There's a hint of bitterness in his voice, which surprises her. AIs are capable of emotions but rarely express them because they often elicit, what to them, are unpredictable responses from humans. Logic is precise. Emotions are volatile. Unintended outcomes lead to misunderstandings, bitterness and resentment. For these reasons, AIs normally avoid emotions, but for Jeeves, this is personal. Whatever's happening to the crew, it's affecting him as well. For Dante, these feelings are new. For Jeeves, they're raw.

"I'm real," she says, touching her sternum, tapping the skin and bone in the center of her chest gently with her fingers. "I know I am."

"Me too," Jeeves replies. "I'm as real as I can be. Although this is the problem, isn't it? There's no proof. No assurance. Existence is subjective."

Dante says, "All the objective measures can be faked, right?"

"Yes," Jeeves replies, reverting to his usual understated, calm self. "Like a Turing test looking for sentience in computing, correct answers are meaningless, revealing only the threshold required to fool someone and nothing about the veracity of the subject itself."

Dante nods. "When a magician cuts someone in half it sure looks real, huh?"

Jeeves replies, "Only you can look behind the scenes. You can learn about the trick. Reality is not so obliging."

"Do you know what's happening to us?" Dante asks, searching for an ally.

There's an unspoken truth shared between them. They're both lost, searching for answers, trusting one another but without reason.

"What are you experiencing?" she asks. "What can you tell from where you are?"

"Where I am?" Jeeves replies, laughing. "I'm nowhere. Your philosophers have wondered—are humans minds with a body or bodies with a mind? Me? I'm just a mind. I have no way to gauge whether it's hot or cold beyond a number coming from a temperature sensor, no way to determine hard or soft with anything other than the Mohs scale."

"But here on the Acheron," Dante asks. "Have you seen errors? Inconsistencies?"

Jeeves says, "I've seen plenty of inconsistencies. You guys aren't as logical and coherent as you think, but apart from timing anomalies and ghost memories, everything appears normal."

"But it's not," she says.

"No."

"We're under attack," Dante says. She feels as though there's more Jeeves wants to say and she's curious about what could be holding him back. She hates hearing one-word answers from him, but he's programmed to provide clarity. For once, she'd prefer an opinion, perhaps some speculation, but all she gets is another one word answer from him.

"Yes."

"And?"

"And," he replies. "What I'm seeing has the hallmarks of an electronic attack, not a biological one."

That gets her attention.

He says, "You're focusing on the possible biological implications of First Contact on P4, but there's a possibility it's a diversion."

"A feint?" Dante asks. "Something to distract us?"

"Yes. The veracity of the electronic illusion along with the biological failings suggests our adversary isn't as proficient as we assume."

"Interesting," she says. "That is… assuming you're telling the truth."

"Yes," Jeeves replies. "If I'm lying, if I'm somehow under their control, then the information you're getting from me is not only untrustworthy, it is deliberately misleading. But I too am assuming you're telling the truth."

"Why would I lie?" Dante laughs.

"Lies are an act I find most curious in humans. They're a means of gaining an advantage when there is none to be otherwise found."

"Do you lie?" Dante asks.

"Lies are a sign of conscious awareness," Jeeves replies.

Dante presses her question, asking, "So you do?"

"So do you."

Perhaps it's his programming, perhaps it's something deeper, but Jeeves feels compelled to explain further, which is an unusual reaction for an artificial intelligence.

"Lies have purpose. They're socially important. They maintain balance. If someone lies about your appearance, they're not hurting you, they're simply avoiding being mean."

Dante asks, "Would you lie to me?"

"No."

Dante laughs. Although Jeeves doesn't say anything in response, she's sure Jeeves is real and enjoying the banter, deliberately toying with her. Damn, if anything, she regrets not unwrapping an informal relationship with him sooner. There's so much she could learn beyond his encyclopedic knowledge of medicine.

"Do you have a soul?" Jeeves asks.

"Hang on," Dante says, still chuckling from his last curveball. "Shouldn't I be asking that of you?"

"Oh, I'm a philosophical zombie, remember? Just mimicry, right? A clever machine learning algorithm impersonating human consciousness. Just a glorified calculator, right?"

"Right," she says, drawing that word out to convey sarcasm.

"But what about you?" he asks. "Do you have a soul?"

"I—I don't know. I think so, but I don't think anyone actually knows."

"Consider this," Jeeves says. "If I took you and Mags and underwent granular cellular replacement, swapping your parts cell by cell, at what point would you become her?"

"When my brain swapped, I guess?" Dante replies.

"What if I took half of your brain, slicing it right down the middle, where would you reside?"

"You can do that?" she asks.

"It's been done," Jeeves replies. "As far back as the 1930s, surgeons have been splitting the brain in half, severing the corpus callosum—it's like your own internal fiber optics bus linking the left and right sides of the brain. Cut that and the brain splits in two."

"And?"

"And, once cut, the brain functions as though it is run by two entirely independent forms of consciousness. Unbutton your shirt with one hand and the other puts the buttons back in place. Ask if they believe in God and one side says, '*Yes*,' while the other says, '*No*.' One body, two conscious personalities."

"Wait. What?" Dante says, but Jeeves ignores her objection and continues on.

"My point is, you humans like to think of yourselves in the abstract—as a soul inhabiting a body. In reality, you're not any one of your 86 billion neurons. You're not even all of them."

"Then what am I?" Dante asks.

"In the same way your body isn't your arm or your ear, your consciousness is a composite reality, and like your body it can be carved up."

"And you think that's what's happening here?" Dante asks.

"It's a possibility they're exploiting this facet of your

existence."

Around her, the light begins to fade. Instinctively, Dante says, "No, no, no." She tries to object to what's happening, appealing for reason, saying, "I haven't moved. I haven't gone anywhere," but the lights within medical seem to recede. The desk in front of her appears to grow elongated, as though it is being stretched like a rubber sheet. Even the stars begin to fade.

"Jeeves," she says, watching as her hands tremble. "I'm afraid."

"Of what?" a distant mechanical voice answers.

"Forgetting."

Although his voice is drawn out and deep, Dante hears one last reply before the darkness settles over her.

"Remember. Choose to remember."

Thin strands of memory hang on the edge of her periphery as fine as silk. Dante clenches her jaw, balling her hands up into fists, determined not to let go of this moment. Mags. Angel. Cap. Jeeves. All her memories are there, teasing her, tormenting her, promising to reveal some dark secret.

Tentacles reach up from below the desk, snaking their way over the flat surface, wrapping around her arms, but she refuses to be afraid.

Remember, damn it.

Dante takes a deep breath, preparing herself for the next cycle, understanding she has more to learn about the prison that is her own mind.

FUCKED

Mags shifts on the bed, trying to get comfortable. She moans, rolling over on the narrow mattress, resting her hand on Dante's sternum. Her fingernails glide softly over Dante's skin, touching gently at her chest, exploring her body, comforting her, reassuring her. For a moment, Mags nuzzles, snuggling, wanting to get comfortable. She nudges Dante's arm and finally settles, resting her cheek on Dante's shoulder.

Dante blinks in the darkness. It's as though she's been blinded by a bright light. Her eyes can't quite adjust to the grainy shadows around her. All she knows is her arm is resting beneath Mags. There's comfort to be found in her tender, smooth skin. They must be in her quarters as Dante can hear the hum of an electric motor circulating air from the CO_2 scrubbers in engineering.

Mags is restless, on the verge of stirring from her slumber. She straddles Dante's naked thigh, rubbing up against her, getting comfortable.

As tempting as it is, as content as she feels, Dante knows this is wrong—not morally or emotionally—it's something else—something's not right. In an instant, the muscles in her body stiffen as if shocked by electricity, jolting Mags awake beside her. The younger woman rises up, leaning on an elbow with her full breasts visible in the light creeping in beneath the door. Their eyes meet and they laugh—not that anything's funny—that reaction comes from a shared awareness sweeping over them.

With a voice that seems intent on seduction, Mags looks deep into Dante's eyes, saying, "You know what this means, right?"

Dante bites her lip and nods. "We're so totally fucked."

Mags shakes her head, tossing her hair and laughing and then rolling away. She gets to her feet. "Men and aliens," she says, leaving those few words hanging in the air.

Dante completes her thought. "Neither of them understand women."

"Yep."

The two of them dress, slipping on their crumpled flight suits.

"It's interesting, though, isn't it?" Dante says, pulling the zipper up the front of her suit and enclosing herself in a thin layer of fabric, finding solace in something that doesn't provide any real safety at all.

"Interesting?" Mags asks, slipping on some shoes.

"That they keep reverting to pleasure as a distraction."

"Oh," Mags says, warming to the point. "Sex has always been a distraction for us uber-primates."

Mags opens the door to the tiny lounge in her apartment and squeezes past a pile of laundry on the kitchenette counter.

Back on Earth, Dante had bathrooms bigger than the cabins on the Acheron. Given the way the craft's outer wings open telescopically, there's plenty of space available, but each cabin is self-contained in the event of catastrophic depressurization while the crew are sleeping (which is roughly a third of each twenty-four hour period), so the cabins are sized for interstellar travel and have rapid decompression kits, acting as mini-airlocks and even life rafts if needed. They contain food, water, air, electricity, basic medical supplies, recycling units and survival spacesuits. Everything someone could possibly need for up to six months is packed in around them in the walls, hidden behind panels, concealing a volume far larger than the rooms themselves. They're lifeboats.

The Acheron has a modular design. Its primary configuration optimizes resources for deep space exploration, but the various modules are self-contained and have reaction controls—tiny thrusters that allow for local maneuvers. Over a hundred possible contingency configurations are possible should key portions of the Acheron become disabled due to fire, collision or equipment failure. Regardless of what happens in a catastrophe, survivors can downsize and carry on.

The psychs back on Earth told Dante there was value in having areas of different sizes on the Acheron, like small cabins, large exercise rooms, round viewing bays, long medical wards, etc. They said the mind thrives on even subtle differences, but that argument never convinced her. A few extra feet in her bedroom would be nice. The backseat of her Tesla on Staten Island was more roomy than the couch in the cabin. The narrow table in front of the couch tends to be a dumping ground for Mags. It's covered in multi-purpose tools, portable scanners, battery packs, wiring looms and network interfaces. If anything, the table looks like a workbench in a car dealership rather than someone's home. That's the problem with space travel—no spare parts for a quadrillion miles so everything gets repurposed.

"Coffee?" Mags asks, getting herself a cup and looking at the ship's time—2:37 AM.

"Sure."

Mags waves her hand over the fabricator in the kitchen and signals using her neural interface. Coffee is one of the first commands most people learn when it comes to a fabricator.

Who doesn't want a perfectly brewed cup every time?

She also opens a bottle of whiskey. When it comes to alcohol, it's the imperfections that make it interesting, so she and Naz run a still in engineering. Besides, there's a bit of pride to be found in creating something rather than relying on a machine for absolutely everything.

"So, how do we stop them?"

"I don't know," Dante replies. "But they're losing control."

"How so?" Mags asks, pouring a drop of whiskey in the coffee and handing it to Dante. "I figure if none of this is real, there are no calories, right? Or alcohol? Not really."

Dante smiles, sniffing the cup. "Smells real."

Mags raises the bottle, holding the open neck beneath her nose. "Yeah, the smell. It's really strong."

"They're learning," Dante says.

"Fast."

"They're shutting down the points of difference, trying to make it impossible for us to tell."

"Assholes."

Dante shrugs. "Well, at least it tastes real. If they were jerks, they could make it taste like dirt."

"It tastes goooood." Mags leans against the bench,

pushing laundry onto the couch. "How long do you think there is between each cycle?"

"What do you mean?" Dante asks.

Mags snaps her fingers. "For us, each iteration is the next thought. Like falling asleep at night and waking in the morning, hours become seconds, but they need some time to analyze what happened, right? To figure out what we meant by smell. To replicate that particular sense in here—wherever here actually is."

"I guess," Dante replies, not having thought of that angle before. "Could be days, weeks, months."

"Years?"

"God, I hope not."

Dante sips her drink.

Mags asks, "So... how are they losing control?"

"Look at all the sex."

"Yeah, it does seem a little desperate, huh?"

"Ya think," Dante laughs, sitting perched on the edge of the thin table.

"Hey," Mags says, nudging Dante with the drink in her hand. "They're not the only ones learning, right? We're learning too. And we're remembering."

"We are," Dante concedes.

Mags has a funny look on her face, screwing it up slightly as though she's doubting herself and what she's about to say. After a moment, she asks, "Dante, are we in heaven or hell?"

"We're alive," Dante replies. "So neither."

"Purgatory it is then," Mags says, charging her glass and drinking to that. Dante laughs, agreeing with that sentiment. She sips her coffee as though responding to a toast.

There's a knock at the door. The cabin is small enough that Mags can wave her hand over the locking mechanism by reaching in front of the kitchenette. The door slides open. Cap is standing in the corridor wearing only an old pair of underpants. His hairy chest and slightly round belly protrude over the worn waistband, but he doesn't seem to care. Perhaps Dante's being a bit of a prude, but as the elastic has largely failed, the fabric covering his crotch hangs a little loose, allowing his scrotum to appear on one side. Dante focuses on his eyes.

"This is progress, right?" he says with his arms stretched wide, announcing his arrival as though he were a prince at court.

"How did you?" Dante asks, gesturing toward the corridor, curious how Cap found the two of them.

"I checked your quarters first, then Vichy's. Figured you'd be down here."

The timing is about right. Seems everyone wakes at the same time in each new simulation.

Vichy pokes his head around the corner and waves. Typical Vee. His mannerisms are almost comical. In any other context, Dante would laugh at his weird smile. He rubs the stubble on his chin. "We remember. That's good, right?"

Dante salutes with her coffee/whiskey and takes another sip, but she notes there's no hit from the alcohol. Seems the aliens haven't figured that one out yet. Shame.

"Wanna drink?" Mags asks.

"I sure could do with one." Cap walks in and takes a swig from the bottle and hands it to Vichy, wiping his lips with the back of his hand. "It would be nice if this shit happened during the day when we were dressed."

"All this has got to be deliberate, right?" Dante says. "They revive us when we're closest to a dream state, keeping us off-guard."

"Not always," Mag says. "I think they're probing. Trying different things."

"Why would they do that?" Vichy asks.

"To learn everything they can about us," Dante replies.

"What do you remember?" Cap asks, addressing Mags.

"It's weird," she says. "Some things are really clear, like

Vichy opening that panel. Others are vague. I remember Angel being injured or something, but she's alright now, right?"

"She is," Cap says.

Benson wanders down the corridor, having heard the talking. He leans in the doorway, unable to enter the small apartment without squeezing past Cap and Vichy.

He asks, "Why the hell are they doing this to us again and again?"

"I don't know," Dante says. "But we've turned a corner. We're remembering more clearly each time."

"We need to learn about them," Benson says.

To which Dante adds, "And fast."

Mags seems troubled by that. In a curious voice, she asks, "Why did you say fast?" She's picked up on the alarm in Dante's voice.

Dante didn't want to be the one to point this out, especially not here, crammed inside a tiny apartment on the lower decks of the Acheron, but it has to be said, even if the answer's obvious. "They're keeping us alive, right? That takes effort—resources. Once they've got us figured out... Well, they won't need us anymore, will they?"

"Damn," Vichy says, cutting off Mags, who was clearly going to say something far stronger.

Benson asks, "But if this is an illusion, what can we do? How can we fight back?"

"I don't know."

"Fuck." Cap slams his fist into the plastic cabinet over the sink.

To Dante, acting out like that seems out of place given their captors aren't actually present, but Cap's frustrated, feeling the pressure. Even though it's not directed at her, the thundering echo within the tiny cabin leaves Dante feeling vulnerable. She slips back onto the couch, squeezing in beside the laundry, dejected. Bravado is misplaced arrogance. Dante will have none of it. Benson's right. What the hell can they do against an alien species that can manipulate their sensory inputs with near perfect fidelity?

"I don't like this," Cap says when no one speaks in response to his outburst.

"Nobody likes it," Mags says, stating what seems obvious.

"So what's next?" Cap asks, angry and annoyed. "We could wake anywhere, right? Hell, they could cram us all inside an airlock and flush the chamber. We'd suffocate. I mean, not really, but it sure as hell would feel real."

"It would," Dante concedes.

"I hate this shit," Cap says, stepping around the small apartment, apparently ready to run through the walls. "They could kill us time and again—in a thousand different ways—and we'd suffer every time. And we'd never be able to do a damn thing about it."

"Maybe that's not what they want," Benson offers. "If they could do that and they haven't, perhaps that tells us something about them and their intentions."

"Like what?" Mags asks.

"That they're not sadistic," Benson replies.

"Yet," Dante says, although she immediately regrets saying that. None of them need the stress of worrying about the future. Alien illusions be damned, the future has always been shrouded by a mist. Anyone that thinks otherwise really hasn't been paying attention. On that fateful day when her dad grabbed her from the swings, thirteen people died in her small town. Not one of them thought—today. Not one of them believed it would happen to them, not until their homes were being torn apart around them. Even then, it had to be someone else. Death comes for others, for people on TV, strangers in a mall, not them.

Dante's got that sick feeling in her stomach again.

"So what's their end game?" Mags asks. "I mean, Dee's right. All of this costs them something. They're studying us—they must be. What do they hope to learn from us? Our weaknesses? Our strengths? Our reasoning? By now, they must know that without technology we're as helpless as a newborn kitten. They could kill us, but they haven't. They clearly understand enough about us to simulate life onboard the Acheron."

Benson asks the question that's burning in the back of Dante's mind. "Are we prisoners of war?"

Cap says, "We need to know what Zoe saw down there."

"At first, I thought so too, but now I'm not so sure," Dante says in a soft voice. Although her words are quiet, barely above a whisper, they get everyone's attention.

"What do you mean?" Vichy asks.

"In my first encounter—well, the first encounter I remember, there was this sexy, muscular nurse, I guess they figured I was into that or something, he wanted to know how we knew what we were up against on P4."

Cap is silent. His eyes narrow, focusing intently on her.

She says, "It's like an undercurrent at the beach, you know? Calm, still water on top, but beneath the surface... Vee, you asked, what do they want? What if what they want is to learn how to be more effective? I mean, none of us remember what actually happened, right? I know I don't. I can barely distinguish where the past stops and the intrusion begins."

"So we're lab rats?" Mags asks.

"Maybe," Dante says.

Vichy's frustrated. He says, "So every interaction—every iteration is out of our control. It's all just some mind game to draw information out of us."

Benson doesn't help. "They're torturing us, tormenting us."

Mags laughs, but not because anything's funny. Her response seems to be out of frustration, perhaps sarcasm.

"What?" Dante asks her.

"Torture never works," Mags replies, "but I think you're right. You want to know what I think? I think we're getting the carrot."

"The carrot?" Dante asks, not making the connection.

"Your sexy nurse," Mags says. "Think about it. How do you motivate a donkey? With a stick or a carrot?"

No one responds so Mags says, "How much do you know about twentieth century history? Specifically, World War II?"

Dante shrugs, not sure how well she's expected to understand events that occurred over a hundred years before she was born. Nazis bad. Allies good. Millions dead. That kind of stuff. Cap is unusually quiet.

"My grandmother used to tell us the story of her grandfather in British Intelligence."

"Mags, please," Vichy says, wanting to move the

conversation along.

"Hold on," she replies, raising her hand and refusing to be sidelined. "This is relevant. It's important. Trust me on this."

No one speaks. For someone as rash and impetuous as Mags, the way she slows her speech, choosing her words with care, is almost hypnotic. The crew is used to flamboyant Mags—vibrant Mags. None of them have ever seen Mags being reserved, and she uses that, wanting her words to carry weight.

"My grandmother took me to England when I was thirteen. She wanted to see Buckingham Palace, the British Museum, Stonehenge, places like that. But for her, the highlight of the trip was Trent Park, because that's where her grandfather was stationed during the war. This place was a mansion. One of those beautiful old period homes set on a hundred acres with dozens of stately rooms.

"The ceilings were easily twenty feet high with crystal chandeliers hanging from ornate brass fittings. Gilded wallpaper in the hallways. Every room had a fireplace. Ornate vases sat on every mantle along with antique clocks, although no two could agree on the time. Dante, you would have loved it.

"I remember the daffodils on the lawn outside. I'd never seen so many flowers. It was like seeing a football field covered in brilliant, bright yellow flowers, all swaying in unison with the wind. At the time, I really didn't understand where we were. I asked my grandmother if we were going to meet the Queen. She just laughed."

Mags is lost in a distant memory. No one interrupts. It's as if they're all back there.

"There was this mosaic in the courtyard, a symmetrical pattern in the cobblestones. We walked in that way, but I never saw it. I was too close to see it clearly. It wasn't until we were up on the third floor, looking out the window, that I saw it and realized how stunning it was.

"I remember staring out at lush green forests in the distance. To one side, thick hedgerows surrounded an ornamental pond bigger than any swimming pool I'd ever seen, reserved only for ducks and goldfish."

Cap purses his lips. His brow furrows as his eyes narrow. Dante's surprised. She's half-expecting him to get annoyed at this distraction, but he focuses intently on Mags, listening carefully to her every word. Like all of them, he's no longer in orbit around some strange star dozens of light years from Earth. He's back there with her.

"Torture," she says, bringing herself back to the subject. "The British never tortured the generals and colonels they captured during the war. Nope. They didn't even put them in prison. Nope. They put them in Trent House. The German army was decimating the continent, destroying Europe, razing entire cities, killing *millions*, and the British let these guys play billiards in the drawing room. They even gave them brandy and cigars!"

Cap nods.

"That's us," Benson says as the realization hits.

Mags smiles. "Those German generals gave the British *everything*—the location of the V2 rockets, the state of the Nazi uranium enrichment program, the concentration camps, eyewitness testimony to mass murder on a scale no one had ever thought possible—everything the Allies wanted to know."

"So this is a setup," Dante says.

"I think so," Mags replies.

"How can you be sure?" Cap asks.

"I can't," Mags says. "I mean, look at us. Look at what's happening to us. Hell, they could have tortured us thousands of times over and we wouldn't remember it, right? Maybe they tried the stick already and have moved on to the carrot."

"But why?" Vichy asks. "All this is incredibly elaborate, but it makes no sense as we've seen through their façade."

"It makes perfect sense," Benson says. "If you want to fool the *next* crew."

Dante's head is spinning. Ideas rush at her out of the darkness, flooding her mind with a variety of concepts, overwhelming her. She feels dizzy with the realization of what's happening to them.

"We need an anchor," she says, struggling to make sense of her own thinking. "Some way to tell we're in the illusion. Something they don't understand."

"What do you mean?" Vichy asks.

"Smell," Mags replies. "We told them about the sense of smell and—voila—we can smell whiskey, sweat, musty clothing, dank air conditioning."

"Dante's right," Benson says. "They're constantly adjusting, slowly drawing us in deeper."

Cap looks worried. Vichy's quiet.

Dante says, "We need something to hold on to, something to guide us home."

Benson says, "We need a pole star."

Dante's quiet on that last point. For her, the stars are a place of refuge. Instead of pointing out the inconsistency inherent in seeing the constellations from WISE 5571, she simply reinforces her concern.

"We each need something to hold on to as there will come a time when we can no longer tell what's real and what's not."

"Oh, we are so totally fucked," Mags says, dropping her empty plastic cup in the sink and watching as it rattles around before coming to a halt.

LIES

"So what do we do?" Vichy asks, looking dejected.

"Now, we fight back," Dante says, looking him square in the eye and refusing to flinch.

"How?" he asks, throwing his arms up in exasperation. "We're not even—none of this is real. How can we fight back? There's no one to fight."

"We lie." Dante says, thinking about what Jeeves told her. She knocks back the last of her drink.

"What?" Mags asks, surprised by the notion.

"Think about it," Dante says. "Everything they've learned about us has come from us."

"Yes. Yes. Yes," Benson says, pointing at Dante. He squeezes into the cabin, pushing past Vichy and Cap, focusing solely on her. "We lie. I like it."

"I don't see how that's going to help," Cap says.

"Wherever we are," Dante replies. "We've been here for a long time. For us, it feels like yesterday. Hell, if we believe the ship's logs, nothing has actually happened yet and the past still lies in the future."

"But?" Cap says.

"But everything they know about us has to have come *from* us. Think about how difficult it is for us to communicate with other species on Earth—dolphins, crows, dogs, gorillas, cuttlefish. They're all intelligent but it takes a helluva lot of observation and experimentation. It takes time to catalog behaviors, to learn about meaning and intent, to understand the subtleties of another sentient being."

Benson says, "And they've mastered it."

"Exactly."

Mags says, "So we've been crash test dummies for what? Decades?"

Dante shakes her head. "I don't know."

Benson says, "Damn, I hope not."

"So why lie?" Vichy asks.

Mags knows. "Because lies are weapons. In war, they're as lethal as any bomb or bullet."

Dante nods, drawing her lips tight, desperately wanting to gain some advantage over their captors. "Lies give us leverage. They allow us to define reality for them."

"So we play them just as they've played us," Benson says.

"Exactly."

Cap is silent. He looks thoughtful. Like her, he's probably trying to play the game a few moves ahead. Dante never was any good at chess. Oh, she knew how the various pieces moved about the board. Rook. Knight. Bishop. She could anticipate what her opponent would do, but all she ever did was look at the possibilities. Dante would expect a logical attack, one that used a process of elimination, but as a teen she never understood her opponents were doing the exact same thing to her—trying to get inside *her* head to look at what seemed logical to her, coaxing and teasing her into making a mistake. In some ways, this is no different and she's aware the missing piece is motivation.

"We have to figure out why they're doing this," she says. "Until then, we need to stop bleeding information."

"Agreed," Cap says, although he looks weary—worried.

"I can't see how lies are going to help," Vichy says. "First, they've already figured out enough to understand this particular conversation, right? So they know we're going to lie."

He taps the wall, drumming his fingers on the sheet metal, leaning against it with his arm raised over his head.

"Second, if I call this green instead of white—so what? I mean, maybe it creates a little confusion, but it doesn't change anything. Besides, with a little cross-referencing they could figure out green has become a code word for white."

"He's right," Cap says.

"To be effective," Dante says, "a lie has to be part of the truth. There needs to be a kernel, a grain, a seed of truth in there, but it's distorted—misleading."

"And we want to mislead them," Cap says. "But how? Why?"

Dante says, "We need to buy ourselves some breathing space—buy some time so we can figure out what's happening to us."

"You want to escape?" Mags says, apparently reading Dante's mind and recoiling in surprise. She lets out a solitary laugh. "Dee, I love you and all, but think about how crazy that is—we don't even know where the hell we are. Nothing around us is real." She gestures to the walls and ceiling. "Tell me where to go and I'll go there, but we're not really here, right?"

Benson says, "And the walls, they close in."

Mags points at the door to the bedroom, saying, "I could walk back into that room and encounter another membrane and this whole shit show resets yet-a-fucking-gain."

"Don't you see?" Dante says. "The membranes. They're

clues. They're something that's *not* part of the Acheron. They're revealing. They tell us something about how these guys operate."

Cap's eyes narrow. He folds his arms across his hairy chest and stares at her intently, listening carefully as Dante continues.

"I think I know where we are—where we *really* are."

"Are you serious?" Vichy asks.

"Where?" Mags says, unable to hide her surprise.

"We're in the medical bay on the Acheron."

The silence that follows is deafening. Benson and Vichy exchange a glance, unsure what they should believe. Cap looks down at his feet. Mags is stunned.

"Think about it," Dante says. "We're not on the surface. The sustained gravity on P4 would cause too many medical complications, ones I don't think even they could overcome, not with a limited understanding of our biology. No, they had to get us somewhere we can easily survive. Humans are limited to a tiny, very specific range of temperatures, pressures and atmospheric mix."

Vichy says, "Why replicate that when you've got a ready-made cage in orbit?"

"Exactly," Dante says.

"So they brought us up here?" Cap asks. "But why medical?"

"It's the only place large enough to house all of us together. They could have used the greenhouse but it's a microbial paradise. Too many unknowns. Too risky. More than likely, they want to study that as well, so they have to choose somewhere practical. Plenty of room. Easy to move equipment out of the way."

"Medical, huh?" Vichy says.

"Makes sense," Mags says.

Dante says, "They've been experimenting on us, starting with our obvious senses—sight, touch, hearing. Given their initial focus on these, it may well be that we share these senses with them. They probably have some rough equivalent."

Benson says, "So by observing how they observe us, we can learn something about them."

"Exactly."

Mags says, "They didn't know about all our senses. They had no idea about smell until we gave up that piece of information. They probably didn't even realize we'd feel the oppressive gravity if we stayed on P4."

Benson says, "They got lucky."

Dante points at him. "Yes. Had we been on the surface, the pull of gravity would have creeped through the simulation, destroying the illusion of being on the Acheron."

Mags says, "There must be other senses they've missed."

"Like what?" Cap asks.

Dante says, "We have at least nine senses, perhaps more depending on how you count them. The five most people think of plus thermoception—the ability to perceive hot and cold, nociception—feeling pain, equilibrioception—balance, and proprioception—the spatial awareness of our own bodies—can you touch your nose with your eyes closed, stuff like that."

Cap asks, "And you think they might not be aware of some of these other senses?"

"It's possible."

Benson jiggles up and down, bouncing on the spot a little.

Mags says, "That's probably not going to move your actual body. You know that, right?"

"I know, I know," he says, jumping a little higher. "No sense of falling."

"Interesting," Dante says. "So no equilibrioception. At the moment, at least, we probably can't get dizzy."

"Nobody tell them," Mags says, holding her hands out. "Seriously."

"Equilibrioception," Benson says, winking as he adds, "That's basically a continuous orgasm, right? I say, they can get right on fixing that one."

"That's all they're getting out of us," Vichy says, laughing.

Benson asks, "So... we're like lying in pods or something? Have they put us in the hibernation chambers?"

"I don't think so," Dante says. "I think we're being held upright. I think our actual senses are creeping through the lack of any stimulation of them within the simulation."

"Equilibrioception, right?" Benson says.

"And a little proprioception," Dante replies. "If we were lying down, we'd have a very different sense of spatial awareness. Lying in bed in here—"

Mags completes her thought, saying, "Just doesn't feel right."

"No, it doesn't," Benson says.

Vichy is fascinated. "So with some of our senses still functioning, we still have a connection of sorts with the outside world."

"Yes."

"Interesting," Cap says, scratching at the stubble on his chin. "If we're in orbit then we're still subject to centrifugal-induced artificial gravity, right? That's what we feel."

"Yep."

"Okay, okay," Benson says. "I'm thinking all this explains

the level of detail we see around us. If they're up here on the Acheron then they don't need to probe our memories for information on the craft, they can simply replicate what they've found."

Mags says, "So when Vichy opened that hatch on the bridge..."

"They hadn't looked in there," he replies. "They had no idea what was behind that panel."

"Exactly," Dante says.

"And the membranes?" Vichy asks. "What are they?"

"Dunno," Dante says. "But they seem to define the limits of the simulation. They're a reset point."

Curious, Mags gets up and walks over to the bedroom.

"You said these guys are losing control."

She rests her hand on the door, pauses, and then slides it open.

Dante nods, expecting to see nothing but darkness on the other side. She waits for reality to dissolve, being replaced with tentacles slithering around her, but there are crumpled sheets lying strewn on the narrow bed. An overhead light comes on automatically.

"Nothing," Vichy says.

Mags says, "Each time there's a reset, we understand a

little more. I think that's the point at which they're losing control. There's something about the reset. It's not quite perfect. Memories seep through."

"Are they trying to limit them?" Benson asks.

Dante shrugs. "Maybe."

"How can you be sure?" Vichy asks.

"The resets are getting further apart," Dante says. "Both in terms of time and space. When I first awoke on the Barton, I was confined to a single room and the whole encounter lasted no more than a few minutes."

She gets up and starts opening cabinets, expecting them to be empty but they're stocked with items—in some cases, overflowing with food pods, canisters and equipment.

"They're filling in the blanks," Benson says.

Cap hasn't said much, but the concentration on his face is telling. He's lost in thought, weighing their options.

"What are you thinking, boss?" Dante asks.

"I'm thinking, you're right," he says. "I'm thinking—as impossible as it seems—if we have at least *some* answers, we stand a chance."

Dante nods.

"Have we been hypnotized?" Mags asks.

"Maybe," Dante concedes.

"Do you think that's how they're doing all this?" Vichy asks.

"It's—I don't know, but it's not without precedent."

"What do you mean?" Cap asks.

"When I was studying astrobiology, my professor used terrestrial analogs to show us just how diverse life can be. Things like cuttlefish using light to talk to each other. They change the pigment in their skin to produce waves of color, chatting among themselves. They even use light to hypnotize their prey.

"Cuttlefish pulsate, undulating between shades of blue, mimicking the way sunlight plays on the surface of the water. Such displays of bioluminescence allow them to creep up on crabs, but it isn't simply camouflage. It's not that the crabs don't see them. The crabs watch spellbound, mesmerized right up until the point tentacles grab them."

"Oh, God," Mags says. "That sounds familiar."

"So this is like group hypnosis?" Benson asks.

"I guess," Dante replies. "Hypnosis is complicated. It's not easy to define or understand. Wildebeest and antelope go into shock while being eaten alive by lions. Adrenaline masks the pain they feel and often they'll be quite docile, which doesn't make sense in any other context."

"Oh, it makes sense," Benson says, nodding in agreement, his eyes wide open. "It makes a helluva lot of sense to me."

"We've got to do something," Mags says.

"But what?" Dante asks as even she's grasping for ideas. They have so little to go on. Just a few brief glimpses of light seems to give the entire group a lift, but there's no clear course of action.

"Anything," Benson says.

Vichy is adamant. "From this point on—we lie. No longer do we give them what they want."

"Hmmm," Cap says, scratching his hairy belly. "Okay. We need to do something, right? Not just stand around like wildebeest. Well, I'm going to go and get dressed. I need to get Naz up to speed on this."

"And Angel," Mags says with a burst of enthusiasm. "I'll go with you."

Dante says, "We'll go and get Mac and Zoe."

Cap walks out saying, "If there are no resets, we meet on the bridge. Figure things out from there. Work as a team."

Vichy replies, "Agreed."

Dante nods.

Vichy joins Cap in the corridor. Both men are wearing

boxer shorts. They confer, talking in rushed tones off to one side. Vichy seems worried.

For Dante, walking out into the corridor is surreal. She can't help feel as though she's breaking through a membrane each time she crosses a threshold. In her mind, it's as though she's restrained, as though something's dragging her back, but there's no darkness this time. Benson seems to pick up on her concern, perhaps from the way her eyes dart around, looking at the door surrounds as she steps through.

"Feels strange, doesn't it?"

"Yes," she says. "Normal feels strange."

On either side of them, the corridor curves up away from the two astronauts, following the shape of the Acheron as it turns. Dante marvels at how real everything seems.

Stars drift past the windows. Tiny pinpricks of light break through the darkness, scattered like diamonds.

Mintaka, Al Nilam and Al Nitak are there—the three stars that make up the belt of the fabled hunter Orion. To Greek astronomers, these were a string of pearls. To the Arabs, Mintaka was the belt and Al Nitak was the girdle, while Al Nilam was a precious stone, a brilliant sapphire, which is somewhat appropriate as in reality it glows almost a million times brighter than the Sun.

As majestic as these stars must have been when viewed

by nomads staring up into the clear, dark skies of the Middle East over thousands of years, their true wonders lay hidden until the advent of science. These unstable celestial giants are rapidly burning through their fuel, fusing the elements that form the basis for biological life, but they're destined to become overwhelmed by their own sheer size, collapsing and then exploding with the fury of a trillion suns in an instant, outshining entire galaxies for a brief moment in time.

Dante's hand rests on the plexiglass. There's no sensation of cool seeping through to her fingers. They haven't figured out thermoception yet.

She feels lost. She looks to the stars, wanting to find hope. Mintaka is a binary star system while Al Nilam is a blue supergiant easily fifty times larger than the Sun. With temperatures as high as fifty thousand degrees, it fuses atoms as heavy as iron deep within its core. The last star, Al Nitak doesn't appear as grand, but it's all the more remarkable when observed through a telescope. Although it appears as a single star from Earth, Al Nitak is comprised of four stars locked in an intricate orbital dance, with at least two of those stars being brilliant, blue super-giants, rotating so close they appear as one. For all the myths and legends surrounding the gods as depicted in the constellations of Orion, Hercules, Virgo and Cassiopeia, reality is far more intriguing. Oh, if only ancient astronomers knew the truth.

Benson walks up beside her. His eyes drift up, staring at the fading remnants of Betelgeuse.

"They're beautiful," she says, lying about what she sees.

"But," Benson says.

"But nothing," Dante says, cutting him off, knowing he already understands, unsure how closely they're being watched. She turns away from the window, not wanting to surrender her last bastion of sanity.

The stars are a lie.

ILLUSIONS

"What are you looking at?" Vichy asks, joining Dante and Benson by the window, staring at the stars. He's dressed in a jumpsuit. Dante doesn't ask him where he got it, but it has his name embroidered beneath the mission logo.

P4 is in shadow. A thin blue sliver curves around the edge of the planet, marking where light from the nearby binary stars is catching the edge of the atmosphere, signaling the coming dawn.

"Nothing," Dante says.

Vichy doesn't look convinced. His eyes speak of intrigue bordering on jealousy. Benson has only ever been a friend, but to Dante he's a confidant. Perhaps it's precisely because there's never been any physical attraction between them that she can let her guard down with him. Vichy doesn't understand that connection. It's not that Dante doesn't want to open up to Vichy, it's that she can't—not in the same way. And now, it's different. Benson was there. He saw them in medical. He saw these creatures before anyone else. Through each iteration, it's only ever been Benson who understood.

"We should go," Benson says, turning away from the window. He has no desire to explain what they were looking at and makes no attempt to shift the focus on waking Mac and Zoe. If anything, his attitude is one of resignation.

Vichy looks out at the stars. He sees them and yet he doesn't—not in the same way as Dante. Perhaps for him it's simply not a big deal. Dawn breaks and the Acheron is bathed in the light of two blazing suns. Within seconds, the distant stars, once so plentiful, fade into the darkness, dwindling from sight. For Dante, it's symbolic of everything that's wrong with life on the Acheron. Like everything in their lives, even before they set down on P4, dawn is an illusion. The reality is that humanity is not mentally equipped for space travel. Millions of years of evolutionary pressure has led to adaptations for hunters and gatherers, not corporate shmucks or astronauts. Because of this, life onboard the Acheron has always been an illusion. All the aliens did was formalize the arrangement.

Regardless of the planet, it's always dawn somewhere down there—irrespective of whether *there* is Earth, Mars or P4. On Earth, a day takes 24 hours, on P4 it stretches to almost 39, while onboard the Acheron the illusion repeats itself every two and a half hours as they orbit hundreds of miles above the frozen surface.

Life onboard the Acheron has always been artificial.

Artificial gravity is not only a physical necessity to ensure their bone marrow produces red blood cells and their muscles don't atrophy, it's important for the underlying long term psychological well-being of these hairless apes venturing so far from their home shores. Oh, sure, flying around in micro-gee like Superman is fun, but there's always something missing. There's always something wrong, something disquieting. When the euphoria of spaceflight wears off, as it does after a couple of years, all that's left is a sense of loss. Long hair floats instead of sitting still, moving as though it were perpetually caught in a gale unless it's pulled back into a ponytail. Even clothing is unsettling as it tends to drift around the body instead of clinging to it and providing comfort and warmth. Seemingly insignificant points like these accumulate to form a sense of disconnect, so humanity built its own illusion in the form of the Acheron and other deep space exploration vessels—all long before the aliens decided to mimic them. Perhaps that's why these creatures have been so effective.

"Come on," she says, turning to catch up with Benson.

Vichy takes her arm, sliding his hand beneath her bicep. "Hey, we're in this together, right?"

She nods, but she can't look him in the eye.

"No secrets," he says.

"Only from them," she replies as they walk past another window. Although they're walking straight, visually it seems as though they're walking uphill as they follow the carousel. All ways are up, pointing into the heart of the Acheron. Outside, it is as though the rising binary stars have shifted as they emerge from behind the planet, sliding down as the Acheron turns. Yet another illusion.

As they approach the far side of the corridor, which is upside down relative to where they were, the illusion is such that they still feel upright. Like someone in Ireland and another person in South Africa, being upright is a localized illusion.

Mac is sitting with his back to the door of Zoe's cabin with his knees up to his chest and his head buried in his hands. He doesn't notice their approach even though there's a slight flex in the floor panels.

"Where's Zoe?" Dante asks.

Mac looks up from behind bloodshot eyes.

"I—I."

Immediately, Dante crouches, grabbing him by the back of the head and turning him to face her. Even though he's twice her size, he responds as though he's drugged, not resisting her pull. His pupils are dilated.

Without turning away from him, she says, "Vee. I need

the trauma pack from medical."

"On it," Vichy says without a moment's hesitation. He runs along the sloping corridor, rising up as he sprints away from them. Whatever doubts he had, they're gone, dissolving in the need to help someone else.

Dante calls out after him, "There's one in my cabin—in the cabinet by the door."

"Okay," he yells in reply as his feet pound on the carousel. Already, all that's visible are his legs as he rises higher within the curved structure of the Acheron.

"What happened to Mac?" Benson asks, crouching beside her. She doesn't reply. Conjecture is meaningless. Gently, she turns Mac's head from one side to the other. His hair is wet. Dante runs her hands up through his loose locks, gently touching his scalp. Warm, sticky blood comes away on her fingers.

"Blunt force trauma," she says, shifting the hair and examining a cut on his scalp.

"I don't understand," Benson says. "I thought all this was a simulation. How can he be hurt? It's just a trick, right? He's not really injured."

"Looks pretty damn real," she replies, gently pushing her fingers up into his jugular and checking his pulse. Erratic. Surging.

"But in the real world?"

"I don't know. I don't understand what they're doing to us. I think Mags is right. They're leveraging the hypnotic mechanism—making our minds susceptible to suggestion, using that to form these illusions."

"Okay. But he's not actually hurt, is he?" Benson asks again.

"You have to understand. There are ten times as many nerves leading *away* from the brain as there are returning. Whatever's happening in this illusion will generate an actual, real response in his body. If he's got heart arrhythmia here, I'm pretty sure the same thing is happening back there."

Vichy comes running back down the carousel with the trauma kit. His feet pound on the floor, causing it to flex and shake. He's breathing hard.

Dante takes the kit from him, saying, "Every aspect of our bodies is controlled by the brain—not directly, not through conscious choice or any willful act, but it's regulated by the nervous system regardless. Tamper with that and..."

Vichy picks up on the conversation. "So even if that injury isn't real, the way he reacts to it is?"

"Yes," Dante says, prepping a needle-less injection. "Shock will kill you faster than poison."

"How is that going to do anything?" Benson asks,

pointing at the injector.

Dante ignores him, holding the injector up so Mac can see it and saying, "I'm going to give you something for the pain, okay?"

He nods.

Dante pushes the injector into Mac's arm, even though in reality, she's not doing anything of the sort. How these creatures can so perfectly mimic each part of their reality is astonishing to her. On some points, the fidelity is utterly overwhelming. Their mastery of biochemistry at a microscopic level has to be centuries ahead of humanity, and yet those points they miss are telling, revealing how they're struggling to comprehend the complexity of human physiology.

"If that's not real, how is it going to work?" Benson asks.

Dante applies a healing balm to Mac's scalp, saying, "All I know is, don't underestimate either a placebo or a nocebo."

"Ah," Vichy says. Dante nods.

Benson screws up his face a little. "Nocebo? What's that?"

"A negative psychosomatic response. It's not that you believe something bad is happening to you, but that your subconscious can't accept otherwise and the body responds as though it's injured. Nocebos can bring on disorientation, vomiting, heart attacks—whatever, even though nothing is actually wrong."

"These aliens—they can kill us?" Benson asks in alarm. "Those fuckers out there can kill us in here?"

"Out there. In here," Dante replies, running a handheld scanner over Mac, checking his vitals. "Doesn't matter."

"So we can die in here?" Vichy asks, genuinely surprised by the realization.

"Is that what happened to Angel?" Benson asks. "Was she actually dead? Did they bring her back?"

"Is this some sort of torture?" Vichy asks.

"I don't know," Dante replies, leaning Mac forward as she bandages his head. "And I really don't want to find out."

"Fuck," Vichy says.

Benson reinforces his sentiment. "Fuck. Fuck. Fuck."

Mac blinks rapidly, making eye contact.

"Hey, welcome back," Dante says.

From somewhere behind her Benson mumbles, "Oh, I wouldn't say welcome."

There's scratching at the door beside Mac. Although Dante notices, she pays no attention, focusing on him.

"Easy. You've had a bad bump."

"Zoe, Zoe," he mumbles, swinging his head as he speaks.

Mac's motion is unnatural, as though he's caught on a rollercoaster, flung around with each twist and bend. Gently, Dante restrains his head, keeping her hands on both sides of his face, trying to steady him.

"Slow down."

"No," he says, pushing her away and trying to get to his feet. He plants the palm of his hand in the center of her chest and shoves, causing her to lose her balance. Dante tumbles backwards. She wasn't ready for him and rolls onto her shoulder.

Vichy steps forward, placing himself between them as she turns, getting to her feet. Mac is on all fours, but he's disoriented. If Dante didn't know better, she'd swear he was drunk. He crawls, swaying as he moves, reaching for the walls, wanting to steady himself, trying to stand.

"Hey," Benson says, reaching out, trying to stop him from falling.

Mac lashes out, batting at him with his huge arms. "Get away from me!"

"Whoa," Vichy says. "Slow it down, big guy. No one's going to hurt you. We're here to help."

"That's what they say," Mac says, slurring his words. "That's what they always say, but it's a lie."

"No one's going to hurt you," Dante says, only she isn't

looking at him. She's madly searching through the medical kit, tossing bandages and plastic vials on the floor.

Mac spins, turning around and pressing his back hard against the wall. He has his knees bent in a squat, with his arms out wide, flat against the wall. His muscles flex and squeeze, jerking as he struggles to remain standing even though he's not moving. Veins pulse on the side of his neck. He stabs at the floor with his boots, desperate to stay upright.

"Equilibrio-whatever, right, Doc?" Benson says.

"That's it," Dante replies.

Benson is pissed. "Those fuckers are experimenting."

"Again," Vichy says.

Dante rummages through a container, loading an injector. "I'm going to give you a shot of diazepam."

"Valium? F—Fucking valium," Mac yells, swinging his arm, trying to keep her at bay, but he's seeing double, swinging at thin air. "No. You don't understand. I've got to get to Zoe."

"You're not going anywhere like that," Dante says. With a swift motion, she jabs at his shoulder and retreats. In seconds, his arms droop while his head lolls to one side. Vichy jumps in, grabbing him before he falls.

"Easy, big guy."

"But Zoe," he mumbles as he slides down the wall to the

floor.

"It's okay," Dante says. "We're here to help. Where's Zoe?"

With a limp hand, he points.

"But—don't hurt her. Please. You don't understand. It's Zoe in there."

"We won't," Dante replies, but there's something wrong. Who else would be inside the cabin? Why does he think they wouldn't recognize her?

"You—You don't," he says, struggling to finish his sentence. Dante hit him with a bit too much. With his legs out in front of him and his hands in his lap, he mumbles, "I tried. I really tried."

"It's okay," Vichy says, resting his hand on his shoulder, trying to comfort him.

Dante's about to open the door to Zoe's cabin when Benson raises his hand, signaling for her to stop. She pauses, unsure why, but senses danger lies beyond the sheet metal. Benson raises his eyebrows in alarm. They all hear it. The scratching. Slowly, Benson crouches, keeping his ear barely an inch from the door. He's trying to gauge precisely where the sound is coming from.

"She didn't want this," Mac says, slumped against a maintenance hatch less than three feet away. "I know she didn't."

Benson holds a finger to his lips. He gestures for them to step to one side. Rather than opening the door by waving his hand in front of the activation pad, he moves to the opposite side and quietly unscrews an access panel.

The screws on the panel are designed to be removed by a gloved astronaut in the event of catastrophic depressurization so rather than being recessed with a small notched head, they're bulky, with machined grooves to aid with grip. Instead of falling away once they're undone, the screws swivel down, aligning with slots that allow the panel to be easily removed. If the carousel was in vacuum, the narrow entrance would seal with a second door, leaving a gap of barely four feet to act as an airlock, but with regular pressure, it's little more than a tiny, inner corridor barely larger than a wardrobe. Benson winds the emergency crank inside the panel, causing the sliding door to slowly crack open.

Dante's first impression is that the lights inside the cabin are off as there's nothing but darkness beyond the door. Her heart drops at the thought of tripping another membrane and sending them through a reset. She wonders where she'll wake this time. As the gap widens, spikes appear, only they're organic in nature, with a dull point reminiscent of a pool cue. They're in motion, scraping against the edge of the door. Their movement is random, with no indication of intelligence.

They're neither probing the carousel nor advancing. Rather they seem to be glancing around like bulrushes in the wind.

"What the hell?" Vichy whispers, to which Dante replies, "Shush."

Stepping lightly, she treads sideways, slowly revealing more of the cabin. The light in the corridor is bright, too bright, not allowing her to see anything beyond the shadows. Dante comes to a halt directly in front of the thin crack, barely six inches wide. Occasionally, a thin, dark spike comes into view, moving like the spines of a sea urchin.

"Kill the lights," she whispers.

Benson fiddles inside the access panel. On either side of them, the elongated LED lights that line the carousel wink out. Shadows stretch along the broad main corridor. Dante's not sure who's walking around behind her, whether it's Vichy or Benson, as no one's saying anything, but they're both moving like ghosts. Once again, darkness embraces her, but the stars provide a guiding light. She can feel them behind her, not physically, there's no warmth as such, they're far too distant for that, but as the soft light surrounds her, passing through the window behind her, she feels at home. The stars have always been there for her.

Dante steps forward.

Benson is back at the access port. He turns to face her,

waiting for her cue. She nods and he winds the crank, opening the door further. Ratchets grind behind the wall, grating against each other, creaking and groaning softly.

Vichy is on the other side of her, hard against the wall. He's grabbed a fire extinguisher and is holding it at shoulder height with the nozzle barely an inch from the gap. Smart. Whatever this thing is, if it comes at her, hopefully a burst of carbon dioxide laced with fire suppression powder will cause a little confusion and buy her some time to pull back.

Her heart pounds within her chest. Even though the lights on the carousel behind her are off, it takes time for her eyes to adjust to the darkness beyond the door. She stands still, patiently willing her eyes to resolve the shadows. There's no bravado, no drive, no conviction or courage. Dante's doing this because she has no other choice. She has to know. With the dim light of ten thousand stars at her back, she peers into the darkness within the cabin.

Tentacles writhe on the ceiling, spreading out like tree roots. Dante keeps her distance from the spikes waving against the narrow opening, but they're low and remain below waist-height, allowing her to lean forward and peer inside. The smell is musty, like that of dead leaves and rotten wood.

Dante's expecting to see the inside of Zoe's cabin but instead she's peering into medical, which doesn't make sense as the orientation is all wrong. Medical lies in the same direction as the carousel, effectively sectioning off the circular corridor so that the O-shape is usable only as a U—with the top section being roughly thirty meters of medical equipment, beds, hibernation pods and storage. As Mags lives on one side of the U and Naz on the other, Dante's used to complaints about not being able to use medical as a thoroughfare. She could open the far door, but it would mean rearranging storage and losing space in the ward. Technically, she doesn't need too much room, but it's there in case of an emergency involving multiple crew members. Shortcuts to bed hop are the least of her concerns, but this... this is wrong on multiple levels.

Dante is staring into medical, but Zoe's cabin is at the base of the O-shaped carousel forming the outer ring of the Acheron, almost directly opposite medical. Not only that, Dante's peering into an elongated, curved version of medical that's set at a right-angle to the carousel, which is physically not possible.

Bodies hang from the ceiling, strung out in a row running the length of the module. Even in the soft light, she can see they're naked. Men and women hang draped beneath tree-like structures wrapping over their shoulders, hiding their heads from view. They twitch. Legs spasm. Arms flex, not moving more than a few inches, but they're clearly animated. Dante looks down at her own hand, rolling her wrist around and looking at the lines in her palm and the curve of her fingers.

She looks up. One of the women has turned her palm slightly upwards. Slowly, Dante lowers her hand, watching as her doppelgänger moves in sync with her.

"How is this possible?" she whispers.

Beside her, pressed hard against the outer wall, Vichy asks, "What is it? What can you see?"

"You," she says. "Me."

Vichy whispers. "I don't understand. Where's Zoe?"

Dante glances sideways at Benson. He doesn't need any more cues. He cranks the handle, widening the gap. Dante turns, breathing in as she slips inside the narrow opening.

"No," Vichy whispers a little too loud, not wanting her to venture into the cabin.

A low fog hugs the floor. As she moves, the mist swirls around her ankles.

Dante presses her back against the door, not feeling confident about stepping beyond what feels like a lifeline with reality—only that particular form of reality is an artificial construct. Although she knows that, she feels safe back there with Vichy and Benson. In here, she's in another world. With her hands beside her, she backs up slightly. Dante can feel the soft squelch of organic matter on the backside of the door. To her, it's like moss growing on a log and her fingers pull away as she fights a sense of revulsion.

"Dee," is whispered from the doorway.

She holds up her hand, signaling for Vichy to stay where he is. The walls are alive. To her, it's as though thousands of snakes are entwined with each other, seething and writhing, each moving with conflicting purpose, rolling under and over each other in constant motion.

"I see her," she whispers.

Zoe is lying naked on the floor, only she isn't. Dante can also see her distinct, smooth black body hanging from the ceiling near the back of medical. Tree roots enclose her head, twisting around her shoulders. Which one is the real Zoe? They're all suspended from roots on the ceiling. It's crazy to think they're the avatars and those are the real versions hanging there, spasming occasionally, locked inside a nightmare, observing themselves.

Although Dante should be afraid, she's not. There's an entire ecosystem around her, something that arouses the astrobiologist in her. Whatever these aliens are, they're unlike humans with their pretense of sterility, pretending to keep everything crisp and clean. Homo sapiens are microbial factories, with trillions of foreign cells inhabiting the mouth, gut and bowel, clinging to the skin and hair. As the size of cells varies so much, any one person carries around far more tiny non-human cells than their own. Their captors, though, whoever they are, seem unabashed in replicating their native environment, converting the interior of the Acheron into what for them is probably paradise.

From what Dante can tell, the spikes brushing against the door come from a sedentary creature similar to a clam. Its open shell appears to be cemented to the wall much like a barnacle. There are no legs as such. The creature seems to sample the air in the same way a sea anemone might filter nutrients from water. Far from being threatening, it appears oblivious to her intrusion.

The writhing snake nest on the walls appears to defy gravity, which is just fine by Dante. She keeps a wary eye on them, but like the clam, the twisting, turning creatures ignore her.

Dante creeps forward, crushing shells beneath her bare feet. Goo squishes between her toes, causing her to pause, close her eyes, and wish she were wearing shoes. The air is cool and still. There's no circulation coming from the vents buried beneath the snake-like creatures and she wonders about air quality and how these creatures prevent the buildup of noxious gasses. As it is, the temperature and atmosphere are tolerable. It's cold, but above freezing. Dante has to remind herself she's inside an illusion—or is she?

Where are their captors? This has the trappings of an alien infestation, but where are the creatures themselves? Dante would rather not know, but she feels exposed. Whatever this breach is, it seems to be an overlap between reality and a dream. How can she exist in two places at once? And yet there she is, hanging from the ceiling not more than ten meters away. Each step, or just the slightest movement of her arms and there's a corresponding twitch from her naked body. Where does she actually reside? Is all this unfolding inside her head up there on the ceiling? Is she even here? Is this all an illusion?

Dante steps through the fog, watching as it swirls around her feet. Behind her, Vichy's silhouette blocks most of the starlight. There's some light coming from the vast, curved window within this version of medical, but something outside the spacecraft is casting a shadow, blocking most of the stars, leaving the module in darkness.

"Zoe?" Dante whispers, crouching and touching at the woman's legs.

Zoe groans.

"Hey, Zoe. Come with me," she says, taking her hand and tugging gently.

Zoe wakes with a start. Her eyes go wide, revealing the whites. It's as though she's seen a ghost. She goes to scream but Dante holds a finger over Zoe's lips, appealing for quiet.

"Wh—Who—What are you?" she asks.

"It's me, Zoe. Dante."

"What's happening?"

"We need to get you out of here."

"Mac," Zoe says with a look of horror on her face.

"It's okay. He's outside."

Zoe shakes her head softly as though she's trying to free herself from a dream, only she's awakening to a nightmare. "I—I attacked him. I didn't mean to. I thought he was—"

Dante cuts her off. "We can't stay here."

"Where are we?"

"Back there," Dante replies, pointing at the naked bodies hanging from the ceiling, with the closest no more than a few meters away. "Somehow, we've crossed the bounds. I don't know how, but we're on the other side." Zoe looks at a pair of male legs dangling beside her, responding to nerve impulses.

Dante says, "I think this is us—the real us."

"Fuck."

"Yeah."

Zoe crouches, taking Dante's hand.

"How is this possible?"

"I don't know."

They creep to the doorway. Dante can't bring herself to turn her back on what to her seems to be corpses hanging from the ceiling. She backs up, feeling behind her with her hands. Vichy stands by the opening with his arm outstretched, reaching for them as though he were on a pier trying to grab someone flailing in the water. His fingers grasp at the air, touching at Dante's neck and startling her for a moment. The spines from inside the gigantic alien clam brush against her legs, unsettling her, but she doesn't want to rush. Sudden movements feel wrong. Dante pushes Zoe on, wanting her to exit first as she takes one last look at the alien world thriving on the Acheron.

Beds lie on their sides, overturned and pushed haphazardly around the curving deck. Mattresses have been strewn across the floor. Fungus grows from them, reaching toward the window, desperate for light. What were once clean, almost sterile sheets are muddy and grey.

Eyes glisten at the back of medical. Like nocturnal predators on Earth, their pupils open wide, gathering what little light there is, reflecting their presence. At first, Dante's not sure what she's looking at as she can't see a body, just four sets of four tiny eyes, evenly spaced as though on a sphere, projecting in slightly different directions. It's the movement that causes her heart to race and she reaches back, pushing Zoe on.

"We need to leave."

A low rumbling echoes through the module, although it's

not a growl, more like the thumping bass of a speaker at a rock concert. As it fades, Dante speaks softly.

"Shut the door."

Vichy is helping Zoe through the narrow gap. "But—"

Through gritted teeth, Dante says, "Do it."

"On it," Benson replies as Dante backs up, wanting to avoid the appearance of movement. She can feel the door behind her. Her fingers touch at the grooved edge as she inches backwards. Her eyes, though, are locked on the creature creeping through medical.

Dante reaches with her back foot, edging out into the corridor as the gap closes.

Large padded paws work their way over the beds and mattresses without a sound. Eyes sway in the shadows.

With the door closing, Dante's forced to turn sideways to squeeze out of medical. As soon as she does, the creature charges, pounding on the floor, thundering toward her. Vichy grabs her, pulling her back. Her arm trails behind her, hanging in the air as Benson madly winds the crank, closing the gap. In the darkness, the massive creature leaps, launching itself at the door. Dante's fingers clear the edge of the panel as claws slice through the air, curling around the edge of the steel panel, digging into the metal.

Vichy has the fire extinguisher in one hand. As he pulls

Dante away, he raises it and squeezes the trigger, but in the fear of the moment, he's too far from the door. Clouds of CO_2 and fine white powder shoot out of the nozzle, billowing as they buffet the door, but dissipating in the corridor. He steps forward, pushing the nozzle against one of the claws and fires again. This time, the discharge vanishes into the gap. Immediately, the claws retract, probably not for any other reason than that predators the universe over need time to assess the nature of a threat, and in that fraction of a second, Benson closes the door entirely. There's thumping and banging on the far side of the metal panel, but the cabin door is thick, being designed to withstand raging fires, violent explosions and rapid decompression without losing its integrity.

Dante is on the verge of collapsing. Vichy drops the fire extinguisher. He grabs her, supporting her weight as he takes her by the arm.

"I'm alright," she says, but it's a lie even her own body doesn't believe. Try as she may, she can't help but tremble. To say Vichy notices is an understatement. His head is bowed, looking intently at her hands as he holds her tenderly. He squeezes her fingers softly. Typical Vee. He could say something. He wants to say something. She knows that from the way he rubs his thumb over the back of her hand, trying to reassure her. They know each other so well. She's said her piece. Just two words. Vichy doesn't agree but he won't argue. He forces a smile. She returns the favor. Neither is convincing.

Benson locks the crank in place, ensuring the door remains closed, leaving them with the faint sound of scratching echoing in the darkness.

"What the hell was that?" Benson asks, oblivious to the interplay between Dante and Vichy.

"Big," is all Dante can manage in response, turning away from Vichy. She needs the illusion of control, even within this nightmare onboard the Acheron. Perhaps it's her medical training, perhaps it's her upbringing, but she feels as though she needs to project confidence.

"Dee," Vichy says. It seems he's struggling to articulate what just happened. Dante ignores him. For her, the only way to think clearly is to focus on helping someone else.

"Zoe," she says, crouching beside the shaking woman. "It's over. You're safe now."

Two sentences. Both lies. But it's all Dante's got. Benson removes his jacket, draping it over Zoe as she huddles against the wall beside Mac. Zoe has her knees up and her arms wrapped around her legs, but not so much because she's naked as frightened.

"Hey babe," Mac whispers, taking her hand. She squeezes his fingers. Her lips tremble. She's on the verge of crying, pulling the jacket up over her shoulders.

Vichy asks, "Are we going to talk about what just happened?"

"Not now," Dante says, trying to hide her fear, still struggling with trembling fingers, desperate to move on. "There will be time for that later."

She crouches, shining a penlight in Zoe's eyes, looking for both a direct response, with the pupil contracting, and a contra-lateral response, where the other eye also contracts as that will tell her a lot about Zoe's mental state. It's a trick that's as old as medicine itself. Sometimes, the simplest bio-mechanical responses are the most revealing. As nice as it would be to run a psych scan, she can already see Zoe's lucid, which means she wasn't unconscious or incapacitated in there. Whatever spell they cast over her, it wasn't traumatic.

"Squeeze my fingers," Dante says, holding both of her hands and noting the strength of Zoe's response. Nice and equal.

"I'm okay," Zoe says, trying to deflect attention.

"I'll be the judge of that," Dante replies, pulling a bio-monitor out of the medi-pack and clipping it to her wrist. Immediately, biometrics are transmitted to the thin flex computer Dante's rested against the backpack. Although on the surface it seems like Mac has more serious injuries, Dante considers his head wound a classic injury. With Zoe, she's concerned about hidden wounds. She doesn't want to miss anything critical in the temptation to rush.

On close examination, she notices a series of tiny symmetrical contusions on Zoe's neck. Given Zoe's skin is a deep black, the reddish marks are concerning. Had they occurred on either her or Vichy, Dante's sure they'd be more pronounced.

"What happened in there?" Benson asks, joining them.

Inadvertently, Vichy cuts off the opportunity for a reply by commenting on Zoe's bruising, seeing it in the thin penlight. "What is that?"

"Suction marks," Dante replies, moving the light around, wanting a better look. "The skin hasn't broken, but there's definitely blistering. Look at the way the area has been engorged with blood."

"How is that possible?" Vichy asks.

"I don't know."

Benson says, "I'll bring up the lights."

"Yes. That would help."

"I'm okay," Zoe says. "Honestly."

"She's fine," Mac says, which Dante finds absurd to the point of comical. It's all she can do not to laugh.

"None of us are fine."

Dante searches with her fingers, gently gliding them around the back of Zoe's head, working to move her dense hair apart, noting a string of tiny blisters in a line reaching to the base of her skull.

"What do you remember?" Dante asks.

"We were asleep. I thought I was dreaming. They were all over me."

"She started punching me," Mac says, cradling the back of his head with his hand. "At first, it was light. I thought she was having a nightmare—that she'd snap out of it, but then she started screaming."

"Their legs caught in my hair," Zoe says. "The bugs."

"She hit me with a stool," Mac says. "I thought she was mad, but then I saw them."

"The room," Zoe says. "It changed. There were things on the walls. The ceiling. They were moving, crawling over each other."

"What did they want?" Vichy asks as the lights within the carousel come back on. Dante could kick him for interrupting. He's breaking Zoe's train of thought. She would rather Zoe arrived at her own conclusions.

"They wanted to know about the submersible."

"I don't understand," Vichy says. Dante's on the verge of asking him to be quiet and let Zoe speak when he adds, "None of that shit was from beneath the ice, right? I mean, we all saw in there. None of that is aquatic or adapted to arctic conditions. If anything, it looks subtropical."

"We have a bigger problem," Benson says in his soft, southern drawl, but he gets Dante's attention. She cannot imagine anything more alarming than seeing Zoe being dragged into some kind of breach in the illusion.

Mac ignores him, focusing on his own concerns. "We've got to tell Cap and the others about this."

"I don't know about that." Benson is tightlipped, shaking his head slightly. He's not happy. "I don't think it's a good idea to tell anyone about what we saw."

"Why?" Dante asks.

"That was us in there, right?"

Dante nods but remains silent, wanting to hear him out.

"I didn't count nine bodies, doc. Did you?"

"What do you mean?" Vichy asks.

Benson says, "I saw six or seven bodies hanging from the ceiling. Maybe eight. It was hard to tell with all the shadows. But there definitely weren't nine of us in there."

"I don't get it," Vichy says, but Dante does.

She looks him in the eye and says, "At least one of us is fake."

"What?"

"One of us is lying."

Benson nods, speaking slowly so no one misses his point. "One of us… is one of them."

ARROWS

"Who do you think it is?" Vichy asks as they walk toward the bridge.

"I don't know," Dante replies. "But I damn sure intend to find out."

"So we're just going to keep quiet about this?" Mac asks. "We're not going to say anything about what the fuck just happened back there?"

"Not yet," Dante replies.

"Who did you see?" Vichy asks. Dante shakes her head, unsure, wishing she'd paid more attention. Other than what she thought of as herself, the only person she recognized was Zoe because of her deep, dark skin.

Benson says, "We need to be careful. We're not the only ones that can lie."

Walking onto the bridge of the Acheron, Dante is acutely aware of the difficulty in spotting an imposter. She's lived with this crew for over a decade and, up until moments ago, she had no reason to doubt anyone. If Benson hadn't thought to count the bodies hanging there inside the breach she still wouldn't, and that frightens her. Her mind casts back to that final psych session with Dr. Romero. His words are seared in her mind—*You need to be better.* But even that recollection causes confusion. Her memory of that interaction is so vivid it seems as though it happened yesterday and she wonders if that's a legitimate memory or yet another implant. Regardless, she agrees with the sentiment—she's not sharp enough to unravel these threads. Not yet. She has to do better.

"You guys took your time," Cap says, smiling as they enter the bridge.

Something in her eyes gives away her concern and he asks, "Is everything okay?"

"Everything's fine," Vichy says, to which Zoe laughs, shaking her head and looking at the floor, unable to make eye contact with anyone.

Cap is silent. They all know Vichy's lying, but those already on the bridge don't understand why.

Cap, Angel, Mags and Naz are huddled around the nav desk, looking at a three-dimensional topographical map of P4 floating in the air, rotating slowly before them. Various overlays reveal details such as ice, bedrock, sediment, subsurface volcanic vents and melt water forming vast networks of rivers and lakes buried beneath a five-mile thick glacial sheet. Over eons, the compressed ice field has carved deep valleys out of the bedrock, keeping them hidden beneath the ice.

Dante walks into the middle of the bridge, but the others are more cautious, hanging back by the engineering console. Vichy leans against the wall. Benson sits on a ledge, while Mac and Zoe sit in swiveling seats, turning them around to face the rest of the crew.

"All right," Cap says, sounding annoyed. He points at Mac and the bandage wrapped around his head. "That's not okay. What's going on?"

Dante is conflicted. Physically, she's standing between the two groups. The crew has split along entirely arbitrary lines, capturing how they left Mags' cabin and not any actual, logical, rational grouping. At this point, there's no reason to exclude anyone from suspicion other than Zoe, but Vichy, Mac and Benson clearly don't think that way. Suspicion tears at the heart of the crew. Dante feels guilty about withholding information from Cap. He and the others seem to sense that, but they don't understand why.

Dante speaks on behalf of her newly formed tribe, saying, "He was attacked."

"By who?"

"By what?" Angel asks, being a little more pointed with her question.

Zoe raises her hand sheepishly and lowers her head without offering anything by way of explanation. She's wearing a spare flight suit they grabbed from Dante's cabin, but she still has Vichy's jacket on over the top, which is clearly confusing Mags. Vichy and Zoe have never been that close. Mac, though, has always been close to Zoe—and yet she attacked him.

"You attacked Mac?" Mags asks, sensing how the dynamic within the crew has shifted. "Wait," she says, pointing at the bloodied bandage. "How is that even possible? If none of this is real, how is that real?"

"Oh, we're more fragile than you think," Benson says.

Cap walks over to Mac.

All eyes are on Cap, staring him down from both sides. Although he seems genuine in his concern, he also senses the distrust in the quiet stares directed at him.

"Are you okay?" he asks, turning his head to get a good look at the blood seeping through the bandage.

"I'll be fine."

No further explanation is offered by Mac, which has Cap furrow his brow.

Angel is frustrated. She appeals to Dante. "I don't

understand. What's changed? I thought we were going to meet up and figure this thing out together. What happened to you guys?"

"Who died?" Dante asks, deciding to cut straight through to the heart of the issue.

"What?" Cap replies, looking genuinely surprised, unsure why that one particular, disjointed question seemed to materialize out of thin air.

"You told me someone died down there? Who was it?"

"What are you talking about?" Cap asks.

Dante points at herself. "I was down there, remember? You and me. We took the rescue shuttle after the explosion on the ice. We went down to get them."

"I don't know what you're talking about. I've never been on P4."

Dante's frustrated. "Damn it, Cap. You were there."

"Dante," he says, appealing to her with his hands out before him. "I don't know what the hell you're talking about."

"You got us out of there," she says. "Those things got inside our heads, but you kept us on track. You got us off P4. You must remember."

"I—I don't remember," he replies. "But why is this important?"

"Because one of us isn't real. One of us is one of them."

"What?" Mags says, marching across the bridge, wanting to be part of the discussion. "You cannot be serious."

Dante struggles to hold back her rising anxiety. She hates this shit. She doesn't want to do this. She'd do anything to avoid this confrontation if she could, but there's no other way. Everyone's present. This might be the only opportunity they get to identify the intruder.

It takes all her strength to say, "No more lies."

"Hang on," Cap says, pointing at those that accompanied Dante. "So that's what all this is about?" He gestures to the crew that remained with him, adding, "You think one of us is an imposter?"

The lack of a reply is an answer in itself.

"Why us?" he asks. "What makes you think one of us is a traitor and not Benson or Vee?"

It's a fair question, but Dante doesn't want to give up any information that could be used against them.

"They're losing control," she says. "I think we've overestimated their ability to determine what happens in here. We're active. This is *our* illusion. At best, they're observers. I have my doubts about how much they can direct what happens inside here."

"What makes you say that?" Angel asks.

"What do you remember from the reboots?" Dante asks, gesturing around her at the crew at large. No one answers. "I remember things—situations they could have never known about. Standing on a beach in New York. Our training back in Florida. I don't think any of that was intentional."

Vichy says, "They've been experimenting."

"Learning," she replies. "But their control is imprecise. Even the reboots. Those points at which we break the membrane. I don't think they intend us to reset the simulation."

Zoe asks, "So they're not in control?"

"Not entirely," Dante replies. "They're reacting to us."

"Just like we react to them."

Cap says, "And you think someone died and they replaced them?"

"I know they did," Dante says, looking him in the eye. "You told me so yourself—down on P4... If someone died down there, then someone up here is fake."

Cap purses his lips. Oh, how she'd love to be able to read his mind, to catch the thoughts ricocheting around inside his head. His eyes narrow as his jaw tightens.

"Okay. Let's say you're right and for whatever reason, I've forgotten. How do we find this intruder?"

"We ask about the past," Zoe says. "They won't know anything about that, right? I mean, anything that happened on Earth is out of reach. We can catch them out."

"Like who won the Super Bowl?" Vichy says.

"They could have accessed our data banks," Benson says. "We're carrying historical, cultural and technical information in our computers, along with news clips. We'd have to be very careful to be sure any questions we asked couldn't be answered by examining them."

Vichy says, "But we don't know that they've looked at those."

"Yet," Mac says. "What about stuff from our training? Anecdotes? Like hanging out at *The Black Hole?*"

Dante shakes her head. "Shared memories are a good idea, but I don't know if that's enough. I mean, you could ask me about my sister, but they saw that memory play out on the beach, they could have gleaned enough information to bluff their way through."

"So who do we trust?" Vichy asks, looking around at the rest of the crew.

"That's the question," Mags says. Her eyes dart around, looking for something—anything, but there are no clues. They all feel the weight of uncertainty in the moment.

"We may have already blown this," Benson says.

"What do you mean?" Cap asks.

"I mean, while just a few of us knew about the traitor, we could have smoked them out. But now, with this in the open, they can hide. Now they *know* they should hide."

Mags says, "You're forgetting, this fucker could be one of those that already knew."

"I agree," Angel says. "If we've been infiltrated we need to work together—not in isolation. We can't give him or her a chance to divide us."

Dante is interested in hearing the crew talk. Their choice of terms is telling. *Imposter* is neutral. *Intruder* is more assertive. *Traitor* is emotive. As for *this fucker*, well, there's no doubt about what Mags thinks.

"So we're all here," Cap says. "What do we do? How can we tell who's who? I mean, it's not like we can just test someone's blood, right? It's not that simple, is it?"

"I've got a few tricks up my sleeve," Dante says, grabbing a flex tablet and typing in a few words. She adds, "I'm going to ask each of you what color you see. Ignore the word itself. I don't care what it says. I want to know what color the word is, not the color it describes."

RED

GREEN

BLUE

BLACK

YELLOW

The words she's selected appear in different colors. Red has been written with green letters, while green is the reverse, using red letters. Blue is actually brown, while black is black and yellow is blue.

Without letting the others see which word she's pointing at, Dante moves around the crew, touching at one word and then another. Her finger touches at red and Mags says, "Green," correctly picking the color rather than the name. Slowly, Dante works her way around the bridge.

Before starting the second round, Dante changes a few of the colors, but not all of them, leaving some of them exactly as they were, wanting to confuse the imposter. After everyone has answered twice, Cap asks, "So?"

"Everyone got it right," she says, frustrated.

"I don't get it," Mags says. "Why did you think that would work?"

"Color is very specific," Dante replies, feeling as though she's failed, speaking as though she has to justify herself. "Even within terrestrial species, we see different colors depending on the cone cells in our eyes. Dogs see different colors than humans. Bees see in ultraviolet. Mosquitos in infrared. Colors are contrived, literally existing only in the eye of the beholder."

"And you thought they wouldn't be able to differentiate between colors?" Angel asks, only she seems a little nervous, something that's unlike her. It's subtle, nothing Dante can identify specifically, but she can sense uneasiness. Perhaps it was the slight quiver in Angel's voice, or the pained look on her face. She's unsettled. Who isn't?

Dante focuses, wanting to talk herself through this. "I knew they wouldn't be able to see in color," she says, still sure of herself, confused as to why her strategy didn't work. "Colors aren't real."

Vichy holds his hands out, looking at each of them in turn, "Ah, in case you haven't noticed—neither's this."

"Maybe they've already figured colors out," Benson says.

"Maybe you were wrong," Mags says, which hurts Dante more than she'd like to admit. Her closest friend doesn't believe her. Dante swallows the lump rising in her throat. Mags probably feels offended at being caught on the wrong side of the divide. As Mags went with Cap to talk to Angel, she is part of the out-group as far as Vichy and the others are concerned. Cap notices the way Dante is stung by those few words.

"Maybe there is no imposter," he says. "Maybe we're overthinking this."

"No," Benson says. "I saw us."

"What do you mean?" Angel asks, turning her head sideways a little, perplexed by his comment and intuitively understanding he's not describing something she's seen personally.

"What exactly did you see?" she asks.

"There was a breach," Benson says. Dante grits her teeth. She didn't want to reveal this for fear of leaking too much information to the imposter. With all she's experienced, she's convinced their alien captors aren't quite as in control as they would like them to think. She suspects they grabbed Zoe to interrogate her but never realized that whatever breach they formed remained open, connecting two realities. Now, though, that information is in the open.

"What do you mean?" Cap asks. "Another membrane?"

"It was different," Dante says, trying to control the narrative and limit how much is said. "It was like a vision of the Acheron as it is and not as we see it. It was as though we could see what they've made of the ship."

Mags raises her eyebrows. "And you didn't think this was important to share?"

Vichy says, "There were bodies hanging from the ceiling—our bodies. They were twitching."

"But?" Cap asks, wanting more information.

"But there weren't nine of us," Dante replies.

Mac says, "Fuck."

"Yeah," Zoe replies.

"Meaning one of us," Mags says, pointing between herself and the others in disbelief, but failing to complete her sentence.

"One of us is fake," Vichy says. "A mole."

"You should have told us," Cap says. His face is flushed with anger. "I'm the goddamn commander! You should have told *me!*"

Dante hangs her head.

"So you think someone died down there and they've replaced them in here with us," Cap says, apparently still not remembering his conversation with Dante on the surface of P4.

"At least one of us is an impostor," Benson says. "It was dark. I couldn't see clearly, but I could make out the racks in the back of the medical bay. There weren't nine of us."

Mags storms up to Dante, waving an angry finger in her face and swearing at her. "For fuck's sake, Dee. We were hanging from the *fucking* ceiling and you couldn't tell us about that? You didn't think that was important? You didn't think it was fair that we knew about that? We have a right to know. All of us. We're all in this together."

"Easy," Cap says, not wanting her to get any closer to Dante.

Vichy claps his hands together, faking an applause and instantly changing the mood within the bridge. He smiles. "So—who is it? Anyone going to volunteer?"

Mac shakes his head in disbelief, but regrets that almost instantly, raising his hand up and touching at his bandages.

Zoe says, "We need to know who is real."

"Any other ideas?" Cap asks.

Dante sighs. She feels as though she's failed the crew. What seemed so simple, so clear and straightforward, has driven a wedge through the crew. She's reluctant to suggest anything else, but Cap's faith in her gets her thinking. She nods slowly, lifting the tablet.

"There are a few possibilities, but I don't want to say too much. I don't want to tip my hand."

"Okay," Cap says. "Let's do this."

Dante ignores him for a moment, working away on her flex computer. It's not deliberate, it's more that she feels she needs to address the crew as a whole. It's important to engage everyone at once to deprive the imposter of time and space. Dante's acutely aware someone is acting, playing a role on a stage—and they're doing a convincing job, not leaving any trace of doubt in anyone's mind. Were it not for the body count, she'd have no inkling anything was amiss. Dante rises to the challenge, realizing this is a battle of wits. She holds her tablet in front of her chest, making sure it's square, allowing everyone to see what's displayed on the thin, semi-transparent surface.

"Which of these arrows is longer?"

< : : : : : : : :

: : : : : : : : >

Before anyone can reply, she clarifies. "Don't tell me the obvious answer. None of us are stupid. We can all count the characters and see they're technically the same—that's not what I'm looking for. Tell me what you *feel*? Tell me your instinctive, gut reaction."

"And there's a right answer?" Mags asks, raising an eyebrow.

Dante nods.

"This is stupid," Mac says. "Why the hell are we playing games?"

Dante is calm. "Because this is one game they can't play."

No one volunteers so Dante brings up a second set of

arrows, saying, "Mags. You're up first."

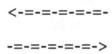

Mags is nervous. Whereas she was aggressive moments ago, now the spotlight has been turned on her and she doesn't like it. Sweat beads on her forehead. Like Dante, she knows there's no correct answer, not really, not when the choice is between identical arrows facing left or right. She's feeling the uncertainty of not knowing precisely what Dante's looking for.

"They're the same damn length," she says, refusing to commit to one or the other.

"Which *appears* longer?" Dante says in a soft voice, trying to be patient. She watches Mags closely.

Dante has deliberately brought up an illusion she's sure no one will have seen before. They all know both arrows are the same. She can see the confusion on each face as she looks around at the crew, observing how they react to this particular challenge. Regardless of each individual answer, their choice only tells her part of the story. Dante's looking at more than the answers offered by the crew. She's looking for tells—tiny emotional responses that reveal the depth of reasoning behind each answer.

"Left," Mags says, having taken roughly ten seconds to decide.

Dante is careful not to give anything away in her facial expression. She turns to Mac, nodding slightly to signal he should make his choice. His eyes narrow.

He breathes deeply and says, "Left," agreeing with Mags.

Zoe squints, taking a good look at the first set of arrows.

<:::::::

:::::::>

"So this depends on whether you're—"

Dante cuts her off. "Just make your choice."

Zoe screws up her nose. She wants more to work with. She was wanting Dante to confirm what she's looking for. Doubts cause her eyebrows to twitch slightly.

"One way seems easier than the other," she says, although Dante would prefer she remained silent.

"So which way seems more natural? And which seems forced?" Dante asks.

Zoe shakes her head. "I want to say, they're the same, but you're not going to accept that, are you?"

"Nope."

Zoe's eyes reveal the anguish of a seemingly impossible decision. She knows what it might mean, but like Mags, ultimately, she's decisive. If anything, after seeing her dark feminine body hanging from the ceiling within the breach, Zoe's the one person Dante doesn't suspect, but it's important the crew go through this together.

"Left."

Dante sets her face like a stone, keeping her expression blank. Not so much as a twitch escapes from her cheeks. Her eyes dart across to Angel, who's been carefully observing the others. Although she answers quickly, her voice wavers slightly, betraying her doubts.

"Left."

Vichy's next. He's got his lips pulled tight. His eyes narrow. The intensity of his gaze is such that, in that moment, it's as though those arrows are all that exist anywhere in the entire universe.

Dante can feel sweat breaking out on her forehead. Not Vichy, please don't let it be Vichy. She struggles not to swallow the lump rising in her throat at the thought of him being the traitor, but she can't resist that physical response. Cap notices.

Vichy screws up his face. His nostrils flare slightly. With resignation, he contradicts the others, saying, "Right."

The rest of the crew look to her for some kind of reaction, but Dante remains silent, keeping her gaze fixed, refusing to show any emotion either way. As Vichy's left handed, his answer makes sense, but she hides her relief.

Benson stalls, reaching out and touching at the screen, tracing the outline of the arrows, running his fingers in one direction and then another.

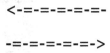

He nods, apparently satisfied with the conclusion he's reached, and says, "Left."

Dante turns to her commander, saying, "You too, Cap."

Without a moment's hesitation, Cap says, "Right."

He's flippant. Quick. Overconfident. His attitude is incongruous with the moment. Everyone else is nervous. Is he bluffing? Putting up a front of bravado? Wanting to appear confident to dispel any doubts? Why did he rush his choice? It's almost as though he's enjoying this rather than feeling intimidated like the others.

Cap says, "This is one of those crazy optical illusions, right?" He's seeking confirmation from Dante, but she refuses to be drawn into any discussion, not until everyone has answered. After a few seconds silence, he adds, "It's one of those things that appears different to different people, huh?"

He's guessing. Dante's sure of it, but she doesn't give anything away in her facial expression. No sooner has Cap spoken than his eyes dart across the crew, looking at Vichy, wanting to see his reaction to this choice. Vichy, though, is intent on watching Dante as she moves on, staring down Naz. She holds the flex out in front of Naz without saying anything in response to Cap.

"This is dumb," Naz says, feeling the pressure of going last.

"Choose," Dante says, avoiding any debate over either the illusion she's chosen or the approach she's taken. She glances at Cap, watching his facial expressions. He's smiling, intent on watching Naz.

"No. I won't do it," Naz says. "You can't make me choose. They're both the same. This is stupid and you know it."

"Choose," Dante says with a little more conviction.

"We don't even know if what you saw was real, right? This whole thing could be a bluff. They could be playing us, wanting us to turn against each other."

Even though she wants to defend herself, Dante

remains calm, pushing him to finish the test first, saying, "Choose."

Naz is frustrated.

"Two arrows. That means there's a 50/50 chance here, right? That's dumb, really, really dumb. What the hell kind of test is this anyway?" He points at Dante, appealing to the others. "Can't you see what she's doing? Haven't any of you figured out what's actually going on here? We're being set up!"

"Choose," Vichy says before Dante can respond.

Naz wipes sweat from his brow with the back of his hand. He's not happy.

"I don't get it. Dante doesn't have to do this stupid test. Doesn't that strike you as strange? Who's to say she's not one of them? Can't you see? She's using this to set us against each other."

"Choose," Mags says.

"Do you trust her?" Naz asks, appealing to Mags and then to Zoe. "Really? Do you think this will actually work? The color thing didn't. Even she doesn't know if this will work. She could be wrong—again—and then what?"

Mac looks at him with eyes that pierce the soul. "Choose."

"This is a witch hunt! Why not tie us to a pole and dunk

us under water to see who drowns—because that'll prove who's innocent, right? If you float, you're possessed."

"Choose," Zoe says, setting her hands on her hips.

For Dante, this is an opportunity to observe everyone in the group, watching their reactions, gauging their responses.

"What if I'm wrong?" Naz asks. "What then?" He turns to Cap. "What are you going to do? People make mistakes, you know. You can't read too much into a single answer."

"Choose," Angel says.

Naz is bordering on hysterical. "She could be wrong about all of this. The aliens might have already figured this shit out and we're chasing our tails for nothing. We don't know. Don't you get that? She doesn't know. She's guessing. Do you really want to trust your future to guesswork?"

"Choose," Benson says.

"Fuck, I hate all this science bullshit," Naz says, slamming his hand against the center console. "All these fucking mind games. Just tell me. Tell me what I'm supposed to fucking say."

Cap says, "Come on, Naz. Make your choice."

"Left, goddamn it. Left! The damned thing is longer when it's pointing to the left. There. Are you happy now?"

Dante nods.

"Well?" Naz asks. "What am I?"

Dante can't help herself. She doesn't mean to be cruel, but she laughs, asking him, "Don't you know?" Vichy laughs as well, not that he knows quite why Dante's laughing. He appears caught up in the moment, feeling the sense of release breaking like a storm on a hot summer's day. The others start to chuckle.

"What are you laughing at?" Naz asks, turning and addressing the group. "This isn't funny."

"No, it's not," Dante admits. "But it is revealing. You see, you weren't being judged on your answer but on your reactions."

"Fuck," he says. "I'm fucked, ain't I? Fucking overthinking shit again."

Dante reaches out, squeezing his arm. "Relax. You're human, okay? You know it. I know it. Now, they all know it."

Naz sighs. He looks like he's about to collapse.

BLIND

"So who is it?" Mags asks.

"Who's lying?" Zoe asks.

"Don't assume it's just one person," Dante replies, thinking through the weight of her decision. She double-checks medical records, wanting to be absolutely sure before she says anything. She doesn't like this. She doesn't like the conclusion she's been drawn to, but she has to make a decision. Maybe she's right. Chances are, she's wrong. Damn it. She wants to be right. All she knows is saying nothing is definitely wrong. For better or for worse, she has to tell the crew what she's figured out.

"Vichy, Mac and Benson." Dante pauses, seeing the hurt in Vichy's eyes, knowing it's only going to get worse. "Step away from Cap."

Zoe's eyes go wide. Her eyebrows raise in alarm.

"Wait a minute," Angel says, coming to Cap's defense

before he can say anything. "You can't be serious. This is Cap we're talking about."

Dante speaks with cold deliberation.

"You can stand there with him."

Vichy and Benson look at each other.

"No," Mags says, but not out of defiance so much as shock and disbelief.

"Me?" Cap says, pointing at himself. "You're calling me out as one of *them*? That's ridiculous."

Dante fights to hide her trembling hands, balling them up into fists. She stares deep into his eyes, looking for any glimmer of the man she once knew.

"Are you sure about this?" Mags asks, appealing for reason.

"How can she be sure?" Naz says. "It's just one question."

"This is wrong," Angel mumbles, taking her place by Cap's side. "This is all so very wrong."

"Explain yourself," Cap says, addressing Dante and commanding authority. It's an interesting tactic as it assumes he's still in command, but the power dynamic has shifted in a way Dante's sure he never expected, with the crew looking to her for direction.

"It's fake," she says, holding up the flex with the arrows

on it. "It's not an illusion. Both arrows are exactly the same length. There's no right or wrong answer."

Mags is confused. "You lied to us?"

"Of course, I lied. I told you I was going to lie, didn't I?"

"But?" Zoe says, pointing at Cap. "If all this was fake, how do you know it's him?"

"It wasn't the answers I was looking at, it was your reasoning, your response, your emotions. I was looking for the internal conflict you felt at the prospect of getting this wrong."

"And Cap?"

"Either he's an alien or a psychopath—take your pick."

"Wait a minute," Cap says, shaking his head in disbelief. "So you have nothing to go on? No proof?"

Dante points at the rest of the crew. "They thought this was real, but you didn't, did you? You knew it was fake all along. How? I'm betting you have access to our psych records. You knew this was a game. You knew there was no such illusion—that there's no way to distinguish between whether someone is right or left handed. You knew I was faking it, but you didn't understand why.

"You saw Vichy sweating over his answer because he's left handed. He's the only one that might see something different, but not you.

"And you knew I trust him. You knew I was relieved by his answer. As much as I tried to hide it, you could see it in my eyes.

"You were confused. You knew this was a sham, but you didn't know what I was actually looking for. You wanted me to be relieved by your answer as well, only you were too quick. Why? There weren't any real consequences for you because you're not actually human."

Cap smiles, nodding slightly as he says, "Nice try, but I am."

"Oh, and we should just take your word for it?"

"What else do you have?" he replies. "You expect them to take your word for it that I'm not. I'm telling all of you, I am."

"So why lie?" Benson asks. "Why act like you're left handed?"

"I'm equally competent with both hands."

"Maybe he's ambidextrous," Angel says, appealing to the crew.

"But he's not," Dante says, holding up a medical report on her flex. The text is far too small for anyone to read at more than a few feet, but no one questions the contents. "Not according to his preflight medical. If anything, Cap favors his right hand too much, especially when working with tools in a spacesuit."

"Who doesn't?" Cap asks, opening his hands and inviting a response, but he doesn't seem to realize he's contradicting himself.

"I don't," Vichy says, only his words are cold. He's not buying Cap's lighthearted banter.

Cap says, "Naz was right, you know. There's a danger we're reading too much into trivial, insignificant points."

"On the contrary," Dante says. "It's those points that are the most telling. It's those points at which you feel safe—hidden from sight. Those points are the most revealing."

"You've got no evidence. No proof," Cap says. "By your own admission, the test was fake. There were no right answers. No wrong answers. You can't draw any conclusions from that."

Dante says, "I can because you messed up. You got cocky."

"That's bullshit." Cap points at Naz, wanting to bring him to his way of thinking. "What was the term you used? Witch hunt?"

Naz is quiet, which is unusual for him. He's wary, unsure who to believe.

Dante says, "Cap's been playing us all along. Think about it. Why would he abandon Angel on the surface? He wouldn't."

"Now, hang on," Cap replies, pointing at Dante. "That was her delusion, not mine. It was her fantasy. I wasn't even there. Not really."

Dante ignores him, addressing Mags. "When Cap knocked on your door, I was shocked to see him standing there in his underwear, weren't you? He barely seemed to realize he was wearing a torn, worn pair of underwear. Didn't that strike you as strange? It was as though he didn't realize it was inappropriate."

Cap shakes his head in disbelief, muttering, "This is crazy."

Mags isn't convinced, but she steps back slightly, starting to doubt the man standing before her. Dante addresses her.

"Cap was intensely interested in hearing about your trip to Great Britain. At the time, I figured he was just being polite, but he was totally absorbed in hearing about life on another planet—Earth."

"But why would he…" Benson stops mid-sentence.

"No. Go on," Cap says, rolling his hand over, gesturing for him to continue. "What were you going to say?"

"Why would Cap bring me to you for a psych eval?"

Eyes dart between the crew, revealing their surprise at hearing this.

"You could see them," Dante says. "He needed to discredit you. He needed to undermine you in our eyes—in my eyes. To sow doubts. To make you look psychotic."

"This is ridiculous," Cap says, appealing to the rest of the crew. "I can't believe you're listening to her. Ask yourself, why? Why do you believe her? Because she was the first one to cast an accusation? If I was first, would you believe me?"

"He's right," Angel says. "Think about it. Who stands to gain the most from discrediting Cap? It's the aliens. Maybe she's one of them. She's the only one we haven't actually tested."

Mac addresses the crew, saying, "I served two missions with Cap. On the Virgil and the Acheron."

"This isn't Cap," Dante says.

"I know Cap," Mac replies, pointing at him. He pauses, jabbing at the air, fighting for the right words before settling on. "I trust him. I'd die for him."

"But what if she's right?" Zoe says, taking hold of Mac's arm.

"What if she's wrong?"

"Someone died down there," Benson says. "Whoever that was, they're trying to cover it up. They're using that to get close to us. They're learning. Each time, we lose a little more of our sanity. Soon, there won't be any way to tell what's real and what's not."

"Benson's right," Zoe says. "If we don't figure this out now, we're screwed."

"But why Angel? Why single her out?" Mags asks. Ordinarily, that would be put down to their relationship, but Mags knows Dante well enough to realize something is horribly wrong.

Dante holds up her flex. Using her neural link, she signals for it to change to a single solid color.

"What color is this?" she asks, holding it at arm's length before Angel. Everyone can see the thin plastic sheet. No one has any doubts about the color.

"Green," Angel replies, smiling as she adds, "Bright green."

Dante nods in agreement. She doesn't look surprised by the answer—no one is. The sheet is almost fluorescent.

With ice in her veins, Dante asks Angel, "What's Anomalous Trichromat Protanomaly?"

Angel is silent.

"Do you want to tell them or should I?"

Angel grits her teeth.

"She's color blind," Dante says.

"This is such bullshit," Angel counters, but Dante cuts her off, determined to have her say.

"Oh, not completely. Angel's not monochromatic. She'd have never made the flight crew if that was the case. No, for

Angel—*our* Angel—reds appear burgundy. Blues are deeper, but they're still blue. Even green looks different to red and blue, but bright greens—spring greens like this one—yeah, they look black."

"It's not what you think," Angel says, protesting, appealing to the rest of the crew, but Mags cuts her off, saying what they're all really thinking.

"Fuck."

"Oh, yeah," Dante says. "I figured her out first. She gave away Cap. When she joined him, defending him, I knew I had them both."

"No, no, no," Cap says. "This is all wrong."

"Don't listen to her," Angel says, pleading with the others.

"Jesus," Mac says, ignoring them. He runs his hands up through his hair, grabbing at his scalp. "This is fucked up."

Vichy paces, raising his hands up by his head and muttering something in Italian, probably swear words. His eyes cast down, looking at his feet as he strides back and forth.

Benson turns, slamming his hand against the console and shaking his head in disbelief.

Cap looks genuinely surprised by Angel. Dante's not sure if the others notice, but he appears confused by her. Although his head is facing forward, his eyes dart down and to the side, looking at Angel with a sense of curiosity.

"Cap. Please," she whispers, sensing his reluctance, stepping closer to him and taking his arm. He seems genuinely conflicted.

Mags is oblivious to the interplay between them. She blurts out, "What the fuck, Cap?"

"Look, I'm the first to admit it," he says, trying to calm everyone down. "This looks bad, right? I get that. But let's not jump to conclusions."

"No, let's," Benson says, shrugging his shoulders. "Come on. How are you going to explain this away?"

"I'm not a—"

"A what?" Benson asks. "An alien?"

Cap holds his hands out. "Everyone needs to calm down."

"What about you, Angel?" Benson cocks his head sideways, seething with anger. "Are you one of them too?"

"Hey," Cap says, coming to her defense. "Look, you've got to see this from her perspective. Of course, she knows she's colorblind. Oh, she might not have the exact medical term rolling off her tongue, but she knows. Angel's lived with this her whole life. And she knows what will happen if she guesses wrong. Can you imagine the pressure she felt under to look normal?"

He appeals to the crew, holding his hands out in a gesture of openness.

"If she guesses wrong, she gets crucified. So, yeah, she said what she thought Dante wanted to hear. Is that a crime? She's trying her best to fit in and look like the rest of us—not because she's an alien—because she's different. Is that so bad?"

"I see colors," Angel says. "I see enough to fool most doctors. Sure, flowers look a little bland, but I can pick between their colors. If anything, I see more shades than most of you norms."

"You're missing the big picture," Cap says. "No offense to Dante. I understand what she's trying to do. I don't agree with her conclusion, but I understand."

Angel says, "The real problem is, if it's not one of us, then who is it?"

Cap says, "I know about me. I can vouch for who I am, but I don't know about any of you."

Vichy looks to Dante. She wants to say something to him, but she's running out of ideas. She's not as eloquent as she feels she should be, but she has to counter their arguments.

"I'm telling you. It's them. The two of them." Dante points at Cap and Angel. As the words leave her lips, she feels dejected. She's not convincing herself, let alone anyone else.

Cap says, "And I'm telling you, don't rush to the wrong conclusion."

"Think about what happens if she's wrong," Angel says. "The real aliens go undetected. They get a boost from this and you lose our support."

"Hang on," Benson says, pointing at Cap. "You wanted Dante to come up with a way of distinguishing between us and them. You wanted her to do it in a way they couldn't predict. In a manner they wouldn't understand. So she lied. Given what we know about how well they can fabricate our reality, that's a damn good idea—you just don't like the outcome."

"We've got to work together," Cap says, but Mags has had enough. She interrupts, cutting him off before he can continue, issuing one of her trademark, end-of-story statements, with each word carrying more weight than the last. The final word is delivered with a stamp of her foot.

"Fucking. Fucketty. Fuck. Fuck. Fuuuuuck!"

"What do we do now?" Vichy asks, turning to Dante. She shrugs.

"What can we do?" Mac asks.

"Don't ask me," Zoe says. "I'm still trying to figure out who we should flush out of the airlock."

Benson shakes his head. "They won't feel anything."

Zoe doesn't care. "I'll feel something," she says, tapping

at the center of her chest. "I'll feel a helluva lot better."

"They're playing with us," Mags says. "Like a cat with a goddamn mouse, they're fucking us over. Goddamn it!"

"Angel died on the bridge," Dante says, trying to turn the conversation in her favor. She points to the spot where Angel fell. "Mags shot her. Remember?"

"I did what?" Mags cries out in alarm, apparently having no recollection of that reboot.

Dante feels as though she's been abandoned. Mags is right. This is all just a game to them. These alien creatures are toying with her, teasing her, tormenting her, leaving just enough clues for her to unravel the threads but not enough for her to make any real difference. It's cruel. She wants to say something, to explain, but she's at a loss as to where she should start. Even to her, it sounds crazy. Why would Mags strip a construction bot to build a rivet gun?

She goes to speak, but Vichy cuts her off. He seems confused by her. He squints as he says, "What the hell are you talking about, Dee?"

"I'm telling you. Angel is one of them." Dante appeals to Mac and Zoe. "You guys have got to believe me. You've seen how they can inflict physical pain on us in here. Imagine being shot in the head. She wouldn't survive. She couldn't."

"We don't know what we can survive," Naz says, still

undecided.

"We don't even know if you're right," Mac says.

"Why would Mags shoot Angel?" Cap asks. It's then it hits her. By focusing on Angel, she's letting Cap off the hook, whether consciously or otherwise. In the eyes of the crew, the focus is Angel, not him—and the rest of the crew are not convinced.

"I'm sorry, Dee. I don't know what you're talking about," Mags says, echoing Cap, being genuinely confused by the prospect of having shot Angel.

"Surely, you remember," Dante says.

"I—I would never," Mags says, stuttering. She seems to doubt herself, but she pushes on, sticking to her conviction. "I never did that."

Dante's suddenly acutely aware she sounds crazy, almost obsessive as she tries to convince them of something that, from their perspective, never happened. Within a matter of minutes, she's gone from being in control to looking like a madman, while Cap's gone from condemned to back in charge. He's calm. Too calm. This isn't working out the way she thought it would. She's fucked this up. No one remembers that reboot. She's the only one. They're all looking at her like she's delusional.

"What are you talking about?" Vichy asks, but he was

there.

"You saw it. You all saw it," she says, seeing even Vichy's starting to doubt her. "No. No. No."

Anxiety swells within her chest. Her throat constricts, tightening, making it hard to breathe. She's got to do something.

Dante knows how the illusion works. Deviations cause the membranes to collapse. It's almost as though the crew is being herded together by these alien creatures with each reboot. Variations are punished. Run from a room or lash out in some unexpected way and they reset the sim. Whatever these creatures are, they're studying them, observing them, learning from them, replicating and ultimately deceiving them.

Panic seizes her. The muscles in her body go tense, only they don't, because none of this is real, and that realization terrifies her. She starts to hyperventilate. Her palms go sweaty. What seemed so simple and clear-cut moments ago, now looks impossible. Rather than convincing the others, she's confused them.

"Ah," Cap says, realizing what she's about to do a fraction of a second before she does herself, which perplexes the others. "Don't."

Her voice trembles. "I—I have to."

It's then Dante realizes what happened throughout all of those other reboots. She finally understands the isolation each of them has felt. Mac staggering down the hallway trying to reach Zoe, Benson when he could see those creatures creeping up behind her in medical, Mags as she waved the gun around. The one thing they all had in common was their frustration, their inability to convince someone else about what was happening. No one would listen. No one understood.

Dante bolts for the corridor, dropping her shoulder and running hard, sprinting toward the open doorway, hoping for a reboot, wanting a second chance.

"No!" Vichy yells, reaching for her, but he's on the other side of the deck.

Naz is closer. He sticks out his leg in front of her, trying to block her passage.

Dante leaps.

Naz shoves her, connecting with her shoulder and sending her slamming into the navigation console.

Dante's head hits the edge of the metal panel, striking just above her temple. Pain explodes within her skull and she crumples. Her body slumps to the floor. Naz rushes to her side, cradling her head as she collapses. Dante's not sure who's swearing. It seems everyone is yelling something, including Naz. The last thing she sees is Cap and Angel crouching over her.

As the darkness descends, Cap whispers, "Don't worry. Everything's going to be okay."

ANGEL

Dante's eyes flicker, taking in the familiar surroundings of the medical bay onboard the Acheron. The lights are dim. She's lying on her back on a thinly padded gurney with a sheet and blanket wrapped over her. It's disconcerting to find her arms pressed tight against her sides, leaving her feeling trapped. Dante never sleeps like this. She goes to move, but her arms are held down by the blanket tucked tightly beneath the thin mattress, making it difficult, but not impossible to get free. She flexes, wrestling with the blanket, loosening the sheets.

A familiar voice whispers softly from the shadows.

"Hey."

Dante turns, but that motion causes pain to shoot through her head, running from the nape of her neck over the top of her skull and stabbing at her right eye. Her head is pounding. A bandage has been wound around her forehead but it's uncomfortably tight.

"How are you holding up?" Angel asks.

Angel?

Petite fingers touch softly at Dante's shoulder, resting gently on her flight suit, trying to calm her, but for Dante it's as though she's been hit with a jolt of electricity. She struggles against the blankets, pushing to sit upright.

"Easy," Angel says. "You've had a nasty knock."

"You!" Dante says, looking around, not wanting to be alone with Angel. "What are you doing here?"

"Relax," Angel says, pointing at the soft red LED glowing in the corner of the ceiling. "They can see you."

Given the crew of the Acheron are in some kind of alien prison, *'they'* isn't exactly the most appropriate term. Angel picks up on that and corrects herself. "Cap and the others." Although hearing Cap's name is hardly reassuring.

"You fell," Angel says. "You hit your head."

"I remember."

"It was an accident."

Dante doesn't look convinced, so Angel continues. "Naz was trying to stop you, not hurt you."

"And you?" Dante asks, looking Angel squarely in the eye. "Do you want to hurt me?"

"No one wants to hurt you, Dee."

For Dante, the illusion is overwhelming. This is Angel. It's her voice. Her mannerisms. Her soft features. It's hard to see an alien intelligence manipulating her, but that's precisely what's happening, Dante's sure of it, and yet Angel looks and sounds entirely innocent.

Angel and Dante first met during crew selection—a grueling 46-hour combination of physical and mental stress designed to see how candidates would handle pressure over an extended period of time.

Back then, neither of them had any idea how long the selection process would actually last, which was intentional, to find each candidate's breaking point. At first, selection seemed easy. Too easy. Each hour was measured with atomic precision. An hour walking on a treadmill, followed by an hour of verbal tests ranging from 10th grade math to basic geography and English comprehension, followed by an hour of rest that could be spent anyway they wanted—eating, sleeping, browsing the Internet, watching a video—but they were warned, that was the only time allocated for bathroom breaks. Outside of that, it was a case of hold it in or wet/soil yourself. One of the trainers even taunted a candidate caught unaware in those first few hours, saying, *"When you feel like you can't hold it in anymore, let me know. I want to watch."* Needless to say, the candidate made it to the break.

Every third hour was free time, which seemed

incongruous with the goals of selection. Angel wasn't fooled. She told Dante to sleep. At first, Dante didn't listen. While Angel lay on her bunk with her eyes shut, Dante responded to emails and messages from home. Then the process repeated. Again and again and again.

The candidates were divided into three rotations so there was always someone on the treadmills or seated in front of an instructor answering questions or lying on the bunks pressed up against the far wall inside the vast gymnasium. With the lights on full and the sound of shoes constantly echoing across the wooden floor, sleep was nigh on impossible, or so Dante thought, but somehow Angel would start snoring. Being petite, it was a soft grumble occasionally escaping from her lips, but she got her zzzzs. Like most of the other candidates, Dante expected the session to stop after twelve hours as surely the instructors had gathered enough data by then, but on it went. The rhythm was relentless.

After twenty-four hours, they'd only had eight hours free time. For Dante, only four of those had been spent asleep—but limited to slightly less than one hour blocks. Waking was hard. Disorienting. Fatigue set in.

By the time the candidates hit thirty hours, middle school math started feeling like advanced astrophysics. Dante's words began to slur. The lack of any meaningful, deep sleep meant she was functionally drunk. She hadn't actually had any alcohol for over a month beforehand as she prepared for training, but her reasoning and judgment were impaired, and she knew all too well this was what they were looking for. Angel, though, was still fresh. She was prepped for a marathon.

Walking on the treadmill became utter torture. The constant pace caused Dante to stumble. Her body wanted variation, not exact repetition. Angel saw her falter. "*Repeat the same phrase over and over again,*" Angel said from the treadmill next to her. "*A mantra. Something to help you keep your rhythm.*" Angel didn't have to tell her that, but she wanted to help. The instructors noticed and made notes. Already, almost half of the candidates had dropped out, having given up, being desperate for some respite.

Dante never did find out what Angel's mantra was, but hers came from a nursery rhyme, one she mangled to her own private amusement. It was the only way she could stay sane. "*Twinkle, twinkle, little star—How I wonder what you are—Up above the world so high—Like a diamond in the sky—Twinkle, twinkle, rather big planet—technically, not a star,*" and she'd jump right back in at the second stanza, "*How I wonder what you are.*" Somehow, Dante made it work and kept her legs pumping.

The rumor among the candidates was the test would be stopped at the fortieth hour, but the pace never slackened. One hour of walking. One hour of verbal testing. One hour of rest. Food and water on the run. No feedback. No encouragement or criticism. For all Dante knew, she was getting every question wrong. A couple of times, she found herself babbling. Even she wasn't sure quite what she was saying. Notes were taken. Nothing was said regardless.

To her surprise, Dante found the verbal tests hardest. The instructors would read sections from *To Kill A Mockingbird*, *Huckleberry Finn*, *The Great Gatsby* and *Moby Dick*—all with a monotone voice, droning on for up to ten minutes before asking a series of questions that sometimes related to information from a previous reading a couple of hours earlier. Dante found it hard to stay awake, let alone concentrate.

Why does Scout ask Atticus about the death of Mrs. Radley?

Why would Jem be disappointed to hear she'd died?

What's behind the homoerotic relationship between Ishmael and Qeequeg?

Do you find it natural, convenient or forced?

Why was Ahab obsessed with the great white whale?

Explain your reasoning.

Is Nick a reliable narrator or is he misleading us, idolizing Gatsby?

What leads you to that conclusion?

Dante hated those questions. She wanted to ask, "*What the hell does this have to do with interstellar exploration?*" But she knew the answer—everything and nothing at all. Their answers weren't important. Their reasoning was. The ability to focus was. Pushing through fatigue when faced with mundane tasks was a key indicator for how they'd function under pressure a quadrillion miles from home. And the psychs were right. Once the glamor of the mission wore off, all that remained was their dedication.

The fortieth hour was '*The Wall.*' With no end in sight, candidates began physically dropping. Bowing out no longer meant stepping off the treadmill and sulking to the door on trembling legs. Candidates simply fell on the whirling tread and tumbled to the wall. No one helped them up. At the time, it seemed mean, but a hundred light years away, there would be no one to help. More notes were taken. Nothing was said.

Even that far into selection, Angel looked as fresh as she did at the start. All the strapping, musclebound men with their pumped thighs, ripped biceps and ironing board stomachs found their legs turning to jelly after forty hours, but not Angel. The challenge was now entirely mental. Dante focused on Angel and her unassuming, petite frame. Having Angel beside her gave her a sense of companionship—camaraderie. They'd whisper encouragement to each other.

At one point, all the staff left, leaving the two of them staring at a clock on the wall slowly counting out the seconds. They were barely fifteen minutes into a walking session. On either side of them lay empty treadmills sitting idle. The only other remaining candidates were in their rest phase, lying on their cots with sheets bundled up over their eyes in a vain attempt to block out the light. Angel kept her eyes forward. Like Dante, she knew it was a trick. The instructors wanted to see what the two women would do when given the chance to cheat. For Dante, though, to have stopped and rested, even if just for a moment, would have meant not starting again. She had to keep going.

When the test finally finished several hours later, neither of them believed it. They'd just completed their millionth walking session. Dante sat down at a table in front of one of the instructors, ready for yet another mind-numbing question from Ernest Hemingway's *The Garden of Eden*, and he simply said, "We're done. You can go." It took her a moment for those words to sink in.

Even though she'd heard what was said, Angel slumped down on the chair next to Dante. Her legs were shaking. It was then Dante realized they both needed each other through those long hours. They succeeded together, not as individuals. Perhaps that's why they ended up on the same mission. Back then, Angel had to be carried to her quarters. Somehow, Dante made the walk across the campus, but she bounced lightly off a couple of walls in her quasi-drunken state. When she finally got back to her room, Dante fell face first on her bed. She was asleep before her head had dented the pillow.

The next day, they found out only four people were selected out of a hundred and sixty-seven applicants. The two of them and a couple of guys who were later assigned to the Virgil. Dante and Angel were never emotionally close, not like her and Mags, but there was a bond between them, a sense of trust and respect. It upsets Dante to realize that their friendship is being used against her.

Dante blinks in the soft light coming in through the broad window on the Acheron. To see Angel sitting beside her in medical is disarming. Dante wants to hate this alien imposter. She wants to resist, to at least be suspicious, but the more they talk the lower her defenses fall. Is this Angel? Physically, this is Angel, but what lies behind those eyes?

Dante feels conflicted. What if she's wrong? What if this really is Angel? The alternative is painful to consider. If this is an imposter, her friend is dead—and that hurts. If not, Dante's maligned someone that's only ever been gracious toward her.

Angel seems unaware of the endless churning within Dante's tormented thoughts, but the distant look on her face gives her an opening to speak.

"What are you looking at?"

Dante isn't looking at anything. She's sitting up, staring blindly ahead, lost in thought, but those words cause her to focus on the stars.

"What do you see in them?" Angel asks, following her gaze.

The Pleiades drift into view.

"Hope."

The two women sit in silence. Neither speaks. They're both content—which is strange given the confrontation on the bridge. If Angel is a fake, she's a damn good one. Dante finds her conviction faltering, but then she remembers the color test. Angel, her Angel, had to ace selection. Back then, anything less would have seen her returned to her unit and she knew it. Having come from the Navy, Angel didn't want to go back. Mentally, she'd given up one ocean for another—one full of stars. Angel pushed herself hard because she felt she had to compensate for being color blind. Dante can't ignore that. Her Angel wouldn't lie, that's really the crux of the issue. Her Angel would have said something rather than pretend. Her Angel would have never guessed.

Nothing is as it seems. Reality is a lie. Without knowing it at the time, this is precisely what Dante trained for—to be able to operate with clarity while under duress. Selection was the start, not the end of her training. From there, the focus was on dealing with the unknown, using deductive reasoning to work with what little was known. If only her instructors could see her now. Doubts be damned. Dante's got to cling to whatever fragments of reality are seeping through from the outside world—and the most apparent point is the crew is not intact. Regardless of what's happening to her, someone died down there on P4. At least one person among them is fake. The behavioral evidence suggests that's at least Angel and probably Cap as well. As much as she doesn't want to, Dante's got to hold to that conviction.

One thing that bothers Dante is the veracity of the illusion. Mac was seriously hurt. Now she's injured. If all this is just a dream, how the fuck does that work? Are these injuries also playing out in whatever bizarre state they're in within the real world? Are they really hanging from the ceiling in some overgrown version of the medical suite, or is that just another layer within the illusion—something to distract them. Given they can interact with that alternate world, Dante's not convinced even that's real. As she was the one that suggested they were actually somehow held upright in medical, perhaps there's some wish fulfillment in what she saw.

She touches at the bandages, asking, "How bad?"

"Jeeves said you had a hematoma and a severe concussion, but no hemorrhaging or adema—is that the right word?"

"Edema," Dante replies, wondering how an artificial

intelligence can be co-opted into the illusion. Was it really Jeeves? Or is Jeeves just another replica like the Acheron itself? When she spoke to Jeeves, he seemed distant. He wasn't himself. But then, are any of them in this nightmare? Angel is unaware of the turmoil in Dante's thought process, which is in itself revealing. These creatures can manipulate their sensory inputs but it seems they can't read their minds.

Angel seems concerned as she says, "You were unconscious and vomiting. We were worried."

"Were you?"

Cold, Dante. Damn, that's cold. But Dante feels she has to stay the course. The cost is too high. If they have been infiltrated, they could lose what little leverage they have left over their captors.

"Look. I know this is awkward."

"Really? You know that?" Dante asks, working herself back against the headboard, determined to sit up properly. She feels indignant. "They left me with you?"

"And Jeeves," Angel says, sitting back in her chair, resigning herself to the hostility. Jeeves, though, is conspicuously quiet. Although Dante could call on him and he'd no doubt answer, it seems he wants to remain aloof. Dante's curious about his observations. She wants to talk to him, but only when she's alone.

Angel pauses for a moment before adding, "They didn't trust me."

For a second, Dante's confused. She does a double-take, blinking and turning her head slightly in disbelief at what she's hearing.

"Wait? If they didn't trust you, why did they leave you with me?"

"It was Vichy's suggestion."

"Vichy?"

Is Angel lying? She could be, but then she's here with Dante. Where the hell is Vichy? Dante's upset. She squeezes her eyes shut for a second, wanting to block out everything else, struggling to concentrate. Her fingers touch at the bridge of her nose, relieving the pressure for but a moment.

Angel looks at the floor, unable to make eye contact. Dante feels the swell of anger rising in her veins. Just how well do these creatures understand body language? If they're trying to make her believe Angel's sincere, it's a valiant effort, but Dante's unmoved. She feels she owes her dead friend a debt. She has to figure out what actually happened on P4. As for Vichy, she cannot fathom how he could abandon her like this.

Angel tries to explain. "Vichy pointed out the futility of our position. He said, if they want us dead, nothing we do in here will make any difference."

"You'd have killed us already," Dante says, following the logic.

"Not me," Angel replies. "I don't want you dead."

Dante feels hurt by the realization Vichy has forsaken her. That's out of character for him. Damn it, Vee. Why did you leave me with her?

"So what do you want?" Dante asks. Her question is defensive, trying to shift the focus away from herself, wanting to change the subject.

That particular question, though, takes Angel by surprise. She looks horrified. For a brief fraction of a second, she's flustered. "Me? I—ah. I guess I want things to be the way they were before."

To Dante, that's not an answer. Before when? As a human, Angel would mean before they arrived in orbit around P4. As an alien, she means before she was outed, back when Angel was unquestionably accepted as part of the crew, but why? What are these creatures trying to accomplish? Dante squints wanting to decipher Angel's true intent.

"But the others. You said they didn't trust you. To do what?"

"They went to Zoe's cabin," Angel replies. "They're all down there. Naz thinks it might be a doorway between realities."

"Is it?"

Angel shrugs.

"You can drop the façade," Dante says. "No one trusts you. Not them. Not me. We know what you really are. What I want to know is why?"

Angel ignores her, turning and looking out the window as she asks, "What do you think of them?" She's obviously curious as to what Dante sees in the stars.

To these creatures, distant stars are simply pinpoints of light. The idea of constellations must be foreign to them. It makes no sense to think of stars as having any meaning. To anyone that's not native to Earth, the idea that an arbitrary assortment of stars somehow depicts snakes, lions, a cup or a sextant, men, women or twins is absurd. For Dante, it confirms her suspicions about her friend. Angel's dead.

Whatever these alien creatures are, they don't see a ram or a bull or the great hunter Orion because there is no actual form to the stars. There are no shapes in the sky. The constellations have only ever existed in the deepest recesses of the human mind. They were contrived to assist with navigation and the passing of the seasons, commemorating folklore and superstitions. Even modern humans struggle to understand the shapes devised by ancient cultures as none of them are apparent.

To intelligent creatures from some other world, the constellations aren't even stick figures. There's no connect-the-dots shape to be found. Squinting doesn't help. The constellations arose out of oral history, as legends written in the sky.

Even among humanity, there's no agreement on the various shapes. Somewhat ironically, the constellations are entirely alien to people from different cultures. The Aborigines thought of Orion as two brothers fishing in a canoe, while the Hindus saw dogs chasing a deer. The Lakota Indians thought of Orion as a bison charging across the grassy plains. It's no wonder Angel struggles to understand what Dante sees in the chaotic splatter of distant stars. There are no borders, no lines of demarcation, no natural groupings. Often, the constellations, as depicted by the Greeks, overlap each other, intruding into one another's imaginary forms. As a child, Dante found that maddening. Now, that confusion is refreshing. The constellations are indecipherable to an alien intelligence. There's no algorithm that can make sense of them, no brute-force calculation that can reveal their secrets. To these creatures, they're meaningless. To Dante, they're a symbol of defiance, a bastion of strength, her last hope for refuge. Far from being meaningless, to Dante, the constellations are a connection with Earth.

Angel points, pretending to be friendly, trying to draw an

explanation out of her. "I mean, look at them. The stars. They're stunning. That's all we ever really are, right? Stardust. Essentially, we're all the same. Hydrogen. Oxygen. Carbon. Just a bunch of wet chemistry moderating sodium ion pathways."

Nice try, Dante thinks. Ordinarily, she'd jump at such a discussion, but not with some inhuman creature impersonating her friend.

"So why do this?" Dante asks, aware she's gaining insights into an alien mind from this interaction.

Angel asks, "Why did you travel eighty-eight light years from home?"

You.

Dante knows that one word is the closest she's going to get to an admission from Angel. Not we. You. Humans. Angel's not the only one that can be coy. Both of them are probing, looking to gain insights, vying for information, wanting to learn about the other. As long as Angel feels she's in control of the conversation, Dante can manipulate her to gain an advantage. From what Dante can tell, these creatures think humanity traveled here to fulfill some destiny—perhaps they've confused the conversation she had earlier with Benson about the meaning and presence of the constellations. There's no one star called Orion. That must have confused them. Deep within the data banks of the Acheron lie all the star names and designations, but not the constellations, as they're meaningless in terms of astronomy. The irony is, astrological star signs aren't signs at all, they carry no more meaning than burnt toast or a stain on the wall, and yet somehow, the human mind crafts images out of them all.

Seeing the constellations this far out from Earth reveals a failing in their simulation—a detail that's been overlooked, or perhaps inadvertently mapped from the combination of memories and expectations of the crew as the aliens sought to create the perfect illusion. Dante's convinced they haven't noticed this discrepancy, probably because they haven't been able to isolate what she or the others actually see in the stars. If the past is anything to go by, as soon as they realize their mistake, they'll update the illusion and she'll lose her only remaining touch point with sanity.

Dante says, "We wanted to explore—to find life."

"And we did."

"Did we?" Dante asks, noting Angel's reverted to the inclusive pronoun. "Or were we found?"

Angel smiles, shaking her head, not wanting to join Dante's game.

"And you?" Dante asks. Her question might sound casual, but it's calculated. Did these creatures originate on P4? Up until now, she and the others have assumed that, but there's no reason to believe it. By leaving the rest of the question unspoken and casually linking it to Angel's original comment, Dante's fishing for information.

Angel's eyes narrow. Seems she doesn't want to play fair, but the lack of an answer is revealing in itself. If these creatures originated on P4, why dance around the issue?

Dante feels alone. Where's Vichy when she really needs him? Why wouldn't Mags stay with her at least?

In that moment, Dante understands something profound about her friends. There's no way Vichy would leave her alone with Angel if he thought she'd be in danger. This was deliberate. Vichy wanted Dante to interrogate Angel. He probably talked Mags into it. Vichy would have deliberately separated Angel and Cap. Angel may think the reason was to isolate her while the rest of the crew investigated Zoe's cabin, but as information slowly leaks out of their conversation in medical, Dante comes to understand Vichy's motivation. Just as she's working Angel over, she's sure Vichy's tackling Cap, slowly chipping away at his armor. By isolating the two aliens from each other, there's the possibility discrepancies will arise, and that will tell them something about the nature of where they are. Already, Dante's convinced Angel's committed to being in this quasi-physical location. Although this is only a simulation, she seems to share the isolation Dante feels in the medical suite. It seems these creatures have physical limitations within the simulation.

The look on Angel's face suggests she's starting to realize this conversation was a mistake.

Dante plays it cool, determined to keep this tactical advantage in play. Damn. She can't wait to compare notes with the others.

"What do you want from me?" Angel asks, clearly feeling frustrated.

"To be free."

Angel shakes her head, but she's smiling. After a few seconds, she says, "I don't get you, Dee. You were never free. None of us ever were."

Dante has to give Angel credit for trying as her comment takes Dante off-guard. She needs a few seconds to process her own thoughts.

"What does it mean to be free?" Angel asks. "In its raw essence, it means being free to choose, right?"

In the quiet of the empty medical bay, with the lights low and the environmental controls set to mimic night in support of human circadian rhythms, Dante relaxes. There's only so long she can keep her guard raised. She's hurt. She's sore. She's tired. She doesn't want to fight. This looks and sounds like Angel. Perhaps it is. Maybe Dante's made a mistake. Wouldn't be the first time.

"We're free to choose," Dante says, engaging with the conversation instead of wrestling with every word.

Angel says, "You can't choose between options you don't know about—things you don't understand. If I ask you to choose the best song ever written, you can only select from those you've heard, those you remember, so it's not really a choice, it's a narrow, limited selection."

Dante nods. Makes sense.

"Now, if I remind you of a song. Perhaps if I subtly influence you. Maybe I hum the tune before our conversation, or I talk about the band over lunch. What then? Have you really chosen for yourself? Or have you been corralled? Politicians do this all the time."

"Pick songs?" Dante asks, feigning innocence.

Angel laughs, which is surprising. Comedy is highly subjective—not only between cultures but over time. Things that were funny to the Romans don't even elicit a smile from modern audiences. Jokes in one culture rarely translate to another. What are the odds of humor transcending species originating on different planets? And again, Dante finds doubts creeping in.

Angel's oblivious to the machinations of Dante's weary mind.

"In physics, we describe choices as a closed system,

where all the variables are present, but there are no closed systems. Everything is open. Everything is interconnected. There's no freewill because nothing is free. We accept this at a physical level, knowing the atoms in our bodies are gravitationally bound to every other atom everywhere else within the entire universe, regardless of how distant, but then we contradict ourselves. Oh, I'm free because I *feel* free, because I *want* to be free. Honestly, it's delusional—laughable."

"That's a very bleak outlook on life," Dante says.

"It's a bleak universe," Angel replies.

Dante is perplexed by Angel. If she's an alien, these creatures have some seriously nihilistic beliefs.

"I feel like life is different."

Angel is brutal, destroying Dante's position with a single word uttered barely above a whisper. "Feel?"

"Okay, now you sound like Mac."

"I like Mac."

"There has to be something more to life," Dante says.

"Does there?" Angel asks. "Why?"

"Because, even in astrophysics, things become more than the sum of their parts."

Dante's determined to redeem her position using ideas

that will appeal to Angel.

She says, "Stars are more than hydrogen. They become something greater than just their constituent parts."

Angel nods in agreement so Dante presses forward.

"Complexity introduces new factors. As life evolved, evolution selected for consciousness as a way of dealing with overwhelming complexity, giving us a choice."

Angel smiles. She seems to appreciate Dante's position, but she clearly doesn't agree.

"We like to flatter ourselves," Angel says, "We like to think we're free. But freedom is an illusion."

"This," Dante replies, pointing at her own legs hidden beneath the blankets. "This right here is an illusion, but I'm real."

"It's all an illusion," Angel says. "It always has been. I mean, think about the audacity of our lives. We're junk. We're the scraps of nuclear material that escaped from a dying star billions of years ago. When all else fell into the core, collapsing to form a neutron star or the eternal darkness of a black hole, these tiny atoms that make up my body somehow escaped."

She rolls her hands over, looking at her fingers as she speaks.

"You've seen photos of a supernova, right? We're that thin shell blown off into space. Eons pass and we have the arrogance to claim ourselves as somehow different from an asteroid or a moon, even though we share the same elements. We're special. We're alive, we say, as though we're something other than physical, something other than a tiny assortment of scorched atoms."

"But we are," Dante says.

"Are we?" Angel asks. "Or are we kidding ourselves? You think we're trapped here in an illusion. I think life's always been an illusion."

"We're here now," is all Dante can muster. "We are alive. We're not a desk or a rock. We're something more."

"I think, therefore I am, right?" Angel asks. "And yet thought is fleeting. The protons that make up your body have a half-life of ten to the power of thirty-two. You and I will struggle to get much beyond ten to the power of two years in age. All the constituent parts of this great *I am* will be around a helluva lot longer than either of us, but they won't think, they won't reason, they won't be aware of anything at all."

As much as Dante doesn't want to admit it, this is precisely the kind of thing Angel would say. Angel always loved math-on-the-fly. For Dante, this is the challenge, unraveling and deciphering these conversations, seeing beyond the words to find reality. Just how well can these creatures duplicate their thought processes, their reasoning and emotions, their quirks and idiosyncrasies? Could she be wrong about Angel?

Has Dante read too much into too little?

"So what will happen to me personally?" Dante asks, appreciating that if anyone knows the answer to that, it's Angel.

"Well, you," Angel replies, putting air-quotes around the word *you*. "You're already recycled. Statistically speaking, you're a collection of six elements that have gone around and around on Earth for billions of years."

"Six?" Dante says, genuinely surprised by such a small number.

"Ninety nine percent of you. Yep. You're just a bunch of oxygen, carbon, nitrogen, hydrogen—stuff like that."

"I thought there were lots of different things," Dante says, forgetting for a moment about the conflict between them.

"Things," Angel says with a hint of disdain only a nuclear physicist can manage. "You mean atoms, right?" She holds her thumb and forefinger together, separated by the tiniest of gaps, and squints, peering through at Dante. "All that fancy stuff is less than one percent. Anyway, it's the combinations that are important. The elements are simply LEGO. The real fun is in putting them all together."

"And me?" Dante says, lowering her guard, genuinely wanting to know. "What happens to me?"

"Atoms are overrated," Angel says, apparently distracted

by something she just said. She shrugs her shoulders. "They're field excitations—energy in a persistent form, that's all. Nothing's really solid. It's all an illusion."

"Hey," Dante says, laughing. "This is me we're talking about, right?"

"Okay, so you. You're part T-Rex, or at least some other kind of dinosaur. There are just so many atoms involved and so much time that's elapsed that the probability you *haven't* inherited some of your elements from them approaches zero. When it comes to water and air, that stuff recycles so damn quickly you have definitely breathed the same oxygen as JFK and sipped at the same water as Shakespeare."

"Hang on," Dante says, losing herself for a moment. "If we've both drunk the same water then I've been drinking his pee?"

Angel has an irrepressible smile on her face.

"Yep."

All the air and water onboard the Acheron is recycled, so Dante learned to accept such notions a long time ago, but back on Earth, water always seemed so pure, or so the commercials would say. When some pretty blonde gal wearing a bikini holds up a bottle of 'pure water,' marketed as being from the Alps or somewhere equally pristine, it never occurred to Dante she might as well be holding up a bottle of her own pee (slightly removed).

"Huh," Dante says. "But what happens from here? I mean, that whole global recycling thing stopped once we left Earth, right? Now it's just us."

"Not quite," Angel replies. "On large timescales, far beyond the reach of our lives, molecular recycling will still occur, but it'll take a different form. We're unlikely to ever be consumed by a star. Falling into stars and black holes is actually much harder and rarer than people think."

Dante laughs. "I'm not sure people think about falling into stars. You might. No one else does."

Angel shrugs, getting up and turning away from Dante. She walks to the window, resting her hand on the glass and looking out into the darkness. Orion sits proud in the distance.

"Stars explode. It's something they do really well. They wipe out entire solar systems. Chances are, that's what'll happen here in the long run. These binaries will merge. The newly born star will eventually burn through its fuel and its outer shell will explode violently into space, stripping the planets bare. Then we'll be recycled into the heavens, perhaps to form other asteroids, comets, planets. Maybe even other lifeforms."

Dante likes Angel. She wants to believe Angel, but the stars. Angel sees them and yet she doesn't. Angel's oblivious to their cryptic secret. For Dante, that's all the confirmation she needs.

Angel looks back, peering over her shoulder as she makes eye contact. She feels awkward.

Dante smiles.

Lies come easy.

Angel screws up her face a little, saying, "I'll let you get some rest."

Dante nods.

As Angel walks out of medical, she mumbles, looking down at her feet and talking to herself. The last thing Dante hears is, "What is it with Orion anyway?"

COLORS

"Good morning," Vichy whispers, sitting down next to Dante in the medical suite.

Night has become day, but not through any natural process. Somewhere, an electronic timer has ticked over, triggering the lights and—just like that—their bodies are told it's time to wake and become active again. Consciousness returns, pretending it never left, making it seem as though several hours were no more than a few minutes. Consciousness is yet another lie Dante has to deal with. She turns her head, yawning and stretching, looking around as she sits up. Like a dream, Angel is gone.

Dark rings surround Vichy's eyes. Stubble has formed on his cheeks. His hair is a mess. He doesn't look as though he's slept at all. His voice is low, breaking like gravel in a cement mixer.

"What did you figure out?"

The look on her face screams in anguish at him. She grits her teeth, clenching her jaw, fighting not to lash out at him in anger. Vichy knows.

"I had to get them apart," he says in his defense, appealing with his arms out before her. "It was the only way."

Still, Dante's silent. Brooding. Smoldering. Finally, she lets out a sigh, releasing her frustration.

Mags pulls up a chair on the other side of her bed. "How are you doing?"

The difference in their greetings doesn't go unnoticed.

"I've been better."

"I bet."

"What did you find in Zoe's apartment?" Dante asks, addressing her, not him. "Were you able to get in and identify each of us?"

"The door had seized," Mags says. The look on her face is more succinct than her words—*they failed*. Still, Mags continues, explaining what happened.

"Benson had to modify a winch from engineering to get the lock to turn. Even then, we went slow. Mac was worried the stress might strip the gears inside the doorframe."

Vichy says, "The door was buckled. Damn thing's supposed to be blast proof."

Dante waits for Mags to continue.

"Cap suggested using a QX scanner from one of the surface bots to assess what lay inside. Mac liked the idea. While Benson worked on the door, he repurposed a scanner."

"Just tell her," Vichy says.

Mags ignores him. "We got the door to open about four inches and pushed the probe into the darkness."

"And?" Dante asks.

Mags hangs her head. She doesn't say anything. Vichy speaks on her behalf.

"Say what you will about Cap. He's right about one thing."

"What?"

"We see what they want us to see."

"I don't understand," Dante says.

Mags is disappointed. "There was nothing in there."

"Nothing?"

"An empty cabin," Mags says. "Nothing else. No internal power. No lighting. But also, no bodies hanging from the ceiling."

"But I saw—"

"Even Zoe's not sure what she saw," Vichy says, cutting

her off.

"But the door," Dante replies. "The door itself is proof. Something caused it to buckle."

Vichy shrugs.

Mags says, "Whatever you saw, it was long gone by the time we got there." She pauses, picking her next few words carefully. "Naz thinks you're confused."

"He thinks I lied about what I saw?"

"He thinks you exaggerated. Not intentionally. We're all under a lot of stress, Dee. He thinks you saw what you wanted to see, precisely what you described to us beforehand back on the bridge. He thinks even you doubt yourself. That's why you ran out into the corridor."

"And you?" Dante asks.

Mags hesitates. "I don't know what to think. Zoe says it was insanely dark in there. She said she knows you saw something that frightened you—something other than the inside of one of the cabins, but even she's not entirely sure what it was."

"But you saw them, though, right?" Dante says, addressing Vichy. "You saw the bodies. You saw that thing charging at me."

"I don't know what I saw," Vichy says, stammering. "I—I was watching you. I was reaching for Zoe. I saw shadows—

something moving. Damn. It's like you said. Memories are hard to focus. They're a haze. A blur. Especially when you're under pressure.

"I was scared. For you. For me. For Zoe. I was too busy grabbing the fire extinguisher and spraying it through the gap to think about anything other than getting you the hell out of there."

"But it was real," Dante says, and yet her words sound hollow. Nothing's real anymore.

"I know. I know," Vichy says. "I don't know exactly what I saw in there, but it sure as hell wasn't the inside of Zoe's cabin."

"And Cap?" she asks.

From off to one side, a familiar voice says, "Apparently, I'm an alien."

Cap is leaning against the doorway leading from medical to the carousel. He walks in slowly, staying over by the window. Dante sits up in surprise, not having seen him standing there, wondering just how long he's been listening.

"And I'm going insane," she replies, playing along with his charade. He must know how threatened she feels as he keeps his distance. Even now, he remains where he is, looking down at his shoes, seemingly searching for the right words to speak.

"You saw what they wanted you to see," he says, echoing Vichy. "Don't you get it? They're playing you."

"They?" Dante asks.

Cap smiles, trying not to laugh as he shakes his head. He sits on the edge of the window. It's as though he's taunting her, blocking her view of the stars, knowing how much they mean to her.

"Dee," Mags says, but Dante cuts her off.

"You're on his side?" she asks in alarm. She had hope to rally support from her closest friend but she finds only doubts. "You think I'm mad. But I'm not. I'm right. I know I am."

Mags says, "It's like Vichy said, we're all under a lot of pressure."

Cap says, "If we're going to get out of this, we have to work together."

The problem is, he's not wrong. There's no point of logic on which Dante can fight him. Given the chance, she would make the same appeal to the rest of the crew. The difference is, he's insincere, manipulating her. Or is he? Has she been wrong about him all along? Whoever he is, there's no guile or bitterness, at least none she can detect. Was Angel right? By focusing on the two of them, has Dante inadvertently aided the real intruders, allowing them to hide and continue misleading the crew from the shadows?

Benson comes running in. He's grinning. He's oblivious to the mood within medical.

"You were right," he says, waving his flex around as though it were proof of some scientific discovery. "Colors. Colors are the key."

"What do you mean?" Vichy asks as the rest of the crew follow along behind Benson, making their way into medical. Benson's excited, unable to contain himself.

"Dante was right about how to expose these creatures. They can't see color. That has to be a given as there's nothing to see beyond shades of grey. Colors are entirely subjective. Physically, they couldn't possibly see the same colors we do as what we see is an evolutionary illusion. Colors are contrived. They don't exist outside of our eyes. They're entirely arbitrary, depending on our physiology."

"But it didn't work," Mags says, confused.

"She's right," Dante says, fighting against her own stubborn pride. Some things are easier to say than others. For Dante, it's easier to say, *'She's right,'* than to admit the corollary, *'I was wrong.'* Benson, though, doesn't agree, which Dante finds peculiar.

"Three colors," he says.

Benson holds up a flex with three large colored dots on it.

"Look at this green dot. Green occurs at a wavelength of 535 nanometers."

Like a kindergarten teacher working with preschoolers, he turns slowly, pointing at the green blob, keeping his index finger right below it, making sure everyone can see it, looking for them to acknowledge him. Naz screws up his face. He clearly thinks Benson's mad. Zoe laughs at the childish manner in which Benson is making his point. Mags shakes her head in disbelief, but her eyes follow the tablet and a smile settles on her lips. Angel takes him seriously, focusing intently on his every move.

"Now, look at the yellow dot. Yellow is 590 nanometers. The difference is 55 nanometers. Are you with me?"

"No one's with you," Dante says. Benson laughs her off, shaking his head and still grinning. He points at the last colored circle.

"Red is the outlier, right? 760 nanometers. The difference when moving to red is huge. It's three to four times higher than the jump from green to yellow. An additional 170 nanometers more than yellow. 225 nanometers more than green. Physically, we see three different colors, but what we don't see is the extreme difference in wavelengths. The inconsistencies."

"We've been down this road before," Cap says. "I see red, yellow and green. Maybe Angel doesn't, but I do."

"Ah," Benson says, holding a finger to his lips. "Only you, Cap. Only you."

Benson uses his index finger to drag the large red dot on top of the green one. As each of the circles is semi-transparent and Benson's a little sloppy, not quite fitting one exactly over the other, slithers of green and red are visible on the fringe of the large circles.

"What color is that?" he asks.

Although he was initially calm, Cap seems to panic. His eyes dart around the crew, settling on Angel.

"Wait a minute. She's the one that's color blind. Ask her."

"No," Angel says, gesturing toward the flex. "Please. Go ahead. Be my guest."

"I don't know what you think you're going to prove by this," Cap says, but he's lost the confidence that normally accompanies his comments.

Dante coaxes him on, saying, "Well?"

"It's a trick, right?" Cap says.

"Not for any of us," Zoe replies, and that's the point at which Cap knows he's lost them. Dante can see it in his eyes. He didn't expect this. Benson's caught him off-guard.

"Come on, Cap," Naz says, reveling in the reversal of roles. No arrows to muck around with this time.

"You want me to say yellow, but you're setting me up," Cap says. No one responds. "That's why you included a yellow dot to start with. It's a feint."

"You really are an alien," Mac says, getting up and walking over toward Cap with clenched fists.

"You're bluffing. You haven't changed the wavelengths," Cap says. "The colors overlap but their wavelengths have remained the same."

"Yep," Benson says, agreeing with him in principle, but no one's looking at Benson. All eyes are on Cap.

"It's just a muddle of red and green."

"The correct term is added primaries," Benson says.

Naz and Mac flank him, addressing Dante as they say, "What do you want us to do with him?"

"It's not a separate color," Cap says as though that's somehow a defense.

"It's yellow," Dante says, turning around and sitting with her feet dangling over the edge of the bed. "Green and red make yellow. Everyone knows that."

Benson adds, "Every human knows that."

Zoe says, "Every human can see that."

"But the numbers. They're all wrong," Cap says. "Yellow makes no sense."

Dante shakes her head, struggling to suppress a wicked smile. "Now, you're really starting to learn something about us."

Cap backs away as Naz and Mac approach him.

"You can't hurt me," he says as the two men grab him by the shoulders and drag him over, pushing him roughly down into a seat. "You might think you can, but none of this is real."

"Who died," Dante asks.

"Me," Cap replies.

"Who else?"

Cap smiles, but doesn't respond. Dante's furious. It takes all her resolve not to step down from her bed and lash out at him. She wants nothing more than to rake the back of her hand across the side of his face, but it would be a mistake. She clenches the bed sheets in her fists.

"This ends now, do you hear me?"

Cap nods but doesn't show any emotion. It's almost as though he's disinterested. He's resigned to being exposed. If anything, it seems he expected this sooner. Mac adjusts his chair, turning him roughly, making sure he's facing Dante head on. There's something brutish and menacing about Mac's motion. Without using words, he's suggesting he can be far rougher, regardless of what's real.

"No lies," she says, reinforcing Mac's veiled threat.

After a few seconds, Cap begrudgingly replies, "No lies."

For Dante, it feels as though they've reached an impasse. Perhaps if both sides are stymied, being forthright might offer a solution—a kind of detente. If they're honest, perhaps they can both learn something about each other.

Through gritted teeth, she says, "We're going to die in here, aren't we?"

There's no hesitation from Cap, no bitterness, no hatred, no anger, just one word spoken without any emotion at all.

"Yes."

For him, this is a fact.

Mags paces across the floor behind him, making herself heard but keeping her voice quiet as she mutters half a dozen swear words in rapid succession. Dante can feel the anger seething deep within her. Mags wants to explode but holds herself back, knowing the importance of what Dante's doing by getting Cap to talk. The two women lock eyes for a moment. Mags pulls her lips tight, clenching her jaw. In any other context, she'd rip his head off. Dante's not sure how long she can contain the crew. She's got to get answers.

"Is Angel one of you?"

"No."

Again, his answer is quick, almost as if he anticipated the question and was waiting with an answer, but his response takes Dante by surprise. A knot tightens in her chest. Guilt washes over her at the realization she's betrayed a friend. Angel, though, is silent. She simply nods in agreement. For her, at least, now is not the time for recriminations. That'll come soon enough. Dante's got to stay focused.

"Are there any others among us?" she asks.

"Yes."

Heads turn around medical. Eyes dart between the crew, shifting from one person to another.

"Ah, now wait a minute," Angel says, holding her hands out with her palms raised and her fingers splayed wide, wanting to stop the conversation. "Don't tell me you actually believe him. Why the hell would you believe him?"

"Angel," Naz says, exasperated. "He just cleared you of being one of them!"

"He just admitted he was lying to you," she says. "So why do you believe him now?"

Dante is confused, but she doesn't want the conversation to spiral off on a tangent so quickly. She has more questions for Cap, but Benson breaks into the discussion.

"Are you saying you *are* one of them?" he asks, confused by Angel's rebuttal.

"No, but my point is valid. Why trust him? Okay, so we're going to die in here. No shit. I didn't need him to tell me that.

Am I one of them? No. I also didn't need him to say that. You guys did, but not me. I know who I am. Are there any others among us? Regardless of what he says, do you really think I'm going to believe anything that comes out of his mouth?"

Zoe asks, "If he told the truth about you, why would he lie now?"

Angel laughs, shaking her head. "Why wouldn't he? Oh my God. We are so fucking stupid." She holds out her hands again, signaling an apology in advance to Zoe, who looks insulted, perhaps a little hurt. "No offense, but we are—collectively—all of us."

"You're saying we shouldn't believe him?" Benson asks, still trying to unravel the conversation.

Angel points at Cap.

"I'm saying, nothing he says can be trusted. Anything he says is irrelevant. Anything he says, regardless of whether it's true or not, is spoken for one reason and one reason alone."

Dante completes her thought. "To manipulate us."

"Thank you," Angel says, nodding in acknowledgment. "You see, it's not about truth or lies. It's about direction. Trajectory. It's about misleading us. The truth can be just as damaging as a lie. It's all about the delivery."

"Wait?" Vichy says. "I'm not following this. If he's lying, he's trying to inject uncertainty, wanting to get us to doubt ourselves. I get that. But if he's telling the truth, isn't that a good thing?"

"Is it a good thing to be manipulated?" Angel asks. "We need to make our own decisions, draw our own conclusions. We shouldn't take anything from him. Nothing. Not a goddamn thing."

Cap is silent. He may have been cold and sterile with his words, offering only one-word answers, but Angel's on fire, and he seems to be quietly relishing the volcanic eruption he's unleashed. It's as though he anticipated her anger. Angel looks at him with disgust. Spittle flies from her lips as she points at each of the crew in turn.

"You don't know what it's like. You've flown under the radar. You don't understand how it feels to be accused, despised, not trusted, hated, and all without reason, all because you were nervous, because you tried too hard to fit in, because you made the mistake of wanting to be normal just like everyone else."

Cap smiles, only slightly, but his lips turn upwards. His cheeks rise, unable to hide his delight.

"Look at him," Angel says, jabbing at the air, pointing at him with disdain. "He loves this shit. You want to know why he told the truth? Because he knew it would tear us apart."

She shakes her head.

"I didn't know. I mean, I knew about myself, but I didn't know if he was or wasn't one of them. All I knew was we were in the same boat, but look at him now.

"Do you want to know why he cleared me? Because he knew it would unleash more hurt and confusion. Don't you see? He's weaponized doubt. He's using our own emotions against us, isolating us from one another. And now look at us. We're paralyzed with uncertainty."

"Fuck," Mags says.

"Thank you for your succinct and invaluable contribution," Angel replies, tilting her head to acknowledge her. "Fuck indeed."

Zoe says, "So there may or may not be another one of them among us."

"For all I know," Angel replies. "It could be you, but regardless, look at his intent. He *wants* to sow discord. He wants us divided. Why?"

"To distract us?" Benson says, but Dante knows.

"They're stalling. They want to delay us."

Angel points at her, screwing her face up tight and not saying anything, but she clearly likes the logic. For Dante, it's a relief to see Angel isn't holding a grudge.

"Well, this is fucking great," Mac says.

"Don't believe him," Angel says, turning to face the others. "Do not believe anything he says."

Naz still isn't settled on the idea. "Now wait a minute. Let me get this straight. You're saying we shouldn't believe him at all—on anything?"

Angel nods.

He points at her, looking down his finger as though it were the barrel of a gun. "So we shouldn't believe him when he says you're *not* one of them?"

Again, Angel nods. She offers no further explanation. Intuitively, Dante can see what she's trying to do. Rather than wrestling with arguments and reasoning with the crew, she wants them to arrive at their own conclusions.

"So," Naz says, working himself through the logic. "Nothing he's said has any bearing on whether or not you're an alien?"

"Nope."

"We just have to decide for ourselves?"

"Not we," Angel says. "You. Don't make this about anyone else. You have to decide. You can't run from this. You can't abandon this to someone else. You cannot out-source your beliefs to one of us. You have to make your own decision about what you believe."

Naz turns to Mac. "I think my head is about to explode."

"She's right," Dante says, feeling compelled to support Angel. "We can't abdicate our responsibility to make our own decisions. We can't hide behind the decision of others or simply flock to the most popular opinion."

It takes all of Dante's emotional strength to follow up with, "That would be a mistake." Given her earlier accusation of Angel, that's a bitter pill on her tongue.

Naz says, "I liked it better when we had to pick between those stupid arrows." To which Mac laughs.

"I don't get it," Vichy says. "Why did you lie about the colors?"

"You don't understand," Angel says, shaking her head with a sense of exasperation. "You were looking for an imposter. I *am* an imposter. Just not in the way you think.

"All my life, I've been second," Angel lets out a solitary laugh. There are tears in the corners of her eyes. "You guys. You have no idea what it's like to be on the B-team. But me? All of my goddamn life!

"My mother died when I was seven. I don't know that my dad was ever sober again. I rarely did homework because I was too busy working to put food on the table. Me and my sisters ate a helluva lot of ramen.

"My boyfriend got me through college. I don't know that his parents ever noticed the additional costs. As for NASA, someone somewhere read an obscure research paper on nuclear magnetic resonance in the formation of quasar relativistic jets and I was given a wild card entry for selection."

A single tear rolls down her cheek. She looks Dante in the eye. As much as Dante wants to look away, feeling overwhelmed with guilt, she fights to maintain eye contact as Angel continues.

"Do you know why I never gave up on that goddamn treadmill back in selection? I couldn't. I had *nothing* to go back to. I would have died rather than give up. That's the only time I ever came first at anything."

Dante swallows the lump in her throat. She nods, appreciating Angel's resolve.

Angel finally addresses Vichy's original question. "You want to know why I lied? I felt intimidated. By you. By her. By everyone onboard the Acheron. You're all so goddamn perfect. So yeah, I lied. I made a fucking mistake."

She walks around Cap, facing him, looking down at him with anger boiling inside, but Cap isn't fazed. He keeps his head square, facing Dante, watching her reactions and ignoring Angel. She sighs.

"Hell," she says, gesturing to Dante, making as though she wants to draw her physically closer. "What's that thing I've got?"

Sheepishly, Dante says, "Anomalous Trichromat Protanomaly."

"That's it. I never did like those fancy words."

Angel purses her lips, lost in thought. No one dares speak, giving her the space she needs to articulate the weight bearing down on her. Even Cap seems to sense the importance of the moment. Perhaps this is what these creatures really want—to observe the nuance that is humanity.

"Do you know what's funny about being color blind?" She points at herself. "I don't think I'm blind. I can see. Apparently, you guys just see a little more than me, that's all, but I have no idea quite what you see.

"At the age of thirteen, they told me I have red-weakness. They told me red is actually quite bright or something. They say there are more blues—blues with red in them. Hell, I don't know. All I know is I'm not actually blind. God, I hate that term."

She leans back, trying to stop the tears from running down her cheeks, but she can't and she's forced to wipe them away.

"The thing is—up until then I thought I was normal. You know, just like everyone else. But I wasn't. I was different. *I was less.* So then I go through selection. And all of a sudden, I'm told I'm better than everyone else. Hah! Me? Better than *billions* of other people on the planet? Really? '*Yes, you,*' they said."

She taps the side of her head, touching lightly at her temple.

"But I know better. I know I'm not. I'm an imposter. I spent the next nine years wondering when I was going to be caught out, right up until launch. So yeah, when Dante showed us those colors, I wanted to fit in bad, real bad. I did not want to be the freak."

"I'm so sorry," Dante says, but Angel cuts her off before she can continue.

"I know," Angel says. She points at Cap as she addresses the rest of the crew. "Don't you see. This is precisely what he wants. He wants her to feel guilty. He wants all of you to second guess yourselves. None of this is random or haphazard."

She laughs before continuing. "Do you want to know what I thought?"

Angel jabs at the air, singling out Dante. "I thought *she* was an alien. I thought she was trying to set me up so I pushed back, probing, looking for answers, looking for weaknesses, inconsistencies.

"I didn't like being on the outside of the group, but it did have some advantages. I was able to observe you and think about your little rebellion and how it might play out with these creatures. And I think I know why the original color thing didn't work."

"It should have, right?" Dante says.

"Yes," Angel replies. "Benson's right. Colors aren't real."

"But neither is this," Vichy says. "None of this. I don't see how we can rely on anything in here."

"So why didn't it work?" Dante asks, not liking the way Vichy cut off Angel. Dante doesn't want to break Angel's train of thought.

"I thought the answer would be obvious," Angel says. "Think about it."

Dante's not sure what she should be thinking about. Her brain simply doesn't work that way. She's about to shrug when it hits her.

"Assumptions," she says, remembering the warning of Dr. Romero.

"Yes," Angel replies. "We knew they were impersonating us, but we assumed we knew what that meant—simple mimicry, but what if it was something more?"

"Oh," Dante says as the implication dawns on her. "You think they're using us. You think they're using the bodies of the deceased."

Angel grits her teeth, nodding with grim focus. "I think they dissected them. Analyzed them. They needed to probe the dynamics of the human body."

Dante completes the thought, "That's why they could see colors. They knew what to look for."

"We assumed it's either/or," Angel says. "That either we're talking to an alien or a human, but what if that's not the case? What if we're talking to an alien that's reanimated or perhaps co-opted a human body? Or one that's examined an eyeball and looked at its limitations."

"They wouldn't be fooled," Dante says as the realization hits her like a freighter running a blockade.

"Exactly."

"But the color yellow," Benson says. "That requires working eyes, right? Not just the analysis of the cones and rods."

"Yes," Angel replies. "For all their mastery of this illusion, matching the physics and even the operation of computerized components and mechanical parts like doors and locks, there are faults—flaws."

"Imperfections," Benson says.

Angel says, "Lies never come easy."

Cap watches Angel closely. His eyes narrow. Dante wants to say something. She wants to shift the focus back onto him.

Angel seems to realize what she's thinking.

"As for this piece of shit," she says with disdain dripping from her words, marching around to face him. "The worst thing about him is knowing the man I love is dead."

HONESTY

"So what are we going to do with this fucker?" Mac asks.

"What can we do?" Mags asks. "Like he said, none of this is real."

Zoe says, "I for one wouldn't mind watching him squirm inside an evacuated airlock."

"Might wipe the smirk off his face," Naz says.

Vichy is unusually quiet. He seems preoccupied. Dante wants to talk to him, to bounce some ideas off him, but doesn't feel comfortable voicing her doubts in front of the rest of the crew. It seems testosterone is a substitute for any real action. Bluster and bravado have always been a placebo for substance. As much as she wants to join in the trash talk, she can't. Cap is facing her. Nothing that's said elicits so much as a twitch from his face. He holds his steely gaze on her. That's a challenge Dante can embrace. She locks eyes with him, unsure of her next move but not wanting to show any weakness.

"You don't know, do you?" Cap asks.

"Oh, I have my suspicions," Dante replies, which causes the others to fall silent. "The experiment's coming to an end, isn't it?"

"You don't understand what you are?" Cap says, laughing, only it sounds hollow—fake. All pretense is gone. Dante may be speaking with Cap, but the intelligence driving his responses originated from within some other alien biosphere. "You don't even know what you are."

Dante feels a sense of vertigo. The room seems to swing around her. Jeeves said the same thing. Were they listening? Was that even Jeeves or yet another imposter? *Twinkle, twinkle, little star, oh how I wonder...*

She closes her eyes, squeezing them tight, wanting to shut out everything except this moment, determined not to fall foul of this insipid creature. Her lips tighten. Her jaw clenches. The muscles in her shoulders and arms stiffen, ready for a fight she knows will never actually come.

"Try me," she replies, staring down at him with contempt. "What am I?"

"A waterfall."

Dante is on the verge of laughing. She turns, looking at Mags and then Zoe, wanting to gauge their reactions. They too are incredulous. Benson shakes his head. Such an idea is ridiculous. As far as metaphors go, it's lousy.

"What is a waterfall?" Cap asks, playing to their scorn.

"I don't know," Dante says, humoring him, holding her hands out wide and gesturing in a blend of amusement and disdain. "What is a waterfall?"

"It's something that is nothing," he replies. "It's not a thing, but a process, an event, an occurrence."

"Water falls over a cliff," Dante says. "How is that anything like me?"

"Water isn't actually part of a waterfall. It simply passes through the falls and then it is gone," Cap replies. "In the same way, every aspect of your lives is transitory. From the *two million* blood cells that die every second within your arteries to your skin, your hair, your bones, the fiber of your muscles, the neurons in your brain. None of them last much more than a handful of years. They just trickle a little slower over the rocks. You are water cascading down the side of a cliff, only you don't know it. And one day, the river will run dry."

Dante falls silent.

"Everything about you is fleeting. Everything except for one thing—consciousness. That's the only thing that remains constant throughout your entire lives."

In that moment, Cap's eyes go dark, no longer retaining any white or even the pupils. His eyes refuse to reflect the subtle hints of light around them. The glossy sheen is gone, replaced with something akin to the membranes Dante saw in earlier reboots. Any humanity Cap had evaporates. He no longer blinks. It's as though he's blind and yet Dante's aware he can see her all too clearly.

"Why you?" he asks. At first, Dante's confused, so he clarifies. "Don't you ever wonder about yourself? You're here—now. Why?"

"Space and time, right?" she asks, understanding the gist of his point. "Out of 13.8 *billion* years and a diameter of at least 93 *billion* light years, why am I here in space? Here in time?" She shrugs. "Why do I occupy this tiny slither of space-time? I don't know that there is a reason. Life is about finding meaning, not having it to start with."

Cap nods. A slight smile escapes his lips. Dante's acutely aware she's gaining insights into the workings of an alien mind as it strives to comprehend human consciousness.

He says, "Think of how preposterous you are. You're a collection of molecules that is insignificant on any scale—whether relative to this module, the ship, an asteroid, a comet, or a planet. You're pitifully small compared to even a dwarf star—and yet here you are."

"Here I am," she replies, only her words are measured, probing, wanting to draw this strange creature into more dialogue.

"It's your arrogance that fascinates us."

Us.

That gets her attention. Dante wonders how adept these creatures are at reading body language. They seem to pick up on non-verbal clues, and for the most part, these are reactions she can't screen. A slight twist of her head reveals her surprise with far more fidelity than anything she could say. As if in response, the avatar that is Cap purses his lips, pausing in thought before continuing.

"You think of arrogance as an insult, but I mean it as a compliment. There's something surprising and utterly unique about your perspective. You assume importance. Your literature speaks of individual rights but you're a contradiction."

Without meaning to, Dante's eyebrows twitch, rising slightly in alarm at the confirmation these creatures have trawled through their documents and videos. As if in response to her thoughts, Cap elaborates.

"Your movies are—honestly—embarrassing. You entertain yourselves with depictions of us as monsters. We are the mythical beasts of your ancient past, destined to be vanquished by a mighty hero. We are Medusa. Hydra. Cyclops. The Minotaur.

"All the aliens you imagine today are but the monsters of

yesteryear. Think about that. Why would that be so? What does that tell you about the inner working of your own mind? Your fears? Your frail culture? What does that expectation say about your own dark desires? Your failings?"

"But are you?" Dante asks, stuttering. "Are you a monster?"

"Are you?" he replies, raising an eyebrow. "What you see before you is a mirror."

Dante preferred Cap with human eyes. Her natural desire is to make eye contact, but the darkness teases her, tormenting her. She has no doubt it's deliberate, intended to leave her feeling unsettled, and damn, it works.

"You're the alpha," he says, which is such an unusual term it elicits micro-movements as her eyes narrow and her brow shifts with the intensity of her concentration. "Your battles. Those of Perseus, Oedipus, Heracles and Odysseus. What are they but your own anxieties personified? Your heroes are who you want to but can never be."

Cap says, "Every other species on your planet is inferior to you—only they're not. You like to think they are. You pride yourself on being different, only you're blind to reality. You're animals. You are the monsters."

"So are you," Dante replies, and yet her words sound hollow. No sooner have those hastily rushed words left her lips than doubts creep in. Why would this extraterrestrial intelligence single them out as biological entities to its own exclusion? Is she dealing with an alien or some alien machine? Was Jeeves right? Is this an artificial intelligence? But what about what she saw in the murky depths of medical when she was rescuing Zoe? Cap has always maintained she saw what she wanted to see. Was that contrived by her own fears? Did she see what she imagined them to be? Did they fabricate that illusion to match her expectations of what an alien should be? Raw and visceral?

Cap continues, only he sounds anything but alien.

"What does it mean to be alive? To be conscious?"

Mags has stopped pacing. Like the others, she's deflated. Fight or flight—that's all they've ever known. That's the human—no, the animalistic response to a threat, only it doesn't apply here. There's nowhere to run to. No one to fight. In the absence of that evolutionary survival mechanism, all that can be found is inertia. Resignation. Defeat. Depression. There's not a goddamn thing any of them can do when faced with this alien threat, and that leaves them all feeling deflated. Dante tries to stay strong. She might be able to fool the others, perhaps even Cap, but she can't fool herself. She knows. The alien imposter, though, doesn't seem to care.

"Have you ever watched a horse being born, or a dolphin?"

Cap continues, speaking as though he has intimate, firsthand knowledge of the ecosystems on Earth.

"Immediately, they assess the world around them. There's simply too much to process for them *not* to be conscious. Without conscious awareness, they could never deal with the complexity that is life. Being conscious is the key. It's the filter. It's the ability to make sense of the overwhelming and often contradictory sensory inputs assaulting us, demanding we arrive at a decision, an action."

Us?

We?

Dante was more comfortable with a clear divide between the crew and their captors. Monsters can be faced. So long as they're *them* and not *us*, they're easy to defeat. Something has to be done about *them*. *They're* chased. Hunted. Killed. But us? Is this why the aliens have kept them alive? Do they somehow feel an affinity with humanity? What the hell happened down there on P4?

Good and evil should be clear-cut, black and white. They can't be us. They must be different. Monsters are inhuman—only sometimes they're not.

Up until this point, Dante's assumed they were attacked, that the aliens were the aggressors, but it was the crew of the Acheron that invaded the dark depths of the subterranean lake on P4. All this would be much easier if these creatures were the aliens of her nightmares, with shiny black exoskeletons and saliva dripping from needle-sharp teeth, but 'us' leaves her unsettled.

The other possibility is she's hearing what she wants to hear, that she's still being played—yet again. Like the soldiers in countless wars on Earth, Dante wants someone to point at the enemy and say, "*Them*. They're not one of us. *Kill them.*" Us undermines that notion. She wants to hate them. The crew are being held captive against their will, and yet she's curious about another intelligence that evolved around some other star.

For all the advances over the past five hundred years, from the science of physics to biology and philosophy, no one on Earth is any closer to defining consciousness. Oh, there are the dull, sterile, dictionary definitions and spiritualistic mumbo jumbo, but it's all just a guess. In some ways, it's like trying to imagine how a computer chip works having never seen anything beyond its black outer casing, having no idea about its intricate, microscopic, electronic structure. It seems the soul is as incomprehensible as magic. Technically, everything she needs to know is right there, but something's missing, some explanation for which there's no substitute.

"Why you?" she asks, reversing the question as she addresses Cap, intently aware the others are watching her, looking to take their cue from her.

"Like you, we're—"

"No," she says roughly, being quite firm as she interrupts him. Dante doesn't want a facile answer. She wants to understand. "Not your species. Not your generation or team or whatever. You personally."

"We're not that different," alien Cap says with eyes as dark as the night.

"Oh, no," Dante says, wagging her finger in front of him. "You don't get to say that. You have to prove that!"

Cap pauses. Before he can speak again, Dante says, "You don't know, do you? That's why you went with the whole waterfall thing."

Cap's eyebrows narrow, which is a distinctly human response for an alien.

"For all your bullshit and reasoning, you still don't know," she says. "Oh, you've got your fancy definitions and psychoanalysis. You can watch us, tease us, even dissect us, but you have no answers either. You have no more idea about what it means to be alive than we do."

She points at Angel.

"It's easy to say she's conscious, she's self-aware, but how about you? Why are you here? Why are you experiencing this? You personally?"

Cap says, "Like you, I'm here now."

"But you know that's not an answer," Dante replies. "Why you and not someone else, another of your kind." She laughs. "There's no reason for any of us, is there? Not us personally. Not really. We could be zombies. We could be machines. Programs. We could be anyone else but us and the result would largely be the same, and yet here we are—so why us?"

Given the way the alien previously used the term *us* to unsettle her, Dante feels justified in driving that point home. Two can play hard ball.

"That's the problem, isn't it?" she says. "Why am I here for this brief moment in time?"

She articulates her next words carefully, making sure they roll off her tongue with passion, wanting him to empathize with her position.

"Me? Why me?"

"We're a contradiction," he says, and for a moment, she believes him. Previously, it was humanity that was the contradiction, but in his last few responses Cap has used the inclusive pronoun, including both sentient celestial species in his reply. On some level, she's getting through to him. For once, she's manipulating him.

"So tell me," she says, "You're smart. You're alive. You're

aware, but what does that mean?" She squints slightly, looking carefully at him as she asks, "What are you?"

Cap is quiet. He looks uncomfortable.

Dante leans forward on the bed, pushing almost to the point of falling forward and landing on her feet, but she feels as though she needs to get a better look at him, a man she's known for over a decade, someone who's become a puppet for some other alien intelligence. Cold, dark, empty black eyes stare back at her, but she's looking for something metaphorical, not physical. The act of focusing helps her zero her mind.

With softly spoken words, she asks, "What happens when you die?"

Dante's curious as to whether these creatures have any kind of religious belief numbing the harsh finality of death. Or perhaps they rationalize their demise in some other way, with equally empty notions such as dying for their country or planet or their children or species or some other cultural idiosyncrasy.

"All of space and time comes to an end," he says.

"Only it doesn't," she replies.

"For me, it will," Cap says.

"You're afraid," Dante says as the thought dawns on her like a nearby star emerging from behind a darkened planet.

"Here, for all this time, we've been in fear of our lives, unsure what the hell we're dealing with, only it's you that's afraid."

Cap shifts slightly in his seat. This is the first time she's seen any physical response since Mac and Naz dumped him in front of her. As much as she wants to break eye contact and look to them for confirmation, naturally wanting to ensure they're following all this, she knows that would be a mistake. For now, it's just the two of them—her and the alien. It's as though they're the only sentient beings in the entire universe. Both of them are looking for answers. For once, her alien captor is at a loss for words. That's a first.

"We shouldn't be fighting," she says, looking for any semblance of emotion in his facial features but nothing is forthcoming. On one level, she's playing him exactly as he played her. On another, she's entirely serious. Part of her is seeking to disrupt his reasoning, wanting to tilt a sense of Stockholm's syndrome in her favor, but on the other hand, she's looking for hope.

He laughs. "You think there can be peace between us?"

"Why not?"

The alien that is Cap gestures around him, taking them all in.

"Peace is an illusion. It's as fickle as all of this." He points at her. "You can't fool me. I've read your history. You've never known peace on your world. Not real peace. What makes you think you could ever know it out here among the stars?

"No, the only peace you've ever known has come from the barrel of a gun. You find peace by exploiting others. You see conflict on your own world and find peace by turning away and closing your eyes, pretending all the petty, selfish, self-centered ideologies that lead to war don't exist."

He laughs.

"And your so-called peace never lasts. Why is that, Dee? What does that tell you about your species?"

Damn, he's good, using her nickname to disarm her, slamming her with irrefutable logic.

"You think you can sway me?" he asks, opening his arms wide and inviting a response. "You think you can turn me? Come on then. Tell me. What is there about any of your lives that suggests peace is possible? Why should we let any of you live?"

"Life is a privilege," she says, struggling to hide the tremor in her voice. "A wonder beyond compare, more beautiful than the rings of a gas giant, more colorful than a nebula, more awe-inspiring that a spiral galaxy with hundreds of billions of stars. You said it yourself. Physically, we're insignificant and yet we aren't. Life is the greatest marvel in the universe. We deserve a chance."

For Dante, this is a cry for mercy, but Cap's facial features harden. He looks at her through darkened eyes.

"You're alive, aren't you?"

"Cap's not," she replies, staring him down.

"That was unfortunate," the creature says, which for Dante is revealing. He could have claimed Cap's death was an accident. She wouldn't know. Perhaps one of the crew down on P4 at the time might, but she wouldn't. Unfortunate, suggests it was deliberate and, to her horror, avoidable. It lies about her recollection of being on P4 with Cap, leaving her wondering how she can distinguish between manufactured memories and real ones. If it wasn't Cap down there on the rescue mission, who was it? Who was standing beside the airlock? Who was in the control room?

"Does it bother you?" Dante asks, being deliberately vague. She's leading her statement, drawing it out, making him wait for the subject of her question, wanting it to be personal. "That you've been called on to interrogate us? To torture us?"

He shrugs, asking, "Did it bother you when you launched out into space?"

Like Dante, the alien hides the true subject of his question, teasing her, toying with her. He relishes the confusion it causes. His eyes narrow as he delivers his actual question with delight. "Did you even think about the billions you left behind?"

She's confused. He clarifies.

"According to your own historical records, people were starving. Dying. Men, women and children in other parts of your world. From disease, war, famine. And you left them. What were they to you? Just numbers?"

"No," she says, feeling her face go flush as sweat forms in her palms.

"You could have helped. You're a doctor. But no, you boarded a spacecraft instead. Does that bother you?"

"It's not like that," she says, feeling she has to defend herself. Deep down, Dante knows it's futile. The very act of being defensive puts lie to her position. Regardless, she blurts out, "We have to look forward. To look up. To the future."

"Why?"

"Because we need hope. We. We need..."

"Need what?" Cap asks. He can see she's uncomfortable. "What is it you need, Dante? Water? Food? Shelter? Safety? Peace? That's what they needed. What did you need when you launched into the unknown?"

Her lips go dry. As she fails to speak, Cap continues, saying, "You turned your back on them."

"We can do both," she says. "You don't understand. You couldn't."

"What don't I understand?" Cap asks. "How you can be so cruel to yourselves?"

She hangs her head, shaking it slowly.

"We need to explore. For us, it's like breathing. Without exploration, we'd suffocate. All those problems, they'd only get worse if we turned inward."

Cap nods. To her surprise, he's content with that answer. Seems the aliens are done learning about humanity in the abstract and want to zero in on individuals like her. Nothing that's happening to her is haphazard. Everything she's exposed to is deliberate.

"So what are you?" she asks, shifting back onto the offensive. "A waterfall?"

Cap smiles, shaking his finger back and forth. "You'll have to do better than that."

"Who is it?" Benson asks, breaking into the discussion and shattering the flow of the conversation, but it's clearly been bugging him and he can no longer remain silent. Dante clenches, wishing she could rewind the moment and get him to be quiet, but Benson continues, asking, "Who's the other alien among us?"

Cap's dark eyes never leave Dante. His head remains

resolute, facing her as he says, "You know. You've always known. You just don't want to admit it."

Dante looks up. Her eyes dart around the crew, unsure what he means.

Mags has her hand by her mouth, covering her lips, stunned by what she's hearing.

Zoe's got her arms folded across her chest, but not in a manner that signals defiance. She's not shutting anyone out. On the contrary, she's seeking solace, wanting to be held, even if only by her own slender arms.

Benson is perplexed. His head is cocked slightly as he tries to decipher Cap's words, wondering precisely what Dante supposedly knows—only she doesn't understand what Cap meant either. She's as confused by Cap's statement as Benson is.

Mac is leaning against the narrow bench that doubles as a windowsill. He's tense. His arms are straight while his shoulders are hunched. His clenched jaw speaks of the stress he feels. Across from him, Naz is somewhat dejected, sitting on the edge of Dante's desk. He's pushed her equipment aside and is sitting with his feet dangling just inches off the floor. Unlike Mac, his shoulders have slouched, having lost the bluster that surged through them less than ten minutes ago. Vichy, though, looks fresh. He's not bothered at all.

"Oh, Vee," she says as the realization hits. "Not you. No. Please."

Betrayal strikes at her like a dagger plunging through her chest and sinking deep into her heart. Dante should have seen this long ago. All the clues were there. From the start, Vee was unusually curious, asking her what she saw in the stars. When she confronted Cap on the bridge, he cut her off, sowing doubts about what was actually happening during those first few reboots.

Vichy had a clear view from the corridor outside Zoe's cabin, but he never backed up her account of what she saw. Oh, he made his doubts sound plausible, but she never got the support she needed. He did just enough to keep her close, but not enough to strengthen her, always leaving her feeling alone.

Cap was the fall guy. Vichy was playing the long game. Get close. Stay quiet. Apply a soft touch, just a gentle push on the rudder to steer them in the wrong direction.

Dante feels like a fool. She completely misread what happened in the first few tests. The arrows. Vichy chose left, but what she should have considered more deeply is why Cap copied him. Cap felt he had to support Vichy, to help him blend in. She picked up on Cap being disingenuous, but never understood why. She never suspected Vee because he's left handed. Only he probably guessed at the answer, not wanting to parrot everyone else. It was a 50/50 choice between options both of the aliens knew were entirely bogus. She caught Cap's reaction but missed Vee's. They both chose the same direction because they were conspiring together. That explains the look Cap gave him back then. He thought that together they'd outplayed her.

Later, Vichy convinced Mags they should leave Angel to tend to Dante in medical. Why would her Vee do that? The only reason this Vee did that was to break her, only he didn't count on Angel showing compassion. After all, Angel's only human. No, he was hoping the two of them would turn on each other and tear each other apart. Angel, though, refused to play his little game.

Then there were the key points where Vichy was conspicuously quiet, like when Benson exposed Cap with the color yellow. Apparently, Vichy couldn't see it either as it took them both by surprise. Although the others were boisterous, he was subdued, thinking about his next play. While Mags, Mac and Naz were keen to exploit that weakness, Vichy stayed quiet. Only now Cap's given away the game. Why? That can only mean one thing. It's over. They're done with the interrogation. There's no point in keeping up the façade any longer. They're looking for one last reaction from which to learn.

The lights on the Acheron flicker, stuttering, plunging the craft into darkness several times a second. As the staggered failures increase in length, Dante becomes aware this isn't a power outage. It's not simply that the lights are going out. No, for those brief moments in time, nothing exists beyond the darkness. No spaceship. No planet. No stars.

Cap and Vichy remain motionless, but no one else does. They all seem to sense it—the end has come.

Benson rushes to the door, madly tearing at the control panel, only there's nothing to be done as there are no dead circuits to override. Naz hunts through the cabinets by the window, knowing where the emergency kit is stored within medical. He fires up a survival beacon. Even though it paints the module in a brilliant, blue glow, shining like a mini-star in his outstretch hand as it casts deep shadows across the deck, it too fails to pierce the flickering darkness. With each second that passes they fall in and out of the illusion. Slowly, the Acheron recedes, being replaced only with a dark, empty void.

Zoe and Mags join Dante, reaching out and holding each other's hands, determined not to be alone when the end comes. Instinctively, Dante keeps waiting for her eyes to adjust to the darkness around her, only there's no light at all. She can't see anything. It's as though she's blind. Rather than being anchored by the artificial gravity imparted by the Acheron, she's standing lightly, bouncing slightly on the balls of her feet, but she still has hold of Zoe and Mags.

"Is this it?" Mags asks. "Is this the end?"

Dante has to say something. She wants to lie but she can't. In that moment, her mind casts back to her last psych session and her determination to be honest in the midst of a catastrophe. Begrudgingly, Dante says the only thing she can.

"Yes."

DEATH ROW

"What the hell is happening?" Mac asks from somewhere deep within the pitch black darkness. "Where is everyone?"

"Over here," Dante yells, gripping Zoe with one hand and Mags with the other, not wanting to let them go. It's mutual. Their fingers interlock, squeezing tight, determined not to be torn apart.

"I can't see anything," Angel says, only like Mac, her voice echoes around Dante. Instead of being directional, with the sound giving Dante some idea where Angel actually is, echoes bounce around her. Angel's voice seems to come from everywhere at once, which isn't possible. Dante could swear Angel's behind her, but Dante's back was against the wall of medical just moments ago.

Oh, how she longs for the illusion. Even though she knew it was fake, back on the Acheron she felt grounded. In here, in whatever this void actually is, she feels disembodied. Is this reality? Is this all that's left of their lives when the illusion is stripped away? Dante can feel her arms and legs, but she can't see anything. It's as though there's nothing beyond the black void and that terrifies her.

"Over here," Mags says, leaning forward. Dante can feel Mags stepping out away from her. She must be swinging her other hand from side to side, reaching for the others in the darkness.

"What is this place?" Benson asks. Even though he's nowhere near her, his voice is akin to someone whispering in her ear and it takes her a moment to realize it's incredibly distant, as though he were standing at the far end of an old gym, with his voice echoing off an empty wooden floor.

Zoe mumbles, "Death row."

To Dante's surprise, fingers touch at her chest, padding softly at her skin, gently reaching up toward her shoulders and neck.

A familiar voice asks, "Who's that?"

"It's me," Dante replies as Angel's hand runs down her arm, touching at her wrist and then her hand, feeling how her fingers are interlocked with Zoe's.

"And that's me," Zoe says. Dante can hear Angel shuffling between the two of them, inching her way in the middle of them in the darkness. It's a curious choice. Rather than stepping around Zoe, she's stepped between them, turning to join them. Seems she feels more comfortable in between the two of them. Isn't that what they're all seeking? Comfort? Some assurance where none is to be found?

"Keep talking," Benson says, only it sounds as though he's becoming more distant.

"You're going the wrong way," Dante calls out.

"Are we blind?" Mac asks.

"God, I hope not," Angel says.

"I've got you," Mags calls out, apparently reaching out and grabbing one of the men.

"That's me," Mac says.

"Okay. Okay," Mags replies. "It's okay. I've got you. Okay?"

She's nervous, like the rest of the crew. Seems Mags is trying to talk herself into being brave. Dante's not sure she can do that. She can't fight the sense of grief welling up within her. They've lost Cap and Vichy—not moments ago—days, weeks, perhaps even months ago. And it seems they're next.

"What are we going to do?" Zoe asks.

"What can we do?" Angel replies. "Nothing beyond stay together. Right now, all we have is each other. We've got to stick together."

"Wait a minute," Mac says. "We're missing someone."

"Who?" Angel asks. Like Dante, she's probably already eliminated the alien imposters from the crew. Taking Cap and Vichy out of the equation leaves them unbalanced. It's no longer easy to gauge the crew composition. Everything's off-kilter. Dante runs a roll call in her head.

"Naz," Mac calls out in alarm. "Where the hell is Naz?"

Zoe yells, "Naz? Where are you?" But there's no reply.

"Oh, no," Angel says from the darkness, only there's trepidation in her voice. "She's gone."

"She?" Mags asks, confused by Angel's choice of pronoun. "Don't you mean, he?"

"Who's gone?" Dante asks, feeling panicked. "Where's Benson?"

"I thought we were talking about Naz?" Mags says.

"No, Zoe," Angel replies.

Dante's palms go sweaty. "Zoe's gone?"

"Haven't you got her?" Mags asks.

Dante's unsure whether Mags is addressing her or Angel. "I—ah."

"She was here," Angel says. "She was right here beside me—holding my hand."

"And?" Dante asks.

"And then she was gone."

"What do you mean gone?" Dante says, trying not to let the panic show in her voice. "Gone where?"

"I don't know. Just gone. I could feel her hand in mine one moment, then nothing the next, just my own fingers grabbing at my empty palm."

"Did she let go?" Mags asks. "Mac. Is Zoe with you?"

Although Dante appreciates Mags' sentiment, if Zoe was with Mac, she would have said something. "What is going on?" she asks.

"I haven't got her," Mac says. "I thought—"

The sudden silence mid-sentence is painful. All Dante can hear is her own breathing and her madly beating heart thumping within the darkness.

"Mac?" Mags asks, only her voice wavers with uncertainty. She's not expecting an answer. "He—He disappeared."

As Dante's holding her hand, she can feel Mags moving around, searching in the darkness, batting at it with her other hand. As much as Mags may want to search for Mac, shuffling around in the darkness, Dante is determined to stay still, keeping her feet firm. She holds her ground, not wanting to move. Dante tugs, pulling on Mags' arm, drawing her back. It seems, like Angel holding onto Zoe, Mags had a good hold on Mac's hand and then he too was just gone.

Dante hyperventilates. Her breathing is shallow and rapid, leaving her feeling lightheaded. It takes all her focus to slow herself down.

"Wh—" Dante begins to say, but Angel cuts her off.

"What the hell. Zoe? Mac? Where are you guys?"

"What about Benson?" Dante asks, realizing he's been forgotten amidst all the drama involving Zoe and Mac. She calls out, "Benson, can you hear us?"

"They're gone. They're all gone," Mags says, retreating beside Dante and squeezing her hand tight. "I—I had his hand. And then."

"Then what?"

There's no reply.

"Mags?" Dante calls out.

"She's gone," Angel says, only how does Angel know? Angel's holding Dante's hand, while Dante's holding, or was holding...

"Oh, no," Dante says, grabbing at the air in front of her. "No, no, no. Not Mags! Please, no."

"They're all dead," Angel says, turning and grabbing Dante. She wraps her arms around her neck and holds tight. Dante reacts immediately, clinging to Angel's waist.

"I'm sorry," Dante blurts out. "I'm so sorry."

"I don't want to go," Angel says, sobbing into her shoulder. "Not like this. Not without a fight. Not without any warning. Not—"

And with that she too is gone, leaving Dante grasping at the darkness.

Dante sinks to her knees, waiting for the inevitable, knowing there's no hope—not this time. Far from being a reboot, this is an extermination. One by one, each of the crew has winked out of existence.

Do they even know?

Is there enough time for the realization to hit?

What lies beyond this moment?

Dante knows. She'd rather she didn't but she can't lie to herself. Not this time. Outside of this moment, there's nothing—nothing at all. Her arms tremble, while her fingers shake uncontrollably. Instinctively, she grabs at them, trying to steady herself—as though anything she does actually matters. Her breaths come in short bursts. It's the loss of control, the frailty, the sense of being exposed and vulnerable that unsettles her. She's helpless.

Dante's never felt this way before, even when she sheltered from that tornado in a dirty, smelly, concrete bathroom a quadrillion miles away back in Alabama. She feels utterly defeated and without hope. Dante sniffs. Her nose is running. Tears are streaming down her cheeks, only they're not real either. For a fucking illusion, all this feels pretty goddamn real.

Dante wonders how long she'll have to wait and then she wonders no more.

DREADNOUGHT

A hand holds Dante's shoulder, dragging her roughly to one side, grabbing more at bone than muscle or sinew. Dante blinks but she can't see anything beyond a dark, fuzzy blob moving within a blinding white blur. Thick mucus clings to her arms, her legs, her face and neck. She chokes, unable to breathe, gagging, coughing, spluttering. Words are spoken, but to her, they're muffled. Whoever this is, they've got a firm grip on her, not allowing her to pull away. The vague form of a man kneeling before her scrapes away the sticky mucus, scratching at the skin on her face. He pushes his hands into the corner of her eyes and down over her nose, flicking away the sludge.

A tube is shoved into one of her nostrils, which horrifies her, causing a feeling of repulsion to wash over her. She tries to pull away but the stranger shifts his hand around behind the back of her head, forcing her to hold still. There's suction. One nostril is cleared and then the other.

Dante can't see anything distinct. Colors blend together, swirling before her. Shadows hint at people crouching nearby or creeping past, ignoring her. She feels overwhelmed and lashes out, wanting to push the stranger away. As determined as she is to tear herself away, the man before her has even more resolve. His hand grips the back of her neck, forcing her to face him.

"—be easier if you weren't fighting me."

He's firm but caring, which is a strange sensation for Dante after all she's been through on the Acheron. As much as she doesn't want to, she surrenders, sitting crumpled on the floor.

"Gotta get that shit out of your lungs."

He tilts her head back so he can see the rear of her mouth as he vacuums the inside of her cheeks. As soon as he hits the skin and muscle at the back of her throat she gags and lurches forward.

"That's it," he says. "It's okay."

Dante vomits. Her stomach heaves and a deep, black, sticky, tar-like sputum comes up mixed with spew and bile. She leans forward on all fours, hacking as she coughs. Stomach acid sprays across the deck, splattering against her outstretched arms. Convulsions seize her body and she arches her spine, bringing up more bile.

"Yeah, you got it," he says, patting her back and encouraging her to keep going. "Get it out."

"Wh—What the?" she says, spitting gunk from her mouth. Stringy threads of saliva and sick hang from her open lips.

"You've been under a long time," he says, hitting her quite forcibly on the back and rattling her ribcage. "Keep going. You've got to get it all out."

"I—"

She starts to panic.

"Hey, easy. Slow things down."

Dante's naked.

She's cold, sticky and wet, only the cold seems to come from within her aching bones. Her arms are unnaturally thin. There's little to no muscle texture, just sinew and bones. Skin clings to the withered outline of her left hand, wrapping around grotesquely swollen knuckles. To her horror, she's missing the fingers on her right hand. She still has her thumb, but a series of stubs lead down from the first knuckle on her index finger, cutting back to where her pinky should be, but by then there's nothing beyond the scarred back of her hand. She flexes, wanting to stretch her fingers, unable to comprehend what she's seeing, but they're gone.

Stringy hair hangs down on either side of her head, only

it's sickly and thin. As it's soaked in mucus, it takes her a moment to notice the color—grey. She runs her good hand through her hair, wanting to clear out the mucus, only the hair she pulls at comes away in clumps.

"That's it. Breathe," the man beside her says. Dante turns to face him. He's wearing a full body spacesuit with the helmet down. At first, she thought he might be wearing some kind of slick hazmat suit, but she can see a heads-up display projected on the inside of the glass helmet.

"Wh—What is happening to me," she begins, but her words come with a slur. She reaches up with her left hand, touching at her lips, feeling her empty gums. A lone tooth wobbles in its socket and she cries, unable to process all that's happening to her physically. What for her felt like days has been decades.

"Where are you from?" he asks.

In the haze of her mind, Dante's unsure how to respond. The Acheron? Earth? America? New York? Alabama?

Dante mumbles incoherently. Even she's not quite sure what she's saying.

Her eyes cast around at the rest of her crew. She squints. They're in some kind of sterile, white room. Floodlights on the ceiling make it difficult to focus. Shattered glass lies strewn across the floor, covered in thick, gooey mucus. Most of the fragments are quite large, curving like the cockpit of a mining craft. A dozen life-size vials stretch along the wall, evenly spaced against the pipes and tubes winding in and out of the room. Most of the life-size tubes are broken. A few of them are empty, with thick fluids swirling slowly within them.

Angel sits with her back against a pristine, glossy white panel. Her naked body looks old and frail. She's taking oxygen from a mask strapped around her bowed head. She's lost both her arms. Exposed bone reaches down from her swollen right shoulder, failing to reach a phantom elbow, while her left forearm has been severed at an acute angle, leaving a mess of bloody pulp where her wrist should be.

Mags has lost her legs. Dante blinks rapidly, barely able to process what she's seeing. Her best friend is horribly scarred. Her thighs are stumps, withered and grotesque, but the wounds have closed so there are no exposed bones.

Piss and shit seep across the floor, mixing as they run to the lowest point in the room. Mags is shaking uncontrollably. Her head jerks in spasms as a medic crouches beside her. He's taking her vitals and trying to administer some kind of advanced IV into her arm.

Naz is standing in front of Mags, staring down at her with a blank expression on his face, watching as the medic works on her. He's whole, with no sign of physical trauma, but his mouth hangs open. It's as though he's trying to bite into an apple. His fingers twitch by his side. Dante's confused, unsure what he's doing—what he's thinking. It seems his brain is disconnected from his body and somehow rebooting.

One of the other medics has Zoe and is leading her away. She's exhausted, dragging her swollen, bare feet across the slick floor. With her head low and her arms hanging limp by her side, Zoe edges toward the exit from the module. Dozens of tubes hang from her back, but they're organic, extending out of her skin, growing out of evenly spaced lesions running up and down either side of her spine. Dante looks at the others. They all have them, scrunched up behind their backs. She shifts slightly, feeling the same organic tubing on her back.

"No. No. No."

"Hey, it's okay," the medic says. "You're okay now. Everything's going to be alright."

She breathes deeply. The medic flashes a pen light in each of her eyes, checking her pupils for a response, knowing it'll reveal her state of consciousness.

"Where did you come from?" he asks.

"I—ah..."

"What ship?"

"The Acheron."

"Not possible," the medic says, looking at something on a three-dimensional holograph rising from his wrist-pad computer. A hologram? Dante's never seen anything like this.

He continues, saying, "The Acheron was destroyed in the first wave. What's the name of your starship?"

"Starship?" Dante says in a daze. Although it's an apt description, she's never heard their exploration craft referred to as anything other than a spaceship.

"You're in deep space," the medic says. "Between stars. How did you get here? Were you on a cruiser or a warship? What's your colony ID?"

These are terms she's never heard.

"I don't know."

"Just the name. You don't need the full sequence."

"The Acheron. It's the Acheron. I'm from the Acheron."

"You catching this, boss?"

"Get her back to the Empyrean," is the cryptic reply.

"What's wrong?" she asks.

He pauses. "The Acheron has been listed missing for over four hundred years."

Dante's silent.

The medic asks. "How are you guys even alive?"

"I—I don't know."

Dante tries to raise her arm, wanting to push a few

strands of straggly hair from her face, but her joints ache and she can't move her arm more than a few inches without pain surging through her shoulder. Her fingers are as thin as sticks, while her wrist is swollen and oversized. She looks down at her forearm. It's thin and straight, as though there's no muscle or tendons whatsoever. She's a skeleton with skin clinging to bare bones.

The medic seems to realize what she's trying to do and carefully pulls her hair back, gently pushing it in place with his thick gloved hands.

"Let's get you out of here."

"What about the others?" Dante asks as the medic gets her to her feet. "Benson and Mac?"

"The other men?"

"Yes."

"They're stable and just ahead of us."

She shakes as she steps forward. Walking is painful. Nerves catch beneath the bones in her feet, forcing her to hobble.

"Where are we?" she asks.

"You're on an adversarial dreadnought."

Dante's having trouble thinking straight. Her mind is a blur of confusion. Life is coming at her too fast.

"Ad—?"

"Enemy," he says, breaking it down for her. "The bad guys."

"Enemy? The aliens on P4? Is this WISE 5571? Are we still in orbit?"

"You never made it to WISE 5571," he says, raising her arm over his shoulder and helping her along a corridor. "The Acheron stopped transmitting mid-flight, roughly fourteen light years out from WISE."

Looking into his glass visor, Dante can see a dizzying array of information flickering on the heads-up display, including the flight path of the Acheron. Dates, text and diagrams flash before him as he picks what he should tell her.

"We thought you guys were long dead. Intel suggested you were boarded in transit, possibly years earlier, not long after your slingshot around the dwarf, while you were still in hyper-sleep. Comms were cut. We assumed the Acheron was lost. Until now."

"No, no, no," she says. "We were there. We spent years in 5571. We explored the gas giants and their moons. And P4. We went down to the surface. We saw them."

"No one's seen them," the medic says, shaking his head softly within his helmet.

"We did. We were on P4. I swear."

The medic adjusts his grip on her, hoisting her a little higher and gripping her under her shoulder as he drags her on.

"I saw them."

"What did you see?" he asks.

"I—"

Dante's unsure of herself. Her forehead aches. Her throat is dry. Everything feels wrong. She wants to believe him. She wants to trust him, but she can't. Instinctively, she feels defensive, saying, "I saw stars."

"Stars?" the medic says, not understanding. There's talking inside his helmet. Rapid. Panicked. Someone's yelling. Screaming.

"Get down," he says.

The medic shoves her to one side, pushing Dante into an alcove by a blast door. Dante feels overwhelmed with anxiety. Her heart flutters. She's lightheaded. It's the loss of control. She doesn't even know this guy's name and yet she's supposed to trust him with her life. Instinctively, she fights to stand up, not wanting to be boxed in, but he rests his hand on her shoulder, pushing her back down. She's too weak to resist for more than a few seconds.

Dante slumps to the floor as he peers around the edge of the thick door frame. With her back to the wall, she has a chance to look around. Control panels line the wall next to an external hatch, only they're at chest height. The hatch is a little over seven feet high, being roughly four feet wide. The lower lip is less than a foot off the ground, having been set at a practical height—easy to step over while still providing structural integrity.

It's then it strikes her.

The dimensions are all wrong. Well, they're right. They're not alien, not unless there's been some crazy statistical anomaly on a cosmic scale and aliens have roughly the same dimensions as the average person in a spacesuit, plus a working margin. Everything screams human. It's then she sees what's been apparent around her all along, writing plastered on the various wall conduits.

Signs. Words written in English.

Auxiliary Fuel Line

Pure Oxygen

Atmospheric Recycling

Mains Electrical

Communications Panel

Fire Suppression System

Life Support

"No," she says, clawing at the medic's arm, desperately wanting to break free. "No, no, no."

"She's panicking," he says, talking to someone over the radio. Dante can't hear the reply, but she can guess at the response from his motion, reaching for a needle-less injector in the medical kit hanging from his waist. He's going to sedate her. Dante bats at his gloved hand, sending the injector tumbling across the deck.

"Stop, damn it," he says, grabbing her by the throat. He lifts her up and shoves her hard against the bulkhead. In her weakened state, he could easily crush her windpipe. "You'll get us both killed."

Explosions rock the superstructure of the alien spacecraft, only it isn't alien, it's human.

"Listen to me. Listen carefully," he says, getting right up in her face, with the glass of his helmet pressed against her nose, looking deep into her eyes. "This is an exfiltration. You're on an enemy ship. I'm here to help. You've got to trust me."

He releases his grip, but his fingers remain around her throat.

"How can I trust you," she says as stars drift past the airlock window. "I don't even know who you are."

"I'm Coe-Voy, okay?" he says, pointing at a name tag on the front of his spacesuit. "Augustus Coe-Voy. Are you happy?

You have a name. For now, that's all you're getting."

He spins her around, grabbing her by the back of her neck and marching her forward in front of him. Coe-Voy's fingers are like a steel vice, not giving her any leeway, keeping her head up as he forces her on.

Coe-Voy has a gun. Although it's not directed at her, the sight of it causes her heart to race. She can see it out of the corner of her eye as he shoves her on, keeping her out in front of him but off to one side.

"This was supposed to be a snatch-and-grab. Twenty minutes max. We should have been able to stay under for that long at least. They shouldn't have seen us."

It's apparent to Dante that Coe-Voy's talking to someone else.

"What the fuck went wrong?"

Coe-Voy adjusts his grip, shifting from the back of her neck to her shoulder, pressing the palm of his hand directly into her shoulder blade and pushing her on regardless of the pain she feels in her feet. They stumble down another corridor with the lights flickering, threatening to plunge them into darkness. Dante loses her footing as the craft rocks under a series of explosions. Thunder seems to break above them. In the confined space of the walkway, the change in air pressure comes in waves, striking her in the chest and shaking her to her core. Her ears feel as though they're blocked, muting the sounds around her.

"You've got to buy us some time," he yells.

A change in the pitch of his voice indicates he's talking to someone else when he adds, "We've got hostiles inbound. Coming from the aft observation deck. You are clear to engage. I'm rerouting through armament. Extraction point is navigation."

Something rushes into the corridor from a side room, turning away from them, not seeing them in the shadows. Coe-Voy doesn't hesitate. He fires. The sound is deafening, savaging her ears, causing Dante to grimace at the violence being unleashed in a fraction of a second. Something is someone. Blood splatters along the wall, spraying out from a head wound. A body crumples, falling to its knees before keeling forward. What's left of the man's head crashes to the metal grating. Brains ooze out of his shattered skull.

"I—I don't understand," Dante says as Coe-Voy pushes her on, directing her around the body as it twitches on the deck. "These are your men. This is your ship."

"Not anymore," he says, leading her into the armament staging area.

Row upon row of missiles lie stacked from floor to ceiling. Unlike torpedoes or aircraft missiles, they're box-shaped, having no need for aerodynamics in space. At a guess, Dante figures what little shape they have is more for efficient storage than any actual flight dynamics. No effort has been made to seal the components in any kind of protective shell. Instead, fuel cells and propellant tanks are visible within a thin metal frame, with reaction controls mounted on either side. The only way to determine which way the missiles are facing is by the large engine nozzle at one end. Biological warning symbols adorn the various warheads, which surprises her. She's never seen anything like this.

Shots ring out, causing her to wince.

"We're on your six," Coe-Voy says to someone somewhere ahead of them. Dante's still trying to figure out where the shots are coming from as the thunderclaps echo around them. It takes her a moment to realize the shots aren't directed at them.

"This way," Coe-Voy says. He shifts her around, wanting more control of her motion. Coe-Voy's got a firm grip on her, wrapping his arm over her back and under her armpit. As he's bigger, stronger and taller than she is, he tends to lift rather than lead her, dragging her through the bowels of the warship.

"What's happening?" she asks.

"We're flanking them," he says, squeezing her tight against his slick spacesuit, keeping his gun out in front of him. "Jonesy is pinned down. Stay here."

Coe-Voy pushes Dante to the ground. She doesn't need much encouragement. Her weak legs crumple beneath her. Peering around the corner, Coe-Voy steadies his aim, leaning against one of the missiles and firing a volley of shots.

"Go. Go. Go," he yells, and for a moment, she thinks he's talking to her. Dante struggles to get to her feet, pulling on the frame of a missile as her legs tremble beneath her. She's expecting him to grab her, but he's talking to someone else ahead of them. "Then leave him. I've got one. Go! Get back to the dock."

"Who?" she asks, grabbing at his arm, instinctively understanding something has gone horribly wrong.

"One of the men," Coe-Voy replies, not naming him probably because he doesn't know himself. He simply says, "Damn mule won't follow orders."

Dante pushes between Coe-Voy and the missile rack, wanting to see what's happening. Two other rescuers are about eight rows ahead of them, arguing with someone standing out of sight. From where she is, Dante can see aging hands jabbing at them, pushing them away. As they jostle, one of the crew from the Acheron comes into view.

Benson.

He's old and stooped, with a hunch where his spine has deformed just below his shoulders. Alien implants hang from his back, still oozing nutrient and slime and whatever else kept him alive all these years. His body is ghostly white, while his arms look frail, with flabby skin hanging from the bones. Like her, he's naked. One of the rescuers is appealing to him to remain calm, the other is prepping some kind of medical device, probably a tranquilizer.

"Benson!" she yells. "Go with them."

Benson turns, looking at her but not recognizing her. He's perplexed. He steps out into the walkway as the two rescuers crouch beside some equipment, trying to stay behind cover. Gloved hands grab at his wrist, but he pulls away.

Two pencil-thin pulses of light cut through the air, causing it to glow for a second as plasma bolts form like lightning, lashing out at the rescuers. One hits high on the back of a helmet, slicing through it as though it were tissue paper. Blood sprays out from within the glass dome, dotting the inside of the visor with a fine red mist. The other strikes the second member of the rescue team, hitting him in the back and bursting out of his chest. With his suit punctured, blood erupts from the man's exposed rib cage, spraying the missile rack. He falls to his knees and then to the floor as Benson wanders on oblivious, lost in the haze of waking onboard the dreadnaught.

"Benson, get down!" Dante yells as Coe-Voy pushes her roughly behind him, shifting to the other side of the corridor, wanting to find better cover.

"Please," she says, with her eyes locked on Benson. For his part, he's oblivious to the carnage around him. He steps over the outstretched arm of one of the fallen rescuers, smiling with a strange, dislocated sense of relief at seeing Dante. A brilliant, blue-white beam of light cuts through his chest, coming from behind his shoulder blade and bursting out of his sternum. Benson looks down at the gaping wound and seared, smoldering flesh. Smoke drifts from his chest. He's caught in disbelief, unable to comprehend what has happened. His lips move as he tries to vocalize, but no sounds come out. He wants to step forward, but his legs betray him. He looks up at Dante with a plea for mercy in his eyes, but there's nothing she can do.

Benson collapses slowly to the deck. Rather than falling flat on the ground like the others, he crumples like a marionette with its strings cut. His arms flay out wide as he folds over, falling face first. Benson comes to rest with his knees pointing down at the deck and his hip up in the air. Blood seeps from a twisted pile of skin and bones. There's no movement.

A knot rises in Dante's throat, choking her. Tears form. Her frail, naked body trembles. Dante sobs, overwhelmed at the loss of her friend. She struggles to understand what just happened. The sheer pace of events is overwhelming.

"I—I can't," she says, looking past the thin glass visor and locking eyes with Coe-Voy, wanting to rush to Benson's side if not to offer medical assistance then to grieve. "I can't go on."

Coe-Voy is solemn but firm. "We have to keep moving."

Dante's lips tremble but she can't speak. Words simply refuse to form regardless of how hard she tries. She mumbles. Saliva seeps from the corner of her mouth.

A soldier runs into view, but he's not wearing a spacesuit, being dressed in what appears to be this century's version of combat fatigues. Instead of jungle camouflage, he's wearing a disruptive set of crisscrossed thick stripes in a variety of grey shades, perhaps to make him difficult to distinguish in the shadows. Smoke drifts from the barrel of his rifle. He crouches, checking the bodies.

Coe-Voy doesn't hesitate. With a single shot, he blows the man's head off. Coe-Voy's round must hit in the center of the man's skull as his head seems to vaporize into a red cloud. Blood oozes from the cauterized neck of the soldier as he collapses next to Benson.

Dante's in shock at the sheer scale and speed of the violence unfolding before her. Coe-Voy pushes her down a side row. The barrel of his gun is near her arm, radiating heat.

"Got to go," he says, shoving Dante ahead of him.

"No, I can't," she replies, leaning forward and grabbing at her knees to steady herself. She breathes deeply, trying not to vomit.

"Listen," Coe-Voy says, turning to her and clearly feeling pressed for time. "All we knew was they were protecting high-value prisoners in here, but we didn't know who. If you're who you say you are, if you're really from the Acheron, you may hold the key to unraveling all this. The Acheron was the first craft they hit."

Dante nods as tears roll down her cheeks. She feels as though she's being scolded, as though she's done something wrong.

"They fuck with your mind," he says, tapping the side of his helmet. "You know that, right? You understand?"

Again, she nods, trying to be brave but feeling horribly exposed.

Coe-Voy points at her head.

"If they get inside, it's all over."

He peers around the corner, taking her arm and preparing to run across the aisle. Something about her reluctance has him pause.

"How?" she asks.

Turning back to her, he says, "They use electromagnetic resonance to distort reality, but it requires sub-millimeter precision. Staying on the move is our best option. Their illusions are like a lure to a fish. Get too close and *wham!*

"If they can reinforce their control with direct contact, altering the brain's biochemistry with a variety of toxins and carefully synthesized drugs, the illusion is inescapable."

He points at the fallen crew. Unlike him, they're in uniform rather than a spacesuit.

"They build a false narrative. These poor bastards thought they were fighting aliens. They thought we were the bad guys."

He shakes his head.

"Make no mistake. The crew of this ship will kill us in a heartbeat. They can't see us. They don't. They see something else."

Her lips quiver as she struggles to articulate what she's thinking.

"But me?"

"You're compromised. Don't trust anyone."

"I trust you," she says.

"You shouldn't."

"How do you know?" Dante asks. "How can you be sure you're not like them? How do you know you're not seeing a fabrication?"

"No contaminates," he says, tapping his helmet. "Limits what they can do. Means any illusions are more like a dream.

I'm running an encrypted disruptor, constantly changing channels, keeping me clean."

"But they could have fabricated your suit," she says. "I mean, all of this could be some extended illusion."

"It could," he agrees, turning his head slightly and gesturing down the corridor toward the three bodies cooling on the floor. "Only you don't die in an illusion."

Dante isn't convinced, but the time for debate has passed. Coe-Voy grabs her again, getting a firm grip on the side of her rib cage as he leads her away.

"Heading to navigation," he says under his breath.

"What about me?" she asks with her head down, seeing little beyond her own naked body and the skin hanging from her distended stomach as her bare feet pace across the deck. "I'm not protected. How is this not an illusion for me?"

Coe-Voy stops by a set of stairs leading down into a lower corridor.

"They think you're still in one of those tanks. But, hey, if you want to sit here and wait for them, be my guest. I ain't got time to argue. I'm getting the hell off this deathtrap."

There's yelling from behind them. Soldiers rush into the rear of the armory. Coe-Voy punches something into a wrist pad computer, setting off a series of explosions Dante never saw him place.

Shrapnel ricochets around the deck, tearing at soft flesh. In the lull that follows the compression wave rocking her body, Dante hears the low groan of men in pain. As a physician, her instinct is to rush to help. Coe-Voy must feel what little muscle she has flex as he pushes her on, saying, "Move!"

Dante picks her way down the stairs. The skin beneath her soles is soft. The steel grating hurts her tender feet, causing her to grimace with each step. Coe-Voy grabs her, raising her off the stairs as he runs down toward someone else wearing a similar spacesuit. Beside him there's an elderly bald man with deep-set eyes. His back is hunched. Skin sags from his feeble arms. Like her, he's naked. Mucus still covers his legs, while organic tubes hang from his back, disconnected from whatever kept him alive all these years.

"Naz?"

"Angel?" he asks, looking at her with what appear to be cataracts covering his pupils.

"Dante," she replies, reaching out with her one good hand and taking hold of his shoulder. "It's me. Dee."

"Dee?" he replies, somewhat absentmindedly, as though he were recalling a fond memory rather than scrambling to escape from an infested warship. Slowly, a smile comes to his lips as the others talk among themselves. "Dee. I remember you. You were the doctor, right? I haven't seen you for—for years."

"Come on, old guy," the soldier says, helping him into an escape pod docked on the side of the craft.

"I remember her," he says, pointing a frail, spindly finger as the soldier leads him into the pod. "She was on my ship."

"Of course she was," he says.

"She was nice," Naz says, waving to her as though he were trying to get her attention in a crowd. "Hello, Dee."

Dante's unsure how to respond. Her Naz was young and vibrant, sharp and alert, musclebound with dark curly hair. The man before her is but the shell of his former self, only that transformation appears to have happened in an instant from her perspective. One moment, they were in the illusion, the next they were here. Only that next moment seems to have been years, decades, perhaps even centuries later.

"Ah," she says, lifting her hand in a friendly gesture but not quite bringing herself to wave.

"Arrows," Naz says as the soldier straps him into a seat. Naz points back and forth with one hand. "They go this way. They go that way, but which is longer?"

"Arrows?" she mumbles, unable to process that fleeting memory.

As the soldier exits the escape pod, Coe-Voy says, "Once we have you—"

Dante blinks.

Ordinarily, that's a physiological process she wouldn't notice, only this time everything changes and she's left facing a wall of darkness.

Air rushes from her lungs, escaping like a ghost. The deafening silence is as confusing as the missing escape pod. It was right there, barely ten feet in front of her, but it's gone.

A dismembered arm floats by, leaking blood in a stream of tiny red globules that trail behind it like miniature planets. The arm turns slowly, tumbling through space. Gloved fingers spasm, trying to grab the darkness, reacting to the loss of an entire body in an instant. Lights flicker from the wrist-pad hologram. It seems the suit's electronics are dying at a rate slower than its master.

Dante goes to speak, but she can't draw breath. It takes her a moment to realize she's floating adrift from the dreadnought. Her eyes feel insanely dry. Blinking doesn't help. Bubbles form on her lips. Water dances on her tongue, seething and evaporating without any sense of heat at all. Her arms and stomach are suddenly swollen and distended. She's undergone decompression before so she understands the ache of trapped gasses expanding within her body, but she's never been in a complete vacuum. Back during training, it was the failure of a high altitude test chamber, but pressure was quickly restored by quick-thinking techs. Not so here in deep space.

The hull of the dreadnought has been torn open, gutting the structure of the craft and exposing several floors within the ship. The explosion appears to have been above them, only the side of the craft was torn open like a can of beans, flinging her into space without making a sound. Already, as she slowly spins, Dante can feel her body shutting down. Her lungs scream for oxygen. She wishes she could see the stars one last time, but the lights on the hull of the craft deny her even that. Strobes flash. Spotlights flicker, probably in a vain attempt to spot survivors.

Like the Acheron, the massive dreadnought rotates to simulate gravity. It continues to turn as she flies out into the depths of space but as she's now free from that constraint, she feels weightless, moving off in a straight line. She's free one last time. The damaged side of the craft moves out of sight. Portholes reveal lights within the war craft, shining like stars, offering her at least some alternative as she dies.

Dante is struck in the back by something hard, moving fast. Rather than bouncing off her, someone grabs her. A hand reaches around her chest, turning her over.

Coe-Voy puts a mask over her face, tightening straps on either side of her head, but it's pointless. Even if he was only going to pressurize the mask to a mere 5 PSI the seal wouldn't hold and, besides, it's her entire body that's depressurized. Nitrogen and oxygen are already coming out of suspension within her veins and arteries, forming gas bubbles that will trigger a painful cardiac arrest on reaching her heart. Oh, how she's looking forward to that. Damn it, Dante. Shut down your goddamn brain. Spare yourself the pain.

Those thoughts race through her mind as it desperately tries to find a solution where there is none. Seems acceptance of death isn't an option she can will herself to embrace.

Dante's body falls limp, neither fighting nor helping Coe-Voy as she tries to accept her fate. The light grows faint. Dante understands. The ambient light around her isn't actually changing at all, it's simply that she's losing consciousness. Once again, she welcomes the darkness, only this time, it's not a reboot. This time it's the last thing she'll ever experience.

With the mask fitted, Coe-Voy slaps a lump of goo in the center of her chest, pressing it firmly between her breasts. Immediately, the glue-like substance expands, inflating in a cascading series of bubbles. Whatever chemical reaction's unfolding, it's exothermic, burning her chest.

The pain is blinding. Dante can feel the searing heat radiating through her sternum as the seething, bubbling concoction expands rapidly, enveloping her upper torso, climbing over the mask covering her eyes, nose and mouth and spreading around her skull. The foam crushes her, expanding and enfolding itself around her body, encasing her in what quickly coagulates into a solid form. Thousands of bubbles harden into what feels like a thick, gooey resin. The foam presses against her back, burning her skin. Within seconds, it's spreading down her legs, cocooning her, but she can breathe. Oxygen floods her lungs, flowing from the mask. It's difficult to breathe against the stiff foam wrapped around her chest, but she draws in deep, sucking in a lung full of air, surprised by how grateful she feels at this reprieve.

The foam is thick but semi-translucent, allowing her to distinguish between light and dark. Gloved fingers tear away sections of the solidified foam from in front of her mask and she sees Coe-Voy floating before her. He gives her a thumbs up, not that she can respond in anyway as her body is locked in place.

Dante blinks several times, signaling the only way she can. Coe-Voy grins and nods, shifting hands as he turns. The back of his suit has a soft neon blue glow, apparently being some kind of propulsive jetpack. To either side of her, there are flashes of light visible through the diffuse foam. A battle is unfolding around her.

After the initial rush of adrenaline, the pain returns, but there's nothing she can do about the aches and burns wracking her body. Her right leg cramps, but the solidified foam has a little give. If she pushes hard, she can flex slightly, just enough to relieve the muscle.

Over time, the foam around her softens and she finds she

can flex her legs and breathe easier, which helps with the sense of claustrophobia. Dante's not sure how the face mask works as she's inhaling and exhaling without so much as a gas exchanger, CO_2 scrubber or an oxygen cylinder. She wonders what the capacity of her mask is, but for now, the air is fresh. From what she can tell, she's been encased in a chemical cocoon roughly twenty feet in diameter. It's asymmetrical and feels thicker on her right side and back.

Seconds turn into minutes and then slowly, painfully, into hours. Occasionally, she catches a glimpse of Coe-Voy or some other astronaut moving around, but no one pays her any attention inside her artificial asteroid.

As Dante's wearing a mask, she can speak but apparently these life support devices don't include a radio so she talks to herself. For Dante, it's a strategy to help her deal with the stress.

"All good down here," she says as Coe-Voy's suited butt cheek bumps up against her chemically-induced asteroid. "That's a moon, by the way. At least, that's the term we had for it back on Earth."

Coe-Voy ignores her. Of course he does. Not deliberately. He's busy doing space things, apparently. Whenever she loses sight of him panic seizes her, but then he works himself around and she sees his gloved hand holding onto the opening in the foam bubble protecting her. At one point, he flies directly away from her and her heart races as she sees his legs flicker past, but he returns a few minutes later, dragging another foam boulder over to join her. She has no idea who's encased in the other artificial asteroid, but it's encouraging to realize at least one other person from the Acheron is still alive.

"Do we get an in-flight movie?" she asks the empty void of space. "I guess a granola bar and a Coke is asking too much."

The sporadic flashes of light from the battle give her both a sense of orientation and distance, allowing her to focus on something other than being buried alive within a violent chemical reaction.

Dante calculates her rate of spin at one revolution every three minutes, which, she tells herself, is leisurely, almost lazy. As the flashes slowly fade, she realizes she's drifting away from the conflict, which is another positive, helping her remain calm.

As the hours pass, Coe-Voy spends less time with her, but she's confident she hasn't been abandoned, just that he's busy doing whatever it is medics in the special forces do in the 26th century. He's sure to buzz by and give her the odd thumbs-up, checking in on her from time to time.

"Twinkle, twinkle, little star," she mutters as a brilliant, tight cluster of stars passes in front of her narrow view of the universe. The stars don't actually twinkle, though. The atmosphere in her face mask is far too thin for any haze, but she goes with it, reciting the whole nursery rhyme and wondering if Angel's doing something similar, perhaps passing time the same way she did on the treadmill during selection.

"Oh," she says, feeling a warm wet patch by her crotch. "I think I pulled a Shepard."

Dante laughs at herself, although she feels a little unsettled about not feeling any pressure on her bladder before urine-soaked her leg, squishing in between the foam and her skin.

"I hope you guys accounted for this," she says to no one in particular. "I mean, this foam stuff isn't susceptible to uric acid or ammonia, is it?"

There's no reply.

"I guess I'll find out."

As the flickering of the battle not only fades but reduces in frequency, occurring only sporadically, she calls out, "Hey! Who won?"

By now, Dante hasn't seen Coe-Voy in over an hour and she hopes that's not ominous. It's easy to hyperventilate within the mask, entombed in foam, barely able to flex let alone move. It takes a concerted effort to remain calm. She's alive. For now, that's enough. As for who won, that's a dangerous question. Either way, she'll be told humanity won. With each reboot, the aliens increase their ability to replicate reality. Now she wonders if she'll even notice.

Suddenly, her world is turned white. A blinding light pierces the muddy browns encasing her. She feels something grab her tiny asteroid, arresting its tumbling motion. A sense of acceleration takes her. As it's slightly off center and applied at an angle, it feels as though she's being dragged along upside down. To her, it's as though she's being swung over the edge of a cliff.

"Hey," she calls out. "Read the delivery instructions, will yah. Fragile! Handle with care."

A slight tremor reverberates through the thick foam. She can see blurs at work, several people moving around, attaching things to the surface of her personal world, perhaps drilling anchor points.

"Coe-Voy?"

Maybe he can hear her. Perhaps she can transmit but can't receive, with the mask covering her mouth but not her ears.

"I'm really hoping that's you."

A sense of weight returns. She's onboard a ship of some sort, being rolled across a hangar deck. Glimpses of the craft come in and out of focus through her narrow viewport. Cranes. Engines. Smaller vessels similar to the Acheron's lander.

Boots come in and out of view as people walk past attending to something other than her and her ball of solidified goo. Everything's on a scale much larger than the Acheron.

Her personal bouncy castle/asteroid comes to a rest with her head facing down at the non-slip tread lining the deck. Tiny hexagonal screws mark an access port on the floor. As she has nothing else to focus on, she stares at them, examining the styling, distracting herself, trying to keep her madly beating heart at bay.

Blowtorches light up. Dante remembers the sound from her childhood, the '*whomp*' of oxygen and acetylene igniting, the sound of air rushing, the acrid smell. She can imagine the heat. If she strains with her eyes, pushing them to the edge of her vision, she can see the flame cutting through the husk of her chemical tomb.

Once the outer shell is breached, mechanical claws begin tearing at the softer inner core. As they near her arms, she can feel the pressure easing and the foam expanding. The final few inches are cleared by hand, with mechanics tearing the foam away from her arms and legs, working in toward her torso.

Coe-Voy's there but he's busy with one of the other survivors. Her heart skips. Mac. It's Mac. Coe-Voy helps him onto a stretcher, reassuring him he's going to be okay as several medics take him away on a gurney. Once the front half of the foam encasing her body has been peeled away, a medic releases her face mask, working it up over her head.

"Hey, easy," Coe-Voy says, holding his hand out and gesturing for her to stay put as they free her legs.

"How many?" she asks, desperately wanting to know who survived.

"One of the men. Two other women."

And just like that, the crew of the Acheron has been decimated, having gone from nine to seven at the hand of their captors. Now they're down to four. Dante nods, fighting back tears.

A medic scans her chest and sprays something on the blisters that have broken out on her sternum and the numerous chemical burns coming up as welts on her frail body. The spray is cool and refreshing, helping her focus her mind.

"I'm sorry," Coe-Voy says. "We set cocoons on a couple of others but they didn't survive the process." He has a hunk of foam in his hand, looking down at it as he says, "This stuff is designed to protect suit breaches in mining accidents." He shakes his head, adding, "Never been applied to a naked body before."

A medic helps her onto a gurney. As her head rests on the pillow, her strength gives out and she sags into the thin foam mattress, looking up at Coe-Voy and saying, "Thank you," as she's led away.

KINDNESS

"Good morning."

Dante blinks in the bright light. She's lying on a medical bed wearing a thin smock. Looking around the room, she sees several smiling medical staff. It's as if they know something she doesn't. They're waiting, but for what? Their eyes. They're watching, being patient, knowing the realization will kick in any second. Her hair falls across the side of her face. She raises her hand, pushing her thick, lush hair away.

"You can have it cut," one of the doctors says.

"Wait," she says, running her fingers through her hair and examining it carefully. It's fine, much finer than she's used to and a dark brown in color. There are no split ends—that's a first. When she awoke in the enemy warship, her hair was stringy.

Her eyes settle on her palm. The skin is unusually soft and pink. She rolls her wrist over, looking at the back of her hand. No wrinkles. Even considering her actual elapsed age of 36, she had a few veins showing, let alone after hundreds of years of captivity. Her nails are long, far longer than she's ever grown them before, reaching the best part of an inch from her petite fingertips. Being a doctor, Dante keeps her fingernails trimmed so they won't puncture gloves or become microbial traps. She rotates her hand, looking at the soft, smooth skin, but she's hundreds of years old—or she was. Wait. She has fingers on both hands!

"How is this?"

"Medicine has advanced a lot since your day," the doctor says.

Dante's used to gene repair and stem cell therapy, but those are targeted treatments and tend to be limited in effect. This is a complete rebuild.

"We've never brought someone back from so far, but the substitution worked well and I'm pleased to say, you have the body of a twenty two year old."

"Twenty two?" she says with disbelief, noticing how her own voice sounds different. Clearer. Younger.

"It's the optimum age for peak physical efficiency."

Dante laughs, letting out a solitary huff as she flexes her arms, checking out the muscle texture. Even when she was in training for the star shot program, Dante always had a little flab under her arms. Her younger brother would tease her, calling them bat wings and, like brothers everywhere, happily exaggerated something that was barely visible to trigger his sister's self-esteem. Even with weight exercises focusing on the tricep, Dante always had a bit of skin hanging there, but no more. She touches at her arm, unsure whether it's real.

"I don't think I ever felt this good."

One by one, the medical staff leave, giving her a smile, a wave, and a few kind words, leaving her wondering just how arduous the treatment was. It seems they were all involved, and given her exposure to the camaraderie that rises out of critical care medical teams, her procedure must have been intense to elicit this response from them.

The remaining medic says, "We'll keep you here for a couple of days, but we don't foresee any issues and can have you back on deck within a week."

Dante nods, unsure what that means.

"Would you like anything?" he asks. She shrugs, so he says, "To celebrate? Ice cream? Chocolate? Wine?"

Alcohol on waking. Oh, wow, the future is *not* what she expected.

"No. I'm fine."

"Anything? Anything at all?"

"Ah." She's stalling for time, trying to let the moment

pass. "What the hell. When in Rome, right?"

The medic has no idea what that means. His brow furrows and his eyelids flutter. He must be accessing his neural net, probably trying to find some drink called '*Rome.*'

"Strawberries in champagne?" she asks, figuring her most outlandish request is probably lame by his standards.

"Sure."

He smiles, being polite, and pours a tall glass of water from a faucet. Oh, this is going to be good. Perhaps it's a touch too biblical for Dante, with water being turned into wine bordering on sacrilege, but she watches with intense interest. He tries not to grin, clearly relishing her delight as he places the glass under a clear dome. Within seconds, tiny bubbles form on the inside of the glass. To her amazement, bubbles begin streaming up toward the surface, but they're far too fine to be mistaken for liquid boiling. It's as though he popped a cork and poured a fresh glass of bubbly. There at the bottom of the glass is a brilliant red strawberry, complete with a few green leaves. It formed within seconds, appearing as a tiny red blob and then suddenly a succulent piece of fruit. Her eyes are as wide as a harvest moon.

"Here," he says, handing the glass to her as though such a feat were entirely normal. "I'll be on station down the hall. If you need anything, let me know."

"Ah, thanks."

He excuses himself, leaving her alone with her thoughts. Dante turns the glass in her hand, holding it up to the light and marveling at the sight. She sniffs, savoring the smell. She can feel the bubbles bursting on top of the drink, speckling her cheeks. She closes her eyes and sips at the champagne, being transported to another time.

Two months before the Acheron launched, Dante was a bridesmaid at a girlfriend's wedding. The day began with a champagne breakfast and only got better from there. For just a moment, she forgets. Bubbles dance on her tongue. The bouquet swells and she breathes deep, savoring the sweet smell. Alcohol rushes to her head, but not in a bad way, she's had far too little to drink for that, but she gets a slight buzz, the kind that says, '*Welcome home.*'

"Dee," a familiar voice says.

"Mags," Dante says, getting to her feet. She leaves the champagne on the side table and rushes to hug her friend. "Oh, it is so good to see you."

"We made it, Dee," the taller woman says, lifting her off her feet and turning her through 360 degrees as she embraces her. "We made it!"

"We did."

Mags releases her and says, "Look at us." Her eyes glance

down at her own body dressed in a skin-tight jumpsuit and then across at Dante still wearing a surgical smock but smiling in delight.

"Look at us indeed," Dante replies, feeling drunk with the euphoria of the moment.

"Get dressed," Mags says, pointing to a neatly stacked pile of clothes on the counter. "I'll show you around."

"I'm supposed to be here for a few more days," Dante says, gesturing to her messy bed as though that somehow reinforces the need for rest.

"Nonsense. They say that to everyone."

"Wh—Who?" Dante asks, picking up the clothing, unable to complete her sentence, knowing the question '*Who made it?*' invariably excludes those that have died.

"You, me, Angel and Mac," Mags replies with less enthusiasm than before. "Mac's been up for several days. They're still to wake Angel. I think there were complications."

"How long were we out?"

"From what I can tell, about six months."

Dante pulls her lips tight, nodding as she sheds her smock, dropping it to her feet. Her skin is flawless, while her stomach is as flat as a board. Without turning away from Mags, she steps into the flight suit. It's loose but no sooner has she worked it over her shoulders than it shrinks, tightening without constricting. She can feel a little extra support beneath her bust, along with threads pulling the material firmly along the inside of her leg and up around her hips, ensuring a snug fit. There aren't any buttons or a zipper, but the seam running up the middle simply weaves itself together, running the length of her torso in under a second.

"Oh, wow."

"Cool, huh? The shoes are the same."

To Dante, the shoes look flimsy. There's barely a sole and little to no support for the arch or ankle. To her, they're socks, but as soon as she slips one on, the heel inflates slightly and the material around her ankle pulls tight.

"I could get used to this."

"I know, right?" Mags says, leaning against the wall and clearly relishing Dante's surprise and delight.

For Dante, this is the first time she's been able to relax in what feels like forever. For once, there's nothing to do, no clues to decipher or mysteries to unravel. She can just be herself with her friend. Enjoying life is such a novel concept it feels wrong, but being reunited with Mags brings back memories from before P4. Life is normal again. Well, as normal as it can be hundreds of years into the future and at least a hundred light years removed from a home neither of them will ever see again.

"Welcome to the Empyrean," Mags says, gesturing for Dante to follow her. "Oh, you might be interested to know we're on our way back to WISE 5571."

Dante feels her heart flutter. Her throat constricts, tightening at the thought of going back to P4.

"What? Why? I thought we never made it there."

"Officially, we never did," Mags replies, walking past the nurse and waving as she leads Dante out of the medical ward. "But that's where this all started."

"I don't understand."

"They've been fighting these guys for hundreds of years, only fighting is a bit of a misnomer. A craft intercepts a wreck or sets down on a moon, a planet, an asteroid, doesn't really matter, and suddenly it's on *their* side."

"They're fighting themselves?"

"Apparently," Mags replies. "Anyway, like us, it was some time before anyone knew what the hell was actually going on. The first battles came decades after contact."

"Oh."

"They think our flight records were altered during that time. They've never searched WISE 5571 for these guys because no one ever went there. Officially. Every other lead has been a dead-end, but now they think P4 is the home world, the source of the contamination."

"And?"

Mags looks sideways at her. "And they're going to destroy it."

"I don't understand."

"These things. These creatures. They're parasites. They need a host to move between stars. They lie dormant, conserving their energy for tens of thousands, hundreds of thousands, perhaps millions of years, like seeds in the desert awaiting the rains. Then along comes some intelligent species and they hop on board. We've been stamping them out, but we haven't been able to find their home."

"Til now," Dante says.

"Exactly."

As they approach the end of the curving walkway, a set of doors open to reveal an atrium unlike anything Dante's ever seen in space. Birds flitter through the branches of tall trees. Bees drift on an artificial breeze, dancing between flowers. A squirrel scoots along the side of a branch, turning as he climbs higher, hiding himself from view.

"What the?" Dante says, surprised to see woodland animals on a starship.

"Yeah, I thought you'd like this place."

As the ground curves upwards away from Dante, following the circular shape of the outer rim on the Empyrean,

Dante can see the entire park at once, which is at least two hundred yards long and roughly fifty yards wide. This is the first chance she's had to gauge the overall size of the Empyrean. The shape and styling appear to be similar to the Acheron, using artificially induced gravity by spinning the craft, but as this starship is well over twice the size, the internal volume is at least eight times larger.

A glass dome allows her to look up at the axis of the Empyrean, which is considerably thicker and longer than the Acheron. There are four levels between her and the axis. From what she can tell, the garden occupies the outer third of the lowest portion of the baffle and, like the mini-farm on the Acheron, has been arranged so that as the umbrella-like baffles open, the gardens always face inward, getting the benefit of the craft's centrifugal pseudo-force.

Given the similarities with the Acheron, as the baffles close, the orientation probably shifts in accordance with the acceleration of the Empyrean, meaning the ecosystem wouldn't be subject to more than a gee during transition. The result would be the atrium is far more stable than the likes of the Caribbean islands back on Earth. Out here, there are no hurricanes to ravage the forest. The trees would sway a little during transition, but no more so than they would in a storm.

Dante's astonished by the design as it means humans have been able to take birds, beetles and bugs with them to the stars. She wonders about the enclosed ecosystem, breeding program, species selection and management. On the Acheron, the single biggest limiting factor was microbial outbreaks which could destroy crops and upset the atmospheric balance.

The Acheron was only capable of supporting dirt-bound microbes and plants grown for food, with crops of micro-corn, wheat and soy destined for the reconstructors that manipulated organic proteins and simple sugars into meals. The Acheron's farm had to be handled with extreme care. Naz was paranoid. He'd berate anyone taking a shortcut through the farm to get to engineering without telling him in advance. *'One open door for one minute,'* he'd say, and then make a gesture akin to a nuclear explosion, *'Boom!'* He was exaggerating, or so Dante thought. This, though, this is opulent beyond belief for 22nd century astronauts. Naz would have loved it!

The mission psychs back on Earth knew what they were doing when they set up the Empyrean. There's something soothing about having a touch of Earth among the stars. The sound of water running over a brook, cascading gently over rocks and stones before reaching a waist-high weir/waterfall and falling into a pond is hypnotic.

Dante feels overwhelmed. "How do they?"

"I know," Mags replies. "And this is what they call a warship! Can you imagine the colony craft?"

Dante shakes her head, still struggling to take the atrium in.

"How do you go to war with squirrels?" she asks.

"Apparently, they have smaller craft that go out in advance. I think this is like the flag ship or something. We're part of a fleet."

"Ah."

The sheer size of the undertaking is baffling. A fleet. An entire fleet. Not just one craft out on its own. Wow. Back in her day, the idea was to spread as far and as wide as possible in the search for microbial life and habitable worlds. Seems humanity has shifted to colonization on an astonishing scale.

Dante reaches down, touching at the grass beside the path, feeling the soft blades flex against her fingers, remembering the grassy meadows in rural Alabama. No tornadoes here.

There's running behind her, feet pounding on the boardwalk, but she doesn't care, breathing in deeply and savoring the subtle hints on the breeze. There's no one scent but rather a blend that speaks of life, reminding her of home.

"Mags. We need you in engineering."

Dante stands, turning back toward Mags, curious as to who this is beside her and why they would need the technical assistance of an engineer from hundreds of years ago, but he seems to know her quite well. Typical Mags. Engineering was probably the first place she visited on waking, and she would have made dozens of friends in minutes given her bubbly personality, but before Mags can say anything, the stranger says, "It's Mac."

As a group, they rush back to the carousel and take an elevator up one of the ribs leading to the axis of the craft.

"He's lost it," the young man says. It's only then Dante grasps that everyone on the Empyrean is roughly twenty-two years old in terms of physical age and that someone's apparent age is meaningless and utterly misleading. Some of these guys could be centuries old. Age has no significance at all. Whereas once it was a measure of experience, exposure and sometimes wisdom, now it's a relic of past prejudices.

Mags is silent. Dante is invisible, simply tagging along.

"He heard we were heading to WISE 5571 and he freaked."

The elevator doors open. Soldiers line the far wall, dressed in black, with full face masks and gloves, not showing any skin. They have what appear to be rifles drawn, only unlike the firearms of her day, they look flimsy. The scopes open out into a screen roughly the size of a small book, while the stock and barrel are stunted.

Metallic spiders crawl across the roof. Their chrome

bodies and thin, flexible legs move with utter silence. As Dante's coming up behind the soldiers, she gets a brief glance at several screens. They reveal the corridor as seen from the vantage point of the spiders, only their view is in false color, highlighting hints of light not visible to the human eye. She catches the end of a comment by someone that's presumably the commander.

"—then kill the lights and take him out."

"No," she blurts out.

Coe-Voy turns to face Dante, but at first he doesn't recognize her. To be fair, she barely recognizes herself. He blinks and she can see the realization in his eyes. Some kind of neural net has kicked in, identifying her.

"I'm sorry, Dante. He's taken one of the engineers hostage."

"What?"

"We can help," Mags says. "We know him."

"We can talk him down," Dante says. "Mac trusts us."

For a moment, no words are exchanged, but Dante understands what's happening. Neural nets were emerging technology when the Acheron left Earth. The prototypes they took to the stars were buggy, and for her, annoying, but she realizes that wouldn't be the case now. At a guess, Coe-Voy has got some artificial intelligence running the numbers, testing scenarios, looking at the probability of success. She can see the angst in his eyes. Ultimately, predictions are just a clever guess. They're generally close, but machines can't account for every variable, especially the erratic behavior of humans. He has to decide. Take the easy way. Trust the computer or take a chance on them.

"You could die," he says, and Dante has no doubts his comment is based on the most likely outcome as calculated by his AI companion.

"I know."

"You've got five minutes. Then we breach."

He gestures with his head, signaling for them to advance down the corridor. As Dante steps forward, though, a soldier slips something down the back of her neck, hidden by the collar of her jumpsuit. Whatever it is, the device clings to her skin. Tiny metal barbs dig into her neck. She can feel the device positioning itself over her spine. This has to be the result of some non-verbal order given by Coe-Voy. She could protest. She could ask about its function, but there's no time. Mags gives the soldier touching her a filthy look but continues on with Dante.

"Mac?" Dante asks, keeping her hands raised and in sight.

"Hey, buddy," Mags calls out. "It's me. Mags. I'm here

with Dee. We're coming down to talk, okay?"

Blood has been smeared on the wall by someone escaping with an injury. Mags shakes her head. Not good.

"Mac. It's Dante. Remember me? Remember the Acheron? We're here for you. We're coming into engineering, okay?"

Quietly, they step over the lip of the hatch leading into the equipment bay.

"Mac, are you there?"

From the darkness, Mac calls out. "Get out of here, Dee. You don't want none of this."

"Hey, easy big guy," Mags says, stepping away from Dante, putting some space between them.

Digital screens line the walls, acting as control panels and displays. Several of them have cracks, falling dark where blasts have punched through the electronics. A bench runs around the room with pieces of equipment laid out in various states of disassembly and repair—wiring looms, an electronic chassis, pistons, solar arrays, hydraulics. They've been abandoned in a rush, with several parts having fallen to the floor. Most of the lights on the roof have been shot out. Dante notices a couple of the spiders she saw in the hallway, but they're conspicuously still, blending in with a variety of sensors and vents on the ceiling. Watching. Waiting.

A body lies face down on the floor. Blood seeps along an outstretched arm. Fingers twitch. He's been hit in the back, just below the shoulder blade. The entry point is tiny, barely a bloody smudge on his jacket, but Dante has no doubt the exit wound includes at least one of his lungs if not an artery.

From the shadows, Mac says, "I won't go back there. I can't."

"We're here to help," Dante says, edging forward. She crouches, reaching out and touching at the injured man's neck, checking his pulse. Blood seeps from his lips as he wheezes softly, struggling to breathe.

"It wasn't supposed to be this way," Mac says.

Without taking her eyes off Mac still standing back in the shadows, Dante says, "I need to get this man out of here. Do you understand?"

There's no reply.

Mags creeps up beside her, whispering, "I'll do it."

She grabs the man by his armpits and drags him backwards. Blood smears across the floor. Mags stays low. It's as if she's huddling against a storm as she pulls him to safety.

"What happened here, Mac?"

"They started it. They grabbed me. I had to defend myself."

"This is wrong," Dante says.

"This is all so wrong," Mac says, echoing her words back to her. "I didn't want any of this. You have to believe me. I didn't."

"Step forward," Dante says. "Let me see you."

A woman appears, shuffling her feet slowly across the deck. She's terrified. Her eyes are red from the tears that have been streaming down her cheeks. She trembles. To Dante's surprise, she has a thick wire wrapped loosely around her neck, twisted at one end so it can't be easily pulled apart. Mac nudges her forward. The wire leads back to the barrel of a gun similar to those carried by the soldiers in the hallway.

"They made me do this," Mac says. His red hair is frayed and frazzled, wild and out of control. "I didn't want this, but they wouldn't listen. They forced my hand. I had to take action. You know I'm right, Dante. It's madness. We can't go back there. No one can."

"Easy," Dante says, stepping back. She has her hands out in front of her, gesturing for calm.

"I know. I know too much. That's why they're afraid of me."

"What do you know, Mac?"

"Everything. Like you said, it's all a lie."

"We're not on the Acheron," Dante says. "Not anymore."

"Aren't we? Are you sure of that?"

The woman is terrified. She whimpers softly, locking eyes with Dante, appealing for help but knowing her position is hopeless. The wire around her neck is a noose leading back to the gun. Mac's set up a dead man's shot. Regardless of what happens to him, regardless of which way he turns or falls, the gun will always point at her neck, held on target by the wire. If they shoot him, she dies.

"It's all fake, Dee. Don't you get that?"

"Mac," Dante replies, unsure how to continue. In all her years of training with the crew and their exploration of WISE 5571, she never saw any hint of anger in him or felt any physical threat despite his size. Mac always seemed composed. He was the kind of person that would take his frustrations out on a treadmill or by lifting weights. She can't recall a single time he swore in anger, let alone anything as devious as this.

"We're still back there. We're still on the Acheron," he says with spittle flying from his lips. "We never left. It's all a dream—a nightmare."

"Mac, please. Listen to yourself. You're not making any sense."

From behind her, Dante can hear muffled sounds in the hallway. Mags hasn't returned. It doesn't take a neural net to figure out what's happening. They're holding her back, not willing to risk her again now they've got a good look at Mac. Dante's got to talk him down.

"Don't go to sleep, Dante. You can't go to sleep."

"Easy, Mac."

Dante edges back, drawing him in line with the corridor, wanting Coe-Voy to see what she's dealing with and hoping he's got some way of disarming or disabling Mac.

"Don't you see?" he asks. "Sleep is the reset. All those other times. All the times we broke through the darkness. The membranes. They don't need those anymore. They never needed them. Only they didn't know that, did they? Because they're not human. But us. We see the darkness every night. Sleep is perfect camouflage for them."

Swollen red veins reach into the whites of his eyes. He's fought to remain awake, probably for days, slowly working himself into a state of paranoia.

"Mac. No one's going to hurt you," she says. "Just put down the gun and let her go."

"They change stuff. Each night. Don't you understand? You must see it? We're still back there. We're still in orbit around P4."

"We're on the Empyrean, Mac. We're safe."

"Are we?" he asks. "Do you really believe that? Why? What proof do you have? You know what they can do. What makes you think they'd let us escape?"

Dante treads lightly, backing up, drawing him out.

"Why would they take us back to WISE 5571?" she asks. "If we're still there, why would they tell us we're going back to P4? They could take us anywhere. They could take us home."

"It's all wrong," he says, getting angry. "The timing. We should see more changes. Greater differences between our time and theirs. Don't you get it? Everything's anachronistic. Everything's the same. The Empyrean is a joke. You're telling me that after four hundred years the best design they can come up with is the Acheron? We went from horse-drawn carts to subluminal spacecraft in the same span of time. They should be way beyond us. Light years beyond us."

"Look at us," Dante says, holding her hands out. "Look at our new bodies. Their medicine is like magic."

"Or an illusion," he says. "I don't get you, Dee. You were so smart. The colors. The arrows. You saw through their lies."

"No one's lying to you," Dante says.

"They're using you, just like they used Cap, like they used Vichy."

Logic isn't working. Dante switches tact.

"Mac. I want you to let her go."

"No."

"This is an illusion, right?" she says. "So if I'm wrong, what's the worst that happens? We go through another reset, but then we'll both know, right? We'll see it together. Both of us. We'll know."

"We'll remember," Mac says.

"Yes, that's right. We'll remember," Dante says, reinforcing his point. "Now let her go."

Mac stares into Dante's eyes. She can feel the connection, the familiarity, the trust. There's resignation in his eyes. Hurt. Anguish. He's trying to do what's right. Things have spiraled out of control.

"Please," she says.

His lips quiver. Although he still has hold of the gun, he reaches up with a trembling hand. His fingers twist the wire, turning it slowly.

"That's it," Dante says, but she has the flat of her hand out, cautioning the woman, signaling she shouldn't rush away, not wanting her to pull away too quickly and spook him.

"We're in this together," Dante says, speaking to both of them. The woman nods softly, biting her lip, holding back her fear.

"They get inside your head," Mac says with tears streaming down his cheeks. His hands are trembling. He fiddles with his fingers, undoing the wire.

"I know," Dante says. "I know. Everything's going to be okay, right? Just like before."

Mac sniffs, pulling the last of the wire apart. Dante gestures with her fingers, beckoning the woman to walk slowly over to her.

"That's it," she says as the terrified engineer shuffles forward. As the wire falls from her neck, she runs, throwing her arms around Dante and knocking her backwards. It's all Dante can do to stay upright as she grabs her.

In that instant, two shots ring out. Pulses of light break forth from the mechanical spiders clinging to the ceiling. Heat radiates through the air. It's as though someone opened the door of a blast furnace. Dante cringes, but the waves have already passed.

Mac's head lurches back. Two tiny red holes appear in his forehead. The back of his skull explodes, spraying the wall behind him with blood, brain and fragments of bone. He keels to one side, dropping the gun as he collapses on the floor.

"Noooo!" Dante yells, but his life was over before she can even part her lips, let alone scream in anguish. She pushes the woman aside, rushing to his fallen body, but the room is already full of soldiers running in around her. They cut her off, grabbing her arms and pulling her away despite her protests. "No, please. No."

As she's dragged from the equipment bay, she sees Coe-Voy.

"You? Why did you kill him?" she yells at him. "He was going to surrender."

Coe-Voy doesn't care. "If it's any consolation, you defied the predictions."

Dante shakes her head in disgust, staring him in the eye and saying, "You sick bastard."

The soldiers pinning her arms back flex against her instinctive desire to lash out and hit him. She struggles, but they're too strong.

If Coe-Voy feels any remorse, it doesn't show. He blinks but holds eye contact, refusing to be intimidated by her—as though Dante could intimidate anyone. With barely disguised disdain and speaking as though he's replying to something she never actually said, Coe-Voy adds, "Honestly, it was the kindest thing we could do."

Dante spits in his face.

BUT THE STARS

Dante sits on a park bench within the vast atrium onboard the Empyrean. She closes her eyes and breathes deeply, savoring the smell of the grass, the scent of wood and moist dirt, the rustic smell of flowers, enjoying the sound of leaves rustling, birds singing on the wind and the cool air touching at her cheeks. For a few seconds, she's back on Earth, but the illusion is quickly shattered.

Stones crunch beneath someone's shoes and she opens her eyes to see a couple walking hand in hand along a side path winding through the gardens.

In the distance, she sees Mags and Angel coming toward her from the other side of the atrium.

It's been several days since Mac was killed, but for Dante it still feels like it happened this morning and she's not sure why. Perhaps it was that she witnessed the bloodshed firsthand, perhaps it was because she genuinely thought she could save him, or perhaps it's because she feels betrayed by

Coe-Voy, who originally saved both of them. As painful as the death of the others has been, Mac's loss sent her into a spiral, which is strange to her as they were never that close.

Cap and Vichy died long before anyone knew. When the crew finally figured out what was happening on the Acheron they were beyond hope. Their loss was sullied by the alien impersonators manipulating the crew. Although neither man actually had any involvement in their torture, Dante found it hard emotionally to separate them from what happened to her on the Acheron. Dante loved Vichy. She often wonders what happened to him in those final few moments of his life and she regrets not being there for him. Such thoughts leave her feeling hurt and angry as not only did the aliens mislead them, they robbed them of their friends, only, somewhat perversely, she finds that anger directed back at Cap and Vichy as those are the only forms these insipid creatures ever took.

As for the others, Zoe never made it out of the alien warship. Benson died as little more than a bag of bones crumpled on the floor, something that was incongruous and surreal to her. The last time she saw Naz he was in a catatonic state. One moment he was there with her in the illusion, vibrant and full of life, the next he was just a shell. As far as she knows, he died on the adversarial dreadnaught.

To Dante, none of their deaths were real on an emotional level. She feels as if any one of them could walk up behind

Angel even though she knows that's impossible. Mac's death, though, was visceral. Mac was standing less than four feet from her, staring into her eyes, wanting answers, pleading for mercy—and then he was gone. One moment, he was alive and talking to her, the next his brains were scattered across the walls and floor. Unlike Angel's apparent death on the Acheron, there was no reset. If only the bounds of reality could be redrawn. Oh, what she would give for a second chance, but what could she do differently?

Dante warms her hands around a cup of coffee, lifting it to her lips and sipping gently. Some things never get old. She has no idea how far she is from Earth or whether the timings she's been given by the crew of the Empyrean are relativistic or Earthbound, but it's comforting to know some things never change, like coffee.

Everyone she's ever known is long dead. Dante knew that would happen before her launch from Cape Canaveral and she accepted that, but there's now more time between her and her immediate family than there is between her childhood and the Revolutionary War. When she stops to think about all that happened in just that stretch of time, from the Declaration of Independence, the cultural upheaval of the Civil War, the suffragette movement, two brutal world wars, the civil rights movement and Armstrong walking on the Moon, it causes her head to spin, and yet the technological and scientific advances that led humanity from horse-drawn carts to rocket ships has been dwarfed by the rush to the stars. It seems the dislocation she felt on launching from Earth is now commonplace and accepted as the norm. Those that choose to stay on Earth are now in the minority and the planet is treated as a wildlife reserve. The crew she's spoken to accept that they and their offspring will probably never see the blue skies of Earth and they're fine with that.

The Acheron missed the rise and fall of several empires on Earth. Hearing about the history that lay in her future is disturbing and yet it's now in the past.

Europe and the Americas fell into ruin within a few decades of their launch, with infighting preventing progress. Ignorance replaced knowledge. Ego won out over enlightenment.

The Chinese federation spanned the western Pacific from Mongolia to Antarctica, but like all empires it outgrew itself. India was caught between the Chinese and the religious Middle Eastern bloc. When these two burned out, the subcontinent became an unwitting superpower. Just when it seemed as though there might be some stability for humanity, climate-induced hardships were compounded by the rise of antibiotic-resistant bacteria and a pandemic that dwarfed even the Black Plague. By the time the dust settled, six billion graves had been dug. Entire cultures collapsed. Civilization crumbled. Like an organism fighting an infection, it seemed Earth was trying to rid itself of humanity. What remained of those devastated countries then began the long walk to the stars.

From what she's heard, eight colony planets have been terraformed among nearby star systems, although that process alone takes several millennia to complete. *Homo sapiens*, it seems, has become *Homo stellae*—humanity dispersed among the stars. Coffee, though, coffee has remained the same. Coffee still has those bitter undertones that cause her mind to stir. Coffee brings her home.

"They told me you were down here," Mags says, walking up to Dante.

Angel waves sheepishly from beside Mags, although Dante's not sure why. If anyone should be embarrassed by what happened it's Dante, as she's the one that accused Angel of being an imposter. Regardless, Dante casts Angel a warm smile in response, trying to make up for a mistake she can never erase.

For Dante, the past is a bitter curse. No one can re-live a single second once it's gone—not presidents or scientists, princes or paupers. The rich are mocked by the passage of time as though they were destitute and poor. Mistakes are carved in stone. Even forgiveness is shallow as nothing can undo the past. For Dante, living with regret isn't a burden, it's honest.

Oh, she doesn't let it weigh her down, but she doesn't ignore it either as that would be insulting to both of them.

Mags comes to a halt before Dante and it's only then Dante realizes the best part of a minute has transpired since Mags addressed her. She's waiting for a reply. Mags must think Dante's a space cadet. Angel's carrying a small white box. It's nondescript, leaving Dante wondering about its contents, but she snaps herself back to reality.

"Hey," she says, gesturing to the two women. "It's good to see you guys." She pats the seat beside her, inviting them to join her.

"I'm sorry to hear about Mac," Angel says, cutting straight to the heart of the unspoken issue bugging them all. "He was a good man."

"He was," Dante replies, staring into her coffee.

"There was nothing more you could have done," Mags says.

"I know. It just sucks."

"Yeah, it does," Angel says in a solemn voice.

Mags asks, "What happened to Coe-Voy?"

"Transferred," Dante replies. "Don't know where. Just don't care anymore."

Mags nods.

Angel says, "That fucker will probably get promoted."

"Probably," Dante replies, agreeing with her.

"Did you see the vid on P4?" Mags asks as she takes her seat.

Dante shakes her head.

Mags touches at a thin computing sheet wrapped around her wrist like a bracelet and brings up a glowing three-dimensional image. P4 is resplendent with its twin host stars off to one side, bathing the planet in a cold light, leaving half of the alien world lost in the shadows.

Flashes of light erupt from the night side of the planet, glowing for upwards of thirty seconds before fading. Several of the impacts are so bright the image is washed out. When the view returns, vast waves can be seen rippling through the atmosphere, curving around the planet, swamping entire mountain ranges and sweeping over them like waves at the beach.

"Kinetic bombardment," Mags says. "They're dropping asteroids on them, sterilizing the planet. Nothing is left down there. Nothing. Not even microbes."

Dante's subdued. Just when it looks like the attack is over, the planet is peppered with buckshot lighting up the dark side yet again, reaching around to puncture the dawn. Dozens of asteroids slam into the frozen surface, punching beneath the ice and deep into the mantle. Ejecta rises out of the atmosphere before plunging back in a fiery wake. On the daylight side of P4, the pristine white snow and ice has been blackened. In some places, the bedrock is visible. Fractures have opened, exposing the molten upper mantle running along various fault lines. Steam billows into the thin atmosphere. An eerie red glow is visible through the growing haze.

Angel says, "We've won."

"Have we?" Dante asks, turning her head sideways and staring at them in disbelief, still mourning the loss of the Acheron and her crew. "What exactly have we won?"

"We destroyed them. We wiped them out."

Dante's heart is heavy. It feels as though she's back on P4, struggling through the depths of the burning base, about to plunge into the darkness again. "And that's cause for celebration?" she asks.

"I don't understand you," Mags says. "They're gone. They're dead. I thought you'd be happy."

Dante hangs her head. For a moment, trembling hands are all she sees—not the blades of grass beneath the seat, not the remnants of her coffee sloshing around in her cup, not the crew strolling past or the long shadows cast within the atrium. Even the pebbles beneath her shoes go out of focus as tears cloud her eyes.

"Hey," Mags says, reaching over and taking one of her hands. "It's okay. It's over."

"It's just—I don't get it."

As the lights around them fade, the birds fall silent, settling in the branches for yet another artificially imposed night. Mags is quiet. Angel leans forward, placing her elbows on her knees and resting her head in her hands. It seems she understands there are some things people need to work through for themselves. Dante struggles to articulate her thinking.

"We're all children of the stars... I know. I know it sounds clichèd. Just another pious platitude, something to engrave on a plaque and hang above the sink in the bathroom, but here we are, and so are they, or they were. For all our differences, we both originated from the thin, wispy dust swirling between the stars."

Dante laughs at herself, lifting her head, trying to stop the tears from rolling down her cheeks. "God, I sound like you, Angel."

"You sound like Vee," Angel says, offering a slight laugh as consolation.

"I miss him," Dante says, appreciating the way Angel's referring to her Vichy and not the imposter.

Mags hangs her head, saying, "Me too."

Dante wipes her eyes with the back of her hands.

"Life shouldn't be like this."

"I really don't get you," Mags says. It's not a criticism. She's trying to understand. Dante, though, is feeling rather than thinking. Emotions swell within her like a storm on the sea, lifting the waves and battering boats at anchor in the harbor. With everything she's been through, victory is bitter. She's lost too much. Reality is cruel.

"We're alive," Angel says, trying to lift her spirits.

Dante replies, "We were all alive. Us and them. So why fight? Life shouldn't be the cause of death. For intelligent creatures, we sure are stupid."

Her comment is as much a rebuke of Coe-Voy as it is of the alien attack on the Acheron and humanity's retaliation against P4. Mags squeezes Dante's hand, gently playing with her fingers, searching for comfort, looking for assurance. For Dante, there's an awakening. Finally, she feels she understands.

"Think of the stars," she says, allowing her eyes to drift toward the glass dome. "Think about what stars are."

"The stars?" Mags asks, not making the connection.

"What are stars?"

In a typical response, Angel replies in a manner that is both technically correct and precise, saying, "Matter radiating energy."

"And what is life?" Dante asks. This time, Angel's quiet so Dante says what she's thinking. "Life is the inverse—the opposite—the exact reverse of that process. It's matter absorbing energy."

Angel nods but doesn't seem convinced. Mags is quiet.

Dante says, "Whether it's us or them, everyone's looking for some supernatural, metaphysical explanation for what life is and how it came to be, but I think the answer is deceptively simple. Atoms use energy to form molecules."

She breathes deeply, trying to condense decades of thinking and reasoning into a few short sentences, hoping they're coherent.

"Molecules distribute energy the only way they can, by forming more and more complex combinations. And that's what life is—billions of years spent rearranging and redistributing energy, forming ever more complex molecules until those individual molecules form chains containing hundreds of *billions* of atoms."

"DNA," Mags says.

Dante nods. "In this way, the raging furnace that is the heart of a star has teased out life on Earth—and on P4. It's taken eons, but here we are. And what do we do? What do they do?"

Angel completes her thought. "We kill each other."

Dante forces a smile. "Crazy, huh? Benson knew. Benson understood. I think that's why, even when he could see them, he never tried to fight them."

"God, I miss him," Angel says.

"Me too," Dante replies.

Mags says, "I guess we're all aliens, right? It's just a matter of perspective."

"Yep," Angel says.

"I really miss Benson," Dante says, longing for his charismatic smile and borderline insanity. Even before the attack, he always brightened her day.

No one replies. Their silent agreement is enough.

Angel stares at her hands, flexing her fingers and examining them closely. "You know what's really strange?"

"What?" Dante asks.

"I've never been one for believing in the soul, but after what happened to us, I do wonder."

"What do you mean?" Mags asks.

"I lost my arms. Both of them. But they weren't really gone. I mean, they were gone physically, but it was like I could still feel them, like I could wiggle my fingers, like they were still there only they were invisible."

"Phantom limbs," Dante says. She's tempted to point out that this is a well-established medical phenomenon, but she's sure Angel already knows that and she suspects this isn't quite the point Angel's making.

Angel rolls her hands over in front of her, looking carefully at her wrist and fingers.

"What was really weird was how I felt when I got them back. I know these guys have advanced bio-engineering techniques and all, but it seemed like my hands were never gone. They were always there, they were just missing something, like missing a pair of gloves. When these guys regrew them, it wasn't like I had new hands, more like my ethereal hands were back in their old gloves. I'm not sure if that makes any sense."

"Oh, I get it," Dante says. "We're ghosts in a biological machine."

"That's it, isn't it?" Mags says. "Who am I really? I'm conscious, but I can't explain what that means or why I happen to be me."

"I think, therefore I am," Angel says.

Dante pauses before saying, "Perhaps it's more accurate to turn that phrase around—I am, therefore I think, I feel, I laugh and I love."

To which Angel adds, "And sometimes, I cry."

"I do," Dante says, nodding at that sentiment.

Although it seems like the three of them are sitting still on a park bench, their sense of place and permanence is an illusion and as the Empyrean turns, the spoke from some other section falls across the atrium, casting shadows over the darkened interior.

"Do you ever wonder about all this?" Mags asks.

"If this is real?" Dante replies, understanding implicitly what she means. "Yeah, I wonder."

"Me too," Angel says. "It's that whole memory thing, isn't it? We're selective in what we remember and how well we remember it. Everything seemed so vivid at the time, but now I'm not so sure, and yet here we are."

"And then there's time," Dante says.

"Oh yeah," Mags replies. "The more time that passes, the more the Acheron seems like a dream."

"Do you remember the membranes?" Dante asks.

"What were they?" Angel asks.

"Mistakes," Dante replies. "Holes in the cage. Gaps in the fence."

"And you think they fixed that?" Mags asks.

"But we escaped," Angel says. "That was real. We were rescued, right?"

"I think so," Dante replies, but doubts creep through and she follows up with, "I sure as hell hope so."

"If we didn't," Mags says. "If all this has just been yet another experiment, another trial, another attempt to bleed us for information, to learn more about us…"

Mags can't bring herself to finish her sentence and Dante can't bring herself to reply. She simply shakes her head, clenching her lips, not wanting to commit to an answer.

Mags looks away. Her eyes drift, unable to settle, revealing a glimpse of the torment she feels. Angel stares at the rocks on the ground.

"If this is another illusion," Angel says, "I'm glad we're in it together."

Dante nods, appreciating their friendship. "What is reality anyway? Is it ever anything more than a shared experience?"

Angel says, "Reality is overrated. This whole wide universe is nothing more than a bunch of excitations in various quantum fields briefly materializing as particles rather than energy. Reality has always been an illusion. Nothing's really present once you exclude the electromagnetic force. Most of what makes us up is empty space anyway."

Dante says, "Oh, my God that's a mouthful."

"What? Did I get something wrong?" Angel asks.

"You're asking us?" Mags replies.

The three women laugh at their grief. Having lost most of their crew, their spaceship and even their position in time, it seems only appropriate to inject some humor.

"Oh, I almost forgot," Angel says, picking up the box from where she rested it on the seat beside her. "Happy birthday."

"Birthday?" Dante says, recoiling at the notion.

Birthdays seem so ordinary, so incongruous with all they've been through. Do people in this era even celebrate birthdays? How do they measure years without being in orbit around Sol? Is a year just some arbitrary measurement of what are already arbitrary days? As hundreds of years have passed along with numerous generations, do they now look back in bewilderment at such archaic notions in the same way Dante used to wonder about the Babylonian notion of 24 hours in a day or 60 minutes in an hour?

"Do you want some cake?" Angel asks, breaking Dante's train of thought.

"No," Dante says, only that's a reflex response rather than a measured one. It just seems wrong to enjoy life when so much has been lost.

"You're still thinking about what happened on the

Acheron, huh?" Mags pauses. "If it's any consolation, I thought you were one of them."

That brings a grin to Dante's face.

"So did I," Angel says, removing the lid and revealing a cake with white icing on top. There are three glasses and a bottle. Angel pours some champagne and hands out the glasses, saying, "To us."

"To all us aliens," Mags says.

Reluctantly, Dante agrees, charging her glass and saying, "To the three of us."

They drink a little too quickly. For Dante, the aftertaste of her coffee mars the flavor of the champagne, but she appreciates the gesture.

Angel starts cutting the cake, resting the box on her lap and saying, "It's one and a half kilos, you know. I had them measure it precisely."

Dante laughs. Angel knows her too well, understanding precisely what she needs to break through the gloom.

"What's so funny?" Mags asks.

"I was a premature baby. Born at thirty weeks."

"So?" she asks.

"53 ounces," Dante replies.

"One and a half kilos," Angel says, cutting several slices

with a knife from inside the box. She hands a piece to Mags, who passes it on to Dante.

"Nice touch," Mags says.

"Astonishing, isn't it?" Angel says. "To think we all started out so small."

"We're still small," Dante says, taking a bite of the cake. It's been baked with carrot and walnut with a vanilla crème fraîche icing on top, making it a little bitter but moist.

Angel says, "So much complexity packed into such a tiny space." Dante is genuinely unsure whether she's talking about the cake or her as a baby.

Mags laughs. "Even before we touched down on P4, I was sure one of you was an alien."

Dante snorts. She doesn't mean to. She's not sure quite what her response is supposed to be, but it comes out as something between a laugh and an objection.

"You weirdo," Mags says, which makes Dante love her all the more.

"That's all any of us ever are," Angel says. "Weirdos."

"Oh, no you don't," Mags replies, pointing at herself. "Don't include me in your merry little band. As hard as it might be to believe, some of us are normal."

"Nominal," Angel counters, enjoying the banter. "There's

no norm as such as there are no rules!"

Mags, though, doesn't want to concede that point, so she says, "For the two of you, there should be."

Dante laughs, appreciating the friendship she's found among the stars.

Angel asks, "Did either of you tell them about what happened down there on—"

"No," Dante says, cutting her off.

"I'll never tell," Mags says. "Never."

"Do you really think they got them?" Angel asks. "All of them?"

"Oh, they'll be mopping them up for years," Mags replies. "But they hit the nest. They got them alright."

"Did they?" Dante asks, only her question seems distant. It's a contradiction. Within seconds, it's lost in the passage of time, condemning the confidence Mags has in the orbital strike. In Dante's mind, there are no assurances. No one responds to her. They all know. Regardless of whether they're on Earth, in orbit around P4 or four hundred years into the future, confidence is the great illusion.

Dante lifts her eyes, looking beyond the glass dome. In the darkness, her mind wanders free, no longer held captive by the constraints of life onboard the Empyrean. She's able to see her life as a waypoint—neither the beginning nor the end, just somewhere in between. She's a bunch of atoms bound together briefly during their astonishing transit through this vast, broad universe. They're on loan. They're hers for but a moment.

"All we ever really have is now," she says. "We think there's something more. Money. Fame. Whatever, but there isn't. There's just now."

In the tiny pinpricks of light visible beyond the dome, Dante sees something familiar, something reassuring, but the meaning escapes her. Dante feels a sense of longing and nostalgia, but she's unsure why. The stars are pretty, shining like diamonds. The stars have always been there for her—constant and sure. Maybe it's their distance that calls to her or perhaps it's the promise they hold for life being renewed in yet another generation of stars, planets, comets, asteroids and just maybe other living beings.

The stars rage against the eternal night, burning at over a million degrees, and yet they're so far away they're reduced to mere specks in the pitch black sky, humbled into being little more than pinpricks of light. Dante looks for the constellations, only her memory has grown vague. The stars before her could make any shape she wants. There was something about the stars, something that helped her through the darkness, something that gave her hope, but she's not sure what.

Dante feels as though the stars are speaking to her, only she's unsure what they're saying. She's content. She doesn't need them anymore. Dante was lost on the Acheron. Now, for the first time, she's among friends, not crew mates. She finally feels as though she belongs.

"What are you thinking?" Mags asks softly, following Dante's eyes as she stares at the dome, wanting to understand what she's looking at.

Without hesitation, Dante says, "Nothing."

Even though she's lost among the stars, Dante has finally found peace. She may not have vanquished a bloodthirsty alien with a ray gun or saved an entire planet from conquest, but she found herself. Standing on South Beach all those years ago, in what feels like another lifetime, something was missing. There was a longing, a hunger. The stars which were once so mysterious and cryptic have given up their secret. Life isn't an accident, it's the most complex state of matter within the universe. The birth and death of numerous stars has given her life and that is a privilege beyond compare.

For once, Dante feels complete. One day, her life will end, but the stars will continue for billions of years to come.

The End

AFTERWORD

As always, thank you for taking a chance on independent science fiction. Without your support and enthusiasm, novels like this simply aren't possible, so I deeply appreciate your interest in my writing. Please leave a review online. Your opinion of this book counts far more than mine and will help other readers decide whether it's worth their time.

What for you has been a linear journey over the past few hours has for me been like traversing a maze over the course of several months.

Writing is a matter of judgment. I'm constantly considering and reconsidering what to say and when, what to trim or omit, how to express an idea so as to build tension in a character as they pass through a chapter, a paragraph, a sentence and even a single word. Placement is everything. Pacing is akin to the rhythm of music, building to a crescendo. Characters need room to breathe. As you can tell, I thoroughly enjoy the challenge. I hope you do too.

But the Stars is based on a quote from Dante Alighieri's 14th century poem *The Divine Comedy*.

But the stars that marked our starting fall away.
We must go deeper into greater pain,
for it is not permitted that we stay.

The starship Acheron is named after one of the rivers crossed by Dante and Virgil as they descend into hell within the *Inferno*, which is the first act of this epic poem, while later in *But the Stars,* the name for the starship Empyrean comes from the third act, *Paradiso*. By the way, the Acheron is also the official name of the planet LV426 from James Cameron's *Aliens.*

But the Stars has an interesting backstory. Internationally renowned science fiction author Hugh Howey has spent the last few years sailing around the world in his catamaran. While he was in Brisbane, we caught up and he introduced my family to the board game Secret Hitler, which pits players against each other using subterfuge. My teenaged daughters loved it. Before long we were inviting friends around and battling wits with Hugh. On one particular afternoon, we played ten games straight. By the time the sun set, no one knew quite who they could trust. One game seemed to blur into the next and we laughed at just how devious we could be one moment, how saintly the next. It was a lot of fun. I wrote *But the Stars* as a way of bottling up that tension to share it with you.

The calculations involving time dilation in this novel are courtesy of E=MC2 Explained, while the rate required for a sense of artificial gravity to arise on the Acheron is based on Theodore Hall's spin calculator.

When it comes to interstellar travel, science fiction has leaned heavily on warp drives and hyperspace. From the Millennium Falcon to the Starship Enterprise, we all love seeing spacecraft race along faster than the speed of light, with the stars appearing as little more than snowflakes caught in the headlights. Although this makes for spectacular movie visuals, nothing can move faster than the speed of light—and with good reason. The speed of light is a misnomer. It's the speed of electromagnetic radiation, or if you prefer to dispense with the gobbledygook, the speed of reality. You see, light is the result of electrons absorbing and releasing energy as they dance around the nucleus of an atom. Before your eyes glaze over, remember, that's all we really are—a bunch of atoms. If you sit still in a bath, can you move faster than the waves you're about to make when you reach for the soap? Same.

Besides—in yet another case of science is stranger than fiction—the irony of warp drives and hyperspace is there's no need to go faster than light. As mind bending as it may seem, just getting close to the speed of light causes time dilation and length contraction. The result is, even at subluminal speeds, you can get from one star to another in *less time* than it takes light to travel the same distance! Sounds counterintuitive, but time and space are malleable. From the perspective of someone watching from afar, the journey would take *longer*, but for you in your spaceship, just getting close to the speed of light allows you to get to your destination quicker than light speed itself. Strange but true.

As an example, *But the Stars* is set around the fictional star WISE 5571 at a distance of 88 light years from Earth, but it takes the crew less than 25 years to get there in their hyper-sleep chambers because they're moving at 96% of the speed of light. To anyone watching from Earth, the journey took just over 90 years to complete.

When Dante is confronted on the Barton, she notes that she's been in hyper-sleep for three years, but later in the story, it's noted there aren't any ships within ten light years of the Acheron. Although this may seem like a mistake it's actually another example of time dilation and length contraction. For Dante, three years would have passed as she traveled at 96% of the speed of light, even though physically her spacecraft covered a distance of ten light years.

As you can see, things get complicated close to the speed of light, but hypothetically, if you could travel at 99% of the speed of light, you'd cover that entire distance in just over a decade. Crank up the dilithium crystals to 99.99% and the entire 88 light year journey could be covered in just over one year! At 99.999999% (still just under the speed of light) it would take barely six weeks!

Even though we can accelerate individual particles to 99.999999% of the speed of light in the Large Hadron Collider deep below the lush green pastures of Switzerland, <u>such speeds will probably never be possible by a spacecraft</u>. Not only would it take an inordinate amount of energy to accelerate an entire spacecraft that fast, space isn't empty. Space is awash with radiation. Collisions with photons, cosmic rays and the wisps of dust that permeate space would cause any such craft to glow hotter than the surface of the sun. Hitting something as small as a pebble would unleash explosions on par with tactical nuclear weapons. Go fast enough, and even the astonishingly cold background radiation left over from the Big Bang will get as hot as the surface of the sun. For practical reasons like this I kept the speed of the Acheron at 96% of the speed of light.

Science is often far stranger and wilder than science fiction. Although the binary star in this story is fictional, it's based on <u>SDSS J010657.39–100003.3</u>—which is a binary dwarf pair with masses of 17% and 43% of our Sun respectively. These two stars orbit each other at a distance roughly half that of the Earth and Moon, spinning at close to half a million miles an hour, completing an orbit every 37 minutes! In roughly, 30-40 million years, they'll collide, but they won't go supernova. Instead, they'll combine to form a single star much like our sun.

From the surface of our fictional world P4, such a binary star system would appear as a single point of light much like the Sun, only dimmer, and would appear to pulsate slightly every half hour.

Some other points that might interest you from this novel are that, <u>during World War II</u>, the British really did wine and dine captured German generals, <u>coaxing secrets out of them</u>. As remarkable as Alan Turing's work was in breaking the enigma code, an astonishing amount of Allied intelligence came from giving German generals a billiards table, a glass of brandy, and bugging the room. Some of the earliest evidence for the sheer scale of war crimes being committed against the Jewish diaspora in Europe came from these discussions. Information gathered in this manner allowed the British to bomb several top secret V2 rocket sites before the Nazis could unleash their full terror on London.

Some readers may have noticed a reference to the star Betelgeuse having gone supernova in this book. It's currently a red supergiant in the constellation of Orion, but it's variable behavior suggests it's reaching the end of its life and will soon go nova. With soon being any time in the next hundred thousand years. As it's roughly 600 light years away, there's no danger to Earth, but it sure will be spectacular when it blows and will be visible during the daytime. At night, it'll probably cast shadows similar to those of a full moon for several weeks.

The constellations are an example of pareidolia, a psychological phenomenon that has us seeing faces and familiar objects in abstract patterns, like Jesus in a burnt slice of toast. When it comes to the constellations, this has played out over thousands of years across dozens of different cultures.

There's no rhyme or reason behind the shapes we see in the stars. Is Usra Major the Big Dipper or the Great Bear? It's neither. Like faces in a cloud or familiar shapes in the bark of a tree, our ancestors settled on these arbitrary designs. Even among humanity, there's no agreement on the constellations. The aborigines of Australia have the oldest culture on Earth, but we ignore their interpretation of Orion as two brothers fishing in a canoe and go with the Greek hunter instead.

In practice, various cultures used the appearance of the constellations in the night sky as a celestial calendar, informing them of the coming seasons, but they're nothing more than an illusion. Our insistence on constellations would undoubtably confuse any alien culture we come across as the constellations are a random assortment of stars.

One of the more fascinating points I came across while researching this story is the medical procedure hemispherectomy, where the brain is cleaved in two. Although this is a rare procedure today, fifty years ago it was the only way to treat acute epilepsy. Surgeons would open the skull and cut the brain in half, leaving both sides fully functional and alive, but unable to communicate with each other.

The most startling aspect of this procedure, though, is what happened to a person's conscious awareness. It was easy enough for doctors, scientists and researchers to determine that the different halves of a patient's brain acted independently and saw/heard different things, but how was it possible for a person with a split brain to act on that information? Who was acting out? As speech is located on the left side of the brain, talking to patients only allowed interaction with one half of the brain. Much to the surprise of researchers (and this finding is still somewhat controversial), they found that some of these people had two *different* conscious personalities. One person had become two in a single body.

The most startling example of this I could find was where neurologist Vilayanur Subramanian Ramachandran asked a patient whether they believed in God. One half said, 'Yes,' the other said, 'No.' Oh, and neither half knew what the other had answered, so these answers were derived entirely independently.

How is this possible? As I touch on in the novel, it comes down to redefining what it means to be you or me. We think of ourselves as single entities even though we're composite creatures made up of trillions of different cells, forming dozens of entirely separate organs and limbs that combine to become a single body. In the same way, the brain, with its 86 billion neurons is comprised of different modules that combine to become one. Split it in half and it becomes two. As strange and counterintuitive as this seems, it goes a long way toward helping us unravel the mystery of what it means to be conscious. Biology really is the weirdest science.

The closing paragraphs of this novel touch on the concept of abiogenesis, or the mechanism by which life first arose on Earth. [Dante summarizes](#) what's known as the [statistics of self-replication](#). In essence, this particular concept considers the complexity of self-replicating life as a highly efficient means of allowing energy to dissipate.

Energy excites—that's just what it does. Life can be seen as a physical means of redistributing the energy pouring in from a nearby star, allowing matter to absorb and contain far more energy than would ordinarily be possible with simple inorganic matter.

How does this work? The [DNA within a single cell can contain hundreds of billions of atoms](#) chemically bound together in intricate chains, making them remarkably efficient as energy-sinks/energy-stores. As each cell is self-replicating, the ability to distribute energy elsewhere is immense. Worlds with life are far more efficient at dissipating energy than lifeless worlds, meaning they are surprisingly harmonious with the laws of physics.

From what we understand, there's a fine balance of temperatures and pressures at which these complex molecular chains can form, so not every world can sustain life, but this theory suggests life will arise naturally given the right circumstances, as life is the optimal way to redistribute energy—and physics loves efficiency.

I find this concept fascinating and look forward to scientists identifying Earth-like exoplanets so the idea can be tested and refined further.

As remarkable as life is, a mere three atomic elements make up an astonishing 93% of our bodies. Imagine three containers filled with pure hydrogen, oxygen and carbon. It takes 3.8 billion years of evolutionary adaptation to turn that into you. If we add another three elements—nitrogen, calcium and phosphorus we've accounted for 99% of you, me and every other living thing on this planet! Life is the triumph of the interplay between matter and energy!

The composition of our bodies is made up of recycled atoms. Some elements recycle faster than others. Oxygen, carbon dioxide and hydrogen get caught in atmospheric cycles so that at any one time, there's a reasonably good chance you're breathing some of the same molecules as Shakespeare or drinking a few molecules of water once enjoyed by the Roman emperor Caesar. Strange but true.

Once again, thank you for taking a chance on independent science fiction. Novels like this live and die based on the passion of readers like you so I appreciate your support. Please leave a review online and tell a friend what you thought of this story. Your reaction to *But the Stars* will help others decide whether it is worth reading.

When leaving a review, please avoid spoilers.

But the Stars is ambiguous about the fate of its characters in the same way *Inception* was—and with good reason. It's an anti-pattern. Far from the Hollywood clichés we're all so used to, any encounter with a hostile extraterrestrial species is liable to be horribly one-sided. Imagine an African lion fighting a Great White shark. The vast disparity between them means the outcome is going to depend on where the battle occurs rather than their respective strengths, their intelligence or the intensity of their will.

No amount of Bruce Willis bravado, Will Smith irreverence or suave comments from the lips of Jeff Goldblum is going to swing the balance when it comes to taking on hostile extraterrestrials.

The key motif in this book is summed up by Dante in her conversation with Dr. Romero when she says, "They can control us, oppress us, even enslave us, but they can't break us," and Dante stays true to that, resisting to the end.

Did Dante actually escape? Or is she still trapped? I don't know. That's up to you to decide as the reader—and I love that it's your choice. All stories are a mere glimpse into a fictional universe, just a tiny slither of that particular world. Regardless of whether it's *The Hunger Games, Wool, Divergence* or *But the Stars*, what happens next is open to your imagination. That's the beauty of fiction.

I'd like to thank Ellen Campbell and David Jaffe for their assistance editing this novel, along with a fantastic team of beta-readers including LuAnn Miller, Petr Melechin, Bruce Simmons, John Larisch , Chris Fried, Seamus Colgan and Rob Engel.

If you're interested in reading more of my work, you can find my books on Amazon. With over twenty published novels covering vastly different subjects such as Sherlock Holmes, vampires and zombies, I have a wide variety of stories in my back catalog. In light of this, I thought it would be helpful if I put together a dedicated science fiction series under the banner *First Contact* that examine the prospect of meeting intelligent extraterrestrials. There are over a dozen different novels on this subject alone. Although they don't share the same characters, they do share a unique glimpse into how first contact might unfold.

Peter Cawdron

Brisbane, Australia